ALSO BY

ALICIA GIMÉNEZ-BARTLETT

*Dog Day*
*Prime Suspect*
*Death Rites*

# NAKED MEN

Alicia Giménez-Bartlett

# NAKED MEN

*Translated from the Spanish*
*by Andrea Rosenberg*

Europa
*editions*

Europa Editions
214 West 29th Street
New York, N.Y. 10001
www.europaeditions.com
info@europaeditions.com

Translation by Andrea Rosenberg
Original title: *Hombres desnudos*
Translation copyright © 2018 by Europa Editions

Library of Congress Cataloging in Publication Data is available
ISBN 978-1-60945-476-0

Giménez-Bartlett, Alicia
Naked Men

Book design by Emanuele Ragnisco
www.mekkanografici.com

Cover photo © panic_attack/iStock

Prepress by Grafica Punto Print – Rome

Printed in the USA

# NAKED MEN

I don't much care, really—I don't love him anymore. Sometimes I wonder if I ever did. Fifteen years of marriage—that's the bad part, the feeling I've wasted my time, though, really, what would I have been doing during those fifteen years if I hadn't been married to him? I don't know. Nobody can guess the past, much less speculate about what the past might have been like had some elements of our lives been different. I must be a strange sort of woman: instead of crying my eyes out, what I feel most acutely is curiosity. Maybe I'm just trying to be different to avoid ending up a cliché: the wife whose husband has left her. There isn't really any other way to interpret it: they've left me. My husband left me for another woman, one who's younger than I am, prettier, happier, and more optimistic. Apparently she's completely problem-free, fresh and radiant as a flower. She's a simultaneous interpreter. Blond, penniless. Probably inexperienced in love, given how young she is.

Our breakup showdown was intense, like something out of a cheesy soap opera. I was already pretty sure he was having an affair, and when he got all serious and said we needed to talk, I guessed immediately what we'd be talking about. But I never thought he'd crank out such a hackneyed confession, so according to script, so man-having-affair-during-midlife-crisis. It was like it came straight of a manual: *How to Dump Your Wife*. I kind of lost it, but I don't feel bad about that. I've spent my entire life controlling myself. I don't think I even cried when they first brought me into the world. The nurses in the maternity ward loved me: "What a sweet baby girl, so well behaved!" Of course, I didn't have any reason to cry back then: my family was rich, and I was the firstborn daughter of a perfect couple. He was brilliant; she was beautiful. There was no way of knowing then that my beautiful mother would die soon after, ravaged by cancer. But I still had my father. Papá worked long hours at his company, but he always took very good care of me: affectionate, indulgent, he'd give my nannies strict instructions and demand a full report when he arrived home. I never threw tantrums or sulked. Papá was always tired after a stressful day, and I didn't want to do anything to upset him, to make him regret coming home to be with me, since we were so happy and so close. I didn't want him to decide to keep working late the next day so I couldn't even give him a hug because I'd already be in bed. Papá always smelled good, like sandalwood cologne. David never smelled like that. Sometimes he smelled like dense office sweat, like mid-level executives at the end of the workday. He'd have been flat broke if it hadn't been for Papá, the company, me.

"I've been doing a lot of thinking, Irene. Things haven't been good between us for a long time. Sure, we live together, we're polite, we help each other out when problems come up, but that's not enough. Marriage calls for more than that—or at least it should. We don't feel that shared affection that makes life so magical anymore. We never make love. I'm forty-six years old, I'm still young—I don't want to live like this. We put a good face on it in public, but there's nothing between us at this point. What will my future look like if we stay together? I can't just bury myself in my work. I feel a pang of longing when I see couples kissing on the street, when a friend tells me he's in love, when I see the passion people feel for each other. But I'm not going to lie to you—maybe if this other woman hadn't come into my life, you and I would have kept going like this forever. But it is what it is—I did meet her."

It is what it is? What a dick! So he met another woman. How dare he even mention her to me? I wanted to slap him, the way, in an earlier era, you might have corrected a servant who had crossed the line, talked back, stolen some object of value. And he says he's still young, too—right, he's a real stud!

"Her name's Marta. She's a simultaneous interpreter from English. She works for a company. She's never been married. I don't want to carry on a relationship with her while I'm still with you. I fell in love, Irene—it may sound harsh, but it's the truth. We have to be mature about things, face reality. This marriage fell apart years ago. It's so hard to tell you these things, but I have to be honest. Maybe things would have turned out differently if we'd had children, but there's no point in having regrets now. We were happy once, and that's what matters. You're young too, you've got the company, and you'll be able to rebuild your love life if you want to. I know you've always been pretty pragmatic about things. You're solid, a sensible type."

I wanted to lash out at him in the rudest, most obscene terms, but I was too flabbergasted to react. If we'd had children! He'd never complained about that before. Children— what children? What a relief, now, that we never had any! My intuition always told me never to have children with any man—not David or anyone else. After all, there weren't any other men like Papá. When he died, I instantly realized he was the last real man I'd ever have in my life. David says I've still got the business, and that's true—I've managed to keep it afloat—though I tend to think David's leaving me because of the global recession. I'm yet another victim of the crisis. He's convinced I'm going under, and he's trying to jump out of the boat before it sinks. Fine, that's nothing new. I never believed he'd married me for love. He was a pathetic loser when I met him, a two-bit lawyer with no future, a hustler who saw that being with me meant having it made. He's done well for himself working at my company, thanks to Papá, thanks to me. He wasn't a bad worker, but anybody else would have done just as good a job, maybe better. We'll see how he does now in his new life as a still-young man. "You're solid, a sensible type," he tells me. The man has no dignity. Who gave him permission to dump that hokey nonsense on me? Oh, sure, love's so important! "You'll be able to rebuild your love life." Such garbage! Since when does he talk like that, like a B movie, like a goddamn romance novel? What I do or don't do with my love life is none of his business.

But I didn't say any of that. I was finding it difficult to say anything at all—he was a stranger to me. Fifteen years? Clearly, fifteen years aren't enough to get to know a person. We might as well have been introduced the day before yesterday. When he was done talking, I think I gave a mocking smile and declared calmly, "You're fired, of course. We'll find another lawyer—it won't be hard. If you want to sell your stock in the company, I'll make you a reasonable offer."

I paused, and he muttered something about how cold I was being, how it was just like me.

"As for the house, you have a week to clear out your things. Come by and pick them up any morning. I won't be around."

He kept griping. He'd expected me to say that, he knew I was going to act this way. I was made of ice, totally heartless. I told him to get out. I thought a week to pick up his things was more than generous.

"I realize that half of the house is yours," I added. "When the business is on firmer footing again, I'll buy you out. For the time being, I'm staying put."

This time he didn't respond. He headed for the door with his head held high and left. I hadn't actually said all that much—what more was there to say? He'd already used all the melodramatic clichés. There was no way I was going to join him on that foul terrain. I have to be able to live with myself, and I'd lose all self-respect if I sunk to his level. I didn't want to see him again. A note he sent days later went straight into the wastebasket, ripped into tiny pieces:

"Please understand, Irene. I wouldn't be able to look at myself in the mirror if I hadn't made this decision."

That's great, David, you go ahead and look at yourself in that wonderful mirror for the rest of your life. I hope you like what you see. There's nothing to understand.

I didn't reply, obviously.

* * *

They're asleep. The story I'm telling is so boring, they're nodding off. I see their eyelids drooping, their minds drifting away to places I've never visited. Saint John of the Cross, Saint Teresa of Ávila, the Spanish mystic. No wonder they're bored. What relevance do Teresa's visions and the convents she founded have to their lives? None at all. The Internet. Twitter. Facebook. What examples can I offer to give them the vaguest idea of what I'm talking about? I can't think of any—most likely, there are none. In the end, all they get are anecdotes: Saint Teresa levitated when she prayed, rising in the incense-heavy air, and angels appeared to her with flaming swords that they plunged into her heart. Not even these iconic images bring the girls any closer to the real context of mystical feeling. My students import mysticism to their trendy fantastical sub-worlds: they imagine Saint Teresa with extrasensory powers, maybe aboard a spaceship. The angels turn into those beautiful teenage vampires from the blockbuster movies. If I try to tell them that a mystical trance is like an extreme concentration of the mind that leads to the abduction of the senses, I might as well be speaking Chinese. I don't think any of them—not a single one—has ever concentrated for more than five minutes straight. They have a hard time focusing their attention on anything. They live scattered lives, connected to dozens of people at once, even if they have nothing to say. Mystical ecstasy? No idea, no answer. *Ecstasy* sounds like a drug they're not supposed to take, since this is a Catholic school and they've internalized a lot of those kinds of prohibitions. It's the term *mystical* that I futilely attempt to explain.

They no longer care about classic literature as it's taught in school. The past doesn't exist for them; they catch glimmers of it through images from the movies and television, but as far as they're concerned, it doesn't have anything to do with their lives. They don't see anything brilliant about Lope de Vega, or entertaining about Francisco de Quevedo, or interesting about Jorge Manrique. They don't perceive any tragic sense of life in Unamuno, or appreciate the rhythmic sonority of Machado's poetry. "One thousand times one hundred is one hundred thousand. One thousand times one thousand is one million." They don't feel its melancholy beauty.

Sometimes I discuss this with my colleagues in the teachers' lounge, but they don't have anything useful to say. They recite the same litany of complaints I've heard so many times before. The more radical ones write off the entire generation: "They're totally shallow, the lot of them. They get everything they want handed to them on a silver platter. Their parents didn't teach them the value of things." The conformists offer generic platitudes: "You have to be patient. They don't even realize it, but we're showing them the joy of learning, and the effects of that will last a lifetime." I tend to suggest more drastic solutions: changing the curricula or, better yet, scrapping them altogether. Finding works of literature that can accommodate these girls' new sensibility, no matter what movement, period, or country the authors are from. I always get pushback, as if I were a revolutionary attempting to do away with the sacred, natural order of knowledge. Ultimately, they're just trying to keep their jobs, their monthly salary, the barest sense of security.

I should have taken that tack myself, especially given what came afterward, at the end of the school year, right before classes finished. The school director called me to her office.

"Do you know why I've called you in here, Javier?"

"I don't know, Mother Superior. Something to do with my classes, I imagine."

"It is something to do with your classes, but it's not good news. We're happy with your work. The girls like you, you've done a good job with the syllabus, and there's no doubt about your professionalism. But you know what things are like in the country right now. This may be a private school, but we still depend on subsidies from the Ministry of Education. Budget cuts affect us too, same as everyone else. We've got just enough to conduct our core educational program, but we're going to have to cancel our review courses, except in math. Back when we started this new project of offering literature review courses, things were different. I hope you understand—it's become a luxury, something we can't really justify. But you've got all summer to look for another job. You'll get some severance pay, of course, as required by law. It won't be much, since you've just been working part-time. Can your family help you out any?"

"My parents died years ago in a car accident."

"Heavens, how tragic! Did they leave you anything you can use now?"

"They were working-class. The little they left dried up ages ago."

"Do you have any siblings?"

"Just an older sister who lives abroad. She's married, has her own life—we hardly ever see each other. But I live with my girlfriend, and she's working."

"My advice is that you study for the certification exams so you can teach in the public schools. That's your best option."

"There are hardly any job openings, you know that."

"The Lord will look after you, Javier. You're a fine young man. In any event, I'll talk with the administration and have them pay you for the whole summer. That's the best we can do."

"Thank you, Mother Superior."

What an idiot—I ended up thanking her. Not that it would have done much good to kick up a fuss. She advised me to take the certification exams, as if that hadn't occurred to me, but I've always been intimidated by having to prove my worth, having to compete with other people. Plus, studying would require one hundred percent commitment, but I still need to bring in some money every month. My father used to tell me I should be a lawyer. He was a bricklayer, and for him becoming a lawyer meant you'd arrived. It was a strange obsession—he could just as easily have suggested I study architecture or medicine, but for him the law was the ultimate status symbol. My mother, who was more of a romantic, just wanted me to be happy no matter what path I chose. The car they were traveling in veered off a straight stretch of highway. It wasn't raining or foggy. Most likely my father fell asleep. They were on their way to the beach for a few days to stay at a vacation apartment they'd rented. A sad story, but all too common. My sister cried a lot, but as soon as she left the funeral home she went back to her family, and I've barely seen her since. The only family I had left was my grandmother, and I kept visiting her every week until last year, when she died suddenly of a heart attack. And that's where this whole nightmare began. Life is unpredictable—ultimately, really, it's crap.

For the school director, her educational program comes first. The only thing she cares about is that her wealthy students keep learning. That's what I should have told her that when she fired me, but I didn't think of it. Not that or anything else assertive. My father wanted me to be a lawyer, but I wouldn't have been any good at it. I never come up with brilliant retorts. I'm not combative. And anyway, being a lawyer doesn't guarantee you a good job these days. Sandra is an economist, but she's working as an administrative assistant.

That night, as usual, I waited for her at home. She was exhausted when she came in, also as usual. She gave me a kiss on the lips. Given the time of night and the time of year, she was surprised I wasn't grading my students' assignments. I asked her to sit down and told her about my conversation with the school director. She immediately burst into tears.

"Things were going too well!" she said. "I have a job and you were bringing in some money too, even if it was just part-time. Now what are we going to do?"

Then she wiped away her tears and got angry.

"Those damn nuns, tossing people out on their ear like that! They could have at least just cut salaries without canceling any classes! All that nice talk about educating future generations, and then they go and act like real turds."

After a while she calmed down and became reasonable, even encouraging.

"Don't worry, Javier, don't look so glum. We'll figure something out. I got upset because it's so frustrating that these things are happening all over the place, and with total impunity. It seems like anything goes. It's not fair. You always took that job really seriously—you wanted those girls to learn, to read, to understand literature. But we'll figure it out. They'll give you some severance pay for now. Then you've got two years where you can collect unemployment. It won't be much, but it's something. I'm still bringing in my salary, which is enough to live on. Things would have to be really dire for you not to find another job in the next two years. So let's not panic. Everything's going to change."

And that's how that ill-starred day ended. Everything had changed. It was the start of a new era for me. I don't even know why I'm here. I'm the overemotional sort—as my darling grandmother used to call me, "a very sensitive boy." Her best friend survived her by only a year. Neighbors told me about her death. They found my cell phone number on a grubby list the old woman kept on the sideboard. I went immediately, though I knew it was a ridiculous way to honor her. I felt bad for the poor woman. She and my grandmother kept each other company, helped each other as best they could, talked every day. Both of them had suffered great misfortunes. In my grandmother's case, her daughter and son-in-law had died in a car accident. Juana's traumas were more complicated, less presentable, even openly embarrassing: a son dead from a drug overdose and his wife in jail for reasons unknown. But those calamities were so devastating that they marked the women like a curse and set them apart, giving them superior status. The other old ladies living alone in the neighborhood could only gripe about everyday sorts of complaints: loneliness, ailments, progressive decline, money problems, memories of better times. But not my grandmother and Juana—they had a massive reserve of misfortune that weighed as much as an army kit bag. Besides the distresses of aging, which they had to face like anybody else, the two of them labored under the terrible burden of two sons who had died in the prime of life, neither of natural causes. As a result, everybody ascribed great dignity to them, elevating them into the aristocracy of sorrow and old age. That distinction made them the object of their neighbors' devoted attentions: they brought bread and fruit, went to the Social Security office to get the old women's prescriptions renewed, and had formally promised to let the grandsons know if anything happened. Me in my grandmother's case, and Iván in Juana's.

Of the two of us, I was the good grandson. I visited her

every Sunday without fail. I'd arrive around five and leave at seven. My grandmother would serve me an afternoon snack, as if I were a little kid. Always the same thing: chocolate cookies from the supermarket and Coca-Cola poured from a one-liter bottle, a little flat because she'd already opened it. I rarely had any desire to go see her, but I went anyway. Sandra would look at me uncomprehendingly: "Of course, Javier, you've got your morals!" She was right—otherwise I'd have spent my Sundays at home, serenely reading, without being hounded by a sense of moral obligation. I guess losing my parents had made me feel the lack of family more acutely, and that old woman was my only family, apart from my sister, who has her own family and never comes to visit.

Occasionally Juana would join our Sunday cookies-and-Coke parties. That's how I knew her grandson's name was Iván and that he was the bad grandson. He never went to see her. At most he'd go by his grandmother's house on Christmas, at some ungodly hour of the night after poor Juana had already eaten, asking if she was going to offer him a piddly little drink to celebrate the holiday. "The only thing he brings is chaos," she'd say. I'd seen him once, and I recalled him vaguely: a guy about my age, looking like low-rent pimp, slim, wiry, with an earring in one ear and close-cropped hair.

And there I was, in that half-empty funeral home, participating in Juana's funeral rites: a small room that contained her closed casket with a heap of flower wreaths at its foot. The women next door told me that the deceased had made a monthly insurance payment so she could have a decent burial and a cemetery niche instead of being cremated. I guess I ended up going to the service because of their opinion of me. Since I was "the good grandson," it wouldn't be hard to preserve that reputation up to the very end. My grandmother's end. After her friend's death, any vestige of her existence would be extinguished forevermore. But I was itching to get out of there. It was all so horribly cheesy: the priest's formulaic words, with the obligatory references to lowly life on earth and the glories of eternal life. The flowers, all paid for by the dead woman; the lack of real sorrow in everyone there . . . In the first row, I spotted the back of what had to be Iván. And it was he who blocked my escape when the service ended, coming up to me and holding out his hand.

"How's it going, Javier? It's so great you came! I'm really grateful you're here, man. My grandma always talked about you. She said you were the right kind of grandson. She told me you're a teacher. Listen, I don't really know how to go about saying this, but now that this bullshit with the priest is done, we have to go to the cemetery for the burial—my grandma didn't want to be cremated. The neighborhood busybodies aren't coming, of course. So it's going to be just me with that asshole priest. Would you do me a solid and come along? If I'm alone with him, he might tell me off or something."

I should have refused, but I have a hard time saying no. Whenever I have to say it, I feel horrible. Plus I was amused by Iván's notion that the priest was going to give him hell for his behavior—a preposterous idea, but an entertaining one. So I went with him. As we left the cemetery, grateful and happy the priest hadn't scolded him, he invited me to go get a drink at a bar. I agreed to that too; after all, I was now an unemployed loser with nothing better to do.

"So your mother couldn't make it to the funeral, Iván?" I asked, trying to get him talking.

"She's sick."

Shit, this guy knows my mother's in the joint. Grandma must have pounded that into his head. What he doesn't know is that she's nearly served out her sentence and is going to be released soon. She's in the psych ward at the prison, but some-times they let her out. I hadn't wanted to tell her about her mother-in-law's funeral. What for? I would have had to go pick her up. At first I used to go every once in a while. They'd call me from the joint to go out there, social services or something like that. I'd wait for her at the exit, and it was just like in the movies: she'd pass me her bag and I'd open up the trunk. She looked like shit, with repulsive bags under her eyes. The last day I went, she was wearing a short-sleeved top and looked so skinny that it seemed like they'd plunged her arms into the stew pot and pulled them out again once all the meat had fallen off her bones. Anyway, I never went back. I haven't seen her much since I turned fifteen. I managed to make it on my own, damn it. I was sick and tired of her fucking drug problems. And I've seen even less of my father. What a family! The god-damn Holy Family! They should get a church at least as big as Gaudí's. But this Javier dude probably thinks I'm into drugs too. I tell everybody there's no way. To be honest, always hear-ing about how he was such a good grandson, I kind of figured he'd be a dumbass, but he seems like a good guy. Just because he was nice to his grandma doesn't mean he's automatically a dipshit. Sometimes I used to think I should go see the poor woman too—but then I just wouldn't feel like it. I already knew what would happen, exactly what she'd say: "Are you eating healthy? Are you going to bed early? Are you getting into any trouble?" Always hinting everything was my mother's fault. Not her precious son's, of course—her son who croaked of an overdose purely by chance. God carried him straight up to heaven, he was such a good boy. My mother was the riffraff, the junkie, the one who'd reeled my father in and led him down a bad path. Well, fuck you, grandma! If you died believ-ing that, you had it all wrong!

"You're a teacher, right? At a Catholic girls' school?"

"I'm a teacher, yes."

This Iván guy is a piece of work. Who knows what he's imagining when he says "teacher." He's probably the type who watches a lot of American TV shows. Judging from his serious expression, he's probably picturing me wearing a graduation cap. But he must have gone to school at some point. Maybe he was one of those violent kids who would threaten the math teacher or slash the principal's tires. He looks at me in amazement. His eyes are lively and intense. He seems like a smart guy on the whole. I wonder what he does for work. It could be anything: personal trainer, car mechanic. I don't think he's a salesman. He seems proud, like he's got nothing to prove, and is wary of everyone he meets. No matter what, he's got an existential mess on his hands: father who OD'd, mother in jail. Is he a tortured soul? Maybe he never looks back. Now I'm going to have to tell him I lost my job. It'll be the second time I've told somebody. The first person was Sandra. Does it bother me to admit it? I think it does. Before, back when there was no crisis and everybody had a job, being unemployed didn't seem like such a big deal. You just started considering what to do next: look for another job, go back to school, change careers. Not now—now we all know that losing your job means joining a club that is not so easy to get out of. It's like announcing you have an incurable disease. Like admitting you're just another failure who hasn't been able to overcome bad luck, those situations that only the strongest, the smartest, the best survive. But I'm not going to tell Iván any of that, because he'll dump the noble teacher image and realize I'm stuck in the same reality as him. I've decided I like Iván. It's fun listening to him talk.

"The nuns fired you? Shit, man, that's rough!"

Throwing a teacher out on the damn street! How are kids supposed to respect their teachers when they know they can be fired just like that? The thing is, now everybody's getting the ax: doctors, lawyers . . . It doesn't matter how many degrees you've got. The nuns just gave this guy the boot. I knew I liked him! I can't stand nuns and priests. I didn't know any at first because we never went to mass and stuff in my family. But when my mother was hooked on drugs, they told her to go to the parish because there was this young priest there who was really cool and could help her out. I was just a little kid, but sometimes I had to go with her. Sometimes my father came too. The hope was that being with the family would help her get off the stuff faster and start leading a normal life. I think my father stopped going pretty quickly, but I kept on, and I found it incredibly embarrassing to hang out with the other kids there, knowing they were all there for the same reason as me. The cool priest would look at me really sadly, like I was a little lamb being taken to the slaughter: "Poor kid, with a junkie for a mom! Thank God she asked for God's help and came to God's house—now every goddamn thing's gonna be OK!" But my mother had only signed up for that crap with the idea of wheedling some cash out of the cool priest. And she did, just enough for two more months' worth of coke. She didn't go back after that. But by then I had the priests' number, and now Javier here is telling me about the nuns, which must be the same thing but the chick version—meaning even worse. The dude's a good guy. I'm going to see if I can help him out, hell, if only for occasionally putting up with my grandma's bullshit: "Are you eating well, sleeping well, getting into any trouble?" I'm going to help this guy. I like him.

"Say, Javier, give me your cell number. Do you use WhatsApp, are you on Facebook? Let's get together sometime and grab a beer, huh? What are you doing, man? Put your money away. My treat. As if, man!"

\* \* \*

By now everybody knows I'm getting a divorce, and everybody knows why. I haven't told anybody but my closest friends, but it doesn't matter—people know. I go to the company to work, and they look at me funny. They feel off balance when I'm around. Some feel obliged to say something. If David weren't the company's lawyer, they'd keep quiet; they'd pretend. But this is all too obvious, and the ones who work with me on a daily basis feel obliged to offer something in the way of condolences. It's funny, because they can't figure out how to go about it, where to even start. I considered writing a note the way famous people do on their blogs: "Owing to irreconcilable differences and after many years of happiness and lives fruitfully shared, we must announce the end of our marriage. We will, however, remain friends." Then I discarded the idea. I'm not famous; I don't have to explain anything to anybody. I don't care what they think. I called the personnel officer into my office and informed him that David would be leaving the company. The struggle between discretion and curiosity was visible on his face. "Voluntarily," I added. The bastard has put me in a difficult position. I'd love to tell everybody he's leaving me for another woman—but how? Playing the wounded victim, full of rage, trying to be funny, ironic, knowing: "As everybody knows, when men get to a certain age, they need a young girl to tell them how wonderful they are." I don't like any of those approaches, though keeping quiet may be worse. I don't want anyone to think I'm so gutted that I'm trying to conceal what happened.

The reactions of the married friends we used to go out with regularly have been cautious. A lot of them have split up in the past few years. Those of us who were still together—what did we do when they split? Thinking back, I remember a single scene performed on repeated occasions. It didn't matter what the couple in question was going through—the drama always played out the same way. First, solidarity with the more affronted or weaker party, if there was one. Then a display of impartiality: "I'm not going to take sides." Third, we'd relax and the endless gossip about the recently divorced couple would begin. Way deep down, it made you feel good when other couples split up. For those of us who were still married, it confirmed that we belonged to the world of happy people. There were always jokes: "Look out, any day now I'm going to kick this man/woman to the curb. I've had it up to here!" Gentle punches on the shoulder, quick kisses, protests, laughter. We were all proud that we were still in the fight. The fact that our marriages lasted while others fell apart was evidence not just of enduring conjugal love but of emotional stability, maturity, intelligence, responsibility.

I don't really remember what we gossiped about, but it was pretty much the same with every divorce. The tone varied, but there was a script for every occasion: first loves who had stayed together too long, financial difficulties, fatigue from living together . . . It's impossible to be terribly original, since marriage contracts don't allow for much variation—they've been pretty much identical since the Paleolithic. To make up for it, we weren't too vulgar in our gossip. We'd provide commentary on the psychology of the divorcing pair, describe significant details we'd witnessed that had presaged an abrupt end to the relationship. We'd point out ill-judged ways of doing things, whether by one member of the couple or by both. It wasn't a roasting session—nobody was rude or went too far. When we seemed to have exhausted the subject, someone might make a cheeky joke, but there was no malice involved. But the subject wasn't so easily exhausted. It would come up again every weekend we got together. A single divorce provided fodder for a couple of months, even a year if it had some element that made it more exciting than usual.

And now all that civilized chitchat will be about me and David and the long years of our marriage. I'm sure they're hashing out all the mistakes we made as a couple. And they're probably correct in their diagnoses, even in their prescriptions for treatments that might have kept us together. Too late. Since David and I broke up, I've gone out with our group of friends a couple of times, to have dinner at the club. I don't plan to do it again. I'm bored by their fakery, the artificially neutral conversations, the sympathy and deference they show me. I imagine what they must say when I'm not around. It's irksome to discover I'm just like everybody else, utterly unremarkable. That's something I'll never forgive David for: he's turned me into just another abandoned wife, like thousands of others.

Other times I've gone out just with the women. One on one, those female friends have been more bearable. Less hypocritical. The married ones tell me about struggles in their own lives in a compensatory effort, exaggerating problems with their husbands or children to forge a bond of solidarity with me. The divorced ones give me advice: how to weather the initial storm, how to deal with loneliness. They all claim to be delighted to be free of their husbands. They all fully enjoy their newfound independence, their freedom, their not having to answer to anybody. I never ask them what they did to wrangle themselves such splendid lives—I know they'd be offended. I guess ultimately they live their lives the way everybody else does, doing what they can and passing the time. If achieving female happiness meant getting married and then getting divorced in order to understand and appreciate freedom, all women would go that route, but that's not how it is. The ones who get divorced all struggle with financial issues. The ones with children have to find a way to fill the father's role too. Even the ones who are most enthusiastic about their breakups encounter problems they've never had to face before. So don't tell me you're the happiest woman on earth, sweetie. I'm over forty, and I know better.

How do I feel, how am I, how am I doing after the split? I don't know. I enjoy going to bed alone at night. The bed we shared for so many years is all mine now. I stretch out on the diagonal, spread my arms wide. I'm comfortable. I can turn on the bedside lamp in the middle of the night, turn on the radio without worrying about bothering anybody. Going to bed alone gives me peace. Waking up alone in the morning, not so much. I open my eyes and immediately note a clenching in my chest. I think about the things I'm going to do next: get up, shower, make coffee, pick out my clothes, get dressed. I feel an incomprehensible unease, an immense lethargy. I'd rather stay in bed a while longer. I've arrived at the office late three times now.

Do I miss David, David himself—his personality, his way of talking, of walking, of seeing? I don't think so. I feel a certain nostalgia for having someone by my side, that's all. There's a space that seems empty—I guess that must be loneliness. David didn't bother me; I could have stayed married to him my whole life. Even though we worked at the same company, we didn't see much of each other. We had different schedules. I ate dinner, and he didn't. I would watch television, and he'd hunker down in front of the computer. I went to bed early, and he'd stay up reading a while longer. On weekends we'd go to the club, but he always played golf and I played tennis. We'd have dinner in the restaurant with our group of friends, never the two of us alone. On vacations we'd visit a foreign country, just a short stay. Then the summer house: golf for him, tennis for me, and swimming for both of us. We didn't take romantic walks through the countryside or spend intimate evenings together, just the two of us in candlelight. Neither of us seemed to want those things. At the beginning of our marriage, we made love frequently. Later, he still wanted to but I didn't; our encounters grew less frequent and eventually disappeared altogether. I thought it was normal. I've never been a passionate woman. I'd never slept with anyone before David. I wasn't even interested in sex during college, where I studied economics. I never felt attracted to anybody. I'm a cold fish, I know. A psychoanalyst would tell me it's because I grew up without a mother. So stupid. I could have stayed married to David forever.

Papá always used to say to me, "The important thing is to be working toward something. We're lucky because we have the company—it gives us a good reason to keep living." Poor Papá! It's preposterous to die at seventy these days. There are people who make it to a hundred without breaking a sweat. Why did he have to die? Now the company's gradually going under—orders are drying up, bills haven't been paid . . . If he were here, he'd tell me what to do. The thing I've been working toward is crumbling away, and on top of it my husband's left me, same as thousands of other women. I think I'm starting to hate David. I don't think I can forgive him. He's left me in the trenches without ammunition, without the will to keep shooting. He's gone off with his little simultaneous interpreter, and I'm left here in this uncomfortable position—and if there's anything I detest with all my might, it's discomfort. I never wait in line for anything. I take taxis instead of driving so I don't have to look for parking. I haven't switched maids in years because I wouldn't be able to stand having to explain to the new one how I like things done. Plus, discomfort is a waste of time, and I've already wasted too many years with David.

* * *

Who would have thought it would be so hard on me to be officially out of work, to be listed on the unemployment rolls? But it is: I haven't had a job for four months now, and I haven't managed to set up a daily routine to help me get through. I was on high alert for a while after being fired, but that's long gone. Then I figured I was transitioning toward something else and needed to hurry up and find a new school to work at. I visited education centers, sent out résumés, put up a professional profile on LinkedIn, followed up on every opportunity. But even as I was absorbed in that flurry of activity, I realized there was nothing for me. The change was going to be a slow one. I started thinking long-term. I bought the exam workbook for high school teachers, but I didn't feel like studying. Why bother? For the first time in my life, I seriously questioned whether I'm meant to be a teacher. I studied literature because I like reading, analyzing books, discovering writers I've never heard of, revisiting classics from countries around the globe. Teaching seems like the only practical application for my degree. I've considered looking in other fields: the publishing world, literary journals, writing schools. But you need contacts in those places, and I don't have any. I was one of those romantic sorts who choose their majors based on taste and spiritual affinity, not on what's going to earn them a living. I must be one of the world's last remaining fools.

And now I'm screwed. It doesn't seem all that strange for someone who's unemployed to feel a little useless; the problem is it's demolishing the image I had of myself. I saw myself as a modern guy, progressive, committed to social justice, eco-minded, able to live with women as fully my equals. The clichés of Spanish masculinity didn't apply to me. But now I'm finding I'm much more limited than I thought. In the mornings, when Sandra goes to work, I stay home and read. Then I clean the house, do the laundry, hang the clothes out to dry in the courtyard. It bothers me that the neighbors can see me doing the household chores. From their kitchens I can hear the televisions, the endless chatter of the radio. Up on the fifth floor there's a guy who lost his job a long time ago, the kind who won't be reentering the workforce. He's a hipster who writes a music blog as his sole hobby. When I run into him in the elevator, he tells me about bands that are playing in the city, the latest songs he's downloaded from the web. I used to find it funny, but now I avoid him. I don't want to think I'm anything like him. I'm embarrassed to be stuck at home—I feel like an elderly housewife. I thought I was beyond certain prejudices, but apparently not.

Sometimes, to avoid suffocating in the apartment, I go to the park to read. It's pleasant sitting on a bench in the fresh air. When I pause for a moment and look around, I see little kids, too young for school still, and old people of both sexes basking in the sun. There are also South American nannies, a few loafers like me, and three homeless men who always sit together in the same spot. Two of them are young men, and the third is a little older. They pass around the ever-present box of wine, though they never get drunk. They're all bundled up in tattered clothes even though it's hot. They're filthy. They engage in an animated conversation that I can't hear, slap each other amicably on the back. One of them stands up suddenly in what looks like anger, paces around for a little bit, and then goes back to his place, calm again. Sometimes the older man is racked by a flamboyant coughing fit that sounds like he's dying; then he laughs. I don't understand the way they think—they're strange men. After observing them for a bit, I realize I've gotten distracted and am no longer reading. Then I get up and leave; that environment depresses me.

I still see my friends, of course, but they're all busy with their own stuff. Some of them have lost their jobs too. Some have found new ones, and some haven't. Some have even gotten used to never doing a lick of work and claim to be in seventh heaven. Two emigrated to Chile. Raúl, one of my friends from college, scrapes by doing odd jobs here and there. He's remade himself as a plumber, not a bad gig. The other day we got together and had pizza, and he admitted that he's satisfied with his life. "The important thing is not to just sit around, man. Believe me, I couldn't take it anymore," he said. You can tell he knows what he's talking about.

Living with Sandra has gotten harder. We've been living together for five years, and this is the worst we've ever gotten along. She claims it's all because I generate bad energy, and I suppose she's right. She says I'm always tense, grumpy, flying off the handle over trivial things. She says she's never seen me like this before, I'm not myself. She's lucky to know that much—I don't even know who I was or who I am anymore. And there's no need to be too harsh on myself—she isn't acting naturally either. She never talks to me about her work the way she always used to. I guess she doesn't want to rub it in that she's working and I'm not. She treats me the way you do a terminally ill person, someone you can't talk to about your plans for the future. But it's not all eggshells. She may tread lightly when it comes to work, but she doesn't hesitate to throw a fit when I've forgotten to run an errand or done a sloppy job ironing or left the kitchen floor dirty. And then I get pissed, I lash out at her, and we start fighting. She throws my atavistic sexism in my face, casting herself as the victim, and ends up saying, "Just leave it, I'll do it. I'll do it all when I get home from work." They're ridiculous arguments, but they sting. Atavistic sexism! It's no good trying to point out that household chores are monotonous and repetitive regardless of whether you're a man or a woman. After our arguments, it doesn't take us long to make up and then make love. But I'm worried because they're becoming the norm.

Iván, Juana's crazy grandson, has called me a couple of times. He wanted us to go out for a beer and a chat. I wonder what he's after. I doubt it's that he still feels indebted to me from his grandmother's funeral. In any event, I've put him off as best I can. I have no desire to expand my social circle.

* * *

We've had to let go of forty workers, mostly manufacturing and marketing personnel. I feel really bad for them, but a company's purpose isn't to hand out charity. I held out as long as I could, but the numbers just weren't budging. I'm anxious about the future, all the drastic measures we may end up having to implement. Everything's taken a dizzying turn. Just a couple of years ago, nobody would have imagined the country's economy would collapse so completely. My only consolation is that my father didn't live to see it. The only reason I ever regretted not having children was that there wouldn't be an heir to pass the company down to. So naïve!

David wanted to have children from the beginning. I didn't. I thought we were good the way we were: in busy solitude. Parenthood would only make our lives more complicated. Finally, after we'd been married a while, I gave in. Everybody else was doing it . . . But then I didn't get pregnant. We went to the doctor, and it turned out I was the problem. They stuffed me full of pills, without success. After that the treatments became more complicated, and I refused to follow them. I didn't want them trying things out on my body. I put my foot down, adamant. I'd do exactly the same thing today. I'll leave my body to science, but I have no desire to be experimented on while I'm still alive, like a guinea pig or a rat.

David didn't push, but a month after I'd decided to give up on the treatments, he came to me, looking very serious, and said, "Would you be interested in adopting, Irene? I don't mind, if that's what you want." I was astonished. How, when, and why had things turned so completely upside down? I hadn't been the one driving the conception train in the first place, and now my husband was talking to me as if I might be feeling enormously frustrated, as if I'd had to give up my fondest dream. "Adoption? No way!" I answered. I wasn't about to go through the experience of adopting a baby who'd turn out to have a heart murmur or some appalling hereditary disease, or to be the child of an alcoholic or a prostitute, with more problems than a fourth-hand car. And I had no intention of traveling to China to pluck one out of an orphanage. I've seen those adoptions with friends of ours. Forty-something couples who get baby fever because her biological clock tells her time's almost up. (Jesus, even the expression *biological clock* is ridiculous!) And so they dive into a long, torturous process: trips to the foreign country, long waiting periods, paperwork, money—lots of money. You even have to pass evaluations to confirm you'll make a competent parent! They look into every aspect of your lives, rummage through the most intimate details, scrutinize your bank accounts . . . Awful! Even though you're willing to take care of someone else's children from a country on the other side of the globe.

"Are you sure?" David tried to ask again. I don't think I even answered. I imagine by now he's got a baby or two with the simultaneous interpreter. Children that she wanted, since she's young, and that he's accepted, since he's in love. No matter how in love he is, though, it must be a shock to his system. Everyone knows the deal: bottles, diapers, slings if you want to go out . . . and you can say goodbye to golf and your tranquil midafternoon glass of whiskey. The house overrun with baby toys and the smell of sour milk. I can't imagine he's happy— he's as selfish and lazy as I am. I've always thought that when you do something for somebody, it's because you're expecting something in return. What is my dear ex-husband getting in return for spending his days dealing with drool, soggy diapers, teething, and wailing in the middle of the night? But maybe I'm wrong—maybe he's been seized by a fit of posterity and wants to see the fruits of his new love made real. Maybe he's starting to share the masculine desire to have progeny, leave a wake as he passes, have his last name live on after him. Maybe he wants to form a real family, sit at the head of the table, and say grace before eating. He's such a stupid man, I wouldn't be surprised.

My friends with adopted children—charming couples—are also members of the group that offered me "anything I need" after my divorce. And they've made kind and well-intentioned predictions: "You'll see, after a while things will go back to normal. You'll start feeling good, maybe even stronger, more sure of yourself." I haven't seen them since—they haven't called once. Lamenting that my friends have "failed me" would suggest that at some point I had faith in them, which isn't the case. Friends have always mattered to me in a relative sort of way. They're good for taking care of social needs: going out to dinner, whiling away a couple of hours in conversation . . . and that's about it. That's why they tend to be pretty similar, not in personality or ideology but in very concrete things: work colleagues with children around the same age, living in the same neighborhood. They fill an empty space in your life. Myself, I've never witnessed one of those epic male friendships nor the total intimacy they say women can achieve. Lifelong loyalty? Not even dogs provide that.

Genoveva Bernat has called a couple of times. I hadn't told her about my divorce, but of course she found out anyway. The first time, she kept me on the phone for two hours until I finally hung up, pretending I was at the office and had to get back to work. Her endless chatter can be summed up quite briefly: "Let's go out for drinks sometime and celebrate your freedom. Life goes on, girlfriend. Don't shut yourself up in your house like a hermit." Well, at least she didn't get all tragic on me. Her second call was to invite me to a party she was throwing on the terrace of her penthouse. I told her I wouldn't be able to make it. She insisted. I'm sure she would have kept insisting we do something together. She's pretty lonely, and she's delighted there's another woman who's not tied down and is available to go out. Again, the needs that friendship fulfills. Everybody's kind of given Genoveva the cold shoulder. She's older than me, about fifty. In her day, she caused quite a scandal when she left her husband and ran off with her personal trainer, a beefy guy, young and handsome but rather scruffy. They lived together for a while, but the passion dried up relatively quickly. She told me once that the guy would always say things like "for all intensive purposes" and "upmost," and said "utilize" instead of "use." It got on her nerves, obviously. His family lived in this tiny apartment in a working-class neighborhood. A harebrained idea, running away with a guy like that! Genoveva's lucky she inherited money from her family and that her ex sends her alimony every month because he doesn't want to deal with negotiations and lawyers or look bad to our friends. She wasn't the least bit upset when the affair with the gym nut ended. I always thought she'd wanted to break free from her husband, and her loser lover presented an opportunity. That way, she didn't have to give so many explanations or spell out her reasons: "I ran off with a hunk"—everybody gets that, right? Once she was free, she got a full facelift and bought a nice penthouse in a well-to-do area. She's a little slutty, but I doubt that's why our friends have dropped her. I imagine the real reason is she's become kind of vulgar: she wears clothes that are too young for her, and her makeup looks like it belongs on the sarcophagus of a pharoah's mummy. She plays the part of the hot chick living it up, the uninhibited floozy. She says everything is "awesome" and "rough," "amazing," and "fantastic," but it doesn't seem pathetic because she's still got a nice figure, lives in high style, and is completely free of hang-ups. She doesn't care what other people think of her.

Personally I'd never given her much thought, but I realize now how brave she's been, shrugging off everybody's opinions, and I like that. I almost admire her. She has undeniable and nearly unbearable flaws: she talks too much, sometimes way too much. She's always coming up with harebrained business schemes that never materialize. I remember listening to her go on and on about a dance school she was thinking of opening, to be run by some old has-been. She'd even planned out the décor. You just have to let her blabber on. She does have a certain charm.

Genoveva Bernat—she's a real character. The next time she calls, I'll tell her yes, I would like to go out with her. Better yet, I'll call her myself and suggest it. At least with her I won't feel like she's judging me, pitying me, trying to finagle information about my breakup so she can gossip about it when I'm not around. It might even be fun.

\* \* \*

Apparently the guy wasn't really into the idea of going out for drinks. Maybe he thought I wanted something from him. He must be giving me side-eye since I didn't visit my grandma as often as he did his. Today he finally said yes, but this is the third time I've called him—though I'd have kept calling if I had to. He doesn't know me; he doesn't realize nobody gives me *no* for an answer. So maybe he'll get to know me better. Of course, it's a big city and this isn't his scene, or he'd have realized I'm the goddamn king, the top dog, the fucking emperor. I'm going to wear nice clothes when we go out. Last week I bought seven Armani T-shirts at an outlet mall, one for each day of the week. They look great on me: nipped in at the waist and tight across the shoulders, highlighting my muscles. They're made of microfiber, really awesome. Today I'm wearing a khaki shirt, Diesel jeans, and black Nikes. The other day some girls coming out of the middle school stopped to watch me walk by. I spotted them rolling their eyes and elbowing each other. When they realized I'd seen them, they burst into peals of laughter. All in uniforms with their hair pulled back with a headband, but girls enjoy fresh meat. They're like wild animals in Africa. If they catch you, they'll take a bite. Their breasts were already visible beneath their shirts.

I'd arranged to meet him at the Cocoa at seven so it would be clear I'm loaded. I'm pretty sure he thinks I want something from him. Maybe he thinks I'm a junkie and drug dealer like my mother and I'm looking to sell him some product. Maybe I made a mistake at the cemetery and he *is* trying to play a part: intellectual, teacher, bookworm. But he's an out-of-work wimp, a loser the nuns put out on the street. So he'd better not start acting all superior or it won't be a long conversation: I'll have one beer to hold up my end of the bargain and then take off. But hang on, Iván, you're getting ahead of yourself! Slow down. Maybe the reason he didn't want to come out all this time is he was just depressed.

Look, there he is. I raise my hand so he'll spot my table. He smiles my way. Like I said, he's a good dude. He shakes my hand, takes the chair next to me.

"Hey, man, good to see you! How's it going, Javier?"

"Well, I'm alive."

Yeah, he's alive. But the guy's wasting away—he's lost weight and has bags under his eyes. He's obviously having a rough time with the unemployment thing. There's this one friend of mine who took it real hard. He lost fifteen pounds the first year. He looked like a skeleton in sneakers. He used to get high all the time in order to forget. He said his self-esteem was shot. The second year he had an easier time of it, though he kept getting high. I stopped seeing him after that—I'm sure he ended up in a real mess. People get worn out quickly, don't know how to fix their problems, just stand there waiting for the solution to rain down from the sky. And not a drop falls, of course. This is an arid country.

"And how are you doing, Iván the Terrible?"

"Why terrible?"

"It's what they called one of the Russian emperors."

"Oh, OK. Shit, man, we're off to a good start! I'm going to do an Internet search for that guy, and if nothing comes up I'm coming after you."

He laughs, but the poor guy's worn down. I can tell even though it's only the second time we've seen each other. I'll see if I can pep him up a little. He may be a brainiac with a college degree, but I'm an outstanding psychologist. I've got people pegged right off the bat. One look, and I can even tell you what color boxers they're wearing.

"I'm doing OK, man, keeping my head above water. Let's have a few beers, as the good Lord wills it."

"Keeping your head above water?"

"Always!"

I hope the teacher realizes it soon and takes note: there may be a hell of a crisis happening, but not even the entire Nazi army, all firing at once, could sink me. I've always got my head sticking out of the foxhole. Nothing gets me down. I know what's what. Politics and banks bore me to tears. I've always done my own thing, even back when everybody was rolling in dough and it seemed like they were the masters of the universe. I had a few friends who were more useless than the Pope's pecker, but they earned a good chunk just for climbing up a scaffold and slinging some bricks around. They'd go to Cancún on vacation, buy Audis or BMWs, and drink high-end wine. Sometimes at the restaurant they'd taste it and tell the waiter to take the bottle back because it was a little past its prime. Guys who'd never imbibed anything but cheap beer and box wine. I'd think, "One of these days, man, you're going to fall off that cloud, and you're in for a hard landing." And that's what happened. Now everybody's so screwed, it's like they've been worked over with a screwdriver. If they aren't unemployed, all they can find is temporary work that doesn't pay shit. Now it's Cancún Schmancún, and box wine is back on the menu.

"Didn't you see it coming, Javier, this fucking recession?"

"I guess so. But my teacher's salary was already really low."

Iván may be crazy, but he's funny—and he's right too. I didn't see it as clearly as he did, maybe because I was still pretty young during the construction boom. But I did see that people were improving their lifestyles but not their education. The review courses I taught at school weren't considered necessary. They were a luxury. The head teacher had learned that schools in the advanced countries offered those kinds of classes. France, Germany—if the European elite had them, why shouldn't we? But the money isn't flowing freely anymore, and the courses have been dropped. Nobody thinks they serve any purpose.

"The nuns didn't want to pay an extra teacher."

"Don't get me started on nuns and priests! They're all a bunch of fraudsters and freeloaders."

I have to let this teacher know I'm in the same boat; I'm like him, even though I didn't go to college. But life's a funny business—he's been kicked off, and I'm still riding the train. He laughs when I talk, cracking up—he thinks I'm funny. That's good.

"Did you know I take flowers to my grandma's grave, Javier? Yeah, man, don't laugh, I'm being serious. I barely saw her when she was alive, but now I leave her giant-ass carnation wreaths. They don't allow candles in the cemetery, though—I guess they don't want us setting the dead on fire. I know it doesn't do my grandma much good now, but better late than never, right? You didn't know her that well, but you must know my Grandma Juana was a pain in the ass. She used to tell stories that would put you right to sleep—wake me up when it's over. The Civil War, man, if you can believe that shit! How because of that bastard Franco they ate lentils and brown bread every day. And stories about when she got married, to my grandfather, I guess—I never met him. How she wore a white dress and satin shoes, and how her veil was blah blah blah. Shit, man, she told me about every fucking stitch of that fucking dress! It nearly made my head explode, man, really, like a bomb. But the worst was when she'd hand out advice by the fistful. 'Be a good boy.' How the hell am I supposed to do that, grandma? Some assholes can't stop being assholes no matter how hard they try. Anyway, you get it, Javier—my grandma was a real drag, and I'm not going to pretend otherwise just because she's dead. I loved her, though—don't get me wrong. The thing is, I don't understand why we have to go visit the people we love all the time. No matter how often I went to see my grandma, she was still a drag and I was never a good boy, so if nothing was going to change, what was the point? Jesus, man, why are you laughing like that? I'm being serious here."

"I know, I know. Don't mind me. Something came over me."

Iván is quite a surprise. He's no dummy. Everything he says has this sardonic quality that's humorous, refreshing, but critical at the same time. He's like a street cat: clever, quick, able to run away from the enemy or turn to fight as the occasion requires. And from the little I know, he could easily have turned out surly or depressive . . . but no, he seems to have come through all right. I haven't had this much fun in a while. Lord knows how he pulled that off. I'm really curious about how he makes his living, but I'm embarrassed to ask and he's not telling. Maybe it's too soon.

"I have to go, Iván. Maybe we can get together some other time for another beer."

"Of course, man, of course we can get together some other time! I'll call you. Oh, no, don't even think about it! Put down that check. It's my treat."

Even his face has changed. Poor guy, he must be pretty miserable!

* * *

"Genoveva? It's Irene Sancho. How are you?"

"Oh, darling, what a surprise! I'm great, how about you?"

Well, look who's showed up. I don't have to ask, I already know how she is: only the lonely, right? That's why she's calling. Every time I've called her, she's totally ignored me. She didn't even want to come to my party the other day. Maybe she doesn't remember she stopped inviting me to hers. I don't care, though; I'm not losing any sleep over it. Which is why I called her—because I couldn't care less what other people think, and so she'd know I'd heard about her divorce. So he flew the coop—welcome to the club of independent women. There are other fish in the sea, as I hope she's finally figured out. Irene, the perfect woman, always cold and distant, like she's above all these worldly things. The model business-woman, daddy's girl, faithful wife . . . Well, look where that's gotten you, sweetheart: gored by the bull like everybody else. It's true that when I went through mine, she wasn't mean about it. She never looked down on me or took digs at me the way others did. But some attitudes speak for themselves: that pitying look of hers . . . And you know, at least my husband didn't leave me for another woman—I was the one who left him. I imagine our friends have turned their backs on her, which is why she's coming to me. Or maybe she's just bored to death with them. Going out with friends from when you were married is awful. It's like you're a widow, like you've got the plague—everybody seems to feel sorry for you. It's really obvious the relationship isn't natural, and the more they try to fake it, the worse it is. They didn't do that with me, of course, because I was the bad girl, the wild child, the slut who left her husband for a younger guy. Since they were supposedly all progressive and high-minded, nobody ever mentioned it to me, but they treated me with complete disdain. I kept going to their get-togethers for a bit, but after a while I stopped. I stopped because I wanted to. I'd had it up to here with their fakery and sideways looks and pretending to be something they're not. Plus I was bored, like she probably is now. I'd always thought they were boring, right from the start: so proper, so formal. No surprise there: I met them all through my husband, and my husband's the most boring man on earth. *Poor Adolfo,* everybody said when I left him: how he'd always been a gentleman with me, never retaliated or spoke ill of me, still pays me alimony, is having to rebuild his life at this age. Nobody got to the root of the problem. Adolfo is significantly older than I am, and he hasn't aged well. He's broad in the beam and deadly dull. He's quiet, stuck in his ways, a home-body. He repeats the same endless routine: work, home again, and early to bed. You don't need a hot wife like me for that sort of thing. I may be older now, but I'm still attractive and I've got blood running through my veins. Plus I'm lots of fun—people laugh a ton when they're with me. Not like my ex. And don't even get me started on the sex issue: just one quick session once a month, God forbid the man wear himself out. No thank you! If that's what he's after, he can find a caregiver or a Benedictine nun, or become a monk himself.

I won't say Adolfo behaved badly after our divorce because it wouldn't be true, but the only reason he pays me alimony is because he wants to. I didn't ask him for it. I never needed his money during our marriage. When my parents died, my brother and I inherited a wad in property and country estates. Of course, we've sold most of it over the years, but there's still a bit left that we could sell if it came down to it. It's great to have the alimony, of course, because I can leave the inheritance for my old age. But I don't *need* it—I've never had to ask any-body for anything. I wasn't born under a bridge. Sure, Irene's father left her a systems factory, which is nice, and she's an economist, which is great. I didn't go to college because it sounded like a drag, but my father owned the largest scrap metal company in Spain. That might sound bad to refined ears, huh? Like he ran a junkyard or something. Anyway, I figure those friends from the club are envious of me, and that's why they look right past me. And I've heard Irene's company isn't doing so well thanks to the crisis, so off your high horse, princess.

"Oh, of course, darling, let's have a drink at the Manhattan! What time do you finish up at the factory? Perfect, I'll be there."

There's Genoveva. I don't know if I would have recognized her if we hadn't arranged to meet. It's been so long since we last saw each other! She looks different—all dolled up! Low-cut black dress, a thin white blazer, black-and-white shoes. She's got two bracelets on one wrist: one made of ebony and the other of ivory. She looks very sophisticated. She smiles at me. We exchange kisses. She practically shrieks:

"You look gorgeous! I think you've lost some weight. Come on, take a seat. I'll have a gin and tonic with Sapphire and Nordic. And she'll have . . . "

She's not looking well. Bags under her eyes, gaunt—she must be having an awful time of it. It must be a bitter pill to swallow, having your husband leave you for a younger woman, though I could see it coming a mile away. David always struck me as a selfish type. A brilliant lawyer, absolutely brilliant, but the first thing he does is get a job in his father-in-law's company. I heard she fired him. I wonder what he's doing now. Now that he's a high-powered professional, I imagine he'll be able to make it on his own. Men are something else, always looking out for number one. Being here with her, I even feel sorry for her. Whatever her faults, she didn't deserve that.

"How are you doing, darling? What's new?"

"Not much, Genoveva. You know how it is."

There's not much she doesn't know already. Just this: I'm starting to get sick of being the poor abandoned wife, and if she starts pitying me the way everybody else does, this conversation won't last long. Now that I see her close up, it seems like she's gotten plastic surgery again. She used to have crow's feet around her eyes even after her facelift, but now they're gone. Her chin was also starting to sag, I remember clearly. She doesn't look fifty, but she doesn't look younger either. She looks worryingly fragile now, like a glass doll that might break with the slightest movement. She hasn't just gotten a couple of touchups—she must have gotten the full treatment again. What for? Is she hoping to stay sexy? Her cheeks are stretched too tight and her eyebrows are too high. Is she looking for a new lover, or is it that she already has one and is trying to be beautiful for him? How exhausting! It must be awful to fight the aging process every day. I couldn't do it. I go to the gym, try not to gain weight, use high-quality moisturizers, buy expensive clothes, but eternal youth . . . Whatever for?

"Do you see the old gang much, Irene?"

"Well, you know how they are."

Of course she realizes I've called because I'm moving on from that gang. If she asks, it's because she wants a little tribute from me. She wants me to criticize them, to tell her I'm seeking out her company because she is so far superior to the others. That's her price. Fine. I want her to know I'm not afraid of social rejection or idle gossip; the only thing I can't stand is being single in a world full of respectable and supposedly happy couples. I tell her that, tell her I can't bear people's phony offers of impartial moral support. I tell her I don't need anyone to help me stay on my feet: I'm not overwhelmed by crying jags or eaten alive by loneliness or sinking into a depression. I'm not looking for consolation or company. I'm good on my own. David is part of the past now. I don't mention that I feel profoundly that I've wasted my time, failed to take advantage of my life. Instead, I say, "I want to have a good time, Genoveva. I've worked too hard, been too serious and formal. So now I want to go to trendy bars, talk nonsense, laugh, do frivolous things, even dance. Do you know what I mean?"

"Of course I do, honey! How could I not? I understand you better than anybody, believe me."

If a good time is what she's looking for, she doesn't need to worry about that: we're going to have a fabulous time. I'm particularly relieved that she said she doesn't cry. The tears of abandoned wives drag me down like nothing else. The only reason they want to go out with you is to launch into the same old tale of woe: my ex turned out to be an asshole, I never saw it coming . . . such a bore. Life's short, and if you spend it listening to other people's problems, you're wasting precious time.

"I got another facelift, Irene, did you notice? Dr. Martínez Santos isn't just a sweetheart, she's a total superstar, the best of the best. She's used this new technique on me that's really amazing. They stretch out your face muscles too, not just your skin, and the really innovative thing is they insert a mesh of gold wires with these strategic anchor points. That way, when the skin gets loose again after a while, they just tighten the wires and *ta-da!*, everything moves back up, no need for another operation. I'm telling you, it's amazing, though I have to admit it was pretty painful. I had a rough few days, but it was worth it—it took ten years off me. If you want, I can go see the doctor with you and you can get something done. Of course, you're younger than I am—you've got time."

"The first time you got your face done, our friends were pretty hard on you."

"They sure were! I've got new friends now—you can imagine. But it's not like before, where we always used to go out as a group, always to the club and the same few restaurants. I'm much freer. I see my friends here and there, we'll meet up one day and then not the next, we see each other around . . . We're adults—there's no need to go around in a pack all the time. I'm very active. In fact, my life is pretty hectic: gym, massage therapist, beauty treatments, lots of movies . . . But don't think I'm so selfish I think only of myself. Every couple of weeks I go to a poor neighborhood to help serve at this soup kitchen run by nuns. You're surprised, huh? I know, it doesn't seem like me at all, but we have to do something for other people. At Christmas I help out with the 'A Toy for Every Child' campaign, and at Easter I help deliver Easter bread and chocolate eggs to low-income families. I'm telling you all this in case you want to sign up for anything. I get a lot of satisfaction out of this stuff, though I know it's very personal, very much dependent on an individual's own conscience."

"I'll think about it."

"Great."

She listens to me intently, but I don't know what she's thinking. Irene's always been very reserved, indifferent to everything. It's hard to know where she's going, but I like her—or I've never disliked her. In any event, I hope she doesn't want me to be her toastmaster. I can go out with her, but I don't do babysitting. If she starts clinging to my skirts, I'll be forced to dump her. I'm a free bird, and I fly through life uncaged.

"Of course we'll go out together sometime! I'd be delighted. We'll have an amazing time, I'm sure of it."

"Me too."

Lord, if all Genoveva can offer me is the address of her plastic surgeon and the chance to do charity work in poor neighborhoods, I think it was a mistake to agree to meet up.

* * *

Sandra says I could give private lessons. She doesn't have a clue. Sure, maybe years ago someone with a humanities degree could offer private Latin tutoring. Latin was a difficult class and lots of students were taking it, so their parents would get them a tutor. But it's been many, many years since then. Latin's fully part of the past now; students haven't even heard of it. And nobody needs a private tutor for literature lessons. Nobody. It's something you study on your own. She proposes some other options: I could lead one of those reading groups they organize at the public libraries. She's clearly sensed my mounting desperation and has been looking into job prospects I might aspire to. I note that they've also been cutting the book club budget because of the crisis. A lot of the clubs have been canceled, actually, and the ones that are left already have coordinators. She says I could form my own book club on the Internet and charge for it. I tell her that's dumb. She gets mad. She thinks I'm rejecting all her suggestions without even considering them. And she's right, I guess, but her suggestions are ridiculous, completely unfeasible; I wish she'd think about them for a minute before opening her mouth. I know I can be hard on her, I know she's just trying to help, but she needs to realize that offering useless help just wears on the person you're offering it to. She gets mad, and I get worn out. If we keep it up, we'll be at each other's throats by the end of the week. Are our lives so poorly stitched together that they're going to end up bursting apart at the seams at the first serious problem? And what can I do to prevent it? Smile all the time to keep her calm? I don't feel like smiling. I don't feel like doing hardly anything. I've become totally inactive right when I have all the free time in the world. When I was teaching, I always wanted to go back home and read. Now I can't even concentrate on what I'm reading. I'm afraid I'm the most basic kind of guy: I need work because it gives me a connection to the rest of the world. It turns out that all those clichés we've heard a thousand times and mocked another thousand are true. Work gives you dignity, integrates you into society, gives you a place in the world, makes you useful. I guess if I were a more intelligent man, a man who thought more deeply, with a more fully furnished soul, I wouldn't need a job title to feel good about myself, but even the act of reading leads me, thought by thought, into the usual dead end: I'm useless to society; reading doesn't pay dividends.

I've gone out with Iván a couple more times, long enough to have a beer and talk a little. I admitted to him that I'm screwed without a job, and he went off on a fantastic rant in his coarse, roguish, hilarious language:

"Work is just a way to get money in your pocket, man, that's it. Where'd you get that bullshit about how it gives you dignity and makes you more of man? No way. The only thing that gives you dignity is having money in your pocket. Your problem is you're spoiled, man, and you're not seeing things clearly. What really sucks is having a job but not earning jack. That'll really give you a complex about lack of dignity and all that shit! And that's where most people are. They spend their lives in a job they don't give a rat's ass about, and at the end of the month they get some shitty paycheck that won't even buy them a pair of new socks. When you don't have any money in your pocket—that's when you don't have dignity, Javier. Every door is slammed in your face, and you're a goddamn slave, a loser. You might as well be invisible. That's a real problem, man, not dignity! So don't give me that crap about feeling useless to society. What society, man? The one that leaves people out on the fucking streets? Come on, man, that's bullshit! I wouldn't even waste an hour of sleep thinking about it."

It was a practical, unconventional, and accurate analysis. It was also my chance to ask him what he did for work, but out of respect instilled in me by others and my fear of offending him or seeming rude, I kept quiet. It would have made sense for him to tell me of his own accord, but he kept quiet too. Maybe he was making a living with some illegal enterprise, or maybe, despite his anarchomaterialist outburst, he was only a manager at a grocery store and was embarrassed not to be living in keeping with his own impassioned theories. I don't know. In any case, I enjoyed his company. He was so radical, and at the same time so free, that it was a pleasure listening to him talk.

When we met up at a bar for the third time, he caught me off guard by asking for my address. I hesitated a moment, and he got offended.

"Don't you trust me?"

I apologized profusely, and eventually he smiled.

"I'm going to send you a gift that'll make you shit your pants," he said.

And so he did.

\* \* \*

First recreational outing with Genoveva. She's scheduled an activity I rarely find enjoyable: shopping. I generally buy my clothing at stores I've been going to for years. The managers and sales clerks know me; they know what I like and what looks good on me: Max Mara, Armani, Calvin Klein. I'd never choose anything by Versace, Dolce & Gabbana, or any of those other flashy, avant-garde designers. Discretion is paramount for me. Papá used to tell me, "A businessperson is like a banker or a politician: he or she always represents the company. Avoid loud colors, wear suits and blazers, and a more masculine look is always good. Above all, though, no flowery patterns or ruffles. Your mother would never have approved of them." Papá was common sense personified. He never remarried, though any other man in his position would have. As a widower, he faced endless challenges: he had to hire nannies, worry about my education, choose a school, a university . . . every detail large and small. He was always unflinching and meticulous; few men could have done better. The main reason he didn't remarry was that he was shattered by my mother's death. And once he'd gotten over that trauma,

I became his reason for living. Not wanting to force a fake mother on me, he elected not to have more children, not to have a companion or enjoy the comforts of love. Two things seemed to be enough for him: the company and me. I didn't realize how much he'd sacrificed for me until I got a little older. He was an imperturbable man, but he must have occasionally longed for female companionship and the fundamental joy one derives from having a large, happy family. When I was old enough to understand, I started worrying about him, trying to make up for the deprivations I'd unwittingly imposed on him. I threw myself into the company, thinking I could show my gratitude that way. Everything was going well until this economic recession undermined what had so laboriously been built. Luckily, Papá didn't live to see the consequences of such profound destruction. What should I do now? Keep fighting even in his absence: get the business back on its feet, diversify, try to start exporting our products . . . but I'm tired, so tired. David's departure, the way he abandoned me, has completely discombobulated my mind. That's the worst part: I don't really care that he's fallen in love with a younger woman, but having my work be disrupted has plunged me into a depression. I wasn't counting on him to help run the company, but having him there gave me a sense of stability. Now I'm on my own. I wonder what ideas Papá would come up with to keep the firm active, but I have no answers. Fatigue hampers my thoughts.

Genoveva wanted to surprise me. She took me to a bunch of stores that sell cheap clothing for young women: Zara, Stradivarius, Blanco. I'd never been into one of those shops, and they're really something else: blasting music, garish décor . . . And the clothing! The clothing is awful, cheaply made, practically disposable. The sales clerks wandering around look really wild, their eyes so heavily made up they can hardly blink. The clientele isn't any better. I couldn't believe it: young girls dressed up in the tawdriest way, with skintight jeans and high heels, their hair dyed all sorts of colors. And it's pure chaos: everybody paws everything, moves it around, takes it off the hangers and leaves it tossed in a corner. There are no doors in the dressing rooms, just a curtain that anybody could pull aside, exposing half-naked you. Genoveva was being really funny. She was clowning around, imitating the sales staff, giving uninhibited little shrieks. Most amazingly of all, though, we bought a ton of stuff. Geno was in her element—she says she goes to those places sometimes. Most of the clothing she buys she passes on to her assistant to give to her daughter, but she says sometimes one of those cheap garments looks great combined with a designer piece. For example, she chose this military-style jacket with gold buttons that made her look like a Hussar. I was dying with laughter when she tried it on, but then it turned out that in combination with the black skirt she was wearing, it actually looked really nice. I bought a few pairs of skintight pants. Absurd. We ended up walking out with two massive bags full of clothing we'd never be able to wear—but the important thing is it had been ages since I'd had so much fun. Then Genoveva suggested we go get some gin and tonics.

"A gin and tonic in the middle of the afternoon? That will definitely give me a headache."

"Nonsense, woman, don't be silly. It'll do you wonders."

Headache? Please! Irene doesn't have a clue. She's always seemed a bit prudish, but she's worse than I thought. Had she really never been to a fast fashion store, not even for fun? Does she really spend her whole life at the factory, endlessly working like she's being punished for something? Sure seems like it. It's obvious her father took advantage of her. The company was sacred! And Mr. Sancho was always high-and-mighty. I used to see him at the club some Saturdays when he came in with his daughter and son-in-law. That son-in-law! He must have really had it up to here with the old man. I'm sure he celebrated when his father-in-law died. He did well for himself to marry an heiress, but I don't know how aware he was that marrying Irene meant marrying the company, the last name, the father, the whole shebang. Now that I think about it, it took him a long time to dump her. He must have been making sure he had all his financial ducks in a row. And now he's flown the coop. I'd like to see the girl he ran off with, but I doubt he'll bring her anywhere he might run into our friends. The girl is probably dead broke and totally smitten with him. I'll bet you anything David sold the motorcycle he rode away from his wife on so he could live out his undying love with her. After all, that marriage had been dead for ages! But Irene's held her head up and kept going. She's doubled over with laughter right now at our having bought such gaudy clothing. I don't get what she finds so amusing. Has she not noticed the way girls dress these days? But fine, I don't mind taking her with me to a few places—it's not like any of my other friends have the kind of free time that I do.

"When are you going to wear those striped pants you bought? They're perfect!"

"You're nuts! I'll just wear them around the house. Where am I supposed to go wearing something like that? Seriously, where?"

\* \* \*

It was Sandra who gave me the letter. She'd pulled it out of the mailbox when she came home from work. I hadn't retrieved it because I haven't left the apartment for a week. I don't feel like it—I know what I'm going to find, and nothing's going to make me feel any better. Sandra's getting worried; my staying home seems to her like the beginning of the end. To placate her, I tell her it's nothing permanent, just temporary laziness. But my explanations don't assuage her concerns. Her anxiety has led to nearly as many fights as my own mental state.

She was struck by the handwriting on the envelope, rough and hesitant, almost as much as she was by the fact that I'd received a letter. So she gave it to me as soon as she arrived. It was from Iván, and it contained a short note: "Here's that gift. I'll be expecting you and your girlfriend." Along with the note were two tickets for a show: "Diamond Room. Saturday the 12th at 10 P.M. Unaccompanied men will not be admitted." Sandra says the place rings a bell, but she can't place it. We look it up on Google, and what we find makes me howl with laughter. The Diamond Room is a club on the outskirts of the city that specializes in male striptease. "Guaranteed entertainment. Handsome, hot-blooded men. Special discounts for groups of ten or more." Sandra finally remembers, and she laughs too.

"Yes, it's a strip club for women. They almost always go in big groups. One of my coworkers told me you can't take it all that seriously. Women go there for bachelorette parties, birthday parties, to celebrate a divorce . . . I thought it was a just a fad—I'm surprised the place is still open. By the way, who's Iván?"

I remind her who Iván is and tell her he's called a few times to invite me out for a beer.

"Why does he call you?"

"I guess he's grateful because I went to his grandmother's funeral. He's an odd guy. I have no idea why he sent these tickets. Maybe he works as a server there."

"Or maybe he's a dancer," Sandra laughs.

That possibility hadn't occurred to me, but it doesn't seem likely. Being part of that kind of show requires certain qualities—the ability to move to the beat of the music, a degree of sophistication, good looks—and this guy strikes me as boorish, quite incapable of being provocative or attractive. In any case, my suspicions have been confirmed: Iván doesn't work some-where conventional. Not a body shop or a grocery store—a strip club. *Hot-blooded men*. I guess his grandmother never found out about it. The world's a big place, and it's got all sorts. It's just that we don't see it: we move among the mem-bers of our own tribe, our particular social sphere.

"So are we going to go?"

I'm caught off guard by her logical question. I hadn't even considered it. A striptease at the Diamond Room? I look at Sandra with a measured expression on my face.

"You think we should? Does that seem like our kind of joint? You said it's all groups of women looking for a night out. Seems like a couple would be out of place—it'd be awkward."

"We can go as observers. It'll be like a sociological experi-ment."

We'll finally get him out of the house for a bit. He's been refusing for days. When he opened the letter, I saw his eyes light up and heard his laugh. That beautiful laugh I'd almost forgotten. My friend María's brother is a psychologist. I'm sure he's depressed, even though he refuses to admit it. Other peo-ple who get laid off don't take it so hard, but he's really sensi-tive: his parents' death when he was young, his love of being alone . . . If only I could help him! But I can't figure out how. So let's go, let's go to that strip club and have a good laugh. I need it too—it's eating me up seeing him like this.

"I didn't realize you were interested in sociology."

"Maybe what I'm interested in is seeing a bunch of naked men with perfect muscles and flat abs prancing around. I think the real issue here is you're jealous—but we should go, or your friend might worry you look down on him for working there."

I didn't put up much resistance. After all, I was curious.

Just as Sandra had said, the place is full of groups of women, which occasionally include a man or two. Very few couples like us. There's a small stage with a long catwalk extending out among the tables. Dim lighting. All a little shabby, ugly, grungy. A large, gleaming disco ball hanging from the ceiling. Maybe it's an old sixties-era cabaret that's been repurposed. The range of ages among the audience members is actually quite remarkable: teenagers, older women, thirty-somethings. It's noisy. Nobody's talking in hushed tones while they wait for the show to begin. It feels rowdier, more like a beachside bar or Oktoberfest: bursts of laughter, coarse shouts. The waiters bustle around, distributing the compli-mentary drinks included with the tickets. Anything after that, we'll have to pay for. I scrutinize the waiters, looking for Iván, but he's not passing out drinks. And he's not tearing tickets at the entrance or serving customers at the bar either.

Sandra is distracted, scanning the room. She must have begun her sociological observation. She looks beautiful tonight, in a blue dress I haven't seen before and with her eyes carefully made up. A voice comes over the loudspeaker and announces that the show's starting. The house lights go down, and intense spots illuminate the stage. A master of ceremonies appears, dressed like the ringleader of a circus: a fuchsia sequined jacket and shiny black satin pants. He's an older man with a raspy smoker's voice.

"Ladies—and gentlemen too, but especially ladies—wel-come to the land of happiness and freedom. What you're going to see here tonight is not just any show, it's the best show of its kind in all of Europe. Having been chosen through a careful selection process, some of the best-looking men in the city will be appearing on this stage. Enjoy."

Given the dry, formal introduction, the attendees' response is pretty unusual: they scream, howl, roar. They clearly aren't taking the MC seriously. They order him off the stage, bellow-ing at him, "Let's see it! Get out of here! You're wearing too much clothing! We want meat!" The room is in an uproar, a pandemonium of laughter. Sandra looks at me in disbelief and starts cracking up. I'm so startled, I'm not sure how to react. It's not like I've been to a lot of stripteases, either male or female, but this intro seems less like a performance and more like an audience-led riot. The MC's still talking; he tells us the title of the first act. It sounded like he said "At School," but there's such a thunderous din that he really could have said anything.

Next the room plunges into total darkness and the shouts die out. The lights go up on stage, where, as if by magic, someone has set up a classroom with a chalkboard and six red student desks. A young man is seated at each one. All of them are wearing ridiculous school smocks and large silk bows tied around their necks. Their shorts leave their bare legs exposed. A teacher, less youthful-looking than the students, appears on the stage. He's tall, shapely, muscular, and dressed in black. The music pounds through the speakers, rhythmic, steady, sexy. The teacher starts dancing to the beat. His sinuous movement starts with his head and gradually spreads down through his torso, arms, hips, thighs, feet. He looks like an inchworm moving across the floor, pulling back, stretching forward. All of a sudden he stops short, goes toward the seated students, and pulls one to his feet, grasping his hand. He leads him to the center of the empty space and gestures for him to mimic his dancing. The student makes a clumsy attempt. The teacher corrects him but then, having grown impatient, sends him back to his place and tries with another student, who isn't a good dancer either. This is repeated three times, and each time the audience cracks up at the young men's bumbling imitations of erotic dance. When the fourth student fails too, the teacher grows desperate. The music gets louder, the classroom lights dim, and a spotlight lands on him. His dancing becomes frenzied, unhinged, lewd. He moves as if in the grip of a sexual fever, like a male animal getting ready to mate. He removes his clothing piece by piece and throws it furiously to the floor. By the end, only a pair of skimpy briefs covers his member. He turns his back to the room and shows off a small, dark butt, each muscle tightly sculpted. The audience explodes. Then, as if they were on springs, the six students leap up from their desks and imitate the teacher's movements, this time flawlessly. They dance in unison, connected to the rhythm, perfect. They pull off their shorts, which fly through the air. A little while later the school smocks are ripped off with a single yank, and the six young men are left standing there in briefs just like their teacher's. Their bodies are slimmer than his, less defined by age. They are of similar build, similar height. Applause thunders through the club, but the men don't bow or wave to the audience; instead, they race offstage. The house lights come up, dazzling after the semidarkness. There's a flurry of waiters, drink orders; a few spectators get up and visit other tables. Sandra stares at me open-mouthed, stupefied but smiling.

"Did you see that? It's incredible, right? That teacher's dancing is electric, unsettling. I can't believe these things are going on right in our city."

But they are going on, Sandra. People make a living however they can. Though there doesn't seem to be anything sordid about this—I don't see anything like the classic patrons of the female striptease, guys staring lustfully at the dancers while nursing their whiskeys.

Another performance begins, announced by the Mexican-style strumming of a guitar. Bright lights spill across the stage. Entering from stage right comes the legendary Zorro himself, dressed in the obligatory black, with a wide-brimmed hat, a cape that goes down to his ankles, and boots with spurs. Despite the mask, I can tell it's Iván. I would have recognized his pursed, unsmiling mouth anywhere, twisted by the faintest rictus of contempt. I lean over to Sandra and whisper in her ear: "I think that's him."

She nods, her curiosity piqued.

Zorro begins a dance clearly influenced by indigenous styles. He stomps his feet, cracks his whip, pretends to gallop on an imaginary horse. It's pretty ridiculous, so much so that the audience titters. Unexpectedly, then, a man dressed as a prerevolutionary guard bursts through the curtains and attempts to capture Zorro. They draw their swords and run through a showy fencing choreography. Thrusting and parrying, they move along the catwalk that juts out into the audience. Seeing him up close like that, there's no longer any doubt that it's Iván. The dust rises up under their stomping heels and floats suspended in the beams of light. The fighting intensifies, until finally Zorro/Iván starts removing the guard's clothing, item by item, with the tip of his sword. Every time an inch of skin is revealed, the audience bursts out into raucous, if still somewhat mocking, cheers. When the entire uniform is off, standing before us is a body in briefs, a little pudgy, with an incipient belly but sturdy legs. Naked and humiliated, the guard looks down at himself and takes off running. This time it's Zorro who chases him, inspiring a frenzied uproar, until the fugitive disappears behind the curtains. The music gets quieter, the ethnic elements drop out, and it becomes the standard pulsing accompaniment to the traditional striptease. Zorro gracefully swings his hips and drops his cape, ruffled shirt, wide-brimmed hat, and pants. He's left wearing black briefs and boots.

"Your friend is hot," Sandra says, laughing.

And it's true, Iván's got the body of an athlete—or, more accurately, like something halfway between an athlete and a ballet dancer: long legs, sculpted at the gym, a flat belly, muscled calves, a perfect ass. He starts strutting down the catwalk, still wearing his mask. The women stretch their arms toward him and shriek. His movements are calm, impassive. He draws close to the frenzied girls, sliding away when someone reaches out to touch him; he gestures at them provocatively, sticking out his tongue and waggling it around like Mick Jagger. He moves toward us and gives us a thumbs-up. "I'll see you after," I hear him say amid the din. I smile and clap. He continues his triumphal march down the platform, and a middle-aged woman sticks a twenty-euro bill in his briefs. Other women follow suit, and, as if by magic, his genital area is suddenly swollen with banknotes. All in unison, like they've rehearsed it beforehand, the girls start howling, "Take it all off!" and then chant, "Off! Off! Off!" The masked figure imperiously gestures for the music to stop. There's a drumroll. Zorro stands up tall, takes a deep breath, and rips off his mask. Now I can see his whole face, its familiar expression: proud, distant. We're all in suspense, waiting for his briefs to come off too, but that doesn't happen. Iván runs offstage and the house lights go on again.

"Man, your friend's a real professional!" Sandra exclaims in amazement. "He made a wad of cash with that little promenade! And did you see how deep in there those girls were stuffing that money? Shameless!"

With short pauses between each number to allow people to order more drinks, the show goes on. The acts are all pretty similar, though after a while only one dancer comes onstage and the erotic intensity increases. What they all share is the strut down the catwalk. The dancers are often accosted by the alcohol-fueled audience members, who try to kiss the guys on the lips, grope their asses. They stuff cash in the guys' briefs, taking their time about it, which makes the friends who've come with them burst into peals of laughter. The dancers systematically rebuff all of these advances, sometimes visibly irritated and gruff. The only ones not participating in the spectacle are the youngest women, barely out of high school. They just shriek at random, their high-pitched voices getting progressively louder. One of them has vomited on the floor. A waiter appears with a bucket and mop. I want to leave. I've gotten the idea at this point, and the show's starting to drag.

But I know I have to stay, not just to say hi to Iván but also because Sandra is having a great time and wants to meet him.

The MC announces the final act, but he doesn't leave the stage at the end of his introduction. The lights go out and then come on again, and he's still there in his ridiculous sparkly, fuchsia-colored jacket. Sexy music. To the audience's surprise, he starts moving to the beat. He's nearly fifty, not attractive in the least. I assume he's going to perform a comical number, but no: his dance grows repetitive, swaying, hypnotic. He's like an aging orangutan getting ready to mate with his very last female. He removes his jacket and shirt. His torso is tanned dark. Age gives his body a dramatic quality that the young dancers lacked. Slowness is his primary erotic weapon. He's in no hurry: he dawdles, dallies, weaves, goes into a slow trance. His pants vanish in a single movement. He reminds me of classical statues of Roman centurions: beefy, brawny, Herculean. He's so wrapped up in his role that he lives it—you can hardly call it performance at all. His face displays extreme emotions: defiance, superiority, contempt, pleasure: "Here I am, bitches. I'll make you happy for real." The audience members who had been mocking him and inventing rude chants are now holding their breath. He has the room in the palm of his hand, and he knows it. He's moving as if engaged in a slow, majestic, ritualistic sort of coitus. He perspires, delights, finds himself in some private, torrid place. He doesn't range around the stage, get close to people, make the mistake of proximity. I glance at Sandra out of the corner of my eye. She's rapt. I am too, though I sometimes feel an absurd need to look away, finding the whole thing too intense. The indescribable scent of sex saturates the room.

In the final moment, as the beat becomes more regular, more insistent, signaling that we're nearing the end, the MC moves his right hand back and unfastens the last bit of elastic: his briefs fall to the floor. A large penis, now freed, hangs against his inner thighs. His balls are dark, tinted a raucous purplish blue, which gives them an odd, glistening sheen. He spreads his arms in complete surrender. He reminds me of the ecstasy of a person being crucified, a sacrifice recently made. His eyes are closed, and then suddenly he opens them and walks offstage. The mocking, derisive audience now applauds uproariously, as if they had just witnessed a performance by a famous tenor. When the lights go up, the room is pervaded by an awkward unease, like at the movie theater after the screening of an intimate film. The spectators can't look at one another, seized by a strange prudishness.

Fortunately, it's now time for the entire cast to take their bows, and the dancers' appearance onstage prevents the show from ending with an unsettling anticlimax. The young men are wearing black pants and sweaters, nice, everyday stuff, looking utterly normal. Nothing unusual's happened here; we hope you'll come back for another visit. There are twelve of them, including the MC, who's somehow had time to change.

The crowd begins to leave, their voices hushed. Euphoria has given way to fatigue. Only a few patrons remain at their tables.

"No comment," says Sandra, giving me a sardonic look.

Quiet music and the final drink orders: bottles of champagne. It must be a sort of tradition among the regulars. We haven't ordered anything, but a waiter brings us a bottle.

"From Iván. He says he'll be right out."

"How thoughtful!" says Sandra before we toast.

After a few minutes, some of the dancers start to emerge and sit down at tables with people who are clearly their friends. Finally Iván appears. He's got the same expression on his face as always. I stand up and introduce him to Sandra.

"Congratulations," she says. "You were great. You were all really good. I loved it."

"Thanks."

It's a kick-ass show, woman, no shit. The only reason we haven't taken it to New York is that the boss doesn't want to. They've invited us, yeah, but he wants to keep things simple, otherwise . . . we'd all be there on Broadway, buck naked. Though really it's better to stay home—there's lots of competition in America, and here we're the only ones. We fucking rule the roost. The room sells out every Friday and Saturday. During the week it's just a dance club. The city is what it is, and we can't fill it every day. We mostly get groups of women, lots of them. If they had to come alone, they wouldn't do it, they'd be embarrassed, but when they're in a group they go wild. Women sure are something, groping you right in front of everybody like it's no big deal. If things were the other way around, if a guy felt up a female dancer, there'd be a riot. The bouncers would get involved. But we have to put up with it— it's part of the show. And they say things that stop you dead in your tracks, really crude stuff. "Come here so I can suck your cock." I bet they don't talk like that at home. It pisses me off, actually, because they don't really mean it—they're just trying to look cool in front of the other women in the group. Though ultimately I don't give a shit—I just do my thing. My main goal is I want to do a good job. I've been rehearsing the new show for a month solid. We change it all up every six months so people don't get bored. That way if they come back, they don't see the exact same show. We get groups of older women and a lot of bachelorette parties. The waiters tell us what table they're at, and one of us will go congratulate the bride-to-be. Then we're the ones who screw with them: "Touch my thigh, beautiful—once you're married, your husband's not going to let you do that." It's bullshit, but they love it. There are also groups of women who come in to celebrate when one of them's getting divorced. You have to be careful with them because they're bitter and might do something nasty or grope you. And then there are the fucking young ones—they're the worst. Not even hatched yet. They get trashed because they don't know how to drink, and they always order the cheapest thing on the menu: beer or wine. Totally hammered. Just today one of them threw up right there in the room. We've even had to call an ambulance a few times because of alcohol poisoning and so forth. If they left you a lot of money, it wouldn't be a problem, but they never give anything. Mariano, the boss, insists they bring energy and says it looks good to have young people in the audience.

"Do you make decent money?" I ask.

"Shit, man, what can I say!"

That's some question the teacher's asking. If we did a show every day, I'd be all set, but since they're only on the weekends, you do OK, but not well enough to buy a Porsche or anything. And we split the money out of our jockstraps with our dance partners. The guy who plays the guard during my act doesn't stay till the end, so I give him half of what I get. The ones who perform solo make the most. They've been around the longest and have the most experience. I'm not there yet. Anyway, with this fucking crisis that's going on, you make less and less each time. I've only been doing this a couple of years, but the older guys say that four or five years ago, women would be slipping fifty-euro bills into their briefs. Now there's no way. The standard is twenties, but sometimes I've gotten tens or even fives.

"You haven't told me if you liked it."

"It was amazing," Sandra says. "Especially the MC."

"Mariano's a genius."

A genius and a force of nature—the best. He owns the place, and he's the smartest one here, the one who gets all the money. I don't resent him for that, for the record. The dude's a real brainiac. He sets all of this up: he comes up with the ideas for the dance numbers, hires all the performers, keeps the books, and takes care of the rent and décor . . . Shit, he's the one running all the risk. And he's a good guy. He pays in cash, and it's pretty good pay, considering. He doesn't take a percentage of the tips—that's all for us.

"His act is incredible," I remark.

"It sure is."

It always leaves everybody speechless. During the show he seems like the worst one and nobody's paying attention, and then at the end . . . at the end he takes it all off, the bastard, and brings the house down. He's got a gift. With what he makes from the show and then with the dance club the rest of the week, he's got to have plenty to live on just from that, but he likes performing. His moves will turn you to stone. He drives chicks crazy, all cocky, like he's saying, "You want me to fuck you, girls, is that what you want? Well, I'm gonna fuck you good." The chicks get all riled up. He's the best. He learned it in the States. He was in a bunch of shows there. He played the Latin macho better than anybody, even though he had competition from the Mexicans and Colombians—but he beat them all. He even married an American. Then they split up and he came back to Spain. He also got older, of course—aging doesn't spare anybody. He's still got a good body, but if it weren't his show, they'd definitely have booted him by now. He's a smart guy, and he gives good advice. He's always saying, "Think about the future, boys. This striptease business doesn't last forever. If you're not careful, your gut goes flabby or you get a bald spot, and then it's all over. They'll slam the door in your face. And I will too—business is business, and ladies want fresh meat. They've already got their husbands back home if they want a close-up view of human imperfection. The customer is always right, so don't think this is forever. You can do all the sit-ups you want, but it won't save you. Save up or look for another job before it's too late, or set up your own joint, or marry rich." That's Mariano, a fucking genius.

"Don't even think about paying, Javier! It's my treat. Put

that wallet away before you piss me off. It's been a real pleasure having you two, I mean it."

On our way home, Sandra looks at me, suddenly serious.

"I can't believe you're friends with that guy."

"Why?"

"He's a flaming sexist."

"Come on, Sandra, give me a break! So he's sexist. He grew up on the streets, what do you expect? Who were you expecting to meet, Nureyev after a performance of *Swan Lake*?"

Jesus, it's like she doesn't have a clue: mother in prison for drugs, father dead of an overdose, raised in orphanages or by his grandmother, trying to make his way in life as best he could. Sexist!

"He hasn't robbed or killed anybody. He found a way to make money at the club. It's commendable. Good for him—I still haven't figured out how to earn a living."

"I'm not saying he's a bad person. I was just taken aback by the way he talked about women. What do you see in a guy like that?"

"I'm a loser too, don't forget, worse than him."

Sandra's a little younger than I am, but it seems like she's stuck in the past. She doesn't realize things have changed—they'll never be the same again. She thinks they'll go back to the way they were: job, family, social position. Her catechism is carved in stone: don't be sexist or racist or classist. Practice solidarity. The crisis hasn't touched her yet. She earns a regular salary, lives a quiet life, goes to visit her parents on Sundays . . . She thinks my unemployment situation is just temporary. She has no idea, doesn't realize the party's over—or maybe she's closed her eyes so she won't have to face reality, but it's still there. It doesn't matter how many academic degrees you have. Nothing makes a difference now. The old model is dead and buried, but there's no new one to take shelter in. Make do—that's the only option. There is no path.

There is no destination. Everything's wide open. Somebody tricked us—a shepherd led us up to the edge of the cliff and then disappeared. If you fall off, that's your fault. That's it.

"All right, Javier, that's enough! You can't get all worked up over every little comment you don't like! I made a mistake, so sorry. Iván's charming, a real gentleman, a prince, a career diplomat. Is that better?"

We'll see how long I can take this sour mood of his. It seems like it's here to stay. Everything pisses him off, every dumb thing drives him crazy. He used to be so even-tempered! A rational man, deliberate, judicious. Never unpleasant or disrespectful. If I chided him, he responded with considered explanations. Sometimes it was even annoying how sensible he was because it felt like he was trying to teach me something. And now I have to constantly bite my tongue to keep us from fighting! I'd never have believed he was such a neurotic guy underneath it all. Sure, he's always had a tendency to concoct huge theories based on absurd little details, which he loved to analyze in depth until he'd drawn occasionally impossible conclusions, but I never thought much about it. You already know a guy who studied literature's going to be a little odd—he'll never be like a science or technology guy. His outlook on life is always slightly less realistic. But Javier's reaction now doesn't make sense. You lose your job and that's it, it's all gone to shit! Well no, man, chill, it's not the end of the world. Or are people just going to stop working forever and ever? Nobody's going to need literature teachers ever again? But it's no use—all he's got are catastrophic predictions: everything's changed, life as we know it is over. It's no good pointing out that I'm still earning money, that we can keep going, we're going to be OK, a job will come along.

We'll see how long I can stand it. Life's hard for me too. They're pushing people harder at work. I'm hustling every day. It's not a breeze for me; they're not rolling out the red carpet wherever I go. I've got plenty of problems too, but I try to pull myself together and push on without writing a philosophical treatise about every obstacle or blaming modern capitalist society or the forces of evil.

I'll stick around as long as I can, but I have no intention of being his punching bag, getting kicked around and having to put on a happy face too. Like that fuss he kicked up today about his new best friend! Iván—what a jerk! What is he doing hanging out with him? What do they talk about? Where did he find that guy, a dumpster? He's a crude, sexist philistine! Your typical neighborhood pimp. I have no idea what their friendship is based on, but there's Javier with his brow furrowed and his face stony, like his own honor's been attacked.

* * *

The manager nags me all the time. I notice his critiques are getting more and more personal. They're subtle, just the barest insinuations, but at bottom they're all the same. I shouldn't skip the weekly meetings at the office, I should do a walkthrough in the factory every once in a while . . . When things were going well, he didn't demand this kind of dedication from me. Quite the contrary, sometimes I had the feeling my constant presence at the firm bothered him, like he was afraid of any intrusion into his domain. But now that the castle's crumbling, he's constantly demanding I work harder and invoking my obligations. How does he expect me to stroll around chatting with the workers when we've had to let so many go? Does he think they're going to welcome me with open arms, waving palm fronds like I'm Jesus Christ on Palm Sunday? They'll lash out as soon as they see me, I know it: "There's that stuck-up prude who hasn't been able to keep the company going since her father died." I don't want people insulting me to my face. Doesn't that damn manager understand who he's dealing with? I'm a woman whose husband left her, and that's a terminal condition. Whenever anybody finds out, they back away. I might as well be contagious. But the manager keeps thinking the company is the most important thing to me. He never liked David. I'm sure he thought he was an opportunist and that my father had promoted him just because he was my husband. And then what does he go and do? Now that the ship's taking on water, he leaps overboard and leaves me at the helm. So the manager has plenty of reason to act this way. And at least he doesn't pity me. I can't stand pity. Though he could at least give me time to react, time to learn how to wear this new "abandoned woman" outfit I never thought I'd have to wear. He's worried about his future, not about me. He knows that if the company goes under, he'll go under too. Where is he going to find another position like this one? When you've been somebody's right hand, it leaves you marked forever after. Nobody wants a limb that's been severed from another body.

I stay calm when he goes off on one of his diatribes. I act just as I do with everybody else: not worried or sad or desperate. I don't weep, I don't flee into my thoughts, I don't say mean things about my ex, I don't tell anyone about my problems. As far as they can tell, I don't even remember I was ever married, and in a way it's true. That way I keep other people from telling me about their problems, which makes me uncomfortable. But whether I show it or not, I'm still a woman whose husband left her for a younger woman. And I just want to be left alone.

I'm not managing my free time very well. If I were emotionally devastated, I would have tried to find a solution immediately—psychologists, physical activity, a trip abroad . . . — but I'm not doing so badly. I hate feeling like I've failed. The only hard part is the emptiness that yawns in front of me; it makes me dizzy. But I don't want to fill up my free time with any old thing just to fill it. I have friends who, when they get divorced, start taking yoga classes, look for a personal trainer, enroll in a graduate program, take ballroom dancing lessons, join groups of women who travel together . . . and they end up going crazy, of course. Other women immediately look for a new man to replace the old one. At first it's to demonstrate that they can hook another guy and reel him in whenever they want. But after that they go through a phase where that's no longer satisfying and they want to be part of a stable couple. Big mistake. Things fall apart, they end up in ridiculous relationships, and they start taking a dim view of men: "Men just aren't willing to compromise," "It's slim pickings when it comes to men." Whenever I hear these statements, I picture horrible scenarios: the emotional freaks you meet on the Internet, the guys who seem wonderful and then turn out to be nightmares, your first boyfriend you lost touch with a million years ago, now older and balding and with whom you have nothing in common. And it's even worse if these women looking for replacement parts have children: rejections, obligations, the need for mediation . . . What are they hoping to get out of these humiliating situations? Sex? Jesus, a lot of the ones I've met stopped sleeping with their husbands ages ago and seemed happy enough. Why do they suddenly and so urgently need to hop into bed with a man? Are they looking for love, a mature love, a second chance? It doesn't matter that they've gotten divorced: love seems more fundamental than eating or sleeping. I don't get it—I don't feel that way at all. I need a man about as much as I need a gun permit: I wouldn't know what to do with either one. Anyway, I know quite well what I don't want to do, but I'm struggling to manage my free time.

Genoveva called to invite me out. I always accept. At least she doesn't whine to me about her love life. I have a pretty good time with her. She's so superficial that she ends up being lots of fun. She suggested we go to the gallery opening for a painter she knows. I'd never been to one or met a painter before—there wasn't room for that sort of thing in my marital or business life. I went, but I should have declined the invitation. I'm not saying I had a bad time; at least I spent some time in an environment that was new to me. But I was expecting something a little more glamorous. Instead, everybody was talking over each other and they were serving white wine that hadn't been chilled properly. It may have been an intellectual environment, but it felt like an evening at the club: laughter, meaningless comments, and people constantly kissing each other on the cheek. There were a few strange guys, looking grungy or dressed up in loud, garish designer clothes, but nothing terribly original. Worst of all was the artist himself. I'd imagine someone with a bit of personality, but instead he was a total philistine: fat and sweaty, sixty-something, and a total ass-kisser. Disappointing.

Today Genoveva called me for a debriefing.

"I was a little disappointed, especially by the painter. I thought he'd be more interesting."

She cracked up.

"Sweetie, painters aren't starving bohemians anymore! You're behind the times."

Poor Irene! Like I say, she's basically a cloistered nun, a precocious little girl who's never been outside her boarding school. She spent so much energy on daddy and hubby and company and club that she's never figured out what life's all about. It's like she's been in a car, being driven down the highway, and she never looked out the window. She's reached her destination without knowing where she is or how she got there. If I were her, I'd have blown my brains out from sheer boredom. But I've gotten by, figured out how to stand on my own two feet and get what I wanted for myself. I'm not scared of people or what they think of me. I keep pushing forward and refuse to worry about it.

"Irene, darling, you know what? I agree with you. The painter's horrible, and his paintings are even worse. Who cares whether he's had shows in New York or China—would you hang a portrait of a diseased, deformed old woman in your living room? Awful! But the paintings go for a lot of money; people are wild about them."

Her living room . . . If I were her, the first thing I'd do is sell that house. It's this huge apartment her father gave them when they got married, and she lived there with David for so many years. Why stick around? Girl, please, move a little, shake that body! If she asked me, I'd tell her just like that. But she doesn't ask anything—she's locked as tight as a safe and as cold as an ice cube. That's why she doesn't want to go out with her old friends. They'd give her advice and start nosing in her business. Not me. I don't give a damn—people should do whatever they feel like with their lives. But if I were in her shoes, I'd sell that place and buy myself a nice apartment. I'd decorate it with the latest trends and add a lot of flashy details. After all, I love playing house! Last month I changed up the décor in my bedroom. I had a blast! Coordinating fabrics, tracking down some vintage piece of furniture, combining colors . . . I love it! But I know how to get the most of things, how to find enjoyment in everything. I've never been one to just sit in a corner all by myself.

"So I guess you're not going to be buying a painting from the guy."

"Not at the moment, Genoveva, though they weren't all terrible. There was some really strong work there."

"Sure, but a butane delivery guy is strong too, and you don't take him home with you."

Genoveva's completely crazy, but sometimes she makes me laugh. She seems to be managing her ample free time just fine. I picture her swaying from side to side, always surrounded by people, always at some party or opening, always at the gym, the beauty salon, the spa. I wouldn't be able to keep up that pace, listen all the time, talk, smile, choose the right outfits . . . These days, I hardly feel capable of anything. Nothing interests me, not even work.

"And to think I'd considered introducing you to my painter friend to see if you'd hit it off! I don't mean for anything serious, just if you were interested in going out with him every once in a while, having some company . . . I don't know, socializing, as they say nowadays."

"Do you have someone you go out with regularly?"

"Me? Perish the thought, Irene! I'm above all that. I've been living alone for many years at this point, and I'm doing great. I do my own thing, make things work . . . But you're younger, recently divorced—maybe it would be good for you to meet a nice guy . . . What do I know! Don't pay any attention to me—I just thought I'd introduce you to the painter, but I see it would have been a bust."

"No need to introduce me to men, Genoveva. At the moment, I'm good just the way I am."

\* \* \*

Sandra was nervous, euphoric when she got home. I was in the living room reading back issues of literary journals that I'd pulled off the bookshelf. She planted herself in front of me.

"Javier, one of the girls at work told me about something you might be interested in, a teaching job. Listen."

He does, but I'd rather he listened without that skeptical look on his face, with a little more hope or excitement. But no, he's got that perpetual sneer of embittered superiority that makes me feel so atrocious. Can't he try even a little bit? He needs to see that our relationship is just as important as his being laid off, and it's getting harder to make it work.

"They're looking for a full-time literature teacher at Crisol.

My coworker's sister teaches there. She remembered I'd told her you were out of work, and before they start interviewing the other candidates, she set one up for you. What do you think? Aren't people wonderful sometimes?"

"Definitely. But isn't that school Opus Dei?"

I know you're always looking out for me, partner dearest, but before you start flying around like a frenzied moth, beating against a hot light bulb and scorching your wings, you should check things out a little more closely.

"So what if it is an Opus Dei school? You've been teaching at a Catholic school for years now. It's basically the same, isn't it? You can teach your classes without buying in."

"It's not that simple."

If only my little moth understood these things without my having to explain them! Anyone who thought about it for five minutes would realize that an order of nuns dedicated to teaching is not nearly the same thing as Opus Dei. Opus Dei is a breeding ground for fascists, an occult organization, a sect. I have no ideological prejudices—those were done with before I was born—but it's preposterous to think the school would hire a guy like me. They'll want somebody who's devoted to the cause, who's easy to control. I teach literature, not science or Latin. And literature is dangerous stuff. Every line of a poem, every chapter of a novel, every act of a comedy or tragedy contains a moral challenge that would have to be neutralized if I worked for Opus Dei. So they'll make sure the teacher they need is cut from a particular cloth—and that's not me. Do I have to explain all these basic things to Sandra? Can't she think for herself? Why is she so happy, so excited? People may be wonderful, but they're awfully shallow.

"Don't tell me you're not even going to consider doing the job interview because it's an Opus Dei school."

Sometimes I think his inactivity and depression are really just airs of superiority. He thinks he's too intelligent to have to engage in the struggle of the day to day. He doesn't want to lower himself. He wants employers to seek him out, to get down on their knees before him.

"Of course I'll do it! But I don't want you to get your hopes up—they're not going to give me the job."

"You're the one who should be getting his hopes up. You can't go into a job interview with a losing attitude! That's no way to achieve anything, Javier."

She stalks off to the kitchen, irritated. Lately she's been leaving the room in a huff whenever we argue. My pilgrimages to whatever room she's retreated to, my attempts to placate her and smooth things over, are starting to wear on me. I feel like a mountain climber with a heavy pack, toiling endlessly upward and never reaching the summit. But I'll follow her, of course, and yet again I'll tell her what she wants to hear.

"Please, Sandra, don't be angry. I said I'll go to the interview, and I'll make sure everything works out."

She gives me a name and phone number to confirm the appointment and leaves for work, calmer now. The contact is one Mr. Contreras. Contrary Contreras—we're off to a great start!

Iván calls that afternoon.

"Hey, man! I haven't heard from you since the show. Did it put you off, did it make you uncomfortable?"

"Not at all! We had a great time."

"You had a great time, huh?"

Shit, this guy doesn't have a clue. "We had a great time" is probably what he told those goddamn nuns, the Ursulines or whatever. "We had a great time" is what you say after playing petanque like the old grandpas in the park. "We had a great time" is total bullshit. I invite them to see the best naked-dude show in the city, and they "have a great time." This isn't good. Maybe I'm wrong about Javier. I had an idea of who he was, but now he says he "had a great time." You're supposed to say, "The show was awesome, it kicked ass, it totally rocked."

Or you ask questions about it. For instance, people have often asked me, "Are all the dancers queers?" But no, these two "had a great time." Maybe Javier's chick was scandalized, maybe she's a prude. She seemed a little weird to me—she wasn't wearing any bright colors, no low-cut top or anything, and she didn't have on eyeliner or any other makeup. I like chicks who dress like chicks! Open-toed high heels and fluorescent fingernails. Tight pants that show off their ass and leave their belly button exposed. A close-fitting, low-cut top that emphasizes their breasts. And long hair spilling down their back. That chick of Javier's must be a real buzzkill. Maybe after the show, she pretended she hadn't liked ogling men's asses and biceps and told Javier, "It's disgusting, so vulgar!" And of course Javier believed her. He's a teacher, so he's probably OK with these spiritual chicks who don't wear makeup. Well, let's see if they understand that getting an invitation from me is something special—I don't just hand them out. And if this idea I'm working on goes well and I make my proposal, then it'll be like he won the Powerball with a ticket someone gave him as a gift. But this "We had a great time" crap is a bad sign. Maybe he'll be offended by my proposal and tell me to fuck off. If so, too bad for him—at least I'll have fulfilled my obligation: no matter how you look at it, I've bent over backward for him. Though really I'd be the one who's screwed, since for some reason I like the guy. But if he gets all high and mighty on me, that's it—I don't take shit from anybody.

"Yes, great, we had a great time."

"I'm calling because I need to talk to you. Would you be able to meet up tomorrow morning?"

"Sorry, Iván, I've got another commitment tomorrow."

"But this is pretty urgent, and I can't talk about it over the phone."

"I'll call you as soon as I'm done, and we can meet."

I don't feel like calling him, but I'll do it. It might be the last time I go out with him. Sandra's right: we don't have much in common. But I would hate for him to think I didn't want to meet up because I didn't like his show. He shouldn't think I'm passing moral judgment on him, condemning the way he makes a living. I'll call.

\* \* \*

I didn't think I'd have to go through this sort of thing. Don't lawyers complain about having too many cases on their plates? So why hold a settlement meeting for a man and woman who have nothing more to say about their divorce?

I hadn't seen David for months. Having him right there in front of me didn't make me feel anything in particular, but strangely I'd forgotten what he looked like. It lasted just a moment, because then I suddenly recognized the features my eyes had seen so many times. He hadn't changed—maybe he was more resolute now, less pensive. He'd also lost that guilty air he'd adopted after his confession: "I'm in love with another woman." He must have felt relieved once he'd said it. It's uncomfortable keeping secrets like that. I was his problem. It's not pleasant being someone's problem without even knowing it. That hurt me more than his betrayal, his lies, his falling out of love.

I hope he notices how calm I am. I just want to get through this settlement business. I regret how I reacted when he told me, "I'm in love with another woman." I should have been completely impassive. Really, I should have been the one to bring our fictional marriage to an end. It was a familiar problem: how many fictional marriages did I see all around me? Lots of them, and they didn't seem so bad. In theory, a long-lasting romantic relationship goes through a number of different stages: passion, understanding, friendship, support, respect.

Because my mother died so young, I was unable to confirm whether that's the case with my parents' marriage. And now I won't be able to confirm it in my own. I do know one thing, though: we never went through that first stage. When we got married, my main feeling was that we were forging an alliance that would benefit the company, which seemed like a good thing. Women's dreams are so ludicrous. We always add an emotional element to everything.

Luckily, I'm fairly reserved and never shared my unromantic fantasy with anybody: "Joined together in matrimony for the greater glory of the company." Had I been more open about it, I'd now be the object of more ridicule. I only hope God grants me the gift of amnesia.

And here came David, out of the blue. Tanned, probably spending more time outdoors now that he's with the simultaneous interpreter. His hair cropped very short—the simultaneous interpreter probably likes it that way. Casual clothes, which she probably buys for him. He must be thrilled to be freed of the stern suits he felt obligated to wear as my company's lawyer.

We listen with feigned attentiveness to the lawyer's every word as, point by point, he outlines the agreement we've drawn up. There is nothing to amend, add, or put into context. We sign. Like an idiot, I rebuff the gold ballpoint pen he holds out to me, remembering how I gave it to him for his birthday. I pull out my own pen and sign my name. And that's that— from now on, I'll have only memories.

When we leave the lawyer's office, David invites me out for coffee. He's relaxed but not smiling. I tell him no, I'm in a hurry. I hold out my hand, but he doesn't shake it. Another mistake. Luckily, it's the last one I'll be able to make in this story.

Driving back home, I nearly run over a homeless man who appears unexpectedly from behind a trash container he must have been rummaging through. "Nearly run over" may be an exaggeration, but I do have to slam on my brakes and I stop mere inches from him, his shape indistinguishable under the sheer bulk of clothing he's wearing. He looks up blearily, as if he doesn't see me. But he does see me: screaming, he calls me a bitch. The passersby stop for a moment, observing us. A hot wave of blood floods my face. I'm startled to discover that my first impulse is to leap out of the car and fly at his ragged body, kicking and shouting. I don't do it, of course, partly because of the people watching. I swerve around him and continue on my way. My rage gradually dissipates, but I continue to be startled by having imagined such violence. It's not my style. My style is to worry: what would have happened if I'd plowed into that riffraff? An endless series of mounting problems—ambulances, lawsuits, a trial, compensation. Today, though, just for having called me a bitch, I wanted to kick him until I was completely wiped out. It's weird. I'm not quick-tempered, I'm not one to fly into rages, I don't get worked up easily. I've always considered indifference to be a powerful weapon. I guess I'm frustrated after the settlement meeting. Seeing David must have upset me more than I thought. It's unsettling that my personality might be changing without my even realizing it. Switching it up at this point in my life and under these circumstances would be tremendously inconvenient. Being the way I am has allowed me to get to where I am, and it's gone pretty well for me. But signs of a shift to a new personality are piling up. For one, I'm less and less interested in work. I seek mental escape by going out with Genoveva. And I'm getting testy. It's worrying. I don't care about changing hobbies or lifestyles, but I couldn't stand changing my personality. If that happens, I'll despise David for the rest of my life. I'll eventually be able to forget the humiliation of being dumped for a younger woman. I'll no doubt forget the years I wasted being with him. But I won't be able to forgive him for turning me into someone else.

* * *

"Seriously, though, Javier, what did you think of the show the other day? Old fuddy-duddies think it's shit, really filthy stuff. They say it's faggy, when it's obviously not. Not that I have anything against fags. I've got friends who are fags, and they're hilarious, really cool people. But if the show was for queers, I wouldn't be in it no matter how much they paid me. I don't want anybody mistaking me for one. Our show is something else—it's got a happy vibe. It's about having a good time. The women who come to see us with their guys, I know afterwards they must really get it on. And the ones who aren't coupled up must have to look for some kind of release, because we get them all hot and bothered, I can tell. Plus the show's artistic and stuff. You don't have to know a whole lot to be up there, but you've at least got to be able to dance to the beat and stay in good shape. If you're a balding, two-hundred-pound schlub with love handles and a beer gut, you'll have to look for something else. We don't go completely naked, so it doesn't matter if you have a small prick; you can add some padding if you need to. Mariano and the other guys who perform alone at the end of the show do have to know a lot more and be well hung, since they strip all the way. They've all got a gift, see. It's like they were born for this stuff, even though this stuff didn't exist when they were born. They work really hard: working out, looking for new songs and bringing them to the boss, improving their posture, tanning sessions, going to the salon every two weeks . . . But as far as I know, not a single one of them is gay. I think Mariano makes sure of that. Not because he has anything against queers, but so the dances will be more authentic and exciting for the ladies. You can always tell when a guy's a fag: a little smile, a little hand flip—you can tell, and that would be no good here, as I'm sure you understand. Mariano has crystal-clear rules for his business. He doesn't allow drugs at work. Well, you can always do a rail of coke, but if he catches anyone shooting up, they'll be out on their ass. He doesn't give second chances, man, that's just the way he is. And I love it, because drugs wrecked my family. You get that?"

"Of course."

"OK."

The teacher looks at me with an expression I have a hard time reading. It's like he's doesn't give a shit about any of it.

"To be honest, I don't have a gift for this. I strip for the money, and I like that. But it's not my calling—nothing ever has been. When I was in school, all the boys wanted to be soccer players or airplane pilots or Indiana Jones—but not me, man. I had no fucking clue what I wanted to be when I grew up. But I already knew what I didn't want. I didn't want to work like a goddamn mule for peanuts. I didn't want to be an electrician or a mechanic or a plumber or go to a factory and do the same thing every fucking day of my life and not earn jack at the end of the month. I knew that for sure! I know this is going to sound like I'm trying to suck up to you, but I swear it's true: the only thing I ever thought I might want to do was be a teacher. I don't know, man, being with kids and teaching them things and telling them whatever you want and them having to listen to you no matter what—that's pretty awesome. Don't laugh— it's cool to have someone listen to you. You don't notice because you're used to it; you'd still be with those kids right now if the damn nuns hadn't fired you. By the way, how are things going with that? Are you looking for another job?"

"Things aren't great, Iván. An opportunity may come along, but I'm losing hope. Being out of work is harder than I expected."

"That's rough, man. It's like everyone's telling you to your face that you're a piece of shit when none of it's your fault. Telling you you're taking advantage of other people. And if your chick has work—and Sandra's real nice, by the way—then it's even more of a bummer. You'd think it would be better, but no, because you end up getting all screwed up about being a kept man."

"You clearly get how I'm feeling."

"I've been there, man, and it was awful. At the time I was living with this girl who worked as a cashier in a grocery store, and it was fucking miserable. I even had to ask her for money to buy smokes! I started doing odd jobs here or there and was earning a little, but not much. That's when I got involved in the show. A friend of mine told me he was looking for guys, and I took the plunge. It's just a job, I thought, why not? Am I hurting anybody? Is it illegal? It's a job like any other, plus I get to have lots of free time. Don't you think so, Javier? Isn't it just another job?"

"Of course."

"Well, look, that's actually exactly the reason I wanted to see you today. Maybe you're going to think this is crazy and laugh, but I'm going to say it anyway, since we've gotten to be friends and I don't like seeing my friends in a bind. Remember that number with the teacher and students? In the show, I mean. Well, a guy who plays one of the students, this French guy named Georges, came in the other day saying he wants out. Not because he's had problems with the owner or anything like that—his mother died and left him a house, and he wants to try to set up and run a country inn. Being one of the students is the easiest role in the show, so I thought maybe you could do it."

Shit, I knew it. I knew he was going to look all scared—but this is worse than I expected. The bastard looks like he's seen a ghost. Seriously? I offer him a job, and I'm the one who's going to have to apologize.

"I think you've got potential, man: you're tall, slim, no gut . . . Shit, man, you look good. And you don't have to put your heart and soul into it or anything—I think you could do a good job. Just rock those bones in time with everybody else, and you'll do great!"

"Damn, Iván, you really caught me off guard here! I never imagined you'd suggest something like this."

How can I get out of this one—it seems clear he's serious.

"Anyway, you might think I look good, but if I showed up and told Mariano I want that role, he'd tell me to fuck off."

"Not if I ask him—we're friends."

"But I'm a terrible dancer. I've never had any talent for it."

"It doesn't matter."

A terrible dancer? Now I'm the one who's surprised. This dude's a goddamn moron. Does he think he's going to be twirling around in a ballet or something? I'm really tempted to say, "Look, teach, this isn't a damn movie. You just have to waggle your cock back and forth, that's it. Forget about dancing—there's no need. You just have to have the stones to go out there half naked and then get even nakeder."

"See here, Javier, I'm not asking you to join the show so you can be a star or go international. I'm talking about a well-paying job, which there aren't so many of. And since it's just on the weekends, you won't have to give up whatever you're getting on unemployment. Plus the guys in the show are really cool. There's the occasional jackass, but not many. We get along really well for the most part. After the show, a bunch of us always go out for beers and something to eat. We have a good time, talk about the things that happened that night: a woman in the audience who was really hot, another one who acted like an idiot . . . I don't know, we have a good time."

"Don't get me wrong, Iván. I'm really grateful you thought of me for the role. I'm sure it's a great job, and I could certainly use the money. But I can't see myself doing that. It's like . . . "

Careful what you say here, Javier. Careful with your similes. What's the plan for finishing the sentence I've started?

" . . . like if they offered you a job as a teacher"? No way. That would basically be saying "like if they offered you a job as a teacher when you're a total loser who doesn't know his ass from his elbow." Not an option. Nor can I tell him that his dancing buddies, the good-time guys, make my hair stand on end just looking at them, and I'd switch seats on a bus so as not to have to sit next to them.

" . . . like if they suggested something you'd never even considered. How would you react?"

"I don't know, man! Unless they were suggesting I take up the priesthood, I'd probably think about it for a little while, maybe even a day or two."

"No thanks, Iván, really. Being a stripper is as good a job as any, maybe even better, but I can't see myself there. I just can't see it. You understand, right?"

"Of course."

Of course I get it. It must be a real bummer worrying that one of your former convent students might see you. Seeing a girl who once asked you about the assignment now staring at your junk bundled away there in your undies . . . Yeah, I get it, but I've done what I can. He was fucked without a job, right? So I go and offer him one. If he doesn't like it, that's his problem. I've done what I can. Now we're square when it comes to how he checked up on my grandma and went to her funeral. Even Steven.

"I hope you're not mad, Iván."

"No way, man! It takes all kinds. To each his own."

"And let's get together for a beer from time to time."

"Absolutely, man, say no more!"

I won't call again—I did what I can. But I do like him. The teacher's a good guy.

"It's a deal."

I won't call, but I truly appreciate his having thought of me for the stripper job. It's a humorous anecdote I'll never forget. Iván's a good guy.

\* \* \*

An unexpected visit. Unfortunately, I was home and had to ask her in. She's had highlights done in her hair and I'd swear she got Botox injections in her forehead and maybe her crow's feet too. She looks awful. I guess she thinks I'm delighted to see her, happy to have her show up at my house unannounced. I haven't talked to anybody from our circle of friends in months. Teresa wasn't a close friend. I've never had close friends of the sort you confide in or discuss life with. I invite her to have a seat, offer her a coffee. I figure I'll just let her talk:

"I didn't think I'd catch you at home, since it's during the workday . . . "

She's lying. Somebody's obviously told her I haven't been going in to the factory much, that I'm neglecting my sacred duties as a businesswoman. She wants to gossip, pass the scuttlebutt along to other people, corroborating or refuting their claims. Trying to be patient, I lie too:

"You know, with the recession, things are pretty slow. They don't need me to be at work as much as they used to."

She reluctantly accepts my explanation.

"I always thought it was the other way around: the harder times are, the more effort you have to put in."

"That's one way of looking at it."

I have no intention of engaging in a debate with her over the functioning of capitalist enterprises or how to ride out financial crises. I politely ask after her husband and daughters.

"Raúl's doing well. He's always got something going on. Since he travels abroad so much, we hardly see him. Our eldest girl started at Esade. Didn't I tell you? I guess not, since we hardly see you either."

She titters, and I titter back. At this point she's realized I'm not going to open my mouth unprompted. If she wants to get anywhere, she's going to have to drag my confidences out of me by offering up some of her own. Maybe she'll get better results that way.

"So tell me, Irene, how are you doing?"

"I'm great, as you see."

"You look wonderful, though to be honest we're all a little worried about you."

That's the crux of it: "We're all a little worried about you." Teresa has shown up here at my house as the spokesperson for our social group. "We all" are my friends from the club. They're people I'm supposed to keep seeing, the members of my natural tribe. "Worried" means intrigued. They want to know why I'm acting the way I am. The word has another implication too: they're offended they haven't gotten an explanation for my absence since my divorce. From somewhere within me I muster some acting skills I've never used before and didn't even realize I had. I shake my head hard enough that my hair swings back and forth, and let out an incredulous chortle.

"Worried? Whatever for?"

She hastily says exactly what I predicted: they've been hearing from me less and less since my divorce. I haven't accepted any of their dinner invitations. I haven't been back to the club. If anyone calls me to meet up one on one, I always make excuses. As a result of which: they think I'm not OK, that something's wrong. As a further result of which: they're worried about me.

"Well, you know what splitting up is like, Teresa. It's rough going. I was married to David for many years. I need time to think, reorganize my life. We just signed the divorce papers a few days ago."

She keeps interrupting me with comments of her own:

"You can't just brood about things—maybe you need to get out, distract yourself." But when I mention signing the divorce papers, her ears prick up and she asks, "How did it go? Did you two talk? Was it hostile? Did he show up alone? Did you show up alone?"

Naturally, she can't go back to the group without some good gossip. Her maneuvering reminds me of the money changers in the temple. I remember when I learned about them in school. The Old Testament was extraordinarily violent, full of fornication, revenge, passion, and parents willing to slit their children's throats in God's name. In fact, I found God utterly terrifying. At night I would dream about Him and wake up crying and screaming for Papá. The poor man would rush in in his pajamas; he never let my grandmother come instead. When I told him that God was appearing in my dreams and wanted to kill me, he dismissed it: "That's nun nonsense. One of these days I'm going to march over to that school of yours and tell them to stop stuffing your head full of garbage. Go back to sleep. I have to be up early tomorrow." He'd go back to bed, a little irritated at having been woken up, and I'd lie there, still a mess, not knowing whether God truly had all the destructive power the Bible attributed to him or if it was just one of Mother Rodríguez's fantasies.

The New Testament was much less terrifying, though there were a few scenes I had my doubts about. For example, Jesus driving the money changers from the temple. Why did he have to be so mean to people who were just trying to make a living? After all, my father was also a sort of businessman, and I couldn't understand Jesus's reaction. It was only after David left me that I understood. Money changers are those people who want to go where nobody's invited them, who're always inquiring, speculating, poking their fingers into the wound and sniffing at the blood. And now poor Teresa, impoverished in some fundamental way, made it even clearer. Now not only did I understand Jesus's anger at the temple, but I also felt it myself. I pictured myself brandishing a whip, knocking over the stalls full of knickknacks: false friendship, false empathy, false affection. I wanted to shout, "My life is a sacred temple that none has permission to enter!"

Of course I repressed my desire to pummel Teresa with a sofa cushion. It would have been ridiculous and, most compellingly, I didn't feel like explaining to her why I was doing it; she never would have understood.

"Not at all, it was just a formality. There was no tension between us. We're all civilized people, right?"

I sense the frustration in every inch of her vexed skin. I assume the third degree is over, that she's finally going to release her prey and move on. But I'm wrong. As in any good show, she's left the bombshell number for the end.

"I'm thrilled things are going so well for you, Irene. Actually, I also came by to let you know . . . well, you know how people are. Always talking and sticking their noses where they don't belong. People are saying you've been going out partying with Genoveva Bernat. No, hang on, listen: I don't have anything against Genoveva. Everybody's got the right to live their own life and do their own thing. But you know what Genoveva's like, and you hear things about her. She has a pretty bad reputation. I don't care either way, but I wouldn't like to see you end up getting hurt because of that friendship. No one in our group would be able to forgive ourselves if we didn't warn you that she's—how can I put it?—a little dodgy. I thought you should know."

"OK."

I'd never noticed how Teresa talks before. She sounds common, like a grocery store cashier. Do I talk like that too? Probably. I wasn't aware, but seeing it from the outside . . . The farther you get from a landscape, the more perspective you have in surveying it. All the women in my social circle talk like that: a mix of lofty words and slangy expressions heard on the street. That way we sound more modern. It's too late to change my vocabulary, but moving away from my social circle is already progress. Anyway, how should I react to her concern for my reputation? It would be the perfect time to tell her to go to hell and never come back, not her or anybody else from the group. But I don't feel like it. My Christ-like hissy fit at the money changers has passed (*hissy fit* is one of those terms that grocery store cashiers use), and I'd rather say something neutral to get her out of here.

"Oh, thank you, Teresa, I can't tell you how grateful I am for your concern! But actually I've only gone out a couple of times with Genoveva, who's a hoot . . . So as for getting close enough for it to hurt me . . . you can rest easy—I know full well what Genoveva's like. I'm not a child."

"I know, but you've always been so sheltered: your father, your husband, our circle of friends . . . "

I briskly stand up. I'm tossing her out, but doing so in such a way that it's as if she were following me somewhere wonderful. I laugh, cluck, get tangled in a bizarre spiel about how happy I am that she came to see me, that her daughters are so brilliant, that our friends are doing well. I finish up with a string of vague promises: I'll call you soon, I'll drop by the club one of these days. All this time I've been herding her toward the door, and at last she leaves.

Is it true what she said, that I've always been sheltered? I don't know. The life I was living was fine—a little boring, now that I think about it, but fine. I don't want to think. I'm going to pour myself a whiskey and watch an episode of one those new American TV shows that are supposed to be real works of art.

\* \* \*

Sandra's attitude this morning is particularly depressing.

She wakes me up before she leaves for work. She chirps like a bird and hops around the room, also like a bird. She insists we have breakfast together, so I stagger out of bed and go to the kitchen with her. She's made coffee and toast. It's the big day. Such excitement. I'm going to be meeting with Mr. Contreras at eleven for the job interview. Seeing the way Sandra's acting, you might think I was going to meet President Obama so he could name me secretary of state. She's nervous, but trying to seem merely excited. It's a horrible strategy. With every look she's telling me, "The world is your oyster, kid, slurp it down. The job will be yours because you're the best. Convince Contreras of that. Grab him by the lapels and tell him, 'This job is mine. You're going to be blown away when you see what a good teacher I am. I'll bring prestige to your crappy school with my mere presence. You'll see.'" I've read that sort of thing in a self-help book or an article from the Sunday supplement: "How to Face Life with Confidence," "Striding toward Success." Total garbage. I'd rather Sandra treated me like an old-fashioned mother whose son is about to take a tough exam: "Eat a big breakfast, sweetie. Everything comes out better on a full stomach." But no, she's chosen the modern route. She desperately wants them to give me this job because I'd be getting it thanks to her intervention, and that would give her a certain amount of power over me. No, that's an appalling idea. Truth is, she's anxious for them to give me the job because living with me under the current circumstances must be unbearable. I've tried not to take my mental state out on her, but without success. Losing a job may not be such a big deal, objectively speaking, but I haven't been able to bounce back from the blow. Buts and more buts. I listen patiently to the words of encouragement she lobs in my direction before rushing off because she's late for work.

Once I was alone in the house, things improved a little. I took a long, luxurious shower. I made another cup of coffee.

I left the house dressed in my standard clothes, though I did comb my hair carefully so it wouldn't be all messy for the interview. I walked instead of taking the bus, and it was only ten-thirty when I got to the school. I went into a little bar where the upperclassmen probably meet up after classes let out. I ordered a beer to bolster my self-confidence. Maybe there's no call to be so snide about self-help books—they're actually pretty rational. The advice they give may be obvious, but they're written for people who aren't very sophisticated, to help show them what they need to do. I'm not unsophisticated, so I don't need to read them to figure these things out. But that doesn't mean their suggestions are all garbage. It's true, you shouldn't let a bad situation get you down. You do need to be aware of your own worth—and I am a good teacher. I may not have passed the certification exam or gotten fantastic grades in school, but I'm a good teacher. I'm interested in the subject. I take my students seriously. My classrooms have always been a respectful environment, which the kids appreciate. I'm not stuck in my ways. I update my knowledge from time to time, not just by reading books but also in pedagogical terms. I've seen a lot of my colleagues get so burned out on teaching that they couldn't care less whether or not their students learn. Not me. It's my calling. It doesn't matter that it's an Opus Dei school—that job is going to be mine. I can't take the risk of letting these months of despondency intrude on the interview and make me look weak. I may have lost my job, but the economic crisis was to blame there, not me.

I knocked back the beer, which tasted bitter at that time of morning, and walked across the street. Ready for success.

The school has wonderful facilities. Seeing the students moving through the halls, I feel a sort of euphoria: this is the world I belong to. Soon I'll be back in it again, with new rolls of students under my tutelage. I'll appear on their weekly

schedules: Mondays, Wednesdays, and Fridays, Spanish literature.

Mr. Contreras keeps me waiting only fifteen minutes. He
appears through a doorway and waves me into his office. He's
the head teacher, not the principal, but all important matters
go through him, including the hiring of new teachers. His desk
is immaculate. My CV is the only paper resting on it. He gazes
at it a second.

"Oh, yes, I remember you! Tell me, Javier, what can you
offer the children at our institution?"

I tell him about my experience, how much I love teaching.
I explain what it seems to me literature's role is in shaping
young people. Modestly, I list my strengths as a teacher.
Contreras listens, solemn and attentive. When I've finished my
spiel, he looks at my CV, looks at me, and asks, "Is what it says
here true—you just taught review courses?"

"Yes. I wasn't a full-time teacher."

Suddenly he looks like one of his molars has started aching.

"Of course, but when you're not a full-time teacher, you
don't have clear responsibilities: you don't have to give grades,
assess students' progress in class . . . "

I'm caught off guard, uncertain how to respond. I find I
have no goddamn desire to argue with this guy. I shrug my
shoulders.

"As you say, that's on my CV."

"Well, it's not automatically grounds for rejection. We want
to do things right, talk with each candidate. So tell me, Javier,
how are you doing faith-wise?"

"Pardon? What do you mean?"

"Do you believe in God?"

"I'm agnostic," I say like an idiot.

When he hears that, it's not his molars that are aching, but
his heart.

"Oh, don't tell me that! It's so sad! If someone is an atheist, that's a tragedy, of course—but there's the possibility of escape. But agnosticism, being comfortable with not wanting to know God . . . It pains me, because with just a little effort one could find faith. But you have to want it, of course."

"I suppose that puts me completely out of the running for the position."

"I wasn't thinking about the position just now, Javier. I was thinking about you."

"I'm fine, Mr. Contreras, don't worry about me," I say politely.

He, also politely, jots down some notes on my CV.

"All right, Javier. We'll let you know once the staff makes a decision. There are a number of other candidates. We'll write to you at your personal address."

He gets up, smiles, accompanies me to the door of his office, shakes my hand. I'm such an idiot—I don't make a stink, don't tell him to go to hell or say anything that might make him the least bit uncomfortable. I'm as eager to get out of there as he is to see me go.

I go back to the same bar. I have another beer, which tastes wonderful this time. I think back to when I explained *Miau*, one of Pérez Galdós's novels, to my students. The protagonist is an aging, out-of-work civil servant who trudges from office to office begging for a new job until everybody's sick of him. That's me, I think. Then a positive thought leaps out in my defense: I'd never have been able to teach in a school like that. It's a den of dogmatists, a dangerous place. If I started there, I'd just end up quitting later, after having endured any number of unpleasant experiences. At least the nuns never asked me if I believed in God.

Sandra calls. I tell her the interview was a disaster and I'm certain they won't offer me the job. She doesn't ask any questions. She just says, "I'll see you later."

At home that night, I'm anxious about her return, as if I've done something wrong. I ponder how to tell her what happened in a way that makes me come off looking like I'm in the right, freed of any suspicion. But then I wonder what the hell I'm doing, cowering and shrunken, terrified of the boss's ire. No, if Sandra comes at me even a little bit, I'm going to lash out at her and accuse her of wasting my time, making me hang my hopes on false dreams. They gave me that job interview to make her friend happy, but they had no intention of hiring me. Not a chance.

I'm assaulted by the memory of my father, one of the few I still have of him. We were out fishing when, there under the clear water, I spotted a huge fish swimming toward us at top speed. I shouted to alert my father, and he started casting out the hook in its path, over and over, but the fish kept going, unfazed. "He's so useless!" I thought grumpily. "Always catching tiny fish, and now when the opportunity comes along . . . " But it wasn't true—the fish was just passing through, and there was never the slightest chance it would bite. I was unfair to my father, though not too much—in the end, he was just a dumbass for whom opportunities for success never came along. As evidence, consider that not long after that fishing expedition, he totaled his car in an accident and crossed to the other side, taking my mother with him. Epitaph: here lies a dumbass, almost as big a dumbass as me.

Waiting for Sandra at home, I realize I feel profoundly humiliated. I really don't feel like seeing her. I know she's not going to scold me—she's going to start crying. I don't want to hear her say what I know she will: "I'm really sorry, baby, but don't worry, another opportunity will come along." She hasn't figured out that there are no opportunities for me. I put on a jacket and head outside. I look for a bar. I've got my cell phone in my pocket in case she calls. "I'll be back late." Sitting at the bar, I order a gin and tonic. I sip it slowly. I'm feeling better. I pick up the phone and look through my saved calls. There it is. I press the button.

"Iván?"

"Shit, man, I can't believe it's you! Hey, teach! What's up?"

"What's happening with that job you mentioned? Does your offer still stand?"

"The job with the show?"

"Of course, what else?"

"Oh, shit, of course it does! Yeah! This makes me really happy, man. You've got some balls. I'll let Mariano know right now. I swear you won't regret this, man. I'll take care of everything. I'll call you tomorrow."

I keep drinking, filled with a sense of peace. There's nothing for me to worry about now. Tomorrow when I wake up, it will be the first day of my new life.

\* \* \*

It's not trial by fire, but it's pretty close. There are mirrors in the dressing room, and I go over to the closest one. Iván is like a dog obsessed with its owner—he trails after me wherever I go and refuses to leave my side. I find his chatter unsettling:

"You look awesome, man! But they've put you lower down on the totem pole: you used to be a teacher, and now you're playing a student."

Yeah, the guy's not bad. He may not think so, but the school uniform looks great on him. This is the hardest moment. You might expect the hardest moment would be when you go on stage and they throw you to the lions, but it's actually right now—I know what I'm talking about—when you see yourself in your costume and realize you look like a total ass. I hope the guy doesn't go chickenshit and back out, because I put in a word for him with Mariano, and that guy doesn't give anyone a break. He'd have a cow. Now I've got to provide moral and psychological support, the way you do to athletes before the competition. I can take care of that on my own. I could have been a psychologist if it had been in the cards, if I'd gone to college. I've got to get him to notice the other guys so he can see he's not alone, playing the fool dressed in a school smock with his legs exposed.

"Do my legs have to be bare, Iván? They're really pale. I haven't been out in the sun for a while. Wouldn't it be better for me to put on some flesh-colored tights or some panty-hose?"

"No, man, they're fine."

The hell with the teacher! He's gone vain on me. Though actually it's a good reaction. The reaction I was afraid of is "I look ridiculous," but if he's worried about looking good, we're doing OK.

"No, Javier, look, man, the idea here isn't to be Brad Pitt sexy. It's almost the opposite, really. This is like a joke, get it? Goofing around. You're here not to make the chicks fall in love; you're here to give them a good time, and maybe have a good time yourself. Look at it that way, and you'll see it's god-damn gravy train. You have a good time, and afterward they pay you. That's awesome, right?"

The strippers are bustling around me. They're about my age, maybe a little younger. Iván introduces them as they come into the huge communal dressing room: Domingo, Pablo, Fefo . . . One of them is Asian—I noticed him when I saw them perform. His name is Wong.

They shake my hand with indifferent politeness. It doesn't seem to be unusual for them to have a new colleague. Of course, this isn't like a factory floor. Being a stripper isn't a profession, and you don't have to take any exams to get the job. I imagine they cycle through a lot. I imagine they all must have other jobs: bartenders, bouncers . . . what do I know! Maybe some of them are just going through a rough patch, like me.

The atmosphere is like that of any locker room: the guys shout, slap one another on the back as they walk by, joke around. When I put on the absurd schoolboy outfit, the other "students" gather around to gently rib me: "There's a new kid, teacher!" "Those are some grade-A legs!" "If you misbehave, I'm going to tell on you." It must be a sort of ritual with the newbies, because they quickly lose interest in me and wander off. One lifts weights in a corner, another sends text messages on his cell phone . . . Only Wong stays with me a while.

"Is this the first time you've done a striptease?" he asks.

Iván jumps in before I can reply.

"Can you believe this guy? Isn't it obvious, ching-chong? Does he look like he's been dancing in Pigalle?"

"I'm not Chinese, I'm Korean. I've told you a thousand times."

"All right, fine, Korean, who cares!"

I have to keep them all away from him—they're going to scare him off. I don't have a goddamn clue what Javier thinks of us. Probably considers us total cretins. None of us talk like him or move like him. It's obvious from a mile off that he's a guy who went to college and reads books. But he'll get used to it, and if he doesn't he's even more of a dumbass than I thought, and he's on his own.

"Look, the makeup is on those shelves over there."

"I have to wear makeup too?"

"Duh, man. Otherwise, the spotlights'll make you look like a fucking corpse. White light washes out your facial features."

Jesus, so it's all out in the open now! He was annoyed when he asked, too. "Me in makeup?" I've assured him repeatedly that the show isn't for queers, but he has to go all super-macho at the first opportunity. The hell with the teacher! I like him, but he gets on my nerves. I think that's why I didn't study psychology: it requires more patience than I've got.

"You're shitting me, Javier! Everybody has to get made up

to go on TV, even the goddamn king. Don't you know that? So like I said, that's where the stuff is so you can paint yourself up."

"All right."

I'm getting on Iván's nerves, acting like a spoiled brat. I'm forgetting he's brought me here to help me out. I need to keep that in mind at all times: I'm not doing him a favor by being here, I came of my own free will. And if I can't stand it, I can just quit after the first performance. Iván would understand. All I'd have to say is "I tried, but it's not my thing."

"Hey, Iván, is there a rehearsal every week, or is this just because I'm joining the show?"

"We rehearse every Thursday evening, man, like clockwork. Don't make any plans on Thursday nights. Mariano's a perfectionist, you'll see. We always rehearse, even if we've done the show a hundred times. Thursday, rehearsal. Weekend, show."

"Is the rehearsal included in the pay, or is it paid separately?"

"It's included."

The hell with the little prince! Maybe he thinks this is Hollywood or something. Two hundred euros a show. That's four hundred a week. And you only work for the twenty minutes you're on stage, that's it, as long as you stick around till the end to take your bows with the rest of the troupe. That's sixteen hundred a month. Practically tax free too, since part of our pay is under the table. Surely he doesn't think it's too little money. There's no way he made that much teaching. He'd have to wipe a lot of boogers to rake in that amount.

"Does it not seem like enough?"

"Oh, yeah, of course, man. I was just asking to be sure."

"As you should. A worker should always know what he's earning. And this is a job, Javier. It might not be a job like any other, but it's a living."

"Of course."

A job. Even he recognizes it's not a normal one. This isn't sitting behind a bank counter or fixing a broken engine. And it's definitely not analyzing the poetry of Saint John of the Cross or holding forth on *Fortunata y Jacinta*. But it's a job, man, a living.

Mariano, the owner, comes into the dilapidated dressing room, which is really just a storeroom. Up close, he's got a pretty sinister look to him. Dressed in a striped polo shirt and black pants, he has none of the magnetism he emanates when he's up on stage, naked. He's in loafers and white socks, tacky stuff. It's strange because all the guys, including Iván, are dressed rather tastefully, even elegantly: dress shirts, jeans, name-brand sneakers. Maybe Mariano wants to look tacky, not show off the money he earns from the show. When I had my initial interview with him, he didn't even look at me. He just asked me if I was married, if I had a car, and if I liked pop music. Weird guy. Today he comes up and reassures me not to be nervous, says it's just a rehearsal and I won't be performing in public until I feel ready. He eyes my legs.

"Do you work out?"

"No," I reply.

"Well, you should. You've got nice legs, but they could do with a little toning. Can you afford a gym membership?"

"Yes," I say hastily.

"Good, I don't like giving people advances. Anybody here'll tell you that."

"They're also a little pale. I haven't been out in the sun much."

"You've got a lot of hair, so that doesn't matter."

"He's bear-y furry! I'm all yours, teddy bear!" Iván jokes in a falsetto.

He's still glued to my side. Mariano moves from group to group, giving the occasional individual instruction: "Don't gel your hair." "Take that earring out." His tone is harsh, very different from the one he used with me. He's like a general inspecting his troops before battle. He's certainly professional. Since he's not wearing the sequined jacket, I figure he's not going to be participating in the rehearsal. When he's done inspecting us, he claps his hands.

"Rehearsal starts in ten minutes! Everybody be ready!"

Iván, in his Zorro costume, looks at me with an almost tender smile.

"Buck up, teach, this is a walk in the park! Just try to feel the music and let yourself go. Imagine you're up there in front of a bunch of chicks who want to suck you off and you won't let them. Just make them horny."

I'm in the first number, so all of a sudden I find myself on stage. The room is empty, freezing cold. I feel the chill on my bare legs; it curls under my school smock and makes its way up to my belly, my chest. The micro-briefs I'm wearing are uncomfortable, constrictive. The spotlights aren't on; we'll be dancing in the washed-out house lights. Everything looks a little shabby. The tables are bare, no tablecloths or lanterns. The chairs are stacked up in one corner. The walls could use a coat of paint.

I look at my schoolmates out of the corner of my eye. We're all waiting for the teacher to come out, for the music to start. The dancers seem serene, natural. They stretch, do breathing exercises. It's comforting to have them there. It helps me feel less stupid in this hideous outfit in the middle of this empty room. Mariano's sitting on a chair near the stage; I can see his white socks glowing in the artificial light.

The music starts. My instructions are to do the same thing as everybody else. I've got the basic concepts because I've seen the show. In theory it's easy—we don't have to move in sync except at the end, when we're supposed to all stop at the same time. The guy playing the teacher comes out on the stage. It's strange to have him so close, to see his powerful muscles flex and ripple as he dances. I can smell his cologne. He moves to one side and leads each of us to the middle of the stage. We all pretend not to know how to dance. When it's my turn, I try to seem clumsy and timid. I go back to my desk after receiving a pantomimed scolding. I wait for the others to play their part, and when nobody's left, the whole class starts dancing together. I dance with the others, imitating them, swiveling my hips, swinging my pelvis back and forth. It's hard to feel the music—I'm so nervous I can barely hear it. Suddenly it goes quiet. We stand still, expectant. Mariano comes up on stage and addresses me:

"I've forgotten your name. What is it?"

"Javier."

"You removed your smock too slowly, not enough energy. You need to rip it off over your head and then toss it aside like a rag, some piece of crap you never want to see again. Got it? Everything else is good. Let's go again."

I feel panicked at first, thinking I'm the only one who has to go again, but no, the whole group puts their smocks back on. We start over, and this time I rip off the smock, which has concealed Velcro in the back, in one swift, decisive movement. Then I violently toss it aside. We reach the end, and I hear the boss's voice, flat and toneless:

"That's better, Javier. Next week you can join the performance."

A few of my fellow dancers slap me on the back. "Congrats," Wong says. Iván can't say anything because he's about to rehearse his number, but he winks at me as he walks by.

We meet up again on our way out and go to get a beer. He's jubilant. I'm surprisingly tired. My back hurts as if I'd spent the afternoon unloading a truck.

"Congratulations, man, you were awesome."

"I wouldn't go that far. I did my best, but I doubt they're going to name me stripper of the year."

"No way, dude, you did great!"

It's like he thinks you have to go to college to shake your ass or something. I've seen newbies rehearse and rehearse and Mariano still doesn't let them perform for almost a month. And you don't get paid for rehearsals—this isn't a pleasure cruise.

"No way, man, no way! You were perfect! You're a god-damn sex bomb and you didn't even know it!"

"No, I'm here because you recommended me, so I imagine the owner just overlooked my faults."

"Like shit!"

Mariano playing good cop? Not a chance! Javier doesn't know it, but the boss can be a real dick.

"It's true you didn't have to go through the tryout phase because I recommended you. Usually they do a huge casting call and a ton of people come, especially with the economic crisis. But Mariano thinks highly of me—he says I bring good energy to the group because I like horsing around and all that. Plus he owes me some favors."

"I figured it was something like that."

"But don't kid yourself, man—that was all you today. This is the first time I've seen anybody do one rehearsal and then get to debut the next week. I think it's because of the image you project, as they say these days. You look like a good boy who has no idea how he ended up in a bad place like this. And that drives the ladies wild. That's how it is with them: either you go all tough and macho, like you've been around more times than a racecar driver, and they eat that shit up, or you play the naïve kid so they can take you by the hand and teach you about life. Chicks are fucking weird, man, as you must know already. They go from one extreme to the other like a teeter-totter. But you're a rock star, man—the other guys said so too. I'll introduce you soon. Some of them are really cool. After the show some of us go out for a bite to eat. Not on rehearsal days, since everybody's really busy. But today's a special day—you just drove the ball right into the net. Want another beer?"

"No thanks, Iván. I've got to catch the bus. It's getting late, and Sandra will be worried."

"If it's because of the damn bus, we have time for one more. I can drive you. We'll have you home in a flash."

I have one last beer with him. Deep down, I want to. There are a lot of people in the bar, good background music—I'm feeling good. I feel like everything that just happened is getting farther away. A bad patch is ended. Though actually it's just the opposite: the bad patch is giving way to something that's just begun.

We walk to a parking garage and stop in front of a black Volkswagen Golf. I don't know anything about cars, but it seems like this is an expensive model: lots of electronic doodads on the dash, leather seats . . . Iván proudly shows it off.

"My car's pretty rockin', huh? Do you like it? It's awesome. It's got everything, look: GPS, automatic parking system, high-fidelity speakers . . . I bought it less than a year ago with cold hard cash, no financing or any of that boring shit. That's why I always park it in a garage—there are lots of crooks out there."

He drives pretty fast but smoothly, not recklessly, totally in control of the vehicle. He's blasting techno music. He hums to himself. Suddenly he asks, "I don't usually butt into people's private lives, but out of curiosity, what did Sandra say when you told her you were joining the show?"

"I haven't told her yet."

"Damn, man, bad call. She's probably going to be pissed you didn't check in with her about it."

"I don't have to check in with her—it's my life."

Iván laughs. His laugh is metallic, insipid, almost stupid. I don't like it.

"I'll say, man. You're the boss, controlling the play, as it should be."

Get a load of the teacher! He plays the nice guy and all, but it seems he's got balls. Of course, he could be bluffing and he just hasn't dared tell his old lady yet. Well, in that case he's on his own. That's none of my business.

\* \* \*

I'm not sure whether Genoveva is less interesting than I thought she was or if it's just that everything bores me now. Going out to buy trashy dresses in a store with pounding music is all right. Drinking gin and tonics in a trendy bar is entertaining enough. But I always thought her life had a bit more to it than that. As it turns out, I, who according to her have been living on another planet, wasn't missing out on anything special. I wonder what people do to fill up their free time. What do David and his young interpreter do? Stay in bed all day, of course! Is he getting set up in his new job? I imagine he must have found one. Or maybe he's decided to live off his girlfriend's salary, which can't be much. Maybe he wants to lead a frugal life. When he was married to me, we led a frugal life, but we had a nice house and once a year we'd travel to some exotic place. He must be happy with a girl who won't need luxuries. If he lives off of her, it won't be the first time—though, to be fair, I admit he always earned his salary. Work came first for both of us. Anyway, he hasn't called me even once to see how the company's doing. He knows we're going through a difficult period, but not even a simple phone call. He must not have been as interested in the work as he pretended to be, or maybe he's ashamed to have left it under such circumstances. Deep down, I'm not surprised he was fed up. I am too. Fed up with the crisis, the unpaid invoices, the negligent customers, the rejected loan applications. The manager is still hounding me, as if everything would be fixed if I spent more time at the office. He clearly doesn't want to bear the burden of the company's failures alone. He doesn't know what to do—he's distracted, easily upset, groping around in the dark. You need a particular fortitude to keep a company going. Papá had it. However severe the crisis, he would have been able to ride it out, grapple with the setbacks, make the right decisions. For a while I thought I'd inherited his constitution, but I was fooling myself. I'm tired. David really knocked the wind out of me. If Papá had been alive, he wouldn't have dared to dump me like that. Of course, then I would have still been living with a worthless loser. It's for the best that he left me—this way, the truth is crystal clear. Sometimes I get lonely and feel like crying, but not because I miss my husband—I miss my father. I haven't shed a single tear over my husband. I'm really proud of that. Genoveva has it wrong: I'm not a cowardly little girl who's been sheltered from the world all her life. I'm just tired—but I'll perk back up.

Genoveva and I have plans this Saturday. We're going to a private cosmetics demonstration. She says it's really fun: they put makeup on the models in front of an audience and serve you a drink. At the end, they sell products at a huge discount. It's being held at a big hotel. We'll see if it's actually any fun. It doesn't seem like anything special. Probably after the demo we'll go out for drinks. And I'll ask Genoveva point-blank, "So, Geno, is this kind of thing all you do to have fun?"

"What kind of thing, darling? I don't know what you mean."

"Well, the places you take me are fantastic and we always have a great time, but . . . it's all a little shallow."

Genoveva lowered her glass from her lips, leaving the usual red imprint on its rim, and looked at me mischievously.

"So you're looking for powerful emotions, huh?"

"Just ignore me. I'm a little down lately. Everything bores

me—everything seems dull, lackluster. The other day I went to the movies by myself and I didn't like the film. But don't pay any attention to me—the cosmetics demo was a lot of fun, with all those gorgeous girls all made up . . . and the eyeliner I bought, and the eyeshadows . . . I don't know what I want, ultimately—pretend I didn't say anything, really."

But I had said it, and Genoveva took note of my words, and interpreted them in her own way.

\* \* \*

She looks at me with a wounded expression. She knows something's going on, though she has no idea what it is. This is no great talent on her part: all more or less companionable couples who have been together a long time know something's going on when something's going on. My face must reveal some of my thoughts completely transparently. If I'd pretended, she wouldn't have noticed a thing. I thought about it, thought about hiding it, but living in the same house makes it impossible. Then it pissed me off that I'd even considered it. What, is Sandra my mother or something? Why should I try to keep her from finding out about what I'm doing?

There's nothing wrong with being in show business. I just can't handle being unemployed, so I went out and found a job. If that job turns out to be socially awkward, that's the fault of Catholic moralism and fear of gossip. I can feel fine about it. Despite all those absolutely logical considerations, though, I still don't know how to bring up the issue with Sandra. In the end, I decide to be honest and direct:

"Come sit, Sandra. We need to talk."

I told her, and at first she was stunned. Maybe I was too concise, too frank. After a second she started laughing, seemingly skeptical.

"So what you mean is one of the dancers from your friend's

show is sick and you're going to sub in for him a couple of days, right?"

It doesn't take long for the mind to adjust reality to our dreams. I don't like her reaction—it actually ticks me off.

"No, that's not what I said or what I meant. There's an open spot in Iván's show because someone's leaving, and I'm going to fill it. If it were a school, I'd be getting a permanent, full-time teacher position."

"But for how long?"

"No idea. If something in my field comes along, I'll quit the show immediately. But in the meantime, I've got a job, you know? A job. You understand, right?"

"No, I absolutely do not."

How could I understand? What is this, Kafka's *Metamorphosis*? One day you get up and instead of having your partner at your side, you've got a cockroach. Is this new Javier really the same one I've been living with for the past few years? What happened to him—what part of his sudden transformation did I miss? The nuns fired him from his teaching job, fine. He's been out of work for months, also fine—but there are plenty of people in this country right now who are in the exact same circumstances. People with kids to take care of, people whose unemployment may have run out and who are having trouble paying their mortgages and even buying food. And what do they do? Jump at the first job that comes along no matter what it is? We're not in dire straits—we have enough to live on. I've got my salary, and Javier's still bringing in his unemployment check. We can make our rent easily, we have no family obligations, we're not big spenders: the occasional movie or rock concert or pizza or kebab . . . So what's with this stripper crap?

"We don't need the money."

"It's not about the money. I want to have a job."

"A job?"

It's the most ludicrous thing I've ever heard. That's not a job—can't he see that? It's not going to make him feel integrated into society, if that's what he's looking for.

"Javier, it's not a normal job, one that'll make you feel like everybody else. You're going to be out of your element, disconnected from the lives of normal people."

"Why isn't it a normal job? Are you being prejudiced?"

"Be logical, like you always say. If you'd met a lion tamer instead of Iván and after a while he'd suggested you work with him in the ring, how would you have responded?"

"That's not logical in the least. Being a lion tamer requires extraordinary bravery."

"Precisely. But . . . "

"Watch out, Sandra, careful what you say next!"

She'd better be careful—there's no way for the sentence she's just started to end well. I've already finished it for her in my head: "But anybody can bare their ass in a seedy dive—that's a piece of cake."

"No, listen."

He's right, watch out, careful what I say. I don't want to hurt him. I don't want to offend him. I don't want to lose him. But this is so absurd, it can't really be happening, not with Javier. He's calm, stable, has his feet on the ground. I've never seen him do anything foolish or out of line. He always does the proper thing. What's happened to him? How did he end up falling under the influence of a guy he'd normally look down on? Iván: lowlife, misogynist, boor, prole. What kind of joke is this?

"Listen, don't get me wrong. What I mean is if you're looking for an activity to give your life meaning in these difficult times, you could write your dissertation, start another degree program, volunteer teaching Spanish to immigrant children or visiting old people who live alone . . . I don't know, something more in line with your personality."

"I needed a job and I have a job. End of discussion."

"Well, try not to talk to me too much about that amazing job of yours."

"Don't worry, I won't."

"Great."

And now where can I go to cry? I don't want to cry with him in the house. I wish he'd leave; I need to cry my heart out for a good long while. This is like a bad dream, and I know I—indeed, both of us—will wake up eventually.

Well, this was foreseeable to a certain extent. I didn't know how our conversation would go, but now it's clear: to Sandra, working at that club is reprehensible, a disgusting thing done by and for vulgar people who are nothing like me. And nothing like her, of course. Furthermore, it's quite clear now how Sandra sees me: I'm a useless person who can be expected to do useless things. Such as studying something totally pointless or visiting lonely old people or giving classes to inarticulate children. Charity—or solidarity, to use the left-wing term. No real surprise. It's odd how truths are revealed in moments of crisis. My job with the nuns was a shitty one: supplementary teacher at a private school, and not many hours at that. A shitty job with a shitty salary. Sandra has always earned more than twice what I do. Life passes, and we don't ask ourselves questions. It's better that way—we might not like the answers. Appearances are enough: I've got a degree, a job, everything's fine. Underneath, though, several feet down, the truths are throbbing. We've buried them there so we can keep going. I was a mediocre student. I didn't take any licensing exams because I'm a coward and was afraid of failing over and over. I didn't look for a better job because I'm lazy and wanted to have free time for reading, my great passion. I've let myself be carried along by the currents that pulled me most easily. I'm accommodating. I make do with very little, and I've attempted to consider this a virtue when it's actually a flaw. I've never taken on any challenges, whether idealistic or material in nature. I'm nothing to write home about. I've lived in keeping with my personality. I'm not going to change now.

I'm not going to write my own self-help book listing actions that could transform me, make me a man renewed and magnificent. I don't believe in men making themselves—that's not how it works. I believe in being lucky in birth. If you're the child of wonderful parents—wealthy, highly educated, well-adjusted, who love each other—you've got a winning ticket. Mine weren't educated or wealthy. I don't remember if they were well adjusted or not. I don't know if they loved each other. They died very young. That's why I actually consider myself lucky to be who I am—at least I didn't end up being schizophrenic or a mass murderer.

I'm going to be debuting, as Iván calls it, in an erotic striptease. I'm going to bare my ass to a bunch of women—and to society. I doubt that'll leave me marked for life. The day of my debut, I'll dedicate my act to Mr. Contreras, who received me so kindly and whose professional rejection made me heed the call of the stage. "This one's for you, maestro!" I'll say, and then I'll start gyrating and shaking my junk. I've decided this kind of dancing should be included in the curriculum of every school in the country. You never know what fate awaits young students. Life is full of twists and turns, and though today we may be learnedly analyzing Jovellanos's prose, tomorrow we might be forced to wiggle our hips in front of a crowd of liberated women looking for a bit of wholesome fun. Just providing a service to society. The important thing is to stay alive and be able to tell yourself things are OK.

Thank God he finally left! Now I can cry in peace!

Today, Friday, is the big day, D-day or whatever you want to call it. When I wake up, Sandra's already left for work. Our tense conversation last week doesn't seem to have affected our relationship. It's like we've decided to pretend nothing happened. And nothing has happened yet, actually. We'll see if anything changes when I start having to go the club every weekend. I hadn't thought about it, but that's going to affect our usual routine. We won't be able to go out for dinner with friends or to the movies. But that's not so bad. Plenty of occupations have inconvenient schedules: bakers, hotel managers, bus drivers . . . Anyway, I'm free the rest of the week.

I make myself breakfast and eat it in the kitchen. There's a news program on the radio, but I'm not listening. Just the sound of the voices makes me feel less alone. I've got to shed this feeling of impalpable worry, of general defeat. I tell myself today's just another Friday. I'm going to go grocery shopping. Then I'll come back home and read the newspaper on my computer. I'll check my e-mail in case there's something I need to answer. I'll surf the Internet for a bit. At noon, I'll go down to the corner bar for lunch. In the afternoon I'll take a long walk. If Sandra's home when I get back, I'll try to talk to her as little as possible. Then I'll go to my new job for the first time.

I followed my plans to the letter. An hour before the show, I met up with Iván at a café. We'd agreed to meet up and head to the club together.

He's really happy to see me, like it's been ages since we last hung out. I try to order a beer, but he tells me no, no alcohol before the performance. I have tea instead, and he has Coke with lots of ice. He smiles at me.

"Are you ready for your debut?"

I tell him I'm not; I've been trying not to think about it.

"Why's that?"

I say that if I think about it, I'm racked by all kinds of bad feelings. I admit that I'm nervous, uneasy, even a little irritable. He stands in front of me and looks at me with those demented eyes of his.

"You're going to kick ass, man, totally kick ass. By the end of the show, you're going to be an international star. But the biggest thing is you can't let it get to you. What you're going through is normal. You've never done this kind of thing, and since it's your first day you've got your stomach all tied up in knots. But ignore the knots. You do your thing. You have to think of it as just having some fun, like you're just hanging out with some buddies for a good time. Buck up, man! I do get where you're coming from, though. I mean, it's like if I had to play teacher with a bunch of kids! Shit, I'd be freaked out! I can't even imagine: me up there talking about literature this and literature that. It freaks me out just thinking about it! And the squirts staring at you, all quiet like they're saying, 'Come on, teacher, feed us some knowledge—we're starving.'"

He makes me laugh, which is his goal. Abruptly, I ask him, "Do you read books, Iván?"

He's caught off guard.

"Me? Truthfully, man? I don't have time. I'll read when I'm old. Hey, man, get a move on or we're going to be late. We have to be there an hour before the show."

It makes me anxious that he always calls it "el show," using the English word. We leave the bar.

The dressing room is packed. Everyone's arrived. Jokes, laughter, howls . . . I assume it's all business as usual. Mariano is walking around, already in his MC outfit. He's chewing gum, and he doesn't speak, doesn't look at me even once. I put on my ridiculous costume. Wong, seeing my ineptitude, offers to apply my makeup. I let him. Someone looks over at us and laughs. The makeup smells like perfume. It's annoying to have this goo on my skin, like being slathered in mud. There's a coffee machine with some paper cups in one corner. From time to time a guy will pour himself a cup and carry it around. Iván, now transformed into Zorro, comes up to me.

"How's it going, man?"

I shrug.

"It's going."

"Like I said, just don't let it get to you. I forgot to tell you—the spotlights shine right in your eyes and they're really bright, so you won't be able to see the audience. So relax, just do your thing."

A minute before we go on stage, I'm in a huddle with the other dancers in my act. Mariano comes over and heads straight for me.

"Are you all set?"

I nod. He goes out on stage to introduce the show. Why is it only now that he's asking if I'm all set? It's a little late, isn't it? Should I take it as a warning that if anything goes wrong, he'll fire me? At that moment I realize I don't actually like Mariano—he's a pretty shady guy. Suddenly I'm myself again, the person I used to be, the person I've always been. What am I doing here? What kind of joke is this? Where has my head been lately? This is absurd, laughable. But all right—I'll finish the performance and tell Mariano this very night that I'm quitting, I've thought better of it. I won't be coming back. Enough foolishness—let's get back to reality. And as far as Iván goes, he'll see I've tried my best to take advantage of the opportunity he gave me, but that this just isn't my thing. "At least I tried, man," I'll tell him, and I'm sure he'll understand.

Mariano has finished speechifying. We hurry out onto the dark stage. My fellow dancers swiftly adopt studied facial expressions and stylized poses. We're off! I feel the air brushing against my legs. They feel naked. I hear a muffled din around me: the audience's breathing, their whispered comments, the clinking of glasses, the rustling of tablecloths and clothing, the clearing of throats. I'm half blind, but I stare out at one of the tables and see a girl smiling at me. I don't look again. I focus on what I'm here to do. I let myself get carried away by the music. I unfasten the school smock and, when it's my turn, rip it off in a single movement, hurling it far away from me. I perform the sexy movements, thrusting my crotch back and forth. I hear people shouting, the occasional admiring whistle. I watch the other dancers out of the corner of my eye to stay in sync with them. Three more powerful bass notes and . . . it's over! We scamper offstage like frightened rabbits. Out in the room we hear applause, cheers. We run into Mariano, who's striding back onstage. I see Iván getting ready for his performance. He winks at me from a distance, giving me a congratulatory thumbs-up.

Once I'm back in the dressing room, I look down at my penis, which feels strange bundled up in the uncomfortable briefs. I hadn't realized it, but I'm sweating. Wong comes over and hands me a robe.

"Here, put this on. You'll freeze otherwise."

"What about you?"

"I've got a backup. Didn't they tell you to bring a robe?"

"No, they didn't tell me anything."

He explains, in fluid Spanish but with a strong foreign accent, that I should go ahead and shower now. Some of the guys wait till the end of the show and shower after we take our bows, so there tend to be lines.

"The showers are a little horrible, but the water's hot."

I'm amused by the phrase "a little horrible." I'm eager for a shower, but I didn't bring any of the necessary supplies: shower gel, toilet kit . . . Iván forgot to tell me about these logistics.

"No problem. I'll lend you everything you need—a towel too. I'm a public service." Wong smiles.

We head to the showers together. Another schoolboy is showering. He waves, his face covered with foam. It's true the place is a little horrible: six unpartitioned showers with a cement floor and walls that nobody's bothered repainting. The room is cold, but there's plenty of water, and it feels like the most restorative shower I've ever had. I watch earthen-colored water run down my body: the makeup. I wonder anxiously whether I'll have to put that goop back on my face for when we take our bows. And when we bow, will the house lights be up so I'll be forced to see the audience?

I wander around in Wong's robe, invigorated from the hot water. I return his soap and we pour ourselves some coffee. Then Iván, who's just finished, comes in.

"Where did that robe come from?" he asks.

"Wong was nice enough to lend it to me. Shower gel too."

"I see," he says curtly.

"You forgot to tell me to bring toiletries."

"My bad, man. Nobody's perfect."

Wong goes off to another cluster of chatting dancers. It's obvious he and Iván don't get along. Iván pats me on the shoulder.

"Nice work, man, nice work! You did great! How was it?"

"I survived."

"It can't have been that bad. You were oozing sex. I was watching, and there were tons of girls hanging on your every move. I swear, man, their eyes were bugging out of their faces."

"Don't say that or I'll never come back."

He claps me on the back, laughs. Someone calls to him and he moves away. I probably said "I'll never come back" in unconscious anticipation of what I want to tell him: I'm not coming back. But I don't feel like analyzing it now.

The end of the show is approaching, and I'm facing another thorny moment: taking my bows. I'm worried. If the spotlights aren't on, I'm going to see the audience and the audience is going to see me just as I normally am: smiling, bowing my head in acknowledgement of the applause, without music or artifice, without the creepy school smock, dressed in pants and a black sweater, like the others.

But it wasn't so bad. Yes, just as I feared, the house lights were up, but what I saw was a bunch of normal people smiling and laughing in a civilized manner. We dancers were no longer ridiculous and purportedly sexy meat, and the audience was no longer playing its role as a sex-crazed rabble. The Roman circus was striking its tents.

I focused on a few people in detail: nice-looking girls; yawning women, tired after the long show; an older man with his younger girlfriend. They'd seen me shaking my ass like a cheap cabaret dancer, but in that moment, for whatever reason, I didn't care.

Then it was time to change again, to put on our street clothes. Mariano sought us out one by one in the dressing room. He was paying us in cash! I couldn't believe it—it was like something out of those novels about the proletariat and the Industrial Revolution: miners receiving their wages, day laborers lining up for their weekly pay.

"You did great," Mariano said when he got to me.

I took the money he handed me and stuffed it in my pocket.

"Aren't you going to count it?" he asked.

"No, of course not!"

He nodded, pleased by my gentlemanly approach. Iván raced by and pointed at me.

"Don't leave. I'm going to say hi to somebody and then we'll get out of here."

I obeyed. I sat in a chair, feeling a little lost.

Only five minutes later, he was back.

"Let's go!" he said energetically, as if the night was only just now beginning.

El Formidable is a large, rundown bar with garish décor. It serves drinks and cold tapas, and even at two in the morning, it's packed to the gills. It's clear there's a city within my city that I have no idea about. When I walk in with Iván, four guys are waiting for us. I've seen them all at the club, but we haven't spoken to one another. Their names are Andrés, Sergio, Jonathan, and Éric. They all have the same look as Iván: close-cropped hair, expensive athletic clothing, chiseled muscles under their T-shirts. Working-class stiffs who've come up in the world. We order ham, chorizo, cheese, Olivier salad, and beer, lots of beer. Everything arrives quickly and fills our bare table, the platters overflowing. I'm dubious that we'll be able to finish off this feast, but my fellow diners eagerly dive in. They eat like pigs in every sense, chewing with their mouths open, licking their knives . . .

Iván brings up my performance.

"Wasn't Javier awesome?"

A chorus of praise begins: "Really awesome," "Like a professional," "Total rock star." They quickly forget about me and start commenting on the show—like Iván, they all say "show" in English.

"Shit, man! Did you see that group of middle-aged women over to the left, right below the stage? They were so man-hungry it was like they'd been off at war."

"Yeah, I saw them. When the boss was performing, I peeked out from behind the curtain, and they were practically drooling. They'd have taken a big bite if they could."

"Shit! The last dick those old bags saw was probably in a baby photo!"

They laugh. They're talking loudly enough that anybody can hear them. I'm uncomfortable, the food hard to swallow. I want to leave, but I just smile. Tomorrow I'll tell Iván I'm not going to go out with them after the show. I'll make some excuse: I like going to bed early, I need to take a walk before I go to sleep.

"There was an awesome couple in the first row. He was an older guy who looked like he had some scratch. She was a babe, super hot. The geezer probably can't even get it up with a crane at this point."

"That's why he takes her to the show, so she can at least get some eye candy."

"No way, man. He takes her so she'll get some motivation and suck him off real good afterward, thinking about us the whole time."

This comment is uproariously received. Their laughter booms like thunder. Iván laughs hardest of all. He looks at me conspiratorially, as if to say, "I told you these guys were awesome." I smile like an idiot, and it's just my luck that Jonathan suddenly asks me:

"What about you, new guy? What did you think of everything?"

"Shit, it was amazing, really fucking cool!"

I hope the proliferation of swear words is enough to reassure them about my opinions.

"That's right, man, fucking amazing. If Tarantino came to the club, he'd make a movie that'd blow your mind."

"Yeah, but he'd spray fake blood everywhere."

"I can picture it: one of those biddies from today goes up to Mariano to give him a blow job, but he turns around and kicks her in the teeth."

"Yeah, and then Éric shows up with a machine gun and starts blasting away at all the ladies."

"He blows their heads off!"

"And their tits! *Pop, pop,* like balloons bursting!"

"And then Wong comes out throwing knives like in a kung fu movie."

The spontaneous brainstorming session cracks them up. It's like being in a schoolyard. I am overwhelmed by all their stupidity, offended by all their vulgarity, and it must show on my face because Iván looks over at me and chides the others.

"All right, guys, don't go overboard. Teacher here's going to think we're fucking retards. Did I mention Javier's a teacher? He's out of work at the moment; the goddamn nuns put him out on the street. And I'm not talking about computer classes or driving lessons—he's a real teacher. Literature—poems and that sort of thing."

It's clear Iván is proud of me. His friends look at me somewhat jeeringly. They don't seem to share Iván's inexplicably high regard for the profession.

Back home, Sandra was sleeping, or pretending to sleep. I undressed noiselessly, with only the hall light on so as not to wake her. I took off my shirt, and when I was emptying my pants pockets before taking them off too, I came across the money Mariano had given me. I looked at it in surprise. My first thought was to hide it, but I ignored that impulse and left it out on my nightstand.

* * *

Who the hell knows what this woman wants. I don't know if she's looking for a fight or if she's just talking to hear herself talk. When she says nothing's any fun, it's because she's looking for bigger entertainment. But who knows what someone like Irene is after—maybe she'd enjoy hang gliding. In any case, I hope she hasn't mistaken me for a lady's companion. I'll go out with her and make sure she's OK, but I'm not going to let her into every nook and cranny of my life. Sometimes I wonder if she's on to me, though that can't be—I've always been extremely discreet about everything. Maybe she senses it, though I'd be surprised. Daddy's girls like her could never imagine that sort of thing. So I don't know what to think. It would be easiest to just get rid of her, have her find somebody else who can show her a good time. I don't have any obligation to go out with her. After all, doesn't everybody think I'm a slut, a man-eater? Well, they can leave me alone, then! Of course, Irene's never said anything bad about me—it's not her style. The other women in the group did talk about me behind my back. But they'll come crawling back one day when their husbands leave them and they're feeling lonely. Life is long, and they're young still. They'll come back to Genoveva then. I've never cared about people's gossip, but some things do hurt. When everybody turned their backs on me and I wasn't as over everything as I am now, that hurt. That's why I was so pleased when Irene called, looking for company. Now everybody else will see that the good girl of the group has turned to Genoveva to help her get out of her hole. But Miss Goody-Two-Shoes is getting awfully tedious, and that's the issue here. If I take her around with me and she finds out about everything, there's no guarantee she'll keep her mouth shut. That would be really annoying, because there's no need. Or she might be shocked and make a huge scene—though that would be the least of my worries.

Anyway, I'll see. For sure, though, I'm making my life a lot more complicated—but that's the way I am. Despite my reputation for being tough and doing my own thing, I'd do anything for a friend. That's who I am. I don't think a selfish, egotistical person would do all this. What have the other women in the group done to help Irene? Nothing. I'm sure they've called her a few times to gossip about what her ex is up to. As if that's going to help anything! Exes are part of the past, and your life isn't over when your marriage fails. You have to keep looking ahead, and above all take care of yourself. Be really clear that you come first. I take good care of myself. If I don't feel like doing something, I don't do it. I don't make excuses. And I go all out to take care of my body. I'm heading to the gym right now. Today I've got a spa treatment, and then an Ayurvedic massage that always makes me feel as good as new. That time relaxing in the water is like a dream. Even the scent is incredibly soothing. They add seaweed and essential oils, so you come out of the bath smelling like a rose. It's incredible. Other days I go to Latin dance class. We goof around and have a good time, and that's the point. I appreciate the little things in life—those are the things that make you happy. If you aren't willing to enjoy the moments, you end up like Irene: bored by everything. These younger girls don't know what they want. Much less Irene. The two of us have been going out for months now, and she hasn't said a word. I don't know if she thinks about her ex or not, if she's bitter about him, if she still cares about the whole mess or is over it. She's very introverted, very odd. That's why I'm afraid to confide in her about certain things.

Shoot! I got caught up thinking about all this, and now I'm going to be late to the spa. I always end up rushing everywhere. I'd like to change that about myself, but oh well—gotta run! And on top of all that, now I remember I left the car at the mechanic. I'll catch a taxi on the corner. Thankfully, with the crisis and everything, you can always find an empty cab.

* * *

During the week, my life isn't any different. I keep up my usual routines: grocery shopping, walks in the park . . . I've got more money now, so I never eat alone at home. I go down to the bar and order the lunch special. The money I earn at the club doesn't get combined with Sandra's to cover shared expenses. I spend it a little more capriciously. I've bought a ton of books and records, a chambray shirt. At first I thought I was keeping the money for my own whims because I wanted to enjoy the advantages of increased income. Later, upon further consideration, it's become clear I consider these earnings to be tainted, something I don't want to use in my normal life. Contaminated money, blemished with the stain of sin. Seems like I've turned into a sheep: I never would have entertained such a reactionary notion as sin before. Apparently I'm leading two parallel lives with two corresponding parallel selves. If that's the case, I'm in trouble.

Iván, who despite his limited education is as sharp as a tack, has an uncannily accurate sense of what's going on in my head. He's always telling me, "Change your mind-set, man, and stop worrying about everything." But it's not that easy.

I've been performing at the club for a month. The third weekend was the worst. I'd stopped being nervous and started seeing everything really clearly. I saw myself half naked, moving my body to the beat and trying to be sexy and jocular at the same time. I observed my fellow dancers, dumb smiles plastered on their faces. I watched the audience shrieking, clapping, almost indifferent to what was happening onstage, focused only on shedding their inhibitions. It was all too much for me, so I asked Iván if we could get a drink just the two of us, and I launched into it: I couldn't keep going, it was humiliating, it was grotesque. I wanted him to come with me to hand in my resignation to Mariano. He would know how to present the issue without offending the boss. Iván didn't get upset. He told me what I was going through was normal, and then he went enigmatic on me: "We all feel like that the first few times. Your problem is you're trying to do everything straight, and that's no good." He explained the enigma: I always refused the line of cocaine that he and the other strippers did before going out onstage. He continued:

"Doing a little coke doesn't mean you're a junkie or something. Nobody hates drugs more than me—look what they did to my folks. But just a rail, that's it, man—it helps a lot. It gives you some inspiration and energy, though that's not actually the most important thing. Most of all, it makes it so you don't give a shit about what's happening around you. One shot, and it's like you're on another planet. You think shaking my ass doesn't make me feel like a goddamn idiot? But doing a line makes everything OK."

To make things even easier, Mariano himself sold the coke at a special price he got thanks to his contacts. I listened to

Iván and tried it. It was great. I'd never done coke before
because it's expensive. My circle of friends was more into
pot—but there's no comparison. A weed high depends on your
mood at the time. Pot has made me alternately happy, weepy,
anguished, and apathetic. Cocaine is more predictable: it
always perks you up, and it makes you not give a shit, just like
Iván said.

Once I started doing coke before the show, I felt calmer
about everything, fundamentally more realistic. The white
powder freed me from prejudices I didn't even think I had and
put my conscience, my critical mind, to sleep. That way I could
do what I had to do. But the drug also had undesirable effects:
I'd sworn I'd never go out with Iván's gang after the show
again, but I always did. The rowdy gatherings alleviated the
uneasiness that flooded me after the performance. Talking with
people who did the same work normalized the situation. The
hits of coke helped me put up with the sexist comments, the
crude jokes, the cruel pranks.

Today—Friday again—Sandra didn't go in to the office.
Her job owed her a day off because of one of those workplace
arrangements I've never understood. We went out for lunch at
an Italian place. Since I started my new job, we've been seeing
less of each other, talking less—and when we do talk, we never
mention the club. It's not normal. She never asks me anything,
not even a simple, "How was your performance today?" It's
become a taboo subject. If I try to tell her what I'm up to, she
dodges the conversation. She's decided to be Dr. Jekyll's girlfriend and pretend she has no idea she's also dating Mr. Hyde.
It's a fruitless effort, since our silences are charged with everything we're not saying. The worst part, though, is that her attitude doesn't make things better for me; it only increases my
sense of marginalization, which I do my best to ignore.

The Italian restaurant was neutral ground, so I seized the
opportunity to put an end to the pretense. Fully aware of what

I was doing, I said, "Tonight we're including a happy birthday wish in the show."

Quick as a flash, she asks me to pass the Parmesan and starts remarking how delicious her pasta is. As if I hadn't heard her, I kept going: "It's for this girl whose friends are bringing her in for her thirtieth birthday. She doesn't know we're going to congratulate her up onstage. It's a surprise for her from her friends."

"Uh-huh," she mutters like a sick princess, and looks away.

"There's a price for that, of course. The club owner's decided . . . "

Her eyes blaze, and in a pleading yet harsh tone she says, "Javier, please . . . "

Determined, I finish my sentence. " . . . decided to charge for that sort of thing. Otherwise we'd do nothing but wish people happy birthday and read out dedications for our dance numbers."

"Javier, if you don't mind, I'd rather you didn't talk about the show."

I stop eating. I stare at her.

"But I'm part of the show, understand? It's my job."

"You're a teacher."

I wring my napkin in my hands—displacement, since at the moment I'd like to be wringing her neck. I haven't been this angry in years. Swallowing my rage, I spit, "Reality check, Sandra: I don't have a job as a teacher."

"And you're not looking for one, either. How often have you called the employment office to ask if they've got anything for you? When was the last time you sent out your résumé? Have you tried using social networks?"

"It's no use. There are only so many schools in this city."

"All right, if not as a teacher, you could look for some other kind of job."

"I already have a job."

"But seriously, Javier, how do you fit in in that environment?"

"If you'd ever let me talk about it, maybe you'd understand. Look, I'm not a professional stripper, and I'm not going to get naked on stage my whole life. But it's my temporary occupation for now, so I don't see why you have to treat me like I've got the plague."

"I don't treat you like you've got the plague, but I don't like talking about it."

"All right, Sandra, that's fine. Denying reality has always been one of your specialties. Your morals are less offended as long as you don't talk about it . . . "

"It's not a question of morality—it's more complicated than that. It's . . . It doesn't matter. Let's drop it."

"Yes, let's drop it. Do you want dessert?"

Dessert or not, the meal was already ruined, though at least one thing was clear: Sandra hates what I do, can't stand it.

I was so upset, my hands were shaking as we left the restaurant. I could have used a line right then.

We spent the afternoon at home reading. There was some tension in the air, but not enough to disrupt the normality. When it was time for me to go to the club, I kissed her hair and said goodbye.

I stopped in at the bar and ordered some tea. The waiter, who knows me by now, asked, "Anything to eat?"

"No, thanks, I don't have time. I have to go to work soon."

It felt so good to say that! It was true: in a little while they'd be waiting for me to show up at work. Waiting for me, Javier. I had a boss, colleagues, buddies to go out to eat with after the show. For the first time, I felt happy as I headed to the club.

* * *

How does he fit in there? Doesn't he realize? Is this the

same man I met that first day? If someone had told me I'd be going through this, I'd have died laughing. Javier, so mature, well-adjusted, calm, tolerant, realistic . . . What goes on in the guy's heads? I thought I knew, but I don't. He's been in the striptease business for two months now, and that's a long time. I thought he wouldn't last a week—actually, I thought he'd never dare do it at all. Sometimes people in literary circles like to dabble in different experiences. But it seems like he's taking it seriously. Why? Not because of the money—we don't need what he's bringing in. Just to have a job, no matter what? Does it really count as a job?

Some days, there in the office, sitting at my computer, I'm convinced none of this is true: I've just dreamed it. I don't understand Javier's reasons for getting involved in this crap. I guess a lot of it has to do with Iván, that lowlife, that philistine. Javier listens to him. He's flattered. Iván always treats him like his intellectual superior. The other day he called here and I answered the phone. "Is the teacher around?" he asked. The teacher! There's the nub of it: my boy's ego is probably in the gutter, and it probably boosts his self-esteem to have Iván admiring him and calling him "teacher." But I fell in love with Javier because he wasn't your typical vain guy! He didn't need me to tell him, "You're so handsome!" "You're so good at your job!" "You're a stud in bed!" all the time. No, he seemed solid. He did things because he liked them, not because they raised his social standing. I never heard him say he wanted a full-time teaching position. Teaching supplementary classes was enough for him. He'd rather live a quiet life than be number one. His only ambition was to have enough free time to read all the books he wanted.

I liked that he was like that; I can't stand guys who are full of themselves. My older sister lives with a guy who makes a lot of money. He's horrible—all he cares about is work, and he's always going around in a snit, competing with everybody, perpetually caught up in his phone and computer. When he gets home at night, my sister has to tell him he's amazing, number one, the best. Otherwise he gets depressed. His aspiration in life is to become the manager at his company. Horrible.

The whole time I've lived with Javier, I've been very happy. We've lived a quiet life. During the week we each did our own thing, and on the weekend we did the shopping together, drank some wine when we were done, had dinner with friends, went to the movies . . . I don't know, the things normal people do! I always wanted a peaceful life, no anger or tension. I've seen what it's like to live with an ambitious guy, and I wanted no part of it. I've met a lot of guys who are as vain as peacocks, competitive as race horses. Mine wasn't like that. Not till one fine day he lost his job and decided to become a stripper. It would be funny if I weren't so bitter about it! It's like a two-bit vaudeville show!

We don't do much on the weekends anymore. He leaves at seven in the evening and I stay home alone, trying to figure out why a guy like him would prance around naked in some run-down dive. "I already have a job." Some job! If it's such a normal, dignified job, why hasn't he ever encouraged me to come see him perform? I'm tempted to show up one day without warning, sit down at an out-of-the-way table, and record him on my cell phone. When he came home I'd show him the recording so he could see himself looking like a ridiculous clown. The only reason I haven't done it is I don't want to go alone and I'm embarrassed to ask a friend to go with me. I haven't told anybody he's working at a club. He's stopped seeing his friends, probably because he's as embarrassed as I am. Everybody thinks we're fighting over something secret. It's awful to be ashamed of the man you live with, though most disappointing of all has been realizing that Javier's like any other guy, that he needs a numbskull like Iván to call him "teacher" so he can feel like he's somebody.

He's told me he comes home so late because he goes out to eat with a group of "coworkers" after the show. I can just imagine how those conversations go! And what his "coworkers" are like! When he gets into bed, he reeks of alcohol.

This is all too much for me. I could still put this period out of my mind if he quit the club immediately, but I'm afraid to ask him to. He acts like dancing nude is the same as being a company accountant, a sacred professional obligation. I don't get it—we used to be so happy! I've been trying to keep on living as though nothing's changed, but it's not working. I've got the club stuck in my head. We'll see—I don't want to give up all hope. Maybe the problem will resolve itself in the same unexpected way it arose. One day I'll get up in the morning and Javier will tell me, "Here I am, Sandra, the joke's over, I'm me again."

\* \* \*

The rooftop bar at the Hotel Imperio. I've been to this super-high-end hotel before, but never on the roof. It's very elegant, very on-trend. I love minimalist décor. Now that I'm living alone, I should change the décor in my house: switch out the furniture, repaint, even tear down some walls. With David everything was very traditional, though he never chose anything. Papá gave us the furniture as a gift. We ordered it together. David said yes to everything—poor guy didn't have a clue about interior design, nor the time to think about that sort of thing. Still, the two of us did all right. We bought the latest fashions, the ones in all the magazines. It drove Papá a little crazy. I called a decorator at first, but he kept asking me personal questions: "What's the life plan for the two of you?" I didn't know what to say; I felt incredibly uncomfortable. I've never been able to talk about my plans with anybody. So I turned to Papá. And I didn't much care what our house looked like anyway. Maybe if my mother had been alive . . . maybe then I would have been more interested in that sort of thing. But living with Papá, I'd learned to do without extravagances. Papá used to say that extravagance is a very womanly waste of time. Of course I'm a woman, but Papá would sometimes tell me I was "his boy," which I was to a certain extent.

The rooftop bar at the Hotel Imperio. Sometimes I think Genoveva feels obligated to take me out on the town. It bothers me, makes me feel like I'm a silly little girl or an abandoned woman—which I actually am. It doesn't matter, I let her take care of me. Today, with a bit of a mysterious air, she's brought me here—I have no idea what's so special about it. The plan is just to chat for a bit while sipping a gin and tonic.

She's stunning today, dressed all in red and black. Even her shoes combine the two colors. We sit down at a table under a super-modern gas heater, nothing like those crappy ones they pull out in wintertime for outside seating at regular bars. I no longer think this plan is boring: I'll have a couple of drinks, and by the end of the first one I'll be feeling more cheerful and ready for a laugh.

"Why did you choose this place?" I ask Genoveva.

"Just my personal business."

Mine and yours too, honey, or at least I hope so. If she doesn't go along with this, I'm going to have to cut her loose. Spoiled little girls are always getting bored, always wanting more—but when you set an entree down in front of them, they turn up their noses and say they're not hungry. We'll see how she reacts. If she's not OK with it, we have nothing more to say to each other. I'm not her nanny or her mom.

"You know what I was thinking, Genoveva? Maybe I should redecorate my place. But then it seems like such a pain."

Genoveva isn't listening—she's distracted or she doesn't feel like talking. Suddenly she lifts her hand and signals to somebody, smiling. I turn for a moment to see who it is and spot two men walking toward us. Are they here by chance, or did she arrange to meet without telling me? If this is another attempt to set me up, I just might kill her. They come over to us. I repress the urge to get up and leave.

"Hi! What's up, boys? How are you? Let me introduce you: this is my friend Irene, and these two are Rodolfo and Uriel."

"Nice to meet you," I hear myself say.

Rodolfo and Uriel? Where did she find these guys, with their preposterous names? I'm suddenly tempted to laugh. Rodolfo is black, black all over—he's *a* black. They're both young, tall, slim, well dressed. Uriel is darkly tanned with Latin American features—Mexican, maybe.

Genoveva has, as usual, taken control of the situation. She tells them to take a seat, orders them drinks. A surprisingly dispassionate conversation begins: what a beautiful sunset it is, the terrace décor, the brands of gin they selected for their cocktails. Fairly quickly, it becomes clear that Genoveva arranged this meeting. They're prototypical studs, beefcakes. Rodolfo's wearing a pink shirt that contrasts with and intensifies the beautiful color of his skin. Uriel's well-developed muscles ripple beneath his suit. They have silky voices, a sophisticated manner of speaking; they're good at small talk.

After a while, the alcohol has perked us up considerably. We go for tapas in a bar in the historic district, one of those places that's suddenly become trendy. It's packed, so we have to wait in line for a table. We drink red wine. It's clear that Genoveva and Rodolfo know each other quite well—they exchange sidelong glances, their shoulders bumping conspiratorially. Uriel starts discreetly flirting with me. The more we drink, the more nonsense we talk. We're like schoolkids: little jokes, double entendres . . . Luckily, occasionally someone reveals a bit of information about the two guys. I finally learn that Rodolfo is from Cuba and Uriel from El Salvador. How is this expected to play out—are we supposed to go dancing in a dive bar somewhere? I don't really care; I'm starting to get bored with the insipid chitchat.

When the desserts arrive, Genoveva and Rodolfo start nuzzling each other like teenagers: an affectionate tap on the nose, a playful tug on the hair . . . Finally they kiss on the lips. The people around us stare at them. They stand out because she's white and he's black, because of the obvious age difference, and especially because of their ridiculous behavior. Under normal circumstances, I'd have been embarrassed for them, but the combination of the gin and tonic and the wine makes it so I just don't care. At some point it occurs to me that maybe my ex and his current girl, the simultaneous interpreter, also coo at each other in public, and they must look as comical as Genoveva and Rodolfo do.

Genoveva ends up paying the check, just as she paid for our drinks on the hotel terrace. The guys don't protest or make any attempt to pay or split the bill. I'm quite sleepy, so I'm caught off guard when my guess turns out to be correct and they cheerfully announce that we're going out dancing. I flatly refuse, say I'm tired, I'm going to bed. Uriel jokingly performs some dance steps right in the middle of the street. "Come on, baby, life is short." He moves gracefully, and I smile. For a second I think Genoveva's going to insist I go with them, but she's so drunk that she's no longer worrying about me. Perfect. I start to say goodbye and Uriel interrupts me, saying he'll accompany me home. I object, but he insists on doing things the old-fashioned way: "I'm a gentleman, and after an evening out, I take the lady home." Fine, I let him come with me. I give the taxi driver the address to the office. On our way there, Uriel keeps staring at me intensely. When we arrive, I hastily get out of the cab, but he gets out too. I pay the driver. I shake Uriel's hand as a final goodbye, and he won't let go afterward, gazing at me with puppy dog eyes. I pull away somewhat brusquely and say good night. I walk through the main entrance. I don't turn on the light. I stay there in the dark, checking to make sure he's left. After a couple of minutes, I go down to the parking lot and collect my car. I head home.

The next morning I call Genoveva. She answers sleepily.

"I'm still in bed, darling."

"Sorry, I thought since it's almost eleven . . . "

"We partied till four in the morning. What did you think of the guys? They're great, right?"

"Who are they? How did you meet?"

I hear her laugh, which immediately makes her cough, since she's a smoker.

"Jesus, Irene, I can't believe how naïve you are! They're escorts, sweetie."

I'm starting to think she's playing dumb, faking it. How is it possible she's never heard that there's such a thing as male escorts? She's so out of touch, maybe it's possible—the girl is totally clueless. Who did she think they were, friends from college? Please! I'm not surprised her husband left her; even I'm getting fed up with her. Didn't she realize what was going on yesterday? What did she and Uriel do when they left? Maybe she told him her life story: about the company and her dad and how her husband left her. It's almost embarrassing, to be honest.

"Do you mean gigolos?"

"That's an out-of-date concept, Irene. They're call guys, I don't know how else to put it."

Gigolos! What planet does she live on? Françoise Sagan, Sylvie Vartan, convertibles, and the Cote d'Azur. She must have seen it in a movie.

"Male prostitutes?"

Genoveva is gripped by a fit of laughter that lasts too long to be genuine. By the end, her laugh sounds like the clucking of a hysterical chicken. I wait patiently for her to stop.

"Look, darling, if you want we can meet for drinks and I'll

tell you all about it, but you saw them—they're gorgeous, well-mannered guys who will take you on their arm wherever you want and always make you look good. And of course if you want them to accompany you to bed, that's fine too. It's a very discreet network. You meet one, and then another one from there . . . It's not a prostitution ring or anything like that."

"But you pay them."

"That's the arrangement, darling. You pay their expenses for the night and an additional fixed fee. But no cash—it's all done really discreetly. A couple of days after you've gone out, you deposit their fee in a bank account. Nothing dodgy, see? It's all very tasteful."

"Right."

"I see you understand."

Poor Irene sounds frustrated. What did she think, that I'd met the guys on the city bus? Two handsome, well-mannered young men! It's not like good-looking men grow on trees! I'm getting up there, sure, but she's not exactly a catch herself: a divorced middle-aged woman, colder than an iceberg, blander than hospital food. And physically? Well, she's not bad, but she's not going to win any beauty contests or have strangers follow her down the street. But she's rich, right? She owns a company. Well, that's what you have to offer, sweetie—that's the deal. The world is a marketplace in every aspect, not just some. Irene's a businesswoman, so she should know everything has its price, its exchange rate, its valuation.

"So how much do I owe you for last night, Genoveva?"

"It's my treat this time. The next time, if you want there to be a next time, we can split the cost. What did you think of Uriel?"

"Very nice."

"He's handsome, right? Those muscles! Rodolfo's a sweetheart. We've gone out a few times, and he's always been flawless in everything. And when I say everything, you know what I mean."

She laughs again. Her laughter repulses me a little. She's revealed herself now. This is the real Genoveva. It had to be something like this; you don't get that kind of reputation just from drinking in bars and buying cheap clothing. Now a lot of things make sense.

Male escorts. There are probably lots of women who use them, hire them to go to parties, on trips . . . The men know how to fit in, and nobody asks where they came from. Those women must no longer aspire to have a future, I think; they live life as it comes, day by day, at peace. And what about me? Do I aspire to have a future? I'm all mixed up and would rather not think about it. I'm not looking for a new love or a good time or anything like that. I don't have a future. I'm happy to have gone out with an escort. I don't feel guilty. It's silly to think about how my father would be rolling in horror in his grave. Papá isn't in his grave or anywhere else. Papá's not here.

I don't want to think. My head hurts. I don't want to think.

\* \* \*

Shit, man, the fuss this guy's kicked up! And all because of something he brought on himself. Where the hell did this guy come from? Hasn't he ever had any friends? I asked him about that one day, and he said, "Yeah, in college, and a few coworkers . . . but I don't see them anymore." I can guess why he stopped seeing them: he's embarrassed to be working as a stripper. Well, he'll figure it out: if it's so beneath him, he can go back to being unemployed, no problem, just stay home reading books or doing sudokus—I don't care. It's not like he's the scion of the Duke of Crappington or something! He can stop putting on airs—he was born in the same neighborhood as me! And weren't any of those friends of his fags? Hasn't he figured out you have to be on your guard? It's not that hard. With all that education and as much as he's read, he doesn't even know the basics of human psychology?

He comes in yesterday and says, "It was awful, Iván!"

"What's going on, man?" I ask.

"Wong tried to touch me, said he's in love with me. I thought I was going to die. It was horrible! You should have told me he was gay; you should have warned me. You didn't say a word—you just left me in the lion's den."

I step into the shower and after a minute Wong asks me for the soap. We're alone in the showers, and there's no one in the dressing room. During the show, I thought I saw a girl I know in the audience, so I stayed till last to make sure nobody was waiting for me at the exit. Wong must have been watching me and turned up then. I pass him the shower gel, and then he hands it back to me. I've got my eyes closed, my face covered in foam. Suddenly I feel someone stroking my genitals, really soft, really gentle. I step back in the confined space and run my hands over my face, trying to clear my eyes to see. And there's Wong, naked and erect. I don't know what to do, how to react. Then he goes and says, "Don't be scared, Javier. We like each other, right?" I cry *No!* like I've seen the devil, like Wong has a knife to my throat. But that doesn't stop him. He says, "I love you, Javier. You're different from the others. You're sensitive. You're not an animal like them. I love you." "No, Wong, really, you've made a mistake, I'm not into men!" He utters a string of jumbled sentences and then puts his hand on my penis again. Nervous, I shove him—not hard, just to get him away from me. But the floor is wet and he slips. He falls to his knees and stays there a while, looking down, not saying anything, nor me either, with the water from the shower still running.

When he got up, he was crying, and he was crying as he left. My heart was pounding, and I felt utterly rattled. The whole grotesque scene could have been avoided if fucking Iván had said something to me—or did nobody realize Wong was gay?

"Don't try to blame me for your screw-ups, Javier! Understood?"

That's life, man, that's fucking life. Go ahead, do somebody a favor. Cheer him up in his low moments, invite him out for beers. Even get him a job. Put yourself out there for him, convince Mariano he's a cool guy who was born to shake his ass onstage. And if he's hungry, pull out a tit and breastfeed him, because that's pretty much the only thing I haven't done for Javier. When he came after me for not having warned him about Wong, I went ballistic. Didn't he see it coming? It was so obvious! The sidelong glances, the little smiles . . . How was I supposed to know the teacher was such a goddamn idiot? All that studying and reading, and apparently he still doesn't know shit about life. Aren't there any queers in books? Where has he been all these years, in a fucking library? And to top it all off, he gets pissed and blames me!

"I'm not your father, Javier, or your mother either. Didn't you realize the guy was into you? You must be blind, man, seriously!"

"You said the club didn't have that kind of problem!"

"I told you it wasn't crawling with fags, but there's always one who slips through! I can't follow you around like a body-guard."

Frankly, that little scene must have been something to see. Wong went way too far. Getting in the shower and grabbing his dick—damn, if it hadn't been clear already . . . ! If the boss finds out, he'll boot him; he's told all of us he doesn't want any problems in his show—no fights or arguments or jealousy, and definitely no faggotry. But Wong isn't the first, and he won't be the last. This job is for good-looking guys who take care of their bodies, so it's inevitable that we get the occasional queer. All the performers boast about how they're lady killers, but some of them go for both fish and fowl. That must have been rough for Javier. It's one thing to deal with insinuations, glances, "accidental" grazes, but a full-on groin grope is different story. I could go tell Mariano about it. I've never been one to squeal on another guy, but Wong went way too far and should be taught a lesson. Plus, Javier's such a wuss, it'll be really awkward for him to keep running into the guy. But fuck it, I'm not going to be his nanny for the rest of his life. Maybe after thirty guys have come into the shower and tried to fondle his dick, he'll finally figure out what's up. I'm just going to have be patient with the teacher.

"Well, man, I'm really sorry about that, but it doesn't really seem right to blame me. These things happen, full stop."

"I know, I know."

These things happen, full stop. That's a philosophical take, a maxim so profound you could base a school of thought on it. These things happen—to people without any education, without any sense of morals. Careful, though, I must be going crazy. Since when do I put any stock in morality? Haven't I always claimed that the concept was invented to restrict freedom? I'm starting to believe I'm superior to the losers dancing in the buff alongside me, oblivious to the fact that I'm just as big a loser. No, enough, I need a little calm and self-awareness. What right did I have to yell at Iván, demanding explanations? I never go off on people! I'm either crazy or stupid. I don't know what's happening to me. Certainly nothing good.

"I'm sorry I yelled at you, Iván. Things have been rough. I was upset and got carried away. What happened isn't your fault. I'm a total dumbass."

I have no excuse. It had been twenty-four hours since my unpleasant run-in with Wong, long enough for my anger to have passed. But no, as soon I saw Iván I went on the attack. I can't vent to Sandra about my problems, so the toxic humors have been building up inside me. It's not fair to him at all.

"I'm really sorry. Forgive me."

"No big deal, man! Let's forget about it and move on."

Shit, any more of this and he'll be on his knees in front of me. There's no need for Holy Week–style self-flagellation here. This whole Wong situation could have actually been pretty funny, but we turned it into a goddamn soap opera. "It's your fault. No, it's yours! Ew, he touched my dick! Gross!" The hell with the teacher. If he'd had to deal with as much bullshit as I have . . . I even got bullshit from my parents. I don't know what he would have done if he'd been dealt a life like mine: jumped out a window or something. Of course, maybe it's good to have had a miserable life—that way you learn to survive and change your fucking destiny. You learn to turn turds into gold. I've got everything I need now: money, a good car, an awesome apartment . . . No lack of chicks, either. I get laid whenever I want. Maybe that's what Javier's missing, getting laid, and that's why he's in such a bad mood. I don't know how things are going with his old lady. She seems like a total drag, like she wants him all for herself. Maybe she even wants kids! Of course, maybe the teacher wants that too: starting a family and all that bullshit people used to do back in our grandparents' day.

"Look, man, let's stop this crap and go out for some beers. What do you say, teach?"

"My treat."

"You're on, man! Your treat! After all, we have to celebrate you hooking up with Wong."

"Asshole."

"No way, no asshole here! It's been years since anyone joined me in the shower. And I've definitely never gotten a declaration of love! Just goes to show you're the bomb, Javier, and as tasty to Chinese dudes as a bowl of rice. Just think if all those millions of them got together to fondle your cock. They'd wear it out, man!"

"Are you done, dickwad?"

"That's right, man, you need to laugh a little. You can't go around always being pissed off and so miserable it's like you're about to burst into tears. Everything's fucked enough as it is— no need to make it even worse!"

\* \* \*

Our friends are surprised that Javier's stopped coming out with us. They ask about him all the time, so I've started lying to them, saying he's tutoring on the weekends. Lying was always the one thing I refused to do. Lies indicate that, on some fundamental level, you can't bear reality. I've tried—I tried telling people that he works at a strip club. I even imagined how I might present it. Humor seemed like a good approach—it would ease some of the shame. "You're going to love this! The ninny was tired of twiddling his thumbs, so he . . . " But I couldn't do it. So I lied—which is ridiculous and risky. If a friend runs into him on the street one day, the cat will be out of the bag. Javier definitely wouldn't lie about it. I doubt he's proud of his job, but I can't see him making something up. He prefers silence: he just disappears, ignoring the fact that I'm still in the world. Sometimes I even wonder whether one of our acquaintances is going to see him performing at the club. That would be a disaster after my tutoring dodge. Maybe I should find new friends. After all, why am I going out alone every weekend in a group where everybody's coupled up?

I've got the same problem with my parents. We used to to their house to eat sometimes, but now Javier refuses to come with me. My parents are nice people who've never interfered in our lives. They don't even call on the phone very often so as not to disturb us. But they've started asking why Javier isn't coming. It's to be expected—I'd ask too if I were in their shoes. I'm going to end up telling them the tutoring lie too.

The question is: why doesn't Javier want to see anybody? The answer's a cinch: he's embarrassed and doesn't want to show his face. If his job were as normal as he claims, he wouldn't have disappeared like this.

This whole situation is really hard on me. Every day that goes by, I feel more depressed. I don't get excited about anything, and at work I zone out so much that it's starting to worry me. The other day I thought maybe I should go to a psychiatrist, and I even started looking for a friend's phone number so she could recommend one. But then I got mad at myself. He's the one with the problem, so why should I see a psychiatrist? We women are amazing, always ready to take the blame for everything. I'm not unstable, I've just been thrown off balance because the man I live with is acting strange, that's all. He's the root of the conflict—a normal guy doesn't take up dancing naked in some seedy dump.

I think the two of us need to have a serious conversation. I'm too young to have this kind of bad mojo in my life. I've seen a lot of my girlfriends suffering because of their guys. It's terrible for them, always wondering whether their boyfriends love them or not. They'll put up with anything to be with them, to keep from losing them: disdain, infidelity, all sorts of nasty stuff. I'm not that kind of woman; I've got my head firmly on my shoulders and my feet on the ground. I have no intention of spending my life paralyzed with fear and letting people treat me like a doormat. I want a peaceful life, sharing my joys and sorrows—living with another person should be a happy thing. I don't think I'm asking for the moon here. I hope that after our serious talk, Javier will realize he's at risk of losing me. I think he'll reflect on things a little—he's never done anything crazy. Now it's like somebody's taken away his willpower, altered his personality. He's caught up in a preposterous nightmare, but at some point he's got to wake up. This damn recession is going to make all of us morally bankrupt! What a country—what a world! Sometimes I fantasize about going with Javier to live in the smallest, most remote village in Spain, where we'd grow organic vegetables or something. A simple life: work in the fields, bake your own bread, chat with a neighbor out in the street . . . But it's not that easy. Doing anything requires a lot of money up front, and there are already plenty of people growing organic vegetables. And what do I know about vegetables? Absolutely nothing. I'm a city girl, and the only work I know how to do is in the city. Am I going to turn my whole life upside down because my guy's decided to shake his ass in a some kind of strip joint? No way, man, not a chance.

\* \* \*

I can't believe it myself, but I did it. Today I called Genoveva to tell her I'm interested in going out with Rodolfo and Uriel again. She started ribbing me a little: "So you're into that sort of thing, huh?" But I stopped her right there. I'm not going to let people treat me like a prissy little girl who's a glutton for punishment, or a moron who's an easy target for mockery. She goes out with escorts, and so do I. That's all there is to it.

This time we have our date in a cocktail bar called Fuego. At my request, Genoveva and I have met up an hour early. I didn't feel like being with the guys the whole evening. Genoveva still doesn't understand where I'm coming from and tries to make another joke at my expense:

"So my idea of introducing you to a couple of studs wasn't so outlandish after all!"

"Genoveva, everything's perfectly all right, but I'd rather you not bring up the guys again. It makes me uncomfortable."

She doesn't respond or seem startled. She just arches an eyebrow and murmurs, "All right, honey, all right. Whatever you say." I hope she gets it now. I'm not going to talk about this, whether seriously or in jest, when I don't even know why I'm doing it. What's driving me to go out with these guys again? The novelty of it, I guess, and curiosity. I know I'm not doing it because I need the company or want people to see me on the arm of a handsome man. The last time we went out, I felt something unexpected: ease. When you're with a man, whatever kind of relationship you've established with him, you always have to keep in mind that he's a man, treat him a little special, make an effort. But with these guys I was relaxed—I didn't care who they were or why they were there. It would be pointless to share such nuances with Genoveva. But at the very least I'd like her to understand that this isn't some world-changing discovery for me, like gunpowder. I'll be able to keep on living perfectly happily after this, even if I don't set off a single firecracker.

"All right, honey, all right. Whatever you say."

Can you believe this child? "I'm doing it but I won't talk about it." Irene's really something else. A total princess. I don't think she's all that healthy, psychologically speaking. But fine, if that's what her ladyship wants, we won't talk about it. Though I'd like to inform her that it doesn't change anything. It's obvious the little prude likes the same things the rest of us women do—or is the Madonna/whore binary true after all? Such an old-fashioned notion. The thing is, in order to do anything, you have to have clear ideas and a bit of class. Irene might be an amazing businesswoman and all that, but she seems to fall a little short when it comes to mental clarity and savoir faire.

We've barely finished our drinks when the boys, as Genoveva calls them, arrive. They look quite dashing: impeccable chino pants, meticulously pressed pastel-colored shirts, gleaming loafers. Knowing what I know about them now—that we're paying them for their time—I do see them differently. I'm more excited, and I've got a ton of questions: How do they see us, as self-indulgent rich women looking to have a good time? Are they harsh moral judges who think of us as total sluts? Do they find us attractive? Maybe when a man's "on the clock," he doesn't even pay attention to whether a woman is beautiful or ugly. I don't know—the whole situation is weird for me, anomalous. I need to assess them as dispassionately as I do my assistant, my workers: ultimately, they're my employees too. I'd like to know more about the boys' lives, but I get the feeling that if I asked anything, I'd just get a bunch of lies in response.

We order aperitifs. Genoveva gets tispy immediately; she must be a bit of an alcoholic after all these years of unsavory nightlife. She starts flirting with Rodolfo, who responds in kind. A powerful wave of embarrassment runs through my body like a shiver. I'm on the verge of getting up and going home. What am I doing here? On second thought, though, what would I do at home? I stay put, but I adopt a severe expression so the guys can see I'm not like Genoveva.

Uriel starts tossing me little meaningful glances, getting bolder and bolder. The careful reserve he displayed when we first met is gone. That's no surprise, really—agreeing to meet them again means I've accepted the terms. There's no possibility of misunderstanding here. We're paying, they're collecting, and we all realize what's going on.

We have dinner at a Basque restaurant. The boys order fish and vegetables, telling us they don't want to gain weight. I order a steak so it's clear I don't care about gaining weight. We drink two bottles of wine, with a glass of brandy for dessert. If this is the way they drink all the time, their livers must be ready to burst. I take it easy with the wine. I don't need alcohol jangling my nerves. I can get up and leave whenever I want, and pay what I owe the next day.

When we leave the restaurant, I assume we're going

somewhere else for one last drink, but Genoveva and Rodolfo, giggling, say they're in a hurry and take off. I don't find it funny, just crude. Uriel suggests we go to a bar for our last drink. I agree, which is a big mistake: as soon as we sit down, I realize I've got absolutely nothing to say. Seeing my silence, he talks instead, chattering away like a radio host, stringing together only vaguely connected sentences. I down my drink quickly because I can't stand his babbling; it's making me crazy. What is he saying? I tune in for a moment, and he's talking about tennis. I hate tennis! Playing tennis is the one thing Papá made me do even though he knew I loathed it. Every Saturday we'd go to the club together, but he'd play a game with one of his friends while I had to take the lessons he'd signed me up for. We'd spend the whole morning apart, and I didn't like that at all. Poor Papá! What was he supposed to do with me for a whole day? But I made it clear I hated the club, and when I got a little older I stopped going with him. I've regretted it ever since.

The guy sitting across from me—suddenly I barely remember who he is—is going on about Nadal's last match. I pull myself together and say, "Let's get out of here."

"To your house or a hotel?"

The question leaves me cold, though in fact it's the relevant one to ask under the circumstances. "A hotel, of course," I say without pausing to ponder it. "But we don't have a reservation."

"I'll take care of that. Is the Palace all right?"

"Yes, great."

I attempt to sound confident—I can't stand being a rookie. Uriel goes off and makes a phone call.

"Any problems?" I ask, trying to demonstrate that I'm in control here.

"No, it's all good."

We grab a taxi and head to the Palace. Realizing that I've

been irritated by his constant chitchat, he stays quiet. I watch him surreptitiously out of the corner of my eye. He looks calm as he stares out the window. He doesn't seem excited or nervous. He watches the passersby on the street, his expression utterly incurious. I try to imagine what's going through his head. Does he know this is my first time doing this? I imagine he does—there's probably something in my manner that gives me away.

We enter the hotel, and before we reach reception he tells me, "Wait here if you like; I'll get the room." It's scandalously obvious that he's a male prostitute and I'm his customer. Though the age difference isn't that large, we don't have any luggage, and we're dressed in different styles, which doesn't tend to happen with couples. Luckily, he's taken the initiative here, because I would have been petrified at having to face the concierge. I'm not sure whether he's arranging the room because that's the way it's usually done or because he's decided I have no idea what I'm doing.

I pace awkwardly around the lobby and stand staring at a horrible painting as if I found it immensely interesting. Out of the corner of my eye, I note that they're giving him the room without asking for his ID or making him sign anything. He must be a regular guest. Smiling, he comes over and takes my elbow, leads me toward the elevator. The receptionist doesn't even glance at us.

We go up to the seventh floor. He leads, and I follow. He knows exactly where our room is. How many times have they given him the same one; how many women has he brought here before? I don't find the thought depressing—I feel only a twinge of disgust. My primary emotion is still curiosity. I'm tempted to ask him to tell me how they behave, the women who come here with him: Do they pretend to be in love, or are they cold and demanding? Do they act like they're starring in a porn film?

He closes the door and looks at me with a smile I'm not sure how to interpret: reassuring, mischievous? He examines the thermostat. I take off my coat and toss it on a chair. I plaster on a neutral expression that doesn't communicate anything.

"Want a drink?" he asks.

I shrug. He goes to the minibar and pulls out two little bottles of whiskey. He pours the contents into two glasses. He hands me one and leaves his unsampled on the nightstand. He sheds the blazer and loosens his tie. From there, what is clearly a very well-rehearsed performance unfolds. He comes over, places his hand on my neck, and starts to massage it. It feels like being stabbed with a needle, and I quickly step back.

"I'd rather you not touch me, please."

He pouts and says wheedlingly, as if I were a child, "Come on, beautiful, relax. You're so pretty, just gorgeous."

"I am relaxed. I just want you to get undressed."

"And then what?"

"Then nothing. I want to look."

He thinks he's in control of the situation again and smiles. Slowly, he takes off his clothes. When he's down to his boxers, he jokingly hums a bit of striptease music. Finally his black boxers drop to the floor. I see his erect penis. It's huge, or at least it seems huge to me. Beneath it is a very large, dark sac covered thickly with hair. I'm fascinated, hypnotized, stupefied. Absurdly, the thought flashes through my mind that I've never seen a man naked before. A childhood memory comes surging back. One day I sneaked into the bathroom while my father was peeing. I tiptoed up behind him, wanting to see what he was holding in his hands. I looked and saw just another bit of flesh, a stream of urine issuing from it. He covered my eyes and made me leave. When he saw me afterward, he didn't scold me; he acted like nothing had happened. Yes, I have seen naked men. I saw my husband for many years, but I didn't really look at him. It never occurred to me that I'd enjoy seeing a man's naked body so much. I could look at Uriel for hours: his unblemished skin, the curve of his shoulders, his sharply defined leg muscles, his belly button, his pubic hair.

Abruptly he interrupts my pleasure and moves toward me, smiling. He swaggers like a cowboy in an old movie. I've been so rapt, staring at his body, that he's started to feel confident, magnificent. I jolt out of my trance when he touches me, caressing my chin. "Baby," he says. His hand provokes an intense feeling of disgust in me, a physical revulsion bordering on nausea. His calling me "baby" almost makes me laugh, but I'm outraged: where does this lowlife, this scum, this total piece of shit get off, daring to touch me?

"Please don't touch me."

"What's that about?" he asks, surprised but not angry.

"Like I said, I just wanted to look at you."

"And you don't like what you see."

"No, actually, you have a beautiful body, but I just got divorced and I'm not in the mood yet."

"Are you sure? We'll go easy with everything, you'll see. You'll get undressed, we'll lie in bed and talk a while, drink our whiskey. We'll take it slow, no rush."

He strokes my face again as he outlines this plan. Not wanting to offend him, I grit my teeth through the new wave of distaste that sweeps over me. For the same reason, I don't reassure him that I'll pay him even if he chooses to leave now.

"Maybe another time, not tonight. I'm not feeling inspired today, that's all."

"All right, whatever you want. Should I get dressed and go?"

"That would be best. I'll stay—I might sleep here."

He gets dressed pretty quickly. He's annoyed, though he's attempting to hide it. I try to smile to placate him. He's pretty high-maintenance! I wonder if men have these sorts of problems with the hookers they hire.

"See you around, beautiful. *Ciao*. The room's all taken care of, OK?"

He barely looks at me as he leaves. Once I'm alone, I sigh, take off my shoes, sip my whiskey. The experience hasn't been very pleasant, but it's been worth it for a number of reasons. First, I know now that I'm bold enough to do it. Second, I've gotten to see his young, strong, gorgeous body. Next time I'll have to let the guy know from the beginning: no sex, just looking.

I lie down on the bed and relax. The whiskey is delicious.

Two days later Genoveva calls me. She tells me she's sent me an e-mail with what I owe for our night with the boys. The e-mail lists an account number where I can deposit the amount.

"That number includes everything, all right, darling? Drinks, dinner, hotel, fee . . . If you want, I can itemize it."

"That's not necessary, Genoveva. Jesus."

"Did you have any trouble with Uriel, sweetie?"

"No, why?"

"He was a little worried about you."

"About me? He shouldn't be."

"OK, he must have gotten the wrong impression. Are you up for getting a bite to eat tonight?"

There's something fishy going on, and I want to know what happened. Maybe Irene stopped the guy cold. I would believe it—these pampered daddy's-girl types can freak out if anything is the least bit off. Maybe she had second thoughts at the last minute. Rodolfo doesn't know exactly what happened, but he knows things didn't go well. Maybe at the last minute this ninny started thinking, "Me, with a male prostitute? What would my father say?"

"Yes, I'd love to go out tonight for a bit. I'll finish up at the office around eight. Does that work for you?"

Genoveva's dying to know, and I can tell her whatever I feel like, fiction or truth. Trouble is, my truth sounds pretty weird.

How do I admit I couldn't stand having the guy touch me? Even worse, how do I explain that all I wanted was for him to take off his clothes, that I just really liked seeing him naked? She'll think I'm a pervert. I'm starting to think that myself.

We meet up at a café full of gaggles of elderly women all talking over one another: children, grandchildren, health problems. I'm amused to think that we'll be talking about quite a different subject. Genoveva doesn't waste a moment. She starts right in:

"Look, Irene, I know something happened with Uriel. Please tell me—I feel terribly responsible. Did he do something wrong? Was he inappropriate?"

"No, not at all. He's a nice guy. It was just . . . well, all I wanted was to see him naked. I mean, just look at him, that's it. I guess he got frustrated."

Genoveva cracks up. Her laugh always sounds fake. I find it jarring—I never force laughter. I don't laugh all that much, actually; there aren't too many things I find funny.

"Well, listen, honey, if that was what you wanted, you did the right thing."

"Is Uriel offended?"

"No, but Rodolfo called to say he was surprised you were so cold with him. You know how guys are, darling. You always have to reassure them that they're the best and you never knew what making love really was before you met them."

"But these guys get paid."

"Makes no difference. Every game has its rules."

"Well, those rules don't work for me, Genoveva. I'm paying for everything, down to the water they drink when they're with me. Why do I have to pay them compliments too?"

"Ease up a little, sweetie! This isn't a company with salaried employees. You're paying these guys to act out a bit of theater, but in order for it to be believable, you have to play your part too."

"I don't get it, Genoveva. Sorry, but it just doesn't make sense to me."

"So I see."

Of course you don't get it, Irenita. The girl must be frigid. I bet you anything she's never gotten laid properly. She's textbook, right out of a psychology manual: a little girl clinging to her father's pant leg, and just going through the motions with her husband. Until the husband got fed up and skipped out on her. He would have taken off earlier if it hadn't been for her father's money. The girl's a disaster. I've shown her the patience of Job, but from now on she can figure out her own entertainment. She's too complicated for me.

"Are these guys set up like an agency?"

"Why do you want to know?"

"Just curious."

"It's not as straightforward as that, with a phone number and a web page and all. You have a contact, you start getting involved in that sort of thing, the word gets out, you let yourself be seen in certain places . . . Rodolfo and I met at that rooftop bar I took you to. He came up to me and . . . "

"Were you wearing a particular kind of shirt or something?"

"Jesus Christ, honey! You're squarer than a Rubik's cube! The key with this sort of thing is in your attitude, your frame of mind, the way you look at things."

"It's all too complicated for me."

"It's all about subtleties, Irene."

She doesn't get it, and she never will. These forty-somethings nowadays are just awful. The women of my generation know what's good for us, and the younger girls go after what they want, but the forty-somethings . . . I'm almost glad to be older. Life experience gives you confidence.

"I'm no good at subtleties, Genoveva. Oh well!"

* * *

Things are going pretty well at the club. I'm figuring it out.
I'm less and less embarrassed about the dancing. Iván says the
women in the audience like me because, even though I've gotten better, it's obvious I'm not a professional. What a ridiculous concept! Are there licensed strippers, PhDs? Is there a
union or a collective bargaining agreement? I guess he's referring to the fact that I'm not part of the nocturnal world, I don't
hang out in the city's underbelly. Even so, I doubt that's apparent at first glance—or maybe it is. Just look at some of my colleagues: sculpted muscles, skintight clothing, wild haircuts, tat-
toos, ear and nose rings . . . They're members of a specific
tribe, and you can tell. I hope working as a stripper doesn't
mark your face with some particular expression, as sometimes
happens with aging homosexuals after a life of excess. I'd hate
to be a Dorian Gray rerun. I must be turning into a chump—
or a fascist, which is much worse. Where do I get off dividing
people into good and bad, vulgar and refined, scruffy and elegant? I've always considered that way of thinking to be pure
ideological garbage, but I was outside the danger zone at the
time, whereas now it's clear I'm fully ensconced in it.

I don't tell Iván about these musings. He'd berate me, or
simply fail to understand. He's given me the best advice possible for the circumstances: "This is temporary. Take it one day
at a time; live in the present moment. Nothing's forever." It's
the universal suggestion, repeated by psychiatrists, teachers,
witches, fortune-tellers, philosophers, and wise men in general.
But how's a person supposed to pull that off? It seems impossible not to think of your identity as being diamond-hard, built
to last. But all of that's just worries for the wart, mental mas-
turbation, as Iván says. Anyway, my day-to-day life has a clear
weak spot: Sandra.

My girlfriend is upset, lashes out for no reason, views me

with contempt, even hatred at times. She takes digs at me and has gotten super passive-aggressive, something I never could have imagined—she was always so straightforward and easy-going. And all of that makes me feel guilty, as if my job were a vice I'm reveling in, something I'm doing purely for pleasure. Sometimes I even wonder if she's right, if I've merrily ditched my teaching career because I've always had a proclivity for porn. I'm going to make myself crazy! She has no empathy for me. She makes no effort to understand how I'm feeling. I wouldn't have been so surprised if she'd reacted some other way: jealous that I'm getting naked in front of other women, complaining that I'm not spending Friday and Saturday nights with her . . . What I can't bear is her moral condemnation, her fear of what people might say. So long to those liberal-minded ideas she used to have. Her prejudices are tied around her neck like the heavy rock attached to a person who's planning to jump into a river to commit suicide.

We've stayed home for lunch today. She took the afternoon off of work because she wants us to talk. I can guess what the topic will be. Christmas is coming, and she's going to insist we have dinner at her parents' house on Christmas Eve. I can't stand the holidays, or her family either. Her father always asks me, in a pitying tone, how my work is going. In his eyes, being a teacher is a kind of failure. He's in charge of warehouse logistics for a large company. He earns a good wad. Sandra's mother is a fabric cutter in an industrial clothing factory. She makes bank too. They've both kept their jobs despite the crisis. I think their wages are lower now, but during the boom they were living it up: apartment, cars, beach condo . . . Like everybody else in this country, they don't value education, just money. Eating at their house on Sundays already made me feel bad back when I was a teacher—what's it going to be like now that I'm in my new role as a pelvis-thruster in a strip joint? Not that Sandra's told them the truth. She even roped me in as an accomplice: "Best not to say anything, Javier. Why upset them?" Fine, if they don't want to know what I do, they might as well not even see me. I'm sure the future has better times in store where we'll be able to be a model family again.

Sandra arrives at two-thirty. I've gotten some Chinese take-out. I set the table. We sit down and serve ourselves spring rolls and rice. Bland small talk. As usual, she's on edge, and I sense a relentless harangue looming. I was right on the money: Christmas dinner.

"No, Sandra, I'm not going this year. You know this is a crazy time for me. I'd rather stay home. Make some excuse."

"Another one? You haven't been to my parents' house in months. I don't know what excuse to invent at this point."

"Well, then tell them the truth."

"The truth—like that's so easy. Why don't you pick up the phone and tell them yourself?"

"They're your parents, not mine."

"Of course, you don't have parents, so you haven't had to worry about it. Maybe if your parents were alive you wouldn't have agreed to work at that club, so you wouldn't have to tell them about it."

"What exactly are you chastising me for, not having parents?"

It devolves into utter absurdity. This is the kind of argument I despise most—they're useless and therefore dangerous. The core source of the contention no longer matters, and we're seeking only to wound, to harm, to cause pain.

"I'm chastising you because our life was going well and now it's shit."

"It's not like I quit my teaching job. I was fired, if you recall."

"Right, and since you were dying of starvation and sleeping on the streets, you had to become a stripper."

"I wanted a job and I have a job. When things are going better, I can go back to doing my thing."

"Your thing! Have you ever wondered why you lost that job? Well, I'll tell you: because it was a shitty job, one nobody wanted, substitute for the substitute for the substitute. Total crap! Did you ever sit for exams so you could snag a full-time position, look for a job where you had real responsibility? No way: an easy job, books, a tiny paycheck, a ton of free time . . . and that's enough! There's a name for that approach, Javier: lack of ambition."

"You never used to care that I'm not ambitious."

"You're right, I didn't! I accepted you as you were, and that's why I don't understand why you found it so unbearable to be unemployed, your revulsion at being supported by a woman. All of a sudden you get ambition, and it's to dance in a club?"

"You'd rather I sat home bringing in my sad unemployment check?"

"I'd rather you looked for a real job, even as a street sweeper, and act like a guy who's got what it takes."

"Careful, Sandra, your words can cause real hurt."

She stops talking. She stares at me. Her beautiful dark eyes narrow to two furious slits. Her face is growing flushed. She slams her fist on the table, making the rice and the Chinese noodles and the water in our glasses jump. She lets out a howl that's huge and deep, savage like that of a woman giving birth.

"I'm sick of it! Sick of it! I'm through! I can't take you acting like a goddamn saint! You're no saint, Javier, just so you know! You're a goddamn denialist: you deny problems, deny reality. You're directing your own movie about life, but life's not like that, Javier."

She covers her face with her hands and starts to cry. Her right elbow is very close to the bowl of sweet-and-sour sauce. I'm afraid it might stain the tablecloth. I don't know what I'm feeling right now. On the one hand, I'm deeply troubled by her distress; on the other, I don't care. I stretch one hand across the table and touch her elbow. I also move the bowl of sauce.

"Don't cry, Sandra. Let's be reasonable about this," I say soothingly.

She emerges from behind her hands, suddenly serene. She dries her eyes with the napkin. She gets up and goes to the refrigerator. She takes out a beer. She asks if I want one too. I accept. We open our cans. We take swigs directly from them. She starts to speak, her voice calm:

"We've reached a point of no return, Javier. I think we should go our separate ways. Even if you found another job as a teacher, nothing would be the same. I've thought about it a lot. I haven't come to this decision in anger. We don't have any obligations—no kids or mortgages to complicate things. We've had some good years; let's leave it at that."

"You don't see any way for us to stay together?"

"Something has broken. I'm not saying it's your fault—maybe I need a different kind of man, or maybe what I really want is to be alone."

It's so hard to say this to him! I'd like to fling myself into his arms so he can cradle me, comfort me, kiss me, like he has so many times before. "Come on, woman, don't fret. Problems may seem huge in the moment, but time proves they never are." With those simple words, Javier always released me from the anguish provoked by life's little obstacles—but now he's the problem. I don't want to end up like one of those women whose romantic relationships have made them permanently bitter. I don't want to get used to things I fundamentally abhor. I don't want to cry. Javier doesn't consume my whole life—there's room for lots of other things. I'll start over.

"If we can just get through this, maybe I'll find a job down the line."

"Please don't make this harder than it already is, Javier."

Actually, he's making it easier with his attitude. His calm

face, his tender expression, like a man who really wants to make up, are starting to seem pathetic. He's like a lapdog: "Please don't leave me." But what's a lapdog doing dancing naked in a club? No, he knows what he's doing—he's changed his life, and there's no room in the new version for me.

"I'll spend this weekend at my parents' house. That'll leave you the apartment free. Please take all your things with you. Don't leave anything so you can come pick it up some other time—that never turns out well. If you don't have enough time, let me know and I'll stay away longer."

"All right, Sandra, I'll do it."

Very simply: goodbye. There's that pragmatic female spirit that's always surprised me in my friends' breakups. I'll go—maybe it's for the best. If there's any possibility of reconciliation, it'll come with time. It's pointless to try to force it now.

Three days to collect my things. Three days to bring our love to a close. It's not a lot, but why would I need more? Corpses rot. I have no intention of begging or throwing myself at her feet. These last months have been hard on me too. I'm not planning to perform a comic sketch or a Greek tragedy. I'll leave with no soundtrack to play me out. Every object I collect from her house will be freighted with shared memories, and it will pain me. But that's life—every change is experienced as a loss, and every loss hurts. And there aren't too many things here that belong to me alone: my clothing and my books. My books! How the hell am I going to move them? Where will I put them? There's that pragmatic male spirit that's always surprised me in my friends' breakups, and that I never thought I'd have.

* * *

"Don't you worry, man. We'll figure something out."

Out on the fucking street! I can't believe it—this dude's

stepped in shit, but not in a good way. He's got crappy luck, though I already figured things would turn out this way, saw it coming a mile off. But it's rough, man, shit, one day to the next: "Pick up your things and get out." Six years they'd been together, he says. And it's all hunky-dory until the moment of truth: "You have forty-eight hours to vacate the conjugal abode, so beat it." Worse than being evicted, man, because in that case you haven't been living with the judge for six years, sharing table and bed. When I get back, I don't want to see a trace of you or our memories, and sweep the floor on your way out. The hell with that! And if you have to sleep in an ATM booth, that's your problem, bub.

I'm more pleased with my own way of doing things every day. Chicks only work at a distance. What good are they? Romance and coupling and starting a family and all that . . . The people who buy into that crap can keep it. I see this issue as clearly as if I had X-ray vision, but Javier's still got his head in the clouds. He doesn't criticize his girlfriend, hasn't said a bad thing about her. In fact, he makes excuses for her: "Well, Iván, it's no surprise she made this decision. By the end, we were leading very separate lives. She wants something else, an emotional stability I may not be able to provide . . . " She's screwed us, Javier! Of course she wants something else: a guy with a good job who brings in money at the end of the month and goes to the grocery store with her on the weekends. Shit, she's textbook! But he doesn't get upset: "Poor thing, she needs emotional stability." The hell with that! If he'd at least get a little pissed and cuss her out a little, maybe fuck that bitch and the horse she rode in on or something, he'd be more relaxed. I mean, if my approach all this time had just been to grin and bear it when people gave me shit, like he does, I'd have burst like a kid's balloon. I can't do it—I give them a piece of my mind. Of course, I remember the insults afterward. If someone pulls that shit on me, I don't forget it. I'm not saying

I'll follow them around with a sawed-off shotgun waiting for my opportunity, but if I run into them again and have a chance to mess with them, I take it. What goes around comes around. I don't forgive or forget. The damn teacher, though—that's some bad luck! First they run him out of his job, and now his chick has kicked him out too. And what would the guy have done without me? He may not get pissed, but he does worry . . . At the very least, his world would come crashing in.

"I don't know how I'm going to do it, Iván. Do you realize how much stuff a person accumulates in six years?"

"What are you looking to take with you, the mattress?"

"Just my clothing and my books."

"That's a piece of cake, man. I've got a friend who works as a manager at a grocery store. I'll ask him for some cardboard boxes, we'll pack everything up, and you're all set!"

"It's not that easy. Plus, I can't let you put me up in your house. I've been enough of a burden on you already."

"Shit, man, don't be an ass! I've got the space."

"I'll look for a place and get out of your way as soon as possible."

"No rush, teach, no rush."

Like I said, he worries. He's too nice a guy—that's why these things happen to him. If he were a jerk, things would be different. He'd be dealing the cards, he'd be in control. Of course, even when he accepts the invitation to stay at my house for a while, he starts worrying about whether it's a pain for me, so there's no way for him to be even a little bit happy. He should know I only invite people I like, and there aren't many of those. If I didn't like him, I'd keep my trap shut, since I don't give a shit about putting on a good face for other people. So all right, this weekend I'll help him move, and we'll see if he starts worrying because of me too.

I go over to his house on Saturday morning. It's the first time I've been inside. It isn't bad—your standard little apartment. He tells me he's already got the clothing packed up in two suitcases. I went by my friend's grocery store, and he gave me a ton of boxes. We just have to fold them back into shape and reinforce them with tape, which I've remembered to buy. I don't get why he wants to take all these books, though. If he's already read them, he could just leave them here—or sell them to a junk shop. Not that I care, really. If he wants them . . .

He leads me to the kitchen and makes me some coffee. We sip it, sitting pleasantly at a little table. He looks pretty down, which is to be expected. All guys go through it when their chicks dump them. I pretend not to notice so he doesn't start droning on about pointless shit. I hurry him up to distract him from his funk:

"All right, man, show me the stuff we've got to pack up."

"All the books are in the back room."

Fuck me, it's like the library back in school! Rows and rows running along every wall that seem practically endless. Shit, now I get why he was so overwhelmed thinking about his books!

"Hey, man, listen, are these all yours?"

"Iván! They're all the books I've accumulated over my whole life, and there aren't *that* many of them."

"Shit! And have you read them all?"

"Almost."

"Good for you, dude, but if you've already read them, wouldn't it be more practical to just throw them out?"

"Don't be an imbecile, Iván. Books are for keeping, you don't throw them away."

"So how about giving them to somebody?"

"They're mine, I want them—it's like they're part of me."

There must be some mystery here I'm not getting, but let's get on with it! If it's so damn important to take the damn books, I'm not going to stand in his way. Of course, we can't just dump them all over my place, and I don't have any bookcases. We'll leave everything in the boxes till he finds an apartment. I imagine he won't mind if I put them in my storage room, where I keep my bike. Of course, if they're part of him, he might want to keep them close and look at them at night. I think all that studying rotted the teacher's brain. With what rent runs around here, he's going to have to find a huge place to fit everything in.

I had to go get more boxes, of course. Books, books, books, heavy as hell. Six hours hauling books, packing them up, carrying them down to the car! I never dreamed anyone could read so much. To be honest, I didn't even do the required reading at school because I thought it was a drag.

By the end of the morning, we were exhausted, our hands filthy—wiped out. But the fucking books were gone from the shelves. The only ones left were the books Javier said belonged to Sandra. Mission accomplished.

"Let's go eat, Iván, we've earned it."

"Eating's not a bad plan, man, but I could really use a beer."

We went to a bar he knew and got drinks and wolfed down a couple of ham sandwiches so big they barely fit on the plate. They tasted amazing after the hell we'd just been through. Then the teacher goes and gets sentimental on me: I'm so grateful for everything you're doing for me, I don't know what I'd do if you weren't helping me . . . I waved my hand in the air like I was erasing his words. "Don't worry about it," I said. "We're friends, right? Well, a guy will do anything for a good friend."

"I know we're friends, but while I'm living here I'd like to help out with expenses. You know, part of the rent, electricity, water . . . "

He's a cool guy, but this sharing expenses business is a little risky. I want to help out, but I don't want him settling in for good, and if he pays his part, it'll seem like he has the right to stay as long as he wants, and that's not an option. My life plan has me flying solo. I've never thought I might enjoy living with someone else. I don't even live with a girlfriend, let alone a buddy. I'm not a bad guy, but it puts me on edge to have my freedom taken away. I come and go as I please. When I don't want to see anybody, I order in pizza or Chinese food or kebabs and eat in front of the TV, happy as a clam. That's the way I am, and I have no interest in changing.

"Look, man, don't worry about that. You're only going to be here a little while, so there's no point in reaching for your wallet. You're going to need that money for when you find a decent place."

Finally we went to my house and I showed him his room, which is pretty sweet. It has a built-in closet and even some trendy curtains I bought at El Corte Inglés, the department store. Plus there's a guest bathroom. He liked it a lot, of course. He put his stuff on the bed and we went out to the living room to have a beer.

The teacher was a little shy. He looked at all the CDs and DVDs I have, a ton of them. I showed him my collection of Jackie Chan movies. I told him I'm not one of those guys who's obsessed with martial arts, but I like those movies—the dude makes me laugh, and I enjoy the way he leaps around and fucks shit up. Suddenly the teacher asks me if I read books, and I tell him I don't have time: between the gym, TV, the computer, my job, and going out . . . my schedule's packed. He says he'll give me a book and I say OK—what else am I supposed to say? He might be offended if I tell him reading makes me tense since I'm not used to it. He also says I should at least let him buy some food and beer to stock the fridge. I tell him fine, if that'll make him feel better . . . though I hardly ever eat in. Cooking's a drag. I fry an egg from time to time, with bacon and potato chips. When I was first living here, I hired Puri, one of my mother's friends, to come in one day a week and clean the place. She'd cook for me too, soups and that sort of thing.

But then she got annoying, insisting I needed to take care of myself, eat healthy and all that crap, and she'd leave me a ton of food in the fridge. And then what would happen? Well, the soup would go bad and I'd have to chuck it out. How should I know whether I'm going to be eating at home? I don't have to clock in like an office worker. Things come up during the day, and I'm not going to stop doing what I'm doing so I can go home and eat some goddamn soup. I told her to forget about cooking. Plus, I didn't like it that she was getting so familiar. I had to stop her a couple of times, especially when she tried to talk to me about my mother. Puri goes to see her in the psych ward at the prison, and then she comes at me with this spiel about how my mother's not a bad woman, she's had rotten luck in life, the poor thing is getting skinny . . . That was it—I don't want to hear about it. I don't talk shit about my mother or go to the clink to rub her face in it, do I? So bug off.

I'll tell Puri I've got a friend staying with me so she can iron his clothes too, though I don't think Javier ever wears dress shirts, just tees. The poor guy's a little wet behind the ears. I'm going to have to teach him a few things about life. I'm curious to know how much he gets in unemployment. Probably crap. That's probably why Sandra kicked him out. Women love suckers like Javier at first, but after a while they get sick of putting up with them. I bet my balls she met a guy who's loaded. I don't believe she's so narrow-minded she can't handle the idea of her boyfriend working in a club. Come on, girl! Don't ask where money comes from when it's already in your pocket. He should look into it—if I were him, I'd hire a private eye to trail her. It wouldn't take him more than a couple of days to come back with photos of the broad with another dude picking her up from work. In a car, of course.

As part of welcoming him to the house, I've showed him my Facebook profile with my nice-guy photo and my Twitter account. He was amazed because I have a lot of followers. I told him that's a breeze—if you say a lot of bullshit, you're sure to get a bunch of followers. Really, though, this networking business is a waste of time and I don't give a shit. Some of my friends are really into it, but not me. The real stuff happens out in the real world, not on the computer. But a lot of people never have anything happen to them because they're chicken—that's the truth.

By about seven o'clock, we've opened some cans of cockles and tuna to munch on before we go to work. You can't work on an empty stomach. Javier seems to have cheered up by the time we leave the house. When we get to the club, he acts like he's in his element. He never seemed happy to be there before—the look on his face always suggested he hated the place. Not today. Today he said hi to everybody, cracked a couple jokes, practiced some of the moves from his dance number, that sort of thing. I think his girlfriend had him brainwashed and all screwed up. It's probably for the best that she's kicked him out.

\* \* \*

Here I am, with a roof over my head thanks to charity, brotherly solidarity, whatever you want to call it. And my benefactor's a guy with whom I have no familial, social, or cultural bond. A guy who's never read a book in his life. He's proved he's my friend, that's for sure, and the hardest part is I don't know how to thank him. I thought about giving him a book he might like, a book that would immerse him in one of the greatest human pleasures, but I have no idea which to choose. I ruled out the classics: they're not easy reading, and they'd probably remind him of homework. I wonder what kind of student he was, though I can imagine: a troublemaker, written off as the product of a fractured family and with the corresponding conduct. He probably skipped school all the time—I doubt his grandmother, bless her, was able to persuade him to go to class. I also doubt she put much stock in her grandson's education. It was enough trouble just putting up with him, keeping him fed. With the classics ruled out, I also considered gripping contemporary stuff—Palahniuk, Cheever, Carver—but I don't know if he'd be interested. Maybe I should lower my sights a little and buy him a Stephen King novel, or just the opposite, raise them as high as possible and give him *Crime and Punishment* in a modern translation. Sometimes that kind of thing works and pure narrative essence manages to win over even stone.

It's weird, right? Problems are piling up in my life, and my response is to start pondering my host's literary education. The most generous explanation is that I just want to return the favor. He gives me work, a roof over my head, and moral support, while I try to transmit to him the only thing of value I've got: the pleasure of reading. The harsher interpretation is that introducing him to books is just my way of trying to make him worthier of me. Iván is primal, sexist, uncouth, marginal—but what if literature could have some miraculous influence on him? I want to be his Pygmalion; worse, I'm acting like one of those partners in an out-of-sync couple who wants to transform his lover to match his own image and likeness. Pathetic. I've turned into a real jackass.

Where do I get off? Iván is far superior to me. I've tumbled down the social ladder; I'm a pariah, a loser. A man who got fired from his job and whose girlfriend gave him three days to get out. Whereas Iván's managed to make a living, get a move on, turn the difficult circumstances of his past into a comfortable, anguish-free reality. He goes out, hustles, shows his face. And me? I shake my sad bones in a striptease show because he got me the spot.

What would my life have been like if I hadn't gone to Iván's grandmother's funeral? I'd still be unemployed. I'd still have

Sandra. But what for? It's clear our relationship was an arrangement whose rules of operation were dictated by other people. That's always the way things are—when you're standing outside an apparatus, you see exactly how the gears work, the whole mechanism. All the pieces have to be in place. We were a simple case: a young couple, both with jobs. Good collaboration on household tasks. Supportive: you scratch my back and I'll scratch yours. Friends in common. Shared interests. Agreed-on outings: to the movies, to dinner. Laid-back weekends. Safe, realiable sex. Everything in its place. Change just one element of that structure—for example, write "stripper" where it says "teacher"—and the whole thing falls apart. The guy changing jobs is the same—me—but the machine no longer runs smooth. It locks up, no longer functions. No option but to repair or change it out. Sandra has opted to change. I imagine she'll look for a replacement part that says "lawyer" or "paper pusher" or "gardener"—it doesn't matter, anything to complete the mechanism so it will start humming along again as smoothly as ever.

Enough, enough—I don't want to play this game. I don't want to be interchangeable. I have my identity. I am who I am, no matter what. From now on I'm even going to be proud of working at the club. I'm going to take off my clothes with conviction, with professionalism, and anyone who doesn't want to see it doesn't have to look.

\* \* \*

"Business is bad, business is bad." I know, I know! I don't need the manager hounding me constantly with that refrain. No doubt he has more information than I do; even our most recent hire probably has more information. But I'm fed up. They need me there for everything now. The manager spends his days telling me about everything that's going wrong. He's looking to cover his ass. He doesn't want to be accused of being lackadaisical.

"Maybe we should sell," I snapped one day.

"It's too late. The way things are right now, if someone bought us out, we'd lose a ton of money. When your father was still alive and things were starting to go downhill, I recommended he sell. A family business of this size can't go toe to toe with the multinational corporations. Of course he refused to listen to me."

"I wouldn't have listened to you either."

"You don't listen to me now, Irene. Maybe if you were more involved in the business . . . "

Enough, man, I don't want to hear your whining. You're anxious to put the responsibility for the coming disaster on me, but I have no intention of falling into your trap. I don't blame you for anything, but don't you blame me. He's scared. I don't understand how Papá could have trusted him so much. He felt secure under my father's protection, and in theory he'd have given his life for him. All of us would have, though I get the sense that ultimately we've all failed him, even me. Me and, of course, that parasite David. I should be thankful my father isn't here to witness this decline, to see my marriage fall apart, but I'm not. I get angrier and angrier as time goes by. People keep looking at me pityingly: "Poor thing, her husband left her for a younger woman." If they only knew how little I care about that! I've dumped a deadweight. What I really can't stand is the way David's betrayed my father. When David left I was numb, but now the anesthesia's worn off and the pain has kicked in. I guess I should get aggressive and fight for the company, get it back on its feet, bring back the boom times, make everybody's jaws drop in amazement. But I'm tired. I haven't been sleeping well lately. I wake up at four in the morning, get up, drink some water, go to the bathroom, head back to bed, and am unable to fall asleep again.

I've done everything all wrong! After David left me, I was dazed, unable to react. Later, I was aggrieved. Then I started hanging out with Genoveva. And now, just when I'd almost forgotten about David, indignation is keeping me awake. Maybe I should go to a psychiatrist, but I don't want to tell someone all about my life—I don't like to talk.

"Lay off more workers. Do what you have to do to keep the business afloat a little longer."

"I'm not sure that makes sense, Irene."

"I don't care."

"If that's what you want . . . You're the boss."

I read his thoughts: "Spoiled little girl. Silly little girl. She thought the world was her oyster, but now that her father's not around, she's let everything go downhill." He heads toward the door, but I stop him.

"What do you suggest we do?"

"Stop paying the invoices."

"We will do that, but not right now. Wait a bit longer."

I don't want to confirm my failure quite yet. Not after my divorce. It'll happen. There's always time to fall apart. Maybe letting a few employees go is enough. I don't want people laughing at me.

I'm finally going to the psychiatrist. Like everything else, he comes on Genoveva's recommendation. She says he's worked wonders for her. He prescribes her sleeping pills and antianxiety medication. I tell her that's what I want too. She praises him to the skies: pleasant, competent, and discreet. He has an office downtown. He's a nice-looking fifty-something, the standard-issue psychiatrist for wealthy women like us. He doesn't smile, and neither do I. He puts on a poker face, and so do I. He asks if I'm depressed. I tell him I'm not. Am I distressed? No. Am I nervous? No. I tell him I wake up in the night and have a hard time getting back to sleep. He asks if I've had a traumatic experience recently. I tell him my father died a year back, my company's not doing well. He asks if I'm married. Not anymore. Divorced? For a few months now. He asks if I want us to talk about that. I tell him I don't.

"A rough patch," he says.

"Exactly," I say.

He prescribes an anxiolytic and a sleep aid. He explains that the sleep aid isn't as addictive as your typical sleeping pill. He gives me a follow-up appointment in two weeks. We'll see. His receptionist charges me a bundle.

\* \* \*

A lot of the time I'm alone in Iván's apartment. He'll be out somewhere—he never tells me where he goes. I wander through the rooms, shamelessly poking around. I don't open drawers or closets, of course. I just look at the décor, and everything I see surprises me. Iván mixes modern objects that aren't bad with kitschier stuff. He has a nice designer lamp next to his computer and, next to that, several imitation Lladró figurines that are just horrendous: a child shepherdess with a lamb over her shoulders, a lady with a parasol covered in bows. I don't get it. How can that cheesy, sappy stuff appeal to a tough guy like him? Were they gifts? Does he have them on display because they've got some kind of sentimental value, or does he really like the way they look?

Some equally disconcerting paintings are hanging on the walls. There are reproductions of abstract art whose primary hue matches the curtains. He's got atrocious posters of cars and kung fu movies that he's placed in ornate gold frames. The contrast produces a strange effect. It's mind-boggling to think that Iván took these posters to be framed with the clear intention of making them beautiful. This rough-hewn man clearly harbors a love of order and beauty.

I stop and review: rough-hewn man, love of order and

beauty. In my thoughts, I'm starting to use the vocabulary of a bad novel, the kind that pathetic writers self-publish under the delusion that they're fantastic: a melodramatic, hollow vocabulary. I guess I'm terrified that the dangers threatening me in this new situation might crash down on me: vulgarity, bad taste, lumpen sensibilities. My fear proves I'm not above anything or anybody. I thought I'd overcome a lot of prejudices, but I haven't. I feel panicky. In the blink of an eye, all of my benchmarks have gone to shit. First, my job, which, though it wasn't very stable, still gave me a certain status. Gone. Second, my friends, who read Murakami novels and watched Coen brothers movies without dubbing into Spanish. Gone. Finally, I've lost my partner, who slotted me seamlessly into a normal life. As a result of this last and most fundamental loss, I've also lost my house, my books on display, my corner of the world.

I've lost all of it consciously. I took the job as a stripper because I couldn't stand feeling useless. I pulled away from my friends because I was embarrassed about being a stripper. Sandra left me because she can't stand having her partner be a stripper. Every action has consequences, and those consequences lead to further consequences. If you choose not to act, it makes no difference: failure to act has its own consequences. And so it goes until you die. The first mistake humans make is not committing suicide as soon as they achieve the barest use of their capacity for reason.

Iván never shuts down the computer, so I've brazenly glanced through some of his chats. He writes the same crap that everybody else does, uses tons of emojis, posts photos of himself wearing new clothes, recommends records and movies . . . all of it rife with spelling errors and marked by an extraordinary conceptual simplicity. "I like it, I don't like it": that's the prevailing logic in his online conversations.

In the solitude of the apartment, with Iván's personality

always thoroughly present, I've started wondering about him. He leads a mysterious life. We see each other bright and early. He drinks a cup of coffee while chatting on the computer, as I've confirmed, and then takes off. "Later, man," he says, and never tells me where he's going or what his plans are. He comes back at night, generally so late that I'm already in bed. He wears brand-name clothes, snorts all the cocaine he wants, pays his rent, has a car that he can afford to fill with gas, goes out for drinks, I imagine. It's a simple question: where does he get the money? The club doesn't pay that much, as I well know. So . . . ?

Once he asked me to spend the night somewhere else. "I'm bringing a girl back here," he said. I suggested I could just stay in my room and not come out, but he didn't like the idea. "Look, teach, I don't usually bring girls home, but this is going to happen every once in a while, and it'll be better for you not to be around." I took off—it was his house, and I couldn't forget that. I put my book, toothbrush, and pajamas in a duffel bag and got a room in a cheap hotel. According to Iván, I could come back at noon the next day. He hasn't thrown me out again since, but it was like a warning, and that day I started looking for a place of my own to rent.

Finding an affordable apartment is no mean feat with the amount I earn. Prices here in the city are astronomical—I never would have imagined it. I assiduously studied the classifieds, and one day I saw something that might work: a studio in a neighborhood on the outskirts of the city. I didn't really care if it was on the moon as long as there was access to the subway and buses nearby. Living in a studio didn't seem too bad either. I don't need a lot of space, and living in a single room can even be cozy if you get a little creative. When I saw it, though, my stomach dropped. It was shabby, dark, stuffy, pretty noisy. The tiny bathroom was disgusting, and the kitchen consisted of a hotplate in one corner. The lodgings

described in the novels of Victor Hugo and Émile Zola probably weren't any more squalid. I was outraged that someone
could demand money for such a hole.

I told Iván about it—I didn't want him to think I wasn't
trying to find my own place, that I was planning to keep staying in his apartment forever, taking advantage of his generos-
ity.

"Don't worry about it, man, don't worry about it. You'll
find something. For now, you're here. You're not in my way."

The teacher's worrying again, and I get it—it must suck to
be living in somebody else's house. But I don't think the rents
are going to come down with this crisis going on. People who
have an apartment, even if it's a piece of crap not fit for keeping chickens, think they can squeeze money out of poor
schlubs who've been foreclosed on by the bank for not paying
their mortgage and have nowhere else to go. The world's
totally screwed, a pit of pure shit, and eventually you're going
to wind up getting dumped into it and have to find some way
to crawl back out.

"I'll keep trying. I left my contact info with a couple of
rental agencies. They've told me as soon as they have anything
that meets my criteria, they'll let me know."

"Well then, you just have to wait."

But don't hold your breath, Javierito, because all those
agencies are interested in is making their percentage on the
transaction. If you go and tell them you want a closet with
kitchen access that doesn't cost too much, they're just going to
blow you off. They won't say it to your face—they'll be nothing but nice to you—but once you walk out, they'll toss your
information in the wastebasket and move on.

"Have you considered a shared apartment? Sometimes I
see things on the Internet."

"I could look, yeah."

I could, but I never will. I'm too old for that. I wouldn't be able to live with someone I don't know, share the kitchen and bathroom. Best not to think about it—it would be all under-achievers like me or maybe university students whose life is nothing but assignments, chaos, and noise. I'd rather live in a cheap hotel, like a character in a Galdós novel. The problem is, with my paltry resources, I don't really have a choice, so I'll be forced to relinquish my moments of solitary reading, my privacy.

"Don't worry about it yet, man. Things are rough right now, and the club's a drag, so it really can't get any worse. There's nowhere to go but up, otherwise . . . "

But poor teach doesn't perk up—I don't think he ever will. He's a cream puff in a cruel world. I'm going to end up having to lend him a hand again, offer him something else. After that, it's going to be all up to him.

\* \* \*

I've decided to go on my own to the rooftop bar Genoveva took me to. I know it's a place for making contact, but just get-ting a drink doesn't mean any sort of obligation. I sit down at a table and order a gin and tonic from the waiter.

I've brought an issue of *Vogue* magazine to flip through if I can't figure out what else to do. Discreetly, I watch the other tables: an older couple chatting in a corner, a touristy-looking guy who must be staying at the hotel. After half an hour, when it's starting to get dark, more people arrive. I pretend to be fid-dling with my phone, but from time to time I lift my head to look around. On one of those occasions I notice a new cus-tomer sitting by himself: thirty-something, nicely dressed in a cream-colored blazer, dark pants, and gleaming loafers. I don't have experience at this, but I'd swear he might be one of them. I don't dare watch him too long, so I perform a somewhat arti-ficial maneuver, tossing my hair back, and get a better look.

He's handsome, he's tanned, he's staring at me. I start to feel anxious, so I order another gin and tonic to boost my courage. When the waiter arrives, I steal another look, and yes, he's still staring at me. I meet his gaze for a second. Later it's two seconds, maybe three. The alcohol is starting to unravel my tensions. I relax. I start to enjoy the situation. I smile at him, and that's the clincher; he gets up and walks toward me.

In the very brief time it takes him to arrive, my mind is racing. I think: I must be going mad. What the hell am I doing here? What kind of wild tear am I on? What if he's a jerk? What if he thinks I'm a nymphomaniac? What if he takes me for a prostitute offering her services? That would be hilarious, really turn things upside down! I'm asking for trouble, I'm an idiot, I feel like screaming.

"Good evening. Would you mind if I sit down?"

He has big teeth. I feel like crying.

"OK."

OK? I sound like a schoolgirl, a moron. You don't say "OK" to a man in this situation. Maybe something like "It's a free country. Have a seat." I decide not to talk, to let him talk instead. After all, he's the one who came over here.

"The city looks beautiful from here, don't you think?"

"Very beautiful. Do you live here?" I ask.

"I was born here! Did you think I was from somewhere else?"

"Well, we are at a hotel . . . "

"People go to hotels for all kinds of reasons. What about you—do you live here too?"

"Yes, I live here."

He starts babbling on about the city's artistic wonders, its Romanesque and Gothic churches, the Arabic heritage . . . That's enough to convince me he's a male escort. It's the same incessant blather Rodolfo and Uriel offered, this time with a cultural element, probably to show me he's not a rube. I take long sips of my gin and tonic to keep my nerve up. His big teeth, which I found jarring at first, now seem to give him an appealingly naughty air. From Gothic architecture he's somehow moved on to high-end design stores. He knows about that too. These guys, assuming he's one of them, sure do talk a lot. If he's not one of them, he's just a bore. Suddenly he realizes I've stopped listening.

"I beg your pardon," he says, "I'm rambling. I just love this city."

"Oh, no problem, I'm just a little tired. I should go."

He stays where he is even though I've signaled to the waiter. He waits for me to pay, and as I'm closing my purse he says, "If you're that tired, you should probably get a room in the hotel."

He's expectant. I look him right in the eye, an inscrutable expression on my face. He rides it out. He's one of them. It seems incredible: all you have to do is come here, sit down, and that's it. The city must be full of places like this for anyone who knows them and knows what she's looking for.

"Would you come and rest with me?" I take ownership of the situation. I shed the embarrassment. I start to enjoy holding the reins.

"A little rest is always good." He laughs the most forced and foolish laugh I've ever heard.

"Then let's go rest."

I arrange for the room myself. He waits for me by the elevators, discreet. The receptionist realizes what's going on; he doesn't ask me if I have any luggage or how many nights I'll be staying.

We go up in silence, standing very close but without looking at each other. When I'm sliding the card into the slot in the door, he moves toward me and tries to kiss me behind the ear. I brusquely pull my head away, but he doesn't react to my rejection; he's still smiling like an imbecile. But my gesture, which is odd given the circumstances, puts him on guard, and he says, "Resting with me costs money. You know that, right?"

"How much money?" I ask, still unable to believe it's my voice I'm hearing.

"Three hundred."

"No problem."

It's a big room. I take off my jacket and go over and sit down on the bed, just like I did last time. He slowly walks toward me. Now his smile is like that of someone who's daydreaming—or drunk. When he reaches out to unbutton my blouse, I stop him short.

"Don't touch me. I just want you to get undressed."

"What about you?"

"I'm staying like this."

He cocks his head like an alert dog—all that's missing is for him to prick up his ears.

"But if I don't see you naked, I won't be . . . motivated."

"That doesn't matter, I just want to look at you."

"But if I don't get motivated . . . "

"Listen, let's not make this a problem. I'm telling you what I want you to do. If you're not interested, you can leave, no problem."

My heart is pounding in my chest. I feel a faint fear but also enormous pleasure at speaking to him like that, insolent, in a commanding tone.

"All right, honey, don't get mad. If that's what you want . . . "

Slowly, he gets undressed. Feeling awkward, he starts humming a parody of a striptease tune. From beneath his clothing his bulky muscles emerge: thighs, calves, shoulders. He's got a flat belly and strong biceps. He's tanned all over, with no tan lines. He's hairy, but his torso has clearly been waxed. His penis, which is large and very pale, hangs a good way down between his thighs. I like looking at him, but I don't feel the least bit of sexual arousal. If he stayed still and didn't say anything, it would be better, but the moron goes and asks, "Do you like what you see?"

"It's not bad," I say curtly.

He strokes his chest, his hips. He turns his back provocatively. He has a small, round butt, very flat, not too prominent, beautiful. He's still yammering the whole time: "This right here, that over there, half turn . . . " I ask him to be quiet—or rather, I instruct him. His face flushes with rage. I think if he could he'd slap me, but he refrains and finally stops talking. His expression grows serious, concentrated, contemptuous. He moves and twists as if he were hearing some internal music. It's a silent dance, impressive. After a while he starts stroking his penis. He becomes erect. He masturbates. First slowly, then more and more eagerly. He abruptly ejaculates into his own hand, panting. His eyes closed, he says, "Can you pass me a tissue?"

I don't move; I keep watching him. He opens his eyes and looks at me with loathing. Somewhat hunched, he goes to the bathroom. He comes back out after a good long while. He's had a shower. His dumb smile is plastered across his face again.

"Did you enjoy it?" he asks.

I don't even answer.

"Can you lie down on the sofa?"

He lies down and closes his eyes. Now I can analyze his body inch by inch. I don't like it. It's too tanned, too muscular, too tended, too fake. He's sleepy; his head nods to one side.

"You can leave now."

"I was falling asleep, I swear."

While he gets dressed, I rummage for the money in my purse. Three hundred euros. I give it to him.

"What about the drink we had in the bar?"

I hand him another twenty. He takes it, almost snatches it.

"Shall I give you my phone number for another time?"

"There won't be another time."

A mocking, ill-humored expression crosses his face. He adopts a dignified tone.

"Well, you know what? That's a relief! I'm not into weird crap. Plus, I've got all the chicks I want."

I turn my back on him. He leaves, slamming the door. What a rude man, a real nightmare! Arrogant, stupid, vain . . . Evidently it's not easy to find pleasant guys. I wonder how Genoveva does it; she's certainly got more experience. But I'm happy—happy I dared to pick one up on my own, happy I was so firm with him. I'm proud of myself, the way I sometimes used to be when I'd walk down the street on Papá's arm.

* * *

I've gone out to buy some books and take a walk. When I get back home, I'm surprised to discover Iván's already arrived. He's lounging on the sofa in front of the television, eating a pizza. Upon seeing me, he raises his hand in the air for a high five. He signals for me to have some pizza with him. I tell him I've already eaten, and I'm about to say something else when he shushes me with a finger to his lips. Then I notice he's watching a show, engrossed. I walk into the kitchen, grab a can of beer from the fridge, and go back to the living room. I sit down next to him, curious to know what he's watching with such interest. It looks like a reality show. Filling the screen is a close-up shot of a young woman wearing a lot of makeup. The vulgar quality of her appearance is intensified when she starts talking. She strings together clichés, faulty grammatical structures, brash expressions. She's one hundred percent low-class. I listen carefully to what she's saying. She's complaining about her friends Carla and Andrea, who could have said something but decided to keep quiet. Her complaint gradually ramps up to an almost tearful lament. After a few more minutes, I figure out what's going on. A young man has cheated on his girl-friend, and the issue is being debated. Both parties are present, and acting as mediator is a TV host, heavily made up and hairstyled and dressed like a tramp. Rather than seeking reconciliation, it seems like the tramp is trying to make the two young people argue and say horrible things to each other. The cheater is a young, cocky-looking guy who's trying to defend himself. In that effort, he's employing some atrocious clichés: "I was drunk—drunk people aren't responsible for their actions," "Some temptations a man just can't resist," "A one-night stand isn't a threat to true love." A real philosopher, this lowlife. I'm starting to feel nauseated, a sensation that increases when the camera zooms in on the girl again so we can see the tears running down her face. "Is there any possibility you might forgive him?" the horrible host asks. The girl sobs openly. "Baby, I swear it'll never happen again," the asshole says. I'm ready to unleash a barrage of expletives and offer a heaping helping of destructive criticism for this garbage, but when I look at Iván, I find that he's choked up, his eyes damp. What the hell's up with him? Is he as revolted as I am and weeping in disgust, or does he have a screw loose? I opt to utter an exclamation that can be interpreted a multitude of ways.

"Shit!"

He sniffles. He's not embarrassed about showing his feel-ings. He wipes his eyes with the napkin, which is stained with pizza sauce. Still staring at the screen, he says, "Yeah, man, it's a shitshow. This guy's a real bastard and really hurt his girl when he stepped out on her. Look at her, poor thing, she's just wrecked. Of course, it's kind of understandable if you put yourself in his shoes. Say you're a little shitfaced one night and a chick starts coming on to you . . . what guy can resist that? That's why I don't have a steady girl. What for? If a nice quickie comes my way one day, why should I have to hurt somebody or lie to her?"

I am flooded by an irrepressible wave of indignation.

"Hang on, Iván," I start ranting. "I couldn't care less about these people's situation. The really screwed-up part, the thing that really makes me crazy, is seeing those two losers going on TV to tell their sob stories. It's unbelievable that anybody would make a show out of this garbage and broadcast it, and even more unbelievable that anybody else would watch it."

I'd never seen him so surprised, so perplexed. He forgets about the TV. He doesn't react for a few seconds, and finally says, "I'm watching it."

"No way. You're watching it because you were chowing down on some pizza, you turned on the TV, and you got sucked in."

"Not at all, man. I watch this show whenever I get the chance. I know what time it comes on, and if I'm home, I always turn it on."

"I don't get it. What do you see in this crap? Tell me, what's so good about it?"

His close-cropped hair must be standing on end like a cat's.

"What do you mean, what do I see in it, man? It's life, it's things that happen to people. Or do the things that happen to everybody else not happen to you? You special or something?"

"Those guys get paid to go on there and air their dirty laundry in public."

"So what if they get paid? At least they get something out of it! Yeah, they're going on TV to talk about personal stuff, but if they were just doing it for the money they wouldn't cry their eyes out like that—it's obvious from a mile off they're crying for real. And they wouldn't put themselves in a position to come off looking bad either."

"Would you go on that show and talk about your life for money?"

"The hell with the damn money! What about what the two of us do for the damn money? Didn't you used to stand in front of a chalkboard reading poetry to little rich girls? And now you're shaking your naked ass, as am I—and I do things that are even worse. So don't give me that bullshit about what I would or wouldn't talk about. I'm going to hit the hay. To be honest, you've really pissed me off this time, teach."

The hell with the teacher! There are some things I just don't get, man. All that book learning and everything, but he doesn't even have the heart to understand two screwed-up kids who go on a TV show to see if they can fix their relationship. So what if people watch it? So what if they make some money telling their story? Who does he think he is, the prince from the Príncipe cookies wrapper, with the crown and everything? Is he in his palace, protected from the riffraff? He hasn't even been able to rent a room of his own since his girlfriend booted him out. And what does he do? Nothing, mooch off of me till I'm fed up. He could have gone on that show himself to fight for Sandra and see if he could change her mind. But no, young sir couldn't possibly lower himself like that and go on there talking about his problems. He's an intellectual, a teacher—he's superior to the rest of us. I was nice and relaxed with my pizza and my TV show, and now he's got me all pissed off. He'd better find a place to live soon or things are going to get ugly.

He's mad at me. It's obvious I went too far, but it just blows my mind that a tough guy like him could fall for . . . But I went too far, period. He is who he is, and he's not going to develop critical awareness overnight. I didn't mean to offend him, but I did. Still, everything I said seemed so obvious . . . but for him it's not. I'm going to apologize. It's becoming more and more clear that I need to get a place of my own as soon as possible, even if it's a nasty hole-in-the-wall. I can't keep staying here. Living with someone who's so different from me is like sleeping on a powder keg.

I knock on the door to his bedroom. He yells out, "Now what do you want?"

"Iván, I want to apologize. I'm sorry, I really am. I was criticizing the TV show, but there was a misunderstanding and . . . "

"That's enough, man, I'm dead tired!"

"But please tell me you're not mad."

"No."

"No, you're not mad, or no, you won't tell me that?"

"Are you serious? You're like a fucking goat, teach! Go the hell to sleep!"

He laughed. Whew. I'd been feeling guilty.

\* \* \*

I can't fucking stand Christmas. Peace and love. Everybody can just fuck off! But it is what it is: ubiquitous ads for nougat and other seasonal treats, and twinkly lights in the streets. Everybody says "Merry Christmas!" even though they don't know you from Adam and the extent of your relationship is that they're selling you a goddamn pack of cigarettes. It drives me crazy! The only thing I like about it is the lottery drawing on December 22. I never win, but every year I buy a couple of tickets just in case. If I win, I'm going to buy a sweet-ass car! And a mansion with servants from all around the world: a Chinese cook, an Ecuadorian maid, an Arab guy as my bodyguard. I'd know how to spend my loot, not like those goobers who go on TV after winning some lame amount of money and jump up and down in excitement. The dumbass doing the report asks, "What are you going to use your prize for?" and they say, "To fill in some holes in the budget!" Jesus, the holes they should be filling are in their heads!

If I won a big amount, I'd give part of it to social causes— soup kitchens and that sort of thing. But I never win anything, big or small. I don't have that kind of luck. Everything I have,

I had to earn it through my own blood, sweat, and tears. If I'd depended on luck, all I'd have is a turd on a stick. Lady Luck's always mooning me; I've never seen her face.

For starters, take the parents who brought me into the world. My dad, a real asshole who at least had the decency to kick the bucket. And my mom, I don't even want to think about it—I'm about to get the same song and dance I get every year. On Christmas Day they let her out of the psych ward at the prison or whatever it's called. The idea is for her to eat with her family, and I'm her family. The hell with family! In the past I've always taken her to a restaurant, but she always makes a scene: she gets drunk, cries, attacks the waiter. I'm embarrassed to be with her; everybody always stares at us. This year, since the teacher's staying with me, we could have our meal in the privacy of home, as they say. So I ditch the restaurant. Of course it's a real drag for Javier, but oh well, it's a way for him to pay for his lodging, right? To be honest, I'm not thrilled to have him hanging out with my mother, but this way he won't think I'm a bastard for never going to visit her in prison. He'll have a better image of me. Plus, when he meets her he'll see what the world's really like—things may have been shit for him for a while now, but they've been shit for me ever since I was born. With parents like mine, if I hadn't hustled, I'd have been screwed. But I figured that out early on and said to myself, "Shit, Iván, either you change tracks or you're going come out the loser." And I changed. A new life, basically reborn. And I've done pretty well—can't complain! The only crappy thing I have to do is this damn meal at Christmas, but I'm going to ask Javier to help me out, and since he's a good guy, he'll agree. Every year I put up with my mother's visit, but it's harder and harder for me to handle because she keeps getting worse and worse. It used to amaze me to see the way she was falling apart, but now I wouldn't be amazed if the Virgin herself appeared before me. Not anymore.

I'm not going to make things complicated for this dinner. I'll go down to the takeout place and order cannelloni and a nice steak. And I'll spend a little cash on some good bubbly. My mom will get lit because she also takes medicine for her nut, so everything hits her hard. With a little luck she'll pass out quick and we'll be able to lay her down on the sofa and eat in peace. When I pick her up, the social worker always tells me not to give her alcohol, but I never pay any attention. She drives me crazy asking for it, so I just give it to her from the start and everybody's happy. What does it matter at this point whether she drinks or not? For fuck's sake, let her be happy. At least once a year, let her forget the crappy life she's had and still has, the horrible things that have been done to her and that she's done to other people. "Drugs are terrible stuff," my grandma used to say to excuse her dead son. Well, all right, then they shouldn't have taken them; it's a little late now to be sorry about that.

\* \* \*

"No, I don't have plans for Christmas. I can eat with you."

I accepted without hesitation; I was staying at his house, so what choice did I have? But I never dreamed the experience was going to be so terrifying and tragic.

When I woke up on Christmas morning, Iván was already pottering around the house. I was surprised to see *Crime and Punishment* lying open on the sofa. I hadn't been sure he would even read it. I heard noises coming from the kitchen. Iván was making coffee.

"Want some?" he asked.

We were eating breakfast in silence when he suddenly said, "That's some rough shit, that business with the pawnbroker and Raskolnikov!"

"I saw you were reading the book."

"I started last night and couldn't put it down. The story just pulled me in, man! The guy's so strange, so twisted . . . and the streets they're in and the staircases and houses . . . everything so dark and cold, rundown, dirty, poor . . . It must have sucked living in Russia back then! There are people living like that here, too—dead broke, surrounded by filth—but at least it's sunny. But that Raskolnikov's something else. Violence doesn't really bother me—I've seen *The Texas Chainsaw Massacre* twenty times and other movies that are even worse—but when he attacks that old lady with the ax . . . Shit, man, that's intense! I couldn't sleep after reading that."

"You're right, the character of Raskolnikov is amazing, a tormented man, devious, gripped by moral doubt. And the murder scene is bloodcurdling, just brutal."

"Yeah, totally."

Bloodcurdling? Best keep my mouth shut—best not tell the teacher the reason I couldn't sleep is that I was actually thinking how I'm like Raskolnikov, exactly like him. That old pawnbroker bitch was making me fucking sick, and when he started hacking at her, part of me was creeped out but another part was like awesome, go for it, hit her again in case she's still alive. After he'd snuffed her, I felt relieved. One less cockroach on the planet! People get really freaked out about killing, but they're fucking wusses, man, because some people deserve to die, to disappear from the face of the earth. Lots of folks aren't worth shit—all they do is hurt people. What a day to start reading that book, with my mother coming over! If my mother kicked it, it wouldn't make the least bit of difference. She's hurt a lot of people, especially my grandma. That's in the past, fine; at least she had some fun getting high and sleeping around with my father and everybody. But now? Is the life she's got now even worth living? Spending her days locked up and doped up with medicines that make her groggy? All she does is create work for the people taking care of her. If she died, it would be better for everybody—for me too. I wouldn't go after her with an ax because that's heavy stuff, but why not get rid of her without all the blood spatter? It's a good thing the teacher can't hear what I'm thinking, because otherwise . . . !

"Why did you choose that book for me?"

"Because it's a classic. People think the classics are boring, but that's not true at all."

"Way to go, classics!"

"And because you have a Russian name: Iván, Iván the Terrible."

"Uh-huh."

Don't joke around with me, teacher—if you could look inside my head, you'd freak the fuck out. You bet I'm Terrible.

As my contribution to the Christmas party, I'd gone by the neighborhood's Chinese variety store. I bought colorful garlands, Santa ornaments, and a miniature Christmas tree that we could set up on a table. Sandra always used to put one on the console in the foyer. Maybe it was a crazy idea, but I thought Iván might like it.

Before noon, while Iván was out picking up the takeout he'd ordered, I spent some time decorating the living room in an attempt to make it feel Christmassy. I draped the garlands around the windows, hung the Santa ornaments on the plastic tree, and set the table as best I could, even putting a red candle in the middle. I thought it looked good, gave the room a cozy feel, though I was worried about Iván's reaction since he's so unpredictable.

When he arrived, loaded down with several containers that gave off a mouthwatering aroma, he was astonished by my decorative endeavors.

"Shit, man, it looks like a luxury boutique in here!"

"Do you not like it? I can take it all down in a flash."

"What are you talking about? I love it! With all this crap you put up, we're going to seem like a real fucking family."

I could smell on his breath that he'd been drinking, and his rapid speech suggested he was agitated, angry. He opened a can of beer and chugged it down. Then he went to the kitchen, where he started moving around aimlessly, with a restlessness that expanded around him. He muttered incomprehensibly to himself, fuming, in a foul mood, brusquely tossing objects aside. I began to realize how upsetting, maybe even unbearable, he found his mother's visit.

At twelve-thirty he went to go pick her up, barely saying goodbye. An hour later, he was back. He introduced her to me with a sardonic surliness that would stick around for the rest of the afternoon:

"This is my dear mother. Her friends call her Elisa. And this is Javier, mommy. He's a real formal guy, a teacher. Did you hear that? A teacher, just so you know the kind of people I'm associating with. He's living here in my house to give me some culture and make sure I behave myself."

I felt a deep pang. The woman was in terrible shape. Her marginal condition, the aura of madness that haunted her, were immediately apparent. Tall, slender, with very pale, almost translucent skin, she viewed the world through two enormous, empty blue eyes. When she smiled faintly, she exhibited several missing teeth. I shuddered, gripped by the profound horror of misfortune. It was too late to mask this initial reaction. I glanced at Iván and found him watching me intently. I had no doubt he'd perceived my shock.

"What do you think of my mother? Gorgeous, right?"

Alarmed, uncertain what role to take, I shook the woman's hand and murmured, "Nice to meet you" while she kept smiling blankly.

"Well, now that the official introductions have been made, let's have an aperitif to get warmed up. What would you like to drink, Mamá?"

I sure showed him! That look on the fucking teacher's face

was just priceless! What, did he think I was kidding about my mother? A jury of my peers, the kind made up of normal, everyday people from off the street, might find me guilty of being a bad son, but if they saw my mother, that would be a different story. How are you feeling, Javier? Sometimes he seems less like a buddy and more like just a damn snob. Books may give you culture, but they obviously don't teach you shit about life, which is the only thing you really need to know about.

"Want a beer, Mamá? Nice and cold, the way you like it. Do they serve beer where you're living now? No? So stingy! Well, look, we've got everything you could possibly want here. Even Christmas decorations! Did you see them? The teacher here put them up himself."

Elisa glances vaguely around the room, and I hear her voice for the first time.

"Very nice. They've put up Christmas things at the residence, too, and a nativity scene."

Her intonation was that of a little girl, but her voice was the low, raspy voice of a smoker. Iván solicitously removed her checked jacket and placed a beer in her hand.

"Let's sit for a while, make sure you're comfortable and happy."

She sat down on the sofa and, restless, turned to her son.

"Do you have a cigarette?"

"Of course I have cigarettes on the day my darling mother comes! Look, I bought Luckies, your favorite."

She opened the packet, and I could see her hands trembling.

"Thank you, son. You're always so good to me."

I gave her a light. She took the first few drags one right after the other, eagerly. The three of us sat there with our cans of beer, not talking. To break the awkward silence, I asked politely, "Don't they let you smoke in the residence?"

She took a while to respond, as if she had a hard time understanding the words' meaning.

"Only two cigarettes a day," she said finally. "One after lunch and another one after dinner. We have to go out to the courtyard if we want to smoke. Inside there are signs everywhere that say 'Smoke-free zone.'"

"Of course, Mamá! They're looking after your health; they don't want anything bad to happen to you or for you to be putting crap in your body."

"Yes," she murmured. She looked pleading, almost fearful when she spoke to Iván.

"What about medication? Are you still taking all those meds?"

"I don't know how many I take—whatever they give me."

Iván let out a harsh laugh, fake and hysterical. He patted his mother on the back.

"That was funny, Mamá! You're a piece of work! No counting pills for you—whatever they put in front of you just goes right down the hatch!"

She smiled with a frightened grimace. Iván leaped to his feet.

"Let's eat! We don't want to burn the cannelloni!"

He disappeared into the kitchen. I looked at Elisa, uncertain what to say. It wasn't really necessary to say anything; she looked serene, detached. Iván reappeared, melodramatic and tense.

"Ohhhh!" he exclaimed, practically yelling. "Would you take a look at that? Cannelloni stuffed with pure meat—veal, pork . . . No filling it out with hot dogs or chicken feet or cat ears. Doesn't it smell good? Real Christmas food!"

He slopped cannelloni onto the plates while I uncorked a bottle of red wine. He was still talking nonstop. I was afraid his nonsensical chatter might continue throughout the entire meal.

"Nothing like family on Christmas! Family's the best, I always say—the sacred host and the blessed ciborium put together."

"Aren't you spending Christmas with your family?" Elisa asked me hesitantly.

"I just have one sister, and we don't see each other much, just once or twice a year, but never at this time. She's always got a lot of obligations at Christmas."

"Are your parents not alive?"

"No, they died a long time ago in a car accident. I was still little."

Iván pounced on the conversation like a wildcat:

"Isn't it horrible, Mamá? Just imagine if the same thing had happened to me, if you and Papá had died in a car accident and left me an orphan. I wouldn't have been able to bear it! Dreadful! I mean, just think how happy my life with my parents has been. Papá's dead now, but I've still got you, momkins. And things are just awesome for us now!"

She smiled faintly, lit a cigarette, and stopped eating. I threw Iván a stern glance, and he, delighted by my disapproval, started to enjoy himself.

"Goodness, Mamá, I'm just delighted to see you, seriously. The two of us are like the teacher here and his sister: we don't see each other much because you've got so many obligations, but when we do see each other . . . it's a real festive affair!"

I got up, my nerves jangling.

"I'm going to get some water," I muttered.

Iván came into the kitchen after me. He'd gathered up the plates; his mother's food was practically untouched.

"Aren't you being pretty hard on her?" I asked quietly.

He looked at me mockingly, but then he grew serious, his eyes transmitting a wave of pure hatred.

"People can treat their mothers however they want."

I turned around in a huff and went back to the living room.

Was this why Iván had invited me, so I could witness his churlish performance?

From there, the meal became even more uncomfortable. Luckily, Iván turned on the TV, which eased the tension in the air. The silence was less painful. Our guest had begun to disconnect from everything around her, including us. She barely tasted the meal. She just drank and occasionally smoked a cigarette, anxiously puffing it down. Iván took her plate as soon as we finished. He didn't remark on her lack of appetite. At least he wasn't tossing harsh barbs at her.

We ate the traditional nougat for dessert and opened a bottle of sparkling wine. We said as little as possible: "Pass me your glass," "Can I pour you a little more?"

"Let's go over to the sofa and have coffee," Iván announced abruptly.

He helped his mother, who now needed a hand, get up from her chair and over to the sofa. He went to make the coffee and served it alongside a glass of whiskey, which I turned down. Feigning interest, we watched a piece on what Christmas is like around the world: the beaches of Brazil, the Swedish snow . . . people smiling wherever they were. Suddenly I see Elisa nod off for good and fall asleep. I spot an opening in the clouds— there's no longer any reason to keep enduring the torture. I get to my feet.

"I'm going to rest a while," I say, and head to my room.

I fall asleep immediately, exhausted from the tension, the food, the drink, and the turbulent day.

Iván comes in to wake me up, shakes me. I'm startled, look at the clock. It's almost eight.

"I'm going to take the old lady home. I'll be back soon. Stick around, if you don't mind; wait for me here."

"I'll come out and say goodbye," I say, moving to get up.

"There's no need. She's so zonked she won't even know who you are."

After a minute, I hear the front door close. I wash my face with cold water. I hate naps—I always wake up disoriented and grumpy. I go out to make myself some tea in the kitchen, which is a mess: dirty plates, containers scattered across the floor . . . I load the dishwasher, clean, organize, sweep . . . Then I sit down to have my tea, which I'm really craving. Maybe the cleaning I've just done will be my last act of gratitude toward Iván for letting me stay in his house, because I'm convinced he's going to ask me to go to a hotel when he gets back. That's why he asked me to wait for him. He probably can't forgive me for scolding him about how he was treating his mother. I could tell he was angry with me, really angry. With any other friend, my reprimand wouldn't have mattered, but the friendship between Iván and me isn't natural. It doesn't matter anyway—I'll go to a hotel tonight till I find something else. At my age, I'm not up for sharing a place with anybody; it always causes problems, especially when it comes to two people as different as Iván and me.

Nine-thirty at night. I hear the key in the lock. He's back. He opens the kitchen door and smiles, throws his jacket on a chair.

"Operation Christmas is finished! Till next year! Damn, you cleaned the kitchen! That's awesome, man! The last thing I wanted to do now was start scrubbing. Want a gin and tonic?"

I'm confused. Iván's expression is no longer irritated; his voice is friendly. He doesn't seem angry at all.

"Did they get on your case at the residence?" I ask.

"Why would they?"

"It seemed like your mother had had a lot to drink, and since you say they don't let her have alcohol . . . "

"Those people don't give a damn what happens to my mother. I brought her back quiet and ready for bed. What more could they want?"

We carry the gin and tonics into the living room and sit down. Iván immediately starts talking.

"You freaked out when you saw my mother, didn't you?"

"Iván, you don't need to say anything else. I'm really sorry for butting into your life. I have no right to say anything. It was my fault, and so's this situation. Tomorrow I'll go to a hotel and look for a place to live from there. I should have done it already. You've been very generous with me, and I'm extremely grateful . . . "

Seeing that he's hanging his head and not listening to me, I trail off. I hear his voice, which is unusually calm, monotone.

"My mother was a beautiful woman, believe it or not. Look at her now, just falling apart. I hate seeing her like that too— I'm not a goddamn monster. But I have a mind, you know, a mind that works really well. And I've got everything recorded in there, and there's no way of erasing it. My mother didn't want me. I was born because my father wanted it. He thought he wouldn't be a real man if he didn't have children, such bullshit. But I always got on my mother's nerves; she hated even looking at me. She would park me at my grandma's house whenever she could. She'd leave me there and go off with my father or other guys. When Grandma would protest and lecture her, she'd come and take me away with her for a while. And that was the worst: yelling, fits of rage, hunger . . . She'd go to the bars to drink and I'd sleep on a chair. After a while she'd get sick of dragging me everywhere and take me back to my grandma's. My father was different. He didn't pay attention to me either, and he forgot about his idea that having children makes you a real man pretty much immediately. But at least he didn't yell at me or look at me with that expression on his face that seemed to say, 'I'd kill you if I could.' Sometimes he was even nice to me, saying I was really smart and was going to be rich when I grew up. Not her—she was always shrieking at me, 'Get out, you're always in the way!'

And if I didn't watch out, she'd slap me! She would have gotten more pleasure from a mangy alley cat than she did from me. Once Social Services came by because she'd left me sleeping in a bar. She said she'd forgotten I was with her. They almost sent me away to a foster home then, but I ended up going back to my grandma's house. My grandma was the one who always stood up for me, though I sometimes got mad at her because she called my mother a slut. I would get mad at my mother, too, because she actually was a slut. I don't really know who I was mad at, but in any case I spent my life being royally pissed off."

I couldn't bear to listen to his grisly stories any longer. I wanted to say, "Just drop it, Iván, I don't need to know anything, don't tell me any more." But it was like he was in a trance; engrossed, he didn't seem like he was going to stop. Why did he feel the need to justify himself to me? Fortunately, he paused to light a cigarette, and I took the opportunity to break in.

"Iván, I'm leaving tomorrow."

"Where to?"

"A hotel. I'll look for a place to live from there."

"No fucking way you're going to a goddamn hotel! Look for whatever you want, but do it from here."

So the teacher sticks his nose my business and then on top of it he's the one who gets miffed and wants to leave. I don't get these thin-skinned intellectual types. He rises to my mother's defense like a lion. So I give him a bit of a dressing down. And now he says he's leaving. Well, fine, man, screw you.

"You've done enough for me, Iván. I've got to look for my own place, like anybody else."

"Look, teach, my old lady won't be coming back till next Christmas. So if it's because of that, you don't have anything to worry about; she won't be hassling us anymore."

"How could you think that? Your mother didn't bother me in the least! Plus, this is your house and I . . . "

What can I say? I feel horrible—I feel guilty, foolish. But our worlds are so different, I don't think I'll be able to make him understand.

"You'll go when you have to go, but not like this. I told you I'm not a monster. Lots of guys in my position would never have seen their mothers again, you know, not at Christmas or at Easter or in their whole fucking lives. I know what I'm talking about, believe me."

"Of course you're not a monster! Let's drop it, Iván—this is ridiculous."

"OK, but I'm not a monster. I'm a pretty cool guy."

For the first time since we met, I see tears in his eyes. I don't know what to do. I want to leave. I want to fly off the handle. I can't bear this situation a moment longer.

"Look, Iván, do you think there's a bar that's open today? I thought we might go out and get a drink."

"Hell, man, of course there are bars open! And going out's a great idea. Let's get out from under these bad vibes, get a little fresh air. I fucking hate fucking Christmas!"

\* \* \*

On the morning of December 24th, Papá wouldn't go to work. We'd stay home by ourselves—even the maid went back to her village for Christmas. On the 25th we would eat with my aunts and uncles and cousins, but we always spent Christmas Eve alone, just the two of us. I loved it! In the morning we'd go see a nativity display, and on the way back we'd visit the best bakery in the city and buy nougat for the holidays: Jijona-style, Alicante-style, the toasted egg-yolk variety, chocolate-flavored. Every year Papá let me choose a new kind that wasn't traditional: marzipan with dried fruit, praline . . . We'd have lunch at a nice restaurant, and in the evening, happily back home, we'd put up the Christmas tree. I remember it being really exciting. Papá would go down to the storage room and retrieve the cardboard boxes where we kept all the ornaments, which were made of delicate glass, not plastic like they are today, in all kinds of shapes and colors: Nordic houses, fish, violins . . . Papá had bought them on a trip to Germany. We always managed to break one while hanging them up, and tempted as I was to cry because I wouldn't get to see it again, I never did cry. My aunt, my father's sister, had told me a while back that I shouldn't ever cry under any circumstances. If I cried, my father would feel sad, and he had enough sadness already what with having lost his wife, and enough problems what with having to bring me up on his own. So I never cried again, not even when I was alone in my room. For Christmas Eve dinner, we'd set the table really fancy. We'd heat up the soup and turkey that Asunción had cooked for us before she left, and we'd sit down across from each other like a king and queen.

It's funny, but I don't remember the Christmases where David was with us nearly as well. We'd have dinner at my father's house, of course, but nothing was magical like it had been. We'd exchange gifts and chat once dinner had ended, but even though it was very similar, everything was different somehow.

This is the first Christmas I've spent alone. I didn't accept my aunt and uncle's invitation to celebrate with them at their home. I don't want them to pity me, looking at me with sorrowful faces, or for them to pretend to be happy to see me. I didn't give an explanation for rejecting the invitation. Just no.

Genoveva also invited me to her house. She organizes a "free-verse" Christmas dinner where she brings together all her friends who don't have plans—but I know all those "verses," and they're not my thing. I can't stand their tittering and their inane comments.

Having rejected all of my options, I didn't really know what to do with myself. In the end I decided to make a good dinner at home, all by myself. In the afternoon I went to the market and bought everything that caught my fancy: tender greens for salad, thin slices of salmon cut right there in front of me, cheeses . . . I watched the people hauling around pounds and pounds of food to fill the bellies of all the family members who would gather around their tables. I didn't feel envious, to be honest—they seemed quite unsophisticated. Then I went to El Corte Inglés and chose a miniature Christmas tree, the kind you set up on a table, very cute.

That night, I took out my best white tablecloth and lit a decorative red candle they'd given me at the office. Everything looked great, and I started to eat, but I was feeling bored so I turned on the TV—and that's where I went wrong. I was watching a piece on how they celebrate the holidays in differ-ent countries around the world when suddenly they showed some images from Sweden of a little blond girl and her father leaving the house all bundled up and going to buy treats at a candy store. Like Papá and I used to do. Tears welled up in my eyes, and I couldn't choke down dessert because of the knot in my throat. It was rotten luck they showed that, because it caught me off guard and really depressed me. I'll never forget the Christmases I spent with Papá. But I didn't think about David even once that night, much less cry over him. The psy-chiatrist was asking about that the other day, talking about how I was doing in general: "Are you no longer angry with David?" I told him no, that at first I'd been resentful and pissed off, but afterward I forgot about him, erased him, as if he'd never existed. I never think about him and his simultaneous inter-preter. "Sometimes the mind strives to deny reality, and it man-ages quite a thorough job of it, but it's no good as a way of healing from trauma. After all, if we can't see the problem, how can we make the necessary changes as we move forward?" he asked. He's an idiot, that psychiatrist; he continues to think my problem is that my husband left me, and there's no convincing him otherwise. Also, what's wrong with finding a way to avoid suffering? I'm thinking about not going to him anymore. I don't even tell him the whole truth anyway . . . I've never told him anything about the naked men. I don't think there's any need, though no doubt he'd want to know about it, even if it was just for the titillation factor. I'll keep going a while longer, mainly because the pills he prescribes have been working well, especially the ones for sleeping.

Anyway, it was a mistake to try to celebrate Christmas with all the usual trappings even though I was by myself. What do I care about Christmas? When it was the three of us, they were busy days: buying gifts, planning the meal . . . but now it doesn't make sense. I'm Catholic—is everybody else Catholic? Do people really think Jesus Christ was born on December 25th, and that's why they're so happy? No. I don't want to make another mistake, so I'm not going to do anything out of the ordinary for New Year's Eve. I don't see why we have to go into a state of collective hysteria just because one year's ending and the next is beginning. Getting dressed to the nines and blowing on party horns—it's incredibly cheesy. When I used to go to the club with our friends on New Year's Eve, by one in the morning I'd already be wishing I could leave and go to bed, but things would last till four or even later. I put up with it because David liked that stuff, but now? It would be silly to try to pull something like that off on my own. Maybe what I'll do is order in some decent takeout, have dinner, take a pill, and go to sleep. It'll be the new year the next morning no matter what I do.

I'll talk to Genoveva and tell her I won't be attending her New Year's Eve party either. I'll come up with a good excuse so she won't be offended. If I just tell her I feel like being alone, she'll start hounding me: "I don't want you to start brooding," "You're going to get all down in the dumps." No, I have to tell a baldfaced lie: my cousin and I are going skiing, I've signed up for an overnight hike . . . something she can't disprove easily. She's such a pain! But I don't want there to be the least bit of tension or alienation between us because I'm planning to ask her to take me with her the next time she goes out with the guys. I'm not going to do it alone ever again.

\* \* \*

It's a real drag to have to perform on New Year's Eve! And we've been doing it for years! Since the crisis started, Mariano doesn't want to lose out on a single day; all the money that comes in goes straight into his piggy bank. The problem is the bastard only gives us a bonus if there's a big audience. Otherwise we get the same pay as usual and have to suck it up—he couldn't care less whether it's the last night of the year or the last night of the century. The good part is afterward the rest of the guys go out and party together. The rest of the guys!—because most of them leave, the ones who have girl-friends or celebrate with their families or whatever. I always stick around, especially since it's not a good night for hooking up. Every year we go to a bar called El Paraca. They don't do a sit-down dinner and cocktail party like at the nice restau-rants, but they serve these amazing mini sandwiches and top-notch sparkling wine. Afterward there's an open bar for rum and cokes—all you can drink. And it's not a total rip-off! And the music is awesome! The teacher said he's down for partying at El Paraca. He'd better be, as out to lunch as he is! Actually, he asked me to go with him before the show to take a look at an apartment he's found. If he wants it, he has to put down his deposit right away, and he wanted to get my opinion first.

So we went. First of all, the place is in the middle of fuck-ing nowhere, a dodgy area full of ragheads and greasers, even blacks. So he's off to a bad start, but I didn't say boo. Then, looking at the place, things went from bad to worse. It was one of those crummy buildings with little balconies full of underwear dangling out to dry and bikes hanging on the wall because they don't fit inside. A piece of shit, basically—there's not much else to say. The street was shit too, practically unpaved, with big potholes and herds of children playing ball. But all right, if he wants to live in a dump, he should go for it. I still didn't say anything. I wasn't going to try to persuade him: "Come on, man, come back to my house, you can see this place isn't for you." I wouldn't do that even if I'd gone fag and was desperate to keep him in my guestroom! It's cool, man—if you want to live in a pigsty, you figure it out. I don't give a shit.

The teacher had an appointment with a lady from the rental agency, who had the key. A forty-something broad, really fucking rude, with tiger stripes in her hair she'd gotten in some cut-rate salon and a suit jacket so tight she could hardly breathe. As soon as she arrived, she gave us a look as if to say, "I'm here because I have to be, but I don't usually work with losers like you." All puffed up from fucking showing apartments to ragheads or whatever! As if her agency specialized in VIPs and only occasionally, out of charity, rented out seedy holes-in-the-wall.

The apartment was on the second floor and faced the interior for maximum noise potential. The woman was yammering on to the teacher, since they'd already met when she showed him the place the first time. She didn't look my way or say a word to me, as if I didn't exist. Just like dogs do, she'd already sniffed out that I couldn't stand her.

Even though we didn't have far to go, we went up in an elevator decorated with your standard tacky graffiti: "Paco, I love you" and the date, which clearly nobody's bothered to clean up or paint over in ages because it's from the Franco era. And her still giving her spiel: "The neighborhood's well connected by public transport. Even though it's a mezzanine apartment, it gets a good amount of light. They tore down most of the interior walls and set it up as a loft, so it's spacious. It's got a full American-style kitchen, and there's a built-in wardrobe in the bedroom. The price is very competitive." Well, great, I'm thinking, apparently it's such an awesome place that at some point the fucking queen of England and her fucking hat collection will be moving in. The teacher, polite as always, kept listening to her sales pitch. When the elevator door opened, I realized we'd avoided the stairs to keep us from seeing them: more graffiti, more deterioration. And then . . . ta-da! spreading before us was the apartment in all its splendor. God, they were the crappiest digs I ever saw in my fucking life! A total shithole. They hadn't even bothered to paint. Suffocatingly small. No self-respecting American would ever cook in the so-called American-style kitchen: four crumbling formica cabinets and a food-encrusted stove. "Let's take a look at the bathroom," she says. The bathroom! The bathroom was totally disgusting—even she's embarrassed about it and says, "With a fresh coat of paint and a bit of cleaning, it would be perfect." I'd like to give the bitch a fresh something, that's for sure.

At the end of the visit, she had cheered up and looked me over for the first time. "And how much are they asking for this palace?" I ask my buddy, ignoring her. "Six hundred euros," he answers. Before I can say anything, she jumps in and goes, "It's a bargain at that price." I know I should have kept my trap shut and talked to the teacher instead, but I was so pissed I didn't have time to think. "Look, sweetheart," I said, "to be frank, it doesn't seem like a bargain to me, it seems like a piece of shit. If you catch my drift." The lady freezes, and Javier hisses at me, "Iván, please." But I keep going: "And anyone who's asking six hundred euros for this piece of shit is a crook." The lady blanches, her face beet-red, and spits out, "We have nicer apartments, sir, but obviously not at this price point." "Well, my friend wouldn't live here even if you handed it to him wrapped up all pretty with a bow on top, understood? And your boss can shove this apartment up his ass. Make sure to tell him that, so he'll know what customers think of his goddamn bargains." The teacher tries to smooth things over, gesturing to me to shush and still saying, "Please, please." And then, her eyes on Javier, the bitch goes and says, "Look, this is my job and I don't have time to waste, so if your boyfriend was hoping for a mansion, you shouldn't have come to me." Your boyfriend! At that, I really lost it! "Listen up, you cunt," I said. "I'm not his boyfriend. Maybe you didn't hear me say he's my friend, but just in case your brain's jammed, I'll knock you upside the fucking head." The teacher leaps to stop me, still muttering, "Please, please." The lady takes a step backward and pulls out her cell phone: "Get out of here right now or I'm calling the cops." The teacher, who's even more freaked out than she is, grabs my arm and propels me down the stairs. The two of them were right to freak out: I was ready to go after that twat. Nobody calls me a queer.

So the two of us were walking down the street, not talking. Javier was pissed. I was even more pissed. After a good fifteen minutes without opening his mouth, he says, "You're crazy, Iván, totally crazy."

"You're the crazy one for considering taking such a shitty apartment."

"I don't earn enough for anything better! Get it through your thick skull!"

Maybe it'll never get into that bull head of his. I'd like to ask him how he manages to live the lifestyle he does: a fabulous apartment, clothing, car, nights out . . . I'd have asked any other friend without hesitating, but I'm nervous around him—he might just punch me, or maybe I'd rather not know. Even so, I'm surprised he made such a scene with the woman from the agency; I'm still feeling frightened, uneasy. I could be letting him interfere in my life to a degree that might even be dangerous. After all, I know who Iván really is!

"I need to have my own place, Iván. Do you get that?"

"Of course I do, man, that's obvious."

"Then you'll also get that rents are really high and I can't afford to live the way you do."

"Look, teach, you're the one who doesn't get it, and ultimately that's my fault. I should have told you some things that you might be interested in. But now's not the time. I'm not feeling inspired at the moment—I'm still pissed at that broad. Tonight after the performance we'll talk man to man."

"Don't be so mysterious."

It's terrifying to hear him say that. I'm sure the conversation will lead to even more problems. At this point, my life is just getting more and more complicated. I've ended up in a jam that it's getting harder and harder to extricate myself from.

"No mysteries, man. All out in the open. We'll talk later."

The teacher's right, really. He doesn't understand a thing because he doesn't have all the information. And so he's a mess. I should have talked to him a while ago. With any other friend, I would have said something and been totally relaxed about it, but with him . . . I don't know if he's going to freak out or how he's going to take it. Maybe he'll kick up a huge fuss or start preaching at me, but I've got to give it a shot. I can't let him go off to some pigsty like the one that broad showed us. I wanted to kill her. I'm sure Javier will understand that this is just a shitty situation and be reasonable. If his brain weren't on the fritz, he'd also realize he can't go off to live someplace where he'll be miserable within a week. Does he think he'd be comfortable in a neighborhood like that? The guy's a dumbass! If I were him, I'd have died ten times over already. Lucky he has me to set him straight—that's what friends are for. And I've got a feeling he could do really well—

better than me, even. He's got that wide-eyed good-guy vibe that chicks dig. Even the boss loves him because of all the applause he gets during the show. Any day now he's going to give him a solo number. Javier just needs to be a little more shameless, a little bolder, declare his presence, and I don't know if . . . Anyway, I'm not his mother—we'll see.

That evening, the two of us headed to El Diamante. The teacher was a little down, but I was exuberant. Getting pissed off is like exercising for me, and that bitch gave me a pretty good workout. Plus it was the last night of the year, and the year that's ending is always worse that the one that comes after, or at least that's what we believe. I did a line of coke for some inspiration, and when it was time for the teacher's number, I kept a sharp eye out to see how he did. I'm starting to understand his technique: he goes out on stage looking as if he's embarrassed to be there, reluctantly takes off his clothes, and moves his body as little as possible, super serious the whole time. He doesn't smile even once. So the ladies—you know how they are—start wanting more and more, and they get curious to know who this guy is, the one who doesn't seem to give a shit, and they feel bad for him, seeing how shy he is. And what with their curiosity, their wanting to bone him, and their maternal instinct, the guy's a raging success. Then I perform and really get them hot. I've got my own technique. With me, it's like I'm saying, "What the hell are you girls looking at? You want me, don't you? Well, let's be clear, I'm way out of your league. Go screw your paunchy husband or that boyfriend of yours who can't get it up. I'm out of reach." Unlike Javier, I really shake my ass—I'm not embarrassed, I know right where I am: on the highest level of the podium, gold medal, top ten.

After the show, right before midnight, they pass out the bags of grapes and the sparkling white wine, which are included in tonight's ticket price. The place is packed. Awesome, the boss will have to pay us a bonus. We performers all go up on stage, where they've set up a plank with a paper tablecloth to look like a long table. The tolling of bells sounds over the loudspeakers, and we eat our grapes. We're fully clothed, of course. At the end, everybody shouts and jumps in the air and says Happy New Year and all that crap. As soon as we can, we sneak out through the rear door to avoid the audience's holding us up. Five of us are going out to celebrate at El Paraca.

When we got to the bar, there were already a bunch of people who'd welcomed the new year there, and the place was red-hot: loud voices, music, sparkling wine, mojitos, rum and cokes . . . the whole shebang. We had a table reserved for us, like VIPs. They gave us a platter with a variety of these amazing mini empanadas. Then a fully loaded salmon sandwich: hardboiled egg, tomatoes, shrimp, mayonnaise, pickles . . . so much better than turkey and all that other bullshit people usually eat on New Year's. And endless glasses of sparkling wine, all you could drink, the highest-quality *brut nature*. Some chicks who were there alone tried to hook up with us, but we weren't there to fool around, so we just deliberately led them on, partying hard. The teacher wasn't joining in on the festivities. He didn't like screwing with the chicks—he gets all earnest, the bastard. But I wasn't about to let him ruin my night. The owner of the place knows me and asked if we'd do a little impromptu striptease to get the staff fired up. Maybe it would have been good, but we said no. We were tired, plus we charge good money for baring our asses—we don't do it for free. And it was lucky I turned him down, because when I turned toward Javier I saw he'd gone pale. Just the thought of stripping there had him totally freaked out. To be honest, I don't know if he's ready for what I'm going to tell him; he seems a little wet behind the ears.

We took off at six in the morning. We were totally wasted. I'd done everything: acid, cola-free coke . . . I could have kept going a while longer, but six in the morning was a good time turn in. I took the teacher's arm—the only thing he was on was alcohol—and we headed home.

Once I'd closed the door, I offered Javier one last drink, but he couldn't handle any more and went to make himself a pot of coffee. While he drank that and I downed another whiskey, I got right into it:

"Listen, teach, where do you think I get the money for this lifestyle?"

The guy was startled. He put on a poker face.

"I have no idea, Iván, but that's your business."

"Shit, man, I know it's my business. But I think you've never asked where I get the cash because you've been making assumptions."

"I don't know what you mean."

"Well, maybe you think I'm a con artist or a drug dealer or something."

"It hadn't occurred to me."

His mouth is tight as he says it. He's a good guy, so he's a terrible liar.

"I'm not into drugs, man. I just take them to have a good time, and no hard stuff. I already told you what drugs did to my parents; I have no intention of going there."

"I totally get it."

"I totally get it," the dude says. He has no fucking idea where I'm going with this, so he's starting to freak out. This is actually starting to be fun. What if I tell him I'm a contract killer? Shit, I might do it just to see the look on his face.

"Look, Javier, I've been thinking a lot about your economic situation, and I think you could solve all your problems if you did what I do."

"And what's that?"

"I'm a male escort for rich broads. That's it—the whole truth."

If he lets his mouth hang open much longer he's going to dislocate his jaw.

"A gigolo?" he asks, astonished.

I laugh heartily.

"No, man, no! That's old-school, obsolete. Gigolos are history. Things don't work like that these days. A lot of the women aren't old—more of them all the time. They're executives with big-deal jobs, or they're lonely divorcees who don't want to get involved in any more love affairs, or they're chicks who are just looking to get laid, no strings attached. Stuff like that. So they want good companions. Sometimes it's just somebody to go with them to parties and galas, because they like people to see them with a handsome guy. Other times it's to have a little fun and then screw, and some of them just want to screw without the fun, period. Do you get me?"

"Are you talking about prostitution?"

"Hell, man, prostitution! Hooking is for hookers, and hookers are broads. This is totally different. And you earn a buttload of money and it's all discreet, easy—'classy,' as they say. Look at me: cool apartment, nice car, designer clothing . . . It's a sweet deal! I think you've got a future in it, too: you're polite, well educated, and it's obvious chicks like you. I see it when you're on stage—they get all hot and bothered. It's your attitude, the way you seem to be saying the show isn't your thing and you're doing them all a goddamn favor. Chicks really dig that."

"Are you saying I should get involved in that too?"

"Well, yeah, man, shit! I'm talking to you, right? Or are you made of better stuff than me?"

Careful, Javierito, don't even think about trying to suggest you're superior and I'm just a lowlife prostitute who eats pussy for loose change. Careful, you could start off the happy new year out in the street with your suitcase—I'm a patient guy, but there are some things I won't put up with.

"No, Iván, Jesus, don't get me wrong! It's just that I'm . . . I don't know how to say it . . . surprised! It's unexpected, you know."

"Of course it's unexpected, but you probably could have figured I wasn't earning all my money shaking my ass at the club. You know what that pays. I only stay there because it's a great place for making contacts. Mariano often acts as an intermediary, he lets you know . . . "

"Is it an organization?"

"No, it's not an agency, though there are those too. But I don't like them. It's just contacts, word of mouth . . . plus the chicks who come direct after the show."

"Damn!"

Actually, he probably would have been less shocked if I'd told him I was a contract killer. Not to mention if I'd told him I was a drug dealer—that would have seemed practically normal.

"Nobody gets a commission, see. Whatever you charge goes straight into your pocket. And of course the ladies pay for dinners, drinks, hotels . . . Most of the time you go screw in a hotel. These ladies put a premium on discretion, as you can imagine. You're polite and know how to socialize, so I bet a lot of them would hire you to go with them to galas and dinner parties. Especially once the word gets out that you're a teacher and you read books, that you're cultured. Once they found out you can carry on a conversation and discuss sophisticated topics, things would really take off. Man, I think you'd be a huge success for sure. You'd earn a nice wad. You'd leave me behind in a flash. I'm not trying to convince you here, but the truth is you'd be able to rent a nice apartment in a cool neighborhood, not a shithole in the boonies. And other things too, of course, but mainly the apartment, since you've seen what the housing situation is like. Think about it, Javier, don't be stupid and worry about whether it's immoral—and definitely don't worry what people will think. You know what the deal is with that? People like to talk, they go on and on about what a person should or shouldn't do, but at the end of the day you're the one who has to live with it. And maybe you decide to do what's wonderful and awesome but then you go through shit, and you're the one living your life, Javier—nobody's living it for you."

"Right."

I go through that whole speech and the dude lowers his head, stares at the floor, and the only thing he comes up with to say is "Right." Great! What's that supposed to mean? I should save my breath because it's not his thing? I think he hasn't quite digested it yet—it's too much for his system. It's a pretty hairy subject. If I were that Raskolnikov dude and told him I wanted to off the old lady, he'd have said awesome; he'd have gone after her with the ax himself. But this is different . . . Sin! Sin! Prostitution, gigolo . . . Even if priests don't even use those words anymore. Well, man, I've tossed you the rope. You're going to have to decide whether to grab it or not. You'll figure it out.

"I'll think about it, Iván. I'll think about it."

\* \* \*

My first thought was to call Sandra to tell her about it. An immediate but completely irrational impulse. But I was so surprised, I needed to tell somebody. Iván, a prostitute! I started laughing. In all the speculation I'd done about his supplementary occupations, that possibility had never occurred to me. And yet it was related to our activities in the club, to the demimonde we frequented. It was so obvious. Most likely all of my colleagues at El Diamante were doing the same thing, working as escorts. Who'd have guessed it—Iván was so manly, so textbook macho! Servicing women. Amazing.

According to Iván, really high-end male escorts. But what did "high-end" mean to him? No way of knowing for sure. In any event, he went out with women who had the money and the balls to hire him. After I stopped laughing, the questions I hadn't dared ask him echoed in my head: did he meet up with the same woman more than once? Did he fake loving gestures during the encounters? Did he really go at it when he was having sex? Did he do ménages à trois, orgies? How much did he charge—were they fixed prices, flexible; did it depend on what he did with the women, how much time he spent with them? I was dying of curiosity about the salacious subject, but it hadn't even occurred to me to ask as he was confessing. He could have interpreted it as me clarifying details before accepting his offer. Why did Iván think I might become a prostitute? He knows I still feel really uncomfortable about stripping even though I've been performing at the club for a while. So he offers me something that's a huge step beyond that? He's a strange guy—maybe he thinks it's more shameful to bare all in public than to go to a private appointment. And is it, actually? I don't think so. There's a theatrical aspect to performing at the club, a little like playing a part in a musical or a variety show. But there's no excuse for going to bed with a strange woman and charging for it.

The word "excuse" made me flinch a little when I thought it. Who was I trying to fool? Let's be serious, I said to myself, stripping was total shit, nothing like a variety show or avant-garde theater. I was earnestly playing the fool—and not exactly a Shakespearean fool or a children's clown. No, I was just putting my body on display in a crude, vulgar spectacle utterly devoid of artistic merit. And what had led me to that point? Not so much the need to earn money as the pressing internal need to stop being unemployed. I'd wanted to get out of the house and work with other people, belong to an active group, shed my worry about becoming a social parasite. If I accepted Iván's new proposition now, all those understandable, even laudable motives would disappear and only one would remain: earning money. That's the crux of it: who engages in prostitution if not for money? That's the way it's been since the beginning of time. And is it not an acceptable reason? Ultimately, that whole business about being part of society through stripping was still bullshit, something I could have avoided if it was so important to me to maintain my dignity. No, my dignity was long gone—and now I really did need money, urgently. If I had money I'd be able to rent a decent apartment, smaller and simpler than Iván's—my needs aren't so grand—but at least a place where I'd have my own space to read, to be alone, to find a bit of peace. Iván's obviously going to kick me out any day now. From his perspective, in telling me this, he's offered me the opportunity to earn enough to be comfortable. What excuse could I give to continue staying with him now? If I tell him I don't feel capable of sleeping with a woman for money, he'll go back to his initial reaction: "Are you made of better stuff than me?" And maybe that question is actually pretty rational—am I, in fact, better than him? If it's true that those women hire you just to spend time with them . . . but I don't believe it. There's got to be something else that comes after. Nobody pays for someone just to go to a party. Though women are pretty weird that way. I remember Sandra hated going places alone. What would she think if she found out I was working as a male escort? She'd say she saw it coming, that the path I'd started down led inevitably to such behavior, to a progressively degenerate state. But now I'm thinking about things I swore I wouldn't think about. Sandra's gone and she isn't coming back. The stuff I'm made of is really pedestrian stuff, certainly no better than anybody else's.

\* \* \*

I'm totally flipping out. Yesterday I went out with Irene again because she asked. Went out with the guys, I mean. Not Rodolfo and Uriel. Sometimes you have to switch it up. Rodolfo and I have been seeing each other for too long, and that always turns sour eventually. I don't know, these guys tend to start taking a lot of liberties. Rodolfo got pretty tedious the last few times. He started bugging me: "Let's go to another restaurant—I don't like this one," "You shouldn't wear red—it doesn't look good on you," "Don't drink so much—you'll get sleepy later" . . . A real pain. They need to realize they're at your service, period. Things always go well at the beginning, but then they start getting really overbearing, as if sleeping with you gave them certain rights. Don't they realize what the arrangement is? No, they end up believing the whole charade: phone calls, dinners, they go with you to different places, you call them "sweetie," you give them a tie or a pair of sunglasses one day . . . and they end up believing it! How is that even possible? "Come on, boys," you feel like saying, "haven't you noticed who's been picking up the check at these places? And that I'm also paying for your company?" Unbelievable! Actually, I'm afraid this is a problem with men in general. Husbands, too, forget the original setup and start butting into your affairs. They demand, object, request, are a complete pain in the ass, and show their worst face. They need to cool it! It's awful. They act like marriage isn't just a sort of contract you sign where each party has to respect the terms established. Chill, boys, you're you and I'm me. But things don't work that way—men take sex so seriously, as if sleeping together wiped out everything else. And if we were talking about a husband here, he'd get a pass! But I'm buying this kid off the shelf . . . I need air, man, let me breathe! If red doesn't look good on me, I'll wear blue instead, but only when I feel like it, understood?

I ditched Rodolfo in the middle of a busy avenue, taking advantage of a red light. I didn't even park or pull up to the curb. I told him, "Get out right now!" And he did, though he insisted on getting his bag out of the trunk of my BMW. We were coming back from spending a weekend at the house of some friends of mine. Sixteen people in total. One of those weekends out on a farm where everybody does his own thing during the day and the group comes together for dinner. At first he was fine, normal, as you'd expect, but then he started really screwing things up. He had to stick his oar into every conversation, even took them over. Please! He just kept babbling! He started talking about the witch doctors back in his country, their spells to ward off evil and whatever other nonsense. People listened politely, but after a while he got on people's nerves and everybody started mocking him and looking at me funny. He didn't even notice, probably because he'd been drinking. I called him into the kitchen at one point and told him to keep his mouth shut because he was making me look like a fool. Nothing out of order. And the moron goes and tells me he's not a puppet and he can say whatever the hell he wants. Hilarious—not a puppet! I didn't respond, of course, because the last thing I wanted was to cause a scene, but I'd already made a decision. On Sunday evening, as we were on our way back, I tell him, "Rodolfo, once we're in the city, you're going to get out of the car and we're never going to see each other again." He's proud—all these South Americans are very proud and very sexist—so he says, "OK. But if I get out, we really will never see each other again. You'll see." Unbelievable! He thought I was hung up on him! Sometimes I really don't understand what people are thinking. They don't get it, they don't see what's right in front of their noses, not even their proper place. I'm paying you, right? So lose this not-a-puppet business, and definitely lose the soap opera threats: "You'll never see me again." That's modern life. Things ended with some badly injured dignity—I had to yell at him to get out of the car because he was pretending he didn't understand.

But let's try to focus a little here. The other day: Irene calls, wanting to go out with the guys again. She can't deny she had a good time, even if she is a total prude. I don't have a problem with it, I tell her, but then she says, absolutely unbelievable, "Tell whoever's coming that I'm not interested in physical contact—I just want to see him naked. I don't want there to be any misunderstandings afterward." Amazing, right? Just incredible! Though I already knew about that—I hear things. After the last time the two of us went out with Rodolfo and Uriel, the next day Rodolfo called me all worried: "Hey, what's up with your friend, did she say anything?" I stopped short. "No, she hasn't said a word. What happened?" "Uriel's upset because your friend wasn't interested in anything with him. She just made him strip naked, that's it. So he wants to know if she just didn't like him, or if he did something wrong without realizing it." Good God!, I thought. I told him I had no idea and that I had no intention of asking Irene either—that's a private matter, and you can't just go around asking about it. But I had the information, of course, and I couldn't figure it out. At first I assumed that since it was her first time, Little Miss Sanctimonious was feeling shy and had had enough just seeing him naked without taking things any further. Of course, after her phone call and that business about "physical contact," it's clear there's something else going on. But what? Maybe, deep down, she's got a bit of lesbian in her. Or is it just that she's repressed after living with her father her whole life? I've even contemplated psychological reasons: she's so shattered after her husband left her that she's become bitter and wants to make other men suffer, so she humiliates them. Because even if he's a male escort, a guy is a guy, and making them strip naked and then rejecting them must really do a number on them.

Anyway, Irene's an odd bird. Really odd. Maybe she's still a virgin. She was so in love with her father, maybe she never wanted to sleep with her husband. So many theories, and maybe that's just her kink, seeing men naked. There are lots of kinks, some really twisted ones too. People are really screwed up—and it's so easy to just be normal. Sometimes I think I'm too normal, because I've had plenty of opportunities to make my life more complicated if I'd wanted to. See, the only thing I want is to live a good life, no drama, grow old and all that, just like everybody else.

All right, well, I'll rustle up a couple of guys—it's not going to be on me if this falls apart.

\* \* \*

It's much better this time. Clearly I need Genoveva for these kinds of plans. Plus, ever since we dropped the pretense, things have been a lot more natural. No more dumb outings to go shopping or have drinks. Now she knows what I want her for. And she likes having me around too—I don't judge her, and my being younger helps mitigate the impression that she's a pathetic older woman looking for a lay. It wasn't too hard to come clean with her. Anyway, it's not like not wanting to sleep with guys, just wanting to see them naked, is anything to be ashamed of. The other way around would be worse. And I put it to her in an aloof tone, without a hint of intimacy. I don't want there to be any complicity between us. I think she understands that and will have the good taste to respect it.

She's already being more discreet this time. She didn't announce with great fanfare that the guys were "hunks." She only mentioned that one of them, "hers," was a commercial model. He wasn't famous or anything, didn't appear in magazines. He just does ads when they call him, a freelancer, and he's occasionally done runway work for a well-known designer. Mine—just hearing her say "yours" made my hair stand on end—was a younger guy who'd studied architecture but had lost his job. To earn money, he was working as a bartender at a nightclub and made a little on the side going out with women like us. At least that was the version Genoveva told me—who knows. There was no way of saying for sure who these guys were or where they came from. An out-of-work architect? Perhaps . . . Roberto, Genoveva's companion, was definitely a model. He stood out because he had a great walk, straight as a ruler, and wore a silk scarf knotted elegantly around his neck. He told stories of his occasional work in the fashion world that sounded true. He wasn't full of himself. Actually, he was pretty entertaining. He talked about a TV commercial where he'd played a modern dad and made us all laugh with his descriptions of how annoying the children on the shoot were, with one of them even spilling a jar of baby food on his pants.

The unemployed architect had a lot less personality. I have no doubt he was unemployed, but I'm not sure he was really an architect. I tried to talk to him about the subject, and the only architect he seemed familiar with was Gaudí. He could have at least prepared a little if he was going to fake it! He was a kid from a lower-class neighborhood who mispronounced words, one of those people who think being well mannered means always saying "please" and "thank you." Anyway, what can you really expect? At least he was handsome and he and Roberto didn't already know each other. Rodolfo and Uriel had seemed like a couple from a TV sitcom, but without the humor. This guy was cheerful and laughed a lot. That was enough for me. They say laughter is good for your health.

I realize how little laughing I've done in my life. Papá didn't have a sense of humor. He was always serious-looking, though not taciturn—it's to be expected after the tragedy he'd gone through with the death of his wife. And there was also his job: a businessman with that level of prominence and responsibilities can't go around telling jokes or howling with laughter at every turn. It's different with me, though. Everything in my life is falling apart: my husband left me, my business is going under . . . what can I do but laugh? I don't have the energy to fight, especially since I have no idea who my enemy is. If Papá were alive, everything would be different; he'd know who to blame and devise a strategy for defeating them. But I don't have his skill, and I lack the resources to clamber out of the hole I seem to have fallen into. Fortunately, my father taught me not to cry. The other day I told that to the psychiatrist, and he said crying can be a good release valve and a way of identifying which of our emotions cause us pain. The world's turned upside down: you go to the psychiatrist so he can tell you how to cheer up, and the guy recommends you start crying. I guess this psychiatrist must deal only with wealthy women like me, which is why he offers such ridiculous suggestions.

Anyway, everything went well with the fake unemployed architect. We headed to a hotel that night and, since he'd already been told what I wanted, there weren't any awkward moments. He took off his clothes and started posing and flexing his muscles. I asked him to keep still, and he obeyed.

Genoveva said we're going to switch partners. We'll see.

\* \* \*

It had to happen, and it did. Luckily, he listened to me. Ultimately, everybody listens when money's talking. With money in the picture, shame and dignity and everything else go out the window. The teacher knew he was in trouble. He comes to me the other day and says, "Iván, about what you were saying the other day—I'd like to give it a shot." And I say, "Awesome, man. Given your situation, it's your best option." Then it got a little messy because he starts going on about how it was just a test, we'd see how things went . . . and then says, "Since it's just a test, find me something light." Something light? I didn't really know what he meant by that until he explained. What he wanted was to take a lady to the movies, dinner, or some kind of party, and that's it.

"Well, man, things don't quite work like that. You go out with a lady, yeah, OK, but after that who knows what might happen, and you have to be up for anything, understand? Whatever the lady wants."

"But you said . . . "

"Don't give me that bullshit about what I said!"

Did he really think he was going to get rich taking chicks to dinner? No way, man! Sure, it's a way to earn some easy cash, but you have to clock in, even if you're fucking Brad Pitt—money doesn't grow on trees. Apparently he thinks he can go and set out his terms from the beginning: "You can invite me to an amazing dinner in a twenty-star restaurant, but afterward I'm going to bed alone—my mom's waiting up for me." Shit, man! I should have told him to go to hell a long time ago, but I just can't do it—I feel bad for him and start thinking how if I leave him up to his own devices, he's going to end up getting the shit kicked out of him. How has he made it almost forty years being such a dumbass? It's just incredible. If I'd been him, there'd be nothing left of me, not even my skeleton. His grandmother must have taken good care of him, and his girl-friend too! I guess since he spent all his time buried in his books, he didn't have to struggle to get ahead. But it doesn't matter—however much education you have and however much other people take care of you, at some point you realize you can't live life from behind a pane of glass. They shove you out of the nest even if you don't want to leave it, and there you are, splayed out in the middle of the street.

A week after that argument, when it still wasn't clear whether we should move forward, a great opportunity came up: a bachelorette party at a private home. I hadn't had any of those gigs for a while because, what with the crisis, there aren't as many of them—people don't much feel like celebrating. But they do happen occasionally: chicks who have a good job and invite all their coworkers to a party at their house. That comes out cheaper than renting a venue and hiring in caterers—plus, if you hire some good strippers for dessert, the crowd will have a better time than if you'd invited them to the fanciest place in the city.

I told him that. I said, "Man, it's a private party, totally 'light.' It'll be like performing at the club, but with the girls sitting closer, real cozy." The first thing he asks is "Will I have to talk to them?" You can't take this guy anywhere. He makes it sound like talking to the girls is something horrible, just the worst, absolutely agonizing. Look, man, if you go to a rocking party, you can't just dance your little dance and then sit in a corner reading a book. No, you have to join in a little, say hi, say the kind of things people generally say in those circumstances: "What's up, girls? Who's getting married? Are you sure about this wedding? Have you really thought this through?" You know, sell the act a little. You can't just show up looking to be loved—we have to earn our keep, right? Another thing is he says he doesn't want them teasing him. All right, that can be negotiated. I'll talk with the chick who's hiring us and tell her my partner is shy and doesn't want them making racy jokes. I really hate to say that, but fine, I'll give it a shot. But what I can't do, no matter what, is say, "Listen, tell your friends my partner won't be talking, so don't bother." Anyway, not wanting to tell him to go to hell, I said, "Well, you won't have to talk much, Javier, maybe a few short sentences." I think he realized what an ass he was being and started laughing.

. I gave him two days to consider whether to accept the job. For two days I patiently waited, holding back from offering the gig to someone else and closing the deal for good. Finally he comes with a martyred expression on his face and says, like he's going in front of the firing squad, "OK, Iván, I'm in. I'll go with you to the party." Shit, man, I'll accompany you to the grave, till death do us part, as the priest says. It's a miracle! He probably spent the entire two days fretting about it: "I'll go, I won't go, I'll do it, I won't do it, yes, no, don't know/no opinion." Patience, Iván, patience!

"All right, all right. There's no need to make a big deal about it, Iván—I'm in."

It's unfair to think it's so easy for him. I suppose he must have had a first time too. Was it bad? Who knows! When Iván and I crossed paths again as adults, I immediately got the sense life had treated him worse than it had me. He seemed like an unlucky guy: deprived of the pleasures of education, haunted by his parents' sad history, full of prejudices against women, living from hand to mouth . . . Today I see him differently. Iván is strong and ready to face any setback, he's able to protect himself from misfortune, he doesn't give up in the face of adversity, he's self-confident, and he doesn't cook up moral dilemmas that prevent him from deciding what's best for himself. His world has turned out to be more real than mine. My ideal was a quiet life, a supportive and drama-free love, an endless supply of books that would bring me happiness. But that all turned out to be a fictional dream that collapsed with the first headwinds. Life is as Iván perceived it from a very young age: uncertain, difficult, sad, swift, cruel. Who can allow himself to live a placid existence dedicated to teaching, reading, thinking, living in harmony with others? I guess I'm not the only one who's had to give up this sort of fantasy. We live in a wild jungle where you have to keep moving to avoid being devoured. The time I spent thinking I was happy had little relation to the truth. I was fooling myself. I thought I was showing my students the wonders of literature, but they probably weren't even listening to me. They weren't interested in Shakespeare or Calderón de la Barca—they were counting the minutes till the end of the class, eager to escape to freedom. They wanted to act, interact, log on to a social network, engage with the thousands of things awaiting them outside. And what about love? Is love as I've conceived of it even possible? Is it madness to still believe that calm and repetition might be a couple's ideal bonds? Sandra left me because of extreme circumstances, but I now realize that even if we'd stayed just as we were, she'd have left me anyway.

My values are obsolete. I've been living like a snail, and the shell I once produced no longer protects me. But did I have to be exposed to the elements so brutally? Being a prostitute! Charging money to sleep with a woman! Iván does it, sure, he likes living it up, overindulging . . . but me? All I need is four books and a cot. Is that true? Probably not. I'm not satisfied with whatever comes along—I'd never go live in a fleabag boarding house somewhere. I'm not good for much, and I need money to survive: that's the raw truth, the only truth.

I've got to preserve my sanity, avoid falling into despair. I'm alone. Iván's my only friend. Stripping at a private party isn't much worse than doing it every weekend at the club. Maybe that one gig will be enough to get me to the end of the month—that's as far as I have to make it.

"All right, Iván. I'll go with you—don't offer the job to anybody else. I'll go."

So there we were, high on life and ready to win. The teacher and I agreed I'd go by the house to pick him up at eleven. I told him I had things to do beforehand, though it wasn't true—but I didn't feel like being with him all evening, listening to all his neuroses.

The first thing I did was offer him some professional advice: don't go overboard with the alcohol, don't even think about dropping acid, keep things under control the whole time. It's a good thing I didn't spend the whole evening with him, because he was insufferable! A long conversation with him would have been torture: "Me, a prostitute—it's so awful! So immoral!" I'm starting to know the teacher as well as if I'd birthed him myself, and I'm positive that's pretty much how things would have gone. In any event, on our way to the party, he started nagging:

"Shit, Iván, I don't think I can do this! We should just drop it—it's a ridiculous idea. Plus, my head hurts. I don't feel good."

I ignored him and focused on driving. I acted like I hadn't even heard him. I even put on some music and turned it all the way up. But it was no use—he kept moaning on about how he didn't have the strength and oh his poor aching noggin. The guy's a real fucking pain in the ass! He's lucky we're friends—otherwise I'd have opened the car door right there and kicked him to the curb. Is this really such a trial for him? Being shy is one thing, but getting all worked up about four chicks seeing you in the buff . . . I've done it a million times! Anyway, patience, I told myself.

When we were almost to the house, the teacher really started getting the jitters and asked me to please let him out. I stood firm—no more bullshit. I stopped the car in front of a huge house with a yard and a dog that started barking at the top of its lungs.

"Look, Javier, do me a favor and chill the fuck out. I stuck my neck out and they hired both of us, and I'm not going to let you make me look bad. You're not going to screw me over, understood?"

Seeing how pissed I was, the bastard suddenly relaxed, or maybe the damn dog just incapacitated him with all that barking. I passed him a rail of coke, and he huffed it right down. I did another, and if that shit weren't so expensive I'd have liked to have gone over to the edge of the yard and blown a little snow right in that fucking dog's nostrils to see if it would fucking lay off.

OK, so once we were calmer and clear on where things stood, I started looking for the house where the party was going to be. I slowly followed the GPS directions, and in a few moments we'd arrived. It was a cool place, definitely not a little duplex or a weekend cabin. We parked beside the wall. It was a quarter to midnight, so we had to wait a bit. That's my MO—I like to show up right on time, not a minute earlier or later. It gives you the chance to scope things out. There were a ton of cars parked there, all luxury models: BMW, Mercedes, Alfa Romeo, Audi . . . The party guests were obviously high rollers. All right, so with a little luck we'd be able to earn some extra cash, which always helps with travel expenses.

In my experience, if the house you're going to is kind of crummy, they tend to be super disrespectful and the chicks get way inappropriate: right from the start they're smooching you and groping your crotch. Then, when it comes time to collect, they're reluctant to give you the cash and they start haggling . . . totally tacky. If the place is really posh, that's its own problem: at first they look at you like you're a turd that's stuck to their shoe, and when the party starts up, you always get the feeling they see you as one of the help. That's no fun, and it can really get you down. The best parties are the middle-class ones, where the girls talk to you and ask you if you've got siblings, if you like soccer, normal stuff.

That night, as soon as I switched off the engine, we could hear the noise coming from inside the house: music blasting, shouts, general chaos . . . It's better that way—we'll draw less attention when we go in. I was a little worried: if we got too enthusiastic a welcome, this doofus might just take off running. A girl opened the door for us—she was in her late thirties, which is normal at bachelorette parties these days since people are getting married later. She was pretty hot in a body-hugging black minidress.

"Are you the guys?" she asked like an idiot.

"No, we're with the Civil Guard," I responded, trying to be funny.

She turned toward the living room and yelled, "Girls, it's the Civil Guard!"

She was pretty wasted, but it seemed like it was just from alcohol since her pupils weren't dilated. She waved us inside. I prodded my companion, who was starting to lag behind. Inside there were about twenty chicks, all of them more or less the same age, all of them holding rum and cokes, all of them dressed to kill. As tends to happen, some of them started whooping and yelling.

"Finally, we've got some real men in here!"

Others tried to shush them, apparently thinking they were ruining the ambience. As I always do, I stayed cool and smiling and didn't say anything, just watched them come.

"Do you want a drink?"

We accept the first of several gin and tonics. Once we, too, were holding glasses in our hands, the room seemed to relax some. The bride-to-be—the chick who'd opened the door—asked us warmly if we were hungry. I told her no, that maybe we'd grab something after the performance.

"Oh, are you in a hurry?"

"Not at all."

"I thought maybe you had another performance afterward."

"No way. The night is all yours."

"That's great! I was worried everything was going to be really cold and mechanical."

"We're professionals, and we like to do a good job."

I said the bit about being professionals so there wouldn't be any confusion. We're on the clock; we're not here to make best friends for life. I made a few rounds through the room, chatting and knocking back gin and tonics. The place was already a wreck, with dirty and half-empty plates scattered everywhere. Sure enough, they started asking me questions.

"Do you have a girlfriend?"

I always answer that one in the affirmative to keep them at a distance.

"What does your girlfriend say about you doing this?"

"Nothing, being a dancer is no big deal."

That provoked the same tired old joke: "Dancer! Have you performed at the opera house?"

They all crack up. I coolly respond, "Not yet, but my agent says there's a contract in the works."

"Oh, you have an agent?"

"Of course. He's the one who told me that I should come dance at a party with a bunch of pretty girls instead of at the Russian Opera."

I don't know if there's any such thing as the Russian Opera, but it didn't matter—I needed to neutralize the joke so things didn't get out of hand. And they were all dying laughing at what I'd said.

With all the kidding around, I've forgotten to keep an eye on the teacher. I look around for him and . . . shit! There he is, surrounded by a gaggle of girls who are staring at him and drooling like they might get off from the sheer pleasure of being next to him. What the hell? What the hell is he saying to them? I wouldn't put it past him to start babbling about Raskolnikov. I go over and say, "Hey, man, we're up." The girls scatter around the room, and I hear one of them say to the bride-to-be, "Oh, he's so charming!" And the bastard hadn't even wanted to come! He's a chick magnet, I always knew it.

The owner of the house shows us to a bedroom where we can change. I ask the teacher how he's doing, and he says fine but he's not sure how this "trial by fire" is going to go.

"Are you nuts, Javier? Just do the same thing you do at the club. That's it. Plus, these chicks are drunk off their gourds.

They won't even notice whether you're naked or wearing a fireman's uniform."

"I don't know, I don't know . . . "

He shakes his head, unconvinced. I know he's going to come through, but he likes to get on my nerves, make himself interesting.

We put on some tight black pants with zippers all the way down the legs that come off with a single tug. They're special striptease pants. I already had a pair, but Javier must have had to order some from the seamstress. They cost a wad. If the dude decides he's not into striptease house calls, it'll be a huge waste.

Our white T-shirts are tighter than normal. This outfit looks good on me—it highlights the muscles in my thighs, shoulders, and chest. I glance over at him, and to tell you the truth he looks pretty weird. He's so lanky and skinny that he looks like a schoolkid in gym class—all that's missing is a pair of gym socks. It's a good thing we're barefoot. In any case, it's obvious those chicks are going to eat him right up. I guarantee it.

When we go back to the party, they've cleared the furniture to one side of the room and dimmed the lights to create a more intimate atmosphere. When the girls spot us, they start shrieking excitedly. All in good fun. I give the bride-to-be the CD for our performance. She puts it on and we get ready, but there's no sound. She doesn't know how to work her own system—she's a dumbass, I could tell as soon as we got here. The guy who's marrying her has no idea what a catch he's got. The party guests are lounging around on cushions and couches. They howl and protest over the delay. The music starts and catches us off guard, but finally we can perform. We've rehearsed a little during the week. Since we're not dancing the same number as in the club, we've had to work it out. We move together to the beat; everything's going well. I'd thought the teacher was going to be pretty detached, but no, he throws himself into it, shakes his ass off. Awesome. The girls' whoops and hollers have stopped. You could hear a pin drop—they're not even breathing. We remove our shirts—applause, exaggerated sighs—but that's the last joke those bitches make. When we take off our pants, the air is thick with tension. We dance around in our briefs, and I get hard. I'm watching the girls' reaction, how their eyes are bugging out of their sockets, how they look away when I meet their eyes, afraid I'll guess what they're thinking. And finally, whoosh!, briefs flying through the air, cock in the breeze. Isn't this what you wanted, you sluts? Isn't it? Well, here you go! You're never going to see cocks like this in your lives. Not ever.

The music stops. They all applaud, and they mean it. You can tell they appreciate the effort we've put in. I'm not sure how the teacher's feeling about things since by the end I was focused on my own experience, but I imagine he's good. They demand an encore. Fine, the prearranged price includes up to three . . . but no more—we're not a damn charity organization.

I put on the second piece of music we've prepared. We get dressed again, which is ridiculous with the audience right there watching us, but it is what it is. White powder has started circulating around the room. I request a hit for the performers. They hand it over without hesitation. The girls are all high. It makes me happy to see them that way. I plunge into the music and we start dancing again. It's going really well—we're stoned and feeling hot. Now I do glance over at Javier to see what he's doing. Seems like he's no longer in a rush, and he's loosened up but not trying too hard—very him.

During the final encore, one of the girls suddenly gets up in front with us. With what are apparently supposed to be sexy movements, she wriggles toward us to the beat. The others laugh and cheer. The ninny starts dancing between Javier and me and gradually undresses. She's the ugliest one there, of course: a real cow, with rolls of fat sloshing from side to side. Horrifying, man! When she's down to her bra and underwear, it seems like her friends aren't finding it so amusing anymore. They fall silent, no longer whooping, but she keeps going. She totally coked up, practically drooling. She takes off her bra, and then she really does look like a dairy cow with an udder you'd attach milk hoses to. She's revolting, but none of her friends attempt to stop her. Suddenly the girl turns toward me and acts like she's going to suck me off.

Hell no, I couldn't take it anymore—I gave her a shove and knocked her sprawling. She fell on her back like a cockroach, legs in the air. Holy shit, what a sight! I got really worked up and started roaring like you wouldn't believe. I ran over to the owner of the house and shouted, "Look, lady, this wasn't part of the deal. You need to get your friends under control." But she got all up in my face, calling me a monster and saying how dare I touch one of her guests, she was going to report me, she . . . a ton of threats! Throughout all this, Javier was tugging on my arm, trying to calm me down—both of us buck naked. A fucking train wreck, man! All the girls were glaring at us, and the fat one was sobbing on the floor. So anyway, I say to the bride-to-be, "Hand over the money, we're leaving before I punch somebody." Looking frightened, she went to get the money. I counted it right in front of her, and it was all there. We got dressed, retrieved our scattered belongings, and I heard the teacher saying, "I'm sorry, I'm really sorry. He flipped out, but he's not really like that." The girl didn't seem to be pissed at him, just me, because she said, "It's my fault too. I should have shut this crap down earlier." I don't know how the teacher managed to pull it off, but they ended up besties. Anyway . . .

In the car on the way back, I was seething. I was ranting about those chicks and about chicks in general. I stopped and had Javier take the wheel, I was so agitated. He started driving, not saying a word, but after a while he said, "Calm down, Iván, please. It's not worth being this upset."

OK. I shut up. Both of us shut up. And suddenly he goes and says, "You were right—it was a piece of cake, like you said it would be. Just a little inconsequential carnage. Luckily, nobody died, though next time we should probably wear helmets."

The guy had some balls to say that. Balls! Because when I'm in a foul mood, it's best to just go with the flow and keep your trap shut. But no, damn it, it was funny—I wasn't expecting that, a bit of humor. I put on a straight face and said, "Don't worry about the casualties. Next time, instead of a helmet, I'll bring a gun, and the first one who gets out of line is going down."

"You would have needed a cannon for that one."

The teacher was on a fucking roll! I cracked up and so did he, and we couldn't stop laughing, looking like a couple of dumbasses chortling away. And to think I'd expected him to freak out that I'd pushed a girl and everything. But no, his little jokes cheered me up. That's one of the nice things friendship can offer.

When we got home we grabbed a couple of beers and wandered happily off to bed. But first I gave him his part of our haul. When I gave him the euros, in cold hard cash, his eyes gleamed as if he couldn't quite believe it. Great, mission accomplished.

\* \* \*

It was awful—there's no getting around it! Luckily I was so stoned that when things started heating up, I didn't fully realize what was happening. I think I really woke up when Iván shoved that girl and she fell over. It was horrible, just atrociously violent. Everything else was pretty funny, actually, totally surreal: Iván and me naked in the middle of a throng of women, some of them dumbstruck and horrified and others so out of their gourds they had no idea what was going on. Iván, more The Terrible than ever, yelling at the host, doubling down on his outrage.

I suppose there were a lot of factors that led to things turning out that way. It was a heady cocktail of elements right from the start: cocaine, alcohol, crumbling inhibitions, and girls who probably weren't used to that kind of thing. Even so, the end of the party wouldn't have turned into such a circus if my buddy hadn't had such a visceral reaction. That girl really did offend our dignity, though, and you could even call it assault. Throwing herself at Iván like that! . . . I would have jumped back myself. She was so unattractive: chubby; her eyes rolled back from all the shit she was on; those gyrating, repulsive movements; her tits swinging back and forth . . . Of course, jumping back isn't the same thing as shoving her away like she was a monstrous vermin. A psychiatrist would have a lot to examine when it comes to Iván's relationship with women, though I bet it's actually a pretty simple case, textbook.

Anyway, after that experience, it's clear what I am: just another male escort. When Iván handed me my part of the money, I was stunned. Sure, it was a lot, but most of all it had been easy. None of what had gone wrong was attributable to the job itself. I'd really gotten myself worked up before the party: moral qualms, a sense of humiliation, fear of ridicule. The altercation with the girl should be deemed purely accidental. Going to that house and dancing naked had turned out to be way easier than I'd ever imagined. I'd actually been chatting with those women like just another guest.

I counted the money several times. Yes, now the numbers made sense: if I performed at two or three parties a month, plus what I earned on weekends at the club, I'd have enough to rent a decent apartment and live on my own. I made up my mind and called Iván:

"Two or three parties like that, Iván, that's all I need."

"All right, Javier. That's great, man. You've ditched your neuroses and buried your fears. Only thing is, bachelorette parties, birthday parties, and other little events like that don't come up every day. We're in a recession, this isn't New York, and I don't have exclusive access to all the shindigs in the city."

OK, man, this is awesome. The teacher sure did snap out of it! He's unbelievable, though—wants to sign up for three little parties a month and make out like a bandit. That would be amazing, but things don't work that way. If it were that easy, even the goddamn bankers would be doing this. You have to put up with chicks who are tiresome, ugly as sin, bitter about life. And sleep with them! It's not all blowing out birthday candles.

"All right, I can go to dinner with an older woman or something too."

"Yeah, sure, or to the zoo. But at some point you're going to have to go to bed with one of them."

"Shit, Iván, that's the last resort. If there's any way to avoid it . . . "

"All right, man, I'll keep it in mind. Say no more."

And he kept it in mind. Three days after that conversation, Iván let me know he had what he called "an awesome contact." He was euphoric.

"Russians, man, they're Russians. Russian tourists. Loaded as a baby's diaper. These broads come to Spain by themselves on business or to see the city and are looking for company at night. They pay a fortune. Just think: barrels full of vodka, champagne, and caviar. And they're sure to be hot—Russian women are always hot! I'm going to finish the Raskolnikov book so I can play the sophisticate. What do you think? Are you in?"

"I don't know what to think, man. It's not what we'd talked about."

"Listen, let's give it a try. Just one time isn't a big deal. This is for Thursday. It's two friends looking for a couple of guys to go out to dinner and then whatever else happens. It's a great gig, I'm telling you."

I said yes. There's no way of coming back from this. Degeneration, opprobrium, debasement? Those words sound so old-fashioned, smell like musty wardrobes. I'll keep my eyes closed.

The Russians were two women in their thirties. The prettier one had startlingly blue eyes, very blond hair, and Slavic cheekbones, high and prominent. The other was big: tall, stocky, enormously busty. "She's as large a barge," Iván whispered in my ear. They spoke some English, about as much as I did. To my surprise, Iván was also able to fumble along in the language. It apparently wasn't his first experience with tourists.

I remained numb, trying not to think about the words from the old-fashioned wardrobe. My shyness had been quelled by a line of coke. Everything was going well. I figured Iván would go with the pretty one and I'd be left with the barge, but this wasn't a teenage blind date—it was a business transaction. The customers got to choose, and the pretty one soon gave signs that she'd chosen me. Iván didn't even blink—indeed, anyone might have thought he found the barge absolutely fascinating, that he's always had a thing for Valkyries.

We went for dinner at a tapas bar. According to Iván, tapas dinners foster conversation, plus foreigners' favorite thing about Spain is the tapas. I quickly realized the Russians were hard to talk to. They didn't smile, didn't try to be pleasant, spoke only in their language, and made absolutely no effort to foster anything resembling mutual understanding. They talked mainly to each other in a harsh Russian full of *n*s that sounded like *ny*s. Sometimes they cracked up laughing. They barely looked at us. I got the sense something was wrong—maybe they regretted their decision and no longer wished to spend the evening in male company. I remarked on it to Iván, who was still calmly eating and drinking.

"No way, man, they don't regret a thing."

"Should we leave, Iván?"

"You think we should take off? You're nuts! No way, this is going great. Russian chicks are weird, man, they do their own thing."

Take off right in the middle of the fun? The guy's totally nuts. He worries me, to be honest—if he makes a break for it, I'll kill him. Who knows where he comes up with these ideas.

What did he think, that the Russians were going to greet us with kisses and gift us sets of nesting dolls? Right from the start, I could tell these women are rich and don't put up with anybody's bullshit. But what the hell do we care? The name of this movie is *Take the Money and Run*—nothing else matters. Maybe the teacher will finally get it into his head that this is just a damn job.

After dinner we went out for drinks. They ordered vodka. After that, the ice started to break a little. They showed us how vodka is drunk in Russia. The barge stood up, knocked back the contents of her glass, got up on her tiptoes, and then let her heels thump back to the floor.

"Shit, man!" said Iván. "That way the alcohol goes down faster. Russians really know where it's at!"

He immediately aped the maneuver, his movements parodically exaggerated, and for the first time the girls laughed along with us. There was more laughter, more toasting, more military thumping of heels. We emptied one bottle of vodka, and midway through the second I realized I was drunk. Iván said at last, "These ladies are sponges, teach—they drink like fish. I think that's enough. If we keep going, there's no way I'll be able to get it up. It's time to go."

He turned to them and started loudly repeating, "Hotel! Hotel!"

I'd have preferred him not to yell quite so loudly, since there were other people in the bar. The girls looked at each other, said something, laughed, and stood up. The barge paid the bill and we went out into the damp night. We headed to their hotel on foot, with them walking up ahead of us. It didn't seem like the alcohol had affected them much. My head was clearing a little in the fresh air.

Before we entered the luxury hotel where they were staying, Iván took the arm of his presumed partner and murmured discreetly in her ear. I wondered what language he was using. Whatever it was, she understood, put her hand in her purse, and pulled out a wad of bills that she must have had ready because she didn't count them. Iván did count them, with astonishing swiftness. He smiled, nodded. It must have been the right amount. I wondered what I would have done if he wasn't there. Everything had taken place far from my sight: the contact, the arranging of a price, the choice of places to eat and drink, the agreement to pay us in advance. Iván had taken care of the ugliest, most sordid bit, but I, seemingly without being aware of anything, had been fundamentally complicit. And yet I was still thinking of him as being my corrupter, as if it were his fault that I was debasing myself. In the full flush of the sentimental phase of my bender, I felt like crying. Iván was helping me, benefiting me—he'd taken me in, offered me access to the means of subsistence he knew. What would have become of me if he hadn't thrown me that crude, highly charged lifesaver? Where would I be, sleeping on a park bench? Why did Iván like me so much? I recalled some lines from a Lope de Vega poem: "What do I have that you should seek my friendship? What do you hope to gain, dear Jesus, that at my door, glazed with dew, you spend the dark winter nights?" Clearly, I was still plastered.

The fateful moment arrived. My Russian, who was gorgeous, shut the door of the room behind her and gave me a come-hither look. What was I supposed to do? I'm no idiot, I know what generally happens when you hook up with a girl, but this was different—it was a professional interaction. Maybe there were required prefatory procedures that I wasn't aware of or details that I should avoid at all cost. I'd been too embarrassed, of course, to ask Iván about protocol. Plus, I would have run the risk of being the object of his merciless teasing. No, I'd have to figure this out on my own. With a little luck, if the girl was used to this kind of arrangement, she'd take the initiative and I'd just go with it. Otherwise, I'd have to come up with a strategy, and I hadn't devised one in advance. How should I act—as if we'd met and been attracted to each other by chance, or did she expect me to behave all macho and dominant and controlling?

I was so motionless and lost in thought that she snapped her fingers in front of my nose. Then she made a gesture signaling a shower, waving her hands above her head and imitating the noise of flowing water. I nodded and went to sit on the bed to wait for her, but I had misunderstood—I was the one who was supposed to shower. I felt deeply humiliated: did she think I was dirty, was she afraid she'd catch some kind of disease? She grabbed me by the arm and pushed me firmly toward the bathroom. I was ready to put my jacket back on and leave the room, but I refrained. I'd gotten to this position by overcoming a lot of prejudices, and now wasn't the time to quit. Plus, having paid us in advance, the Russians might start arguing with Iván, and the last thing I wanted was to hurt my partner.

I came out of the bathroom wearing one of the hotel robes. The Russian was lying naked on the bed. She was flipping through a city guide I'd seen lying on the nightstand when I entered. She looked at me and gestured for me to get undressed. I obeyed. She smiled and opened her arms, murmuring. She was

234 · ALICIA GIMÉNEZ-BARTLETT

beautiful, as beautiful as a woman in a painting. The white expanse of her flesh, her slender body, her lips . . . I felt a wild desire—it had been so long since I'd been with a woman. I pulled out the condom I'd brought, went over, and started kissing her thighs, but she pulled at me impatiently. She wasn't interested in foreplay, just fucking. She pushed my cock into her and started to pant. I managed to hold out a good while. At that moment I loved her passionately.

I think I did a good job. When she fell asleep, I left.

\* \* \*

Well, would you look at the teacher! I knew he could do it! Just three months in, and he's already been able to rent his own apartment. It's not as cool as mine, but it's pretty nice: fully equipped kitchen, a living room that's about 300 square feet, a bathroom with a rainfall shower . . . and in a decent neighborhood, not one of those awful slums full of Arabs and blacks he was looking at when he was flat broke.

He left my house, of course. I helped him with the minimove and loading up the books. He could finally have them on shelves and look at them every day like pirate treasure! The first thing he did was hire a carpenter to install bookcases. Apparently that was what he cared about most: arranging his Raskolnikovs. Holy hell! I don't have a problem with it, though. To each his own.

I haven't asked him anything about his on-the-clock screws. I gave it a try the first few times, and he didn't seem to take it well. So I zipped my lip, and that was that. Anyway, it's not like I'm dying to know how he gets on with the ladies—well, maybe just a little bit. Maybe he gives lectures or writes poetry to get them hot. Whatever he does, it seems like it's working. Some women request him, looking for him and no one else. OK, right on. It also seems like his conscience is no longer pricking him. He must be worried about other things now, though. The other day we were hanging out having a beer and I told him:

"Things are really going awesome for you, man. If you keep it up, pretty soon you'll be able to think about buying a car and designer clothes."

"Listen, Iván," he responded, "I already have what I needed: money to live on and a place of my own. I'm not planning to earn more money. If they came to me today and offered me my old classes back for the same or even less money, I wouldn't think twice. I'd drop all of this and be a teacher again. You get it, right?"

"Yeah, I get it."

But I didn't get it, and I still don't. As a teacher, he didn't earn even close to the money he makes now. He got by thanks to his girlfriend's salary, in a crappy little apartment. Not to mention all the work: how many hours did he have to spend in class with those kids to make what he makes now just working weekends at the club and going out a couple of times during the week? Plus, it doesn't seem like he's actually looking for work as a teacher. The truth is it sounds good to say you're doing this because you have to, but no, actually you're doing it because it's a good living, and everybody wants a good living. Of course some people do it out of need—a kid doesn't grow up dreaming of becoming an escort—but once you've tasted the good life, you don't go back. And anyone who tells you otherwise just wants to be a saint—and nobody's more of a saint than I am. I'm Saint Iván himself.

In any case, the teacher's a huge success. He sure did keep it under his hat, the bastard! He must be dynamite in the sack. He probably goes at it all polite, and the ladies love that: "Would you most kindly grant me your permission to fuck you, your ladyship?" Holy hell! Maybe he tells them all they're the most amazing dames he's ever met in his life and talks to them about love. Speaking of which, I have to warn Javier never to use that word. In the heat of the moment, it's OK to say, "I really like you," but no love talk. You never know with women—they read romance novels and watch movies, so they take it super seriously and can really get you in trouble. It happened to me once with this chick who was more loaded than a dump truck. I never said anything to her about love, but she got all hung up on me. She hired me every week. She started telling me about how she was a widow, didn't have any children, and was really lonely. One day she goes and asks me how much she'd have to pay me to get my services exclusively so I wouldn't go out with any other broads. I dodged the question and gradually started pulling back from her. Sometimes I'd tell her I didn't have room in my schedule to see her. I didn't want to be straight with her because I was afraid she'd make a stink and then the word would get out and scare off my other customers. She didn't have my cell number—I don't give it to anybody—but she'd been to my apartment a few times to screw. I really fucked up there—she would wait out on the street at night for me to come home. One day I had to tell her that if she did it again, I'd call the police. She stopped for a while, but then started up again. One night she invites me to have dinner at a hotel, and then plunks down a sheaf of papers in the middle of the table. It was the list of her assets! A house in Mallorca, a downtown apartment, money in the bank, and the pension she inherited when her husband kicked it. She tells me she can't live without me, asks me to move in with her, says everything she owned would be mine if I said yes, swears up and down we'd be as happy as clams. Shit, what a mess! I got up and scrammed without even saying goodbye—maybe she'd figure out how this story went. The next night—at three in the damn morning—I find her waiting at my door. I went up to her and said right in her face, "Look, lady, I don't like you, you're not my type, and you can shove your money you know

where—maybe it'll give you a little thrill." "But I love you!"
the bitch answers, like she doesn't understand Spanish or
something. So then I really did give her a slap that knocked her
over. She was shocked, the cunt—as if she hadn't deserved it.
She started crying hysterically and ran off. I never saw her
again, but it was a real pain in the ass to get rid of her. Some
people might say it was a dumb move because she was so filthy
rich, but I go through life a free agent, and that's not going to
change. Anyway, these broads get demanding after a while. At
first everything's great, but then they start wanting to control
you: where are you going? Who are you calling? What do you
want the money for? It happened to a buddy of mine, and he
ended up getting sick and tired of the lady. Anyway, that's life,
but I've got to warn the teacher so he doesn't get tangled up in
any drama.

Only trouble is, Javier doesn't want to go to these places on
his own—he always asks for the two of us to go together. So he
misses out on work opportunities because there's not always a
need for two guys at once. But between parties, showers, and
tourists, we do OK. It's cool to have him with me when they
ask for two. Actually, it's awesome, because he adds some class.
He's calm, sophisticated, polite. When we arrive, we seem
more like the guests of honor than like two guys who've been
hired to strip or screw. But I still think he's going to have to go
on his own at some point. It'll happen when his wallet starts
itching, you'll see—he can save that bullshit about not needing
any more money for somebody else, because I don't buy it.
Once you get started, the more you make, the better. After a
while you start thinking about having a car, getting better furniture, dressing nicer. And for vacation you'll want to go to the
beach, since nobody sticks around in the city because of the
heat. Not to mention blow, which I'm not supplying anymore.
The truth is I've done a lot for the guy, but I don't regret it.
He's appreciative and dependable, and there are some things

about him that really surprise you. The other day he goes and gives me a gift. He bought me a bonsai. Holy hell, a bonsai! As if I were the sort of guy who had plants and took care of shit. I've got it there in the little window in my kitchen. It's looking pretty sad, since I totally neglect it. But it was nice—him giving me a bonsai means he thinks highly of me, doesn't consider me a clod who's only happy if you buy him soccer cleats.

Anyway, the important thing is he's on track, and any day now he'll be ready to fly solo. He doesn't spend his days whining about how he doesn't have a job and society doesn't need him. Plus he's shed of that awful girlfriend of his, who just wanted to control him. His life has changed—he's not a loser anymore. It's obvious he's going to end up lapping me—girls really like him.

* * *

"Oh, listen, you're going to love him! I've gone out with him a couple of times and he's great. Very funny, totally uninhibited. And he looks like a real man too! Of course, it's not like he's a *gentleman* or anything, but he says things sometimes that are unexpected and witty, and they make me laugh. I'd rather have that than your standard pretty boy who plays the urbane sophisticate and tells you some whopper about his Harvard degree. He'll show you a good time . . . plus he's very skilled in the things he needs to be skilled in. In the end, sweetie, a woman just needs to have a little fun—someone who recharges your batteries, makes your problems go away, makes you laugh. In *Vogue* the other day there was this survey about what women today value in men. I've read a ton of those surveys over the years, and the things that were always valued before were things like 'He makes me feel safe, he's considerate of my needs, he's affectionate.' But times have changed, and the characteristic that trounced all the others in *Vogue* was

'He has a great sense of humor and makes me laugh.' The thing is, women have changed a lot. These days you feel safe because of the money you have in the bank. You look out for your own needs, and affection . . . you only take it in occasional doses, since in excess it can be suffocating, makes you want to take off to the ends of the earth all by yourself. But having someone who makes you laugh is another issue. The world we live in is so grim and depressing: climate change, endangered species, impoverished children in Africa, recession . . . please, enough already! As if there were some way to fix any of that. I do what I can already: I don't waste water, I turn off all the lights before going to bed, I'm on the board of an NGO . . . Just lay off already, let me enjoy life a little—it's way too short! You get what I'm saying, right, Irene?"

"Of course, Genoveva, of course."

I do get it, but what I don't get is what the heck it has to do with me or where my friend's going, trying to sell me on this nonsense—just because she's met a wonderful guy who makes her laugh doesn't mean she's got an identical one ready for me. And I have to say the last few times we've gone out have been a little frustrating. She probably chooses the kind of guy she's into and then requests another one for me without getting into any specifics. They just have to get undressed, so really anyone will do. But the last few times, the guys have been real bores. Nice bodies, sure, but kind of boorish, pure gym flesh. Plus, since they know the only thing I want is a little show, they spend most of the time doing poses that range from comical to pathetic. I've sometimes wondered whether I'd have a better time of it if I just signed up for a painting class and ogled the nude models. The only thing I'd be missing is the sense of power I have now when I tell them, "Sit down, spread your legs, don't smile, get dressed and go because I've had enough for today."

"Well, I'm telling you about the guy because I have a plan."

"Another one of our nights out?"

"Oh, Irene, sweetie, Jesus! You say it as if I were talking about a funeral, not a night on the town."

"Don't take it the wrong way; I just want to know if there's anything new to the plan."

"Well, yes, listen, yes there is! This guy I'm telling you about works at a male strip club."

"I didn't know there was such a thing."

"Right here in the city. Don't picture a regular club like the ones women dance in—this is just a bit of fun. Girls go there for their bachelorette parties; groups of women go to celebrate divorces. The clientele isn't exactly sophisticated—you know, secretaries, cleaning ladies, that sort of thing—but if we don't take it too seriously we could have a great time. I'm thinking we can go on Saturday and have dinner with the guys afterward."

"What guys?"

"The fun guy I was telling you about is named Iván, and he has a friend—the two of them always work together."

"Look, Genoveva, if you haven't even met the friend, I think it would be better . . . "

"Can you hang on a minute? You're just impossible today, honey! Apparently the friend is the cat's pajamas too—handsome, courteous, an unemployed literature teacher who's doing this kind of work as a temporary thing."

"Really?"

Oh, sure, literature teacher, loves painting, goes to the opera every Sunday. I've heard it all before.

"Yes, and this time it seems like it's true."

"How do you know?"

"From the way Iván said it."

"Right."

"Please drop that tone, Irene! Anyway, you don't have anything to lose by just taking a look! He works at the same club as Iván. We're going to see the show on Saturday. Then we'll get a drink with the guys, and you can decide there whether to move forward. No obligation whatsoever. I'll tell Iván your participation is conditional. All right?"

"OK, I guess that's all right."

"I'll call back to give you the time and place."

Unbelievable! This child is really starting to get on my nerves! And with everything I've done for her! She gets more bitter and rude every day. It's been a while since her husband left her at this point—she could pull herself together. Plus, she does whatever she feels like and no one's looking over her shoulder. She's got money. So what more does she want? To get married again? When I suggested I could introduce her to eligible guys, she started shrieking like a hyena and told me she had absolutely no interest in romance. I don't get her, to be honest. As far as I'm concerned, she can keep acting like a spoiled child and things won't end well. You have to be clear on a couple of things in life, just a couple, and I don't see her making an effort to identify what's most important. At any rate, I hope at least she doesn't ruin Saturday night for me. I'm looking forward to going to a dive, seeing new things . . . but I'm not like her—I get excited about things, I'm looking for stimulation. Hell, that's the least you can do if you want to keep from blowing your brains out.

\* \* \*

I hope he puts some real energy into shaking his ass tonight, because we've got visitors. Two broads are coming to see the show, and then we're hooking up afterward. They're not tourists and there's no party involved. They're locals, and they're both loaded. And I think if it goes well they'll be repeat customers at least for a few months. I hope this dude gets his act together, because they want a second. They're total upper-crusties, so they'll love a well-mannered prof type.

"They're super posh—mine's named Genoveva. Genoveva, shit! It sounds like a princess's name, like somebody important. She's getting up there in years, but she takes care of herself and must have a boatload of Botox, so she's not too bad. The important thing is she's a wild one. She's looking to let loose, has a sense of humor—the other day we were busting up laughing. She's obviously been in the air longer than a peregrine falcon, those ones they're always rattling on about how endangered they are. But she's a straightforward bird—there aren't going to be any complications or misunderstandings with her."

"And what does this have to do with me, Iván?"

"Hang on a minute, man, let me finish."

He's already glowering—Jesus, we're off to a great start. It would be nice if he figured out that I'm the one who needs him this time, that sometimes you have to do your friends a solid. I bust my ass looking for good opportunities for him, making sure the little prude doesn't feel defiled, and now he might go and tell me to deal with them on my own. As if these upperclass broads give a shit who you are anyway. They spend the evening with you, have a screw, and ciao. After that you disappear from their heads and they never think of you again. Plus, I don't understand this crap about how he doesn't want to go with Spanish women. He says it gets him down to talk to them, makes him feel like a real prostitute. The hell with this prostitute crap—as if that means anything!

"The thing is, Genoveva—if that's even her real name—has this friend who's shy and she wants to take her out partying. But the two of them have to go out together with two guys—if not, there's no deal. That's the lay of the lay."

"But you know I don't want to go there, Iván. Foreigners and parties are fine, but . . . "

"Hang on a minute! None of what I've said about Genoveva applies to the other one. She's a lot younger. She split up with her husband not long ago. She's got a lot of money and not a lot of life experience—she hasn't been around a single block. You could say she's a virgin with this kind of thing."

"What difference does that make? That makes it even worse."

"Goddammit, Javier, stop interrupting me! I'm trying to tell you this hen isn't looking for cock."

"What do you mean?"

"Just what I said—she isn't into fucking. She wants to see the guy naked, look at him a while, and that's it. But she pays the same—and I assure you she'll pay well."

"I don't get it."

"It's not that complicated, man—are you sure you're a teacher? She's not interested in screwing. She probably has her reasons: maybe she's going through a terrible depression, or maybe she's dealing with a childhood trauma and that's why she split up with her husband, because he wanted to screw properly, or maybe she's got some disease down there . . . What the hell do I know! That's not the point."

Why the hell does the guy want to know why the poor woman doesn't screw? Let's say she doesn't like cock and leave it at that! He can just lie there buck naked for a while until the chick gets tired of looking at him and kicks him out. Then he takes the money, takes off, and the hell with it! What difference does it make why she doesn't want to fuck? I guess it's possible she's a total pervert and not a shy little dove, but I'm not about to tell this moron that—he'll freak out and drop dead right here. And even if she is a pervert who'll go home afterward and screw a ram she keeps in the backyard, what the hell do you care?

"I just don't get it, seriously."

"All right, well, I'll tell Genoveva it's conditional and we'll at least have dinner with them. You take a look and then decide. If you have any doubts, you can give an excuse and take off."

"That's mean, Iván—it would be better to just take a pass."

"Better? It's better to hang me out to dry, make me lose out on a good gig? Thanks a lot, man, seriously! I thought you were my friend, but it's clear the only thing you care about is your own hang-ups, and the hell with me, is that it?"

"Please don't be like that. We agreed from the start that I wouldn't go out with Spanish women."

"Wow, man, that's great! And who do you think you are, the pope? You say something once, and it goes for life? Go to hell, Javier—you're going to screw me out of good business because you don't feel like getting naked in front of a chick. But whatever you say, man, whatever you say. I'm leaving—I've got to run. Bye."

I went home, cursing to myself, without giving him time to say another word. Half an hour later, he was already calling me on the phone—yes, he'd do it, I could count on him, he'd do it. I said thanks. I'd figured that would happen.

\* \* \*

In the beginning, when I'd put on the ridiculous little schoolboy smock for the show, I'd try to avoid catching sight of myself in any reflective surface. Now I don't care anymore, though I'd still rather not come face to face with a mirror. Hence my lack of enthusiasm about today's plan—the damn smock is ridiculous whether I can see myself in it or not, and I know the women we're meeting were watching me in it when I was dancing. Even if I try to make a joke out of it, I still find it humiliating. But how could I refuse? Iván was furious, and I guess he was right: I can't keep tiptoeing around this. Plus, I need the money. I have to keep paying for this life I've set up, which is my life now. Though sometimes I wake up with a start in the middle of the night, thinking it's all just a dream. But no, this is my life now. Sometimes it doesn't even seem real that I ever had another one where I did the things normal people do. That really makes me upset, and I can only shake myself out of it by getting up and going to the living room. I survey the shelves of books, the computer in one corner, the wing chair with an ottoman in front of it that props my legs up while I read. Then I usually go to the kitchen and make myself a cup of warm milk. The refrigerator purrs gently. It's nice. It's my home. I don't have to steal or kill or exploit anybody to keep it. Everything's fine. I go back to bed and fall asleep.

Today there's a festive air in the dressing area. It happens sometimes, for no real reason. The guys tell jokes and slap each other on the back, roughhouse a little, chase each other around the room. Even the owner seems to be in a good mood, rolling his eyes heavenward in an exaggerated display of the patience required to put up with their antics. When the show starts and it's my turn, I dance as usual. I know all the moves by heart, and I always try to perform them the same way. The other day I heard the owner say he wanted to change up the show a little. We'll see what Shakespearean character I'll have to play this time. I don't have a preference, but if the changes get me into a less ludicrous costume, that would be great.

The room is packed. There's not a single table free. When my number's over, I wait patiently for the others to finish. Mariano, the owner, ends the show as usual. He must be totally coked up today, because he's really going for broke: compulsive movements, pure alpha male. He's coarser and more arrogant than other times. He's given his all for his audience, as he says. I've managed to keep from thinking about how, out there in that ferocious, shrieking audience, there's a little dove waiting for me. The line I did has helped. I feel so good, I even know how I'm going to act when I'm face to face with the woman. I'll get to the hotel room and undress like I'm getting ready to put on my pajamas and go to bed after a long work-day. No affectations. If the chick's hoping I'm going to do lit-tle poses or show off my body like Superman, she's in for a dis-appointment. The only problem will be if she gives me orders: spread this, hold that, lie down like this. I'll tell her that wasn't part of the deal—I'll refuse. She wants to see a naked man, and that's exactly what she's going to get. Though I admit I am curi-ous to meet a woman with those sexual predilections.

\* \* \*

I never imagined a place like this actually existed: large, rundown, kitschy décor. I'm surprised it hasn't become trendy with the beautiful people. I have to admit Genoveva's right—it seems like a fun plan. There aren't many men in the audi-ence—it's mostly women between the ages of about twenty and fifty. Some look just like the girls who work in the factory. They're all really done up: tons of makeup, lots of eyeshadow, colored highlights in their hair—appalling. And their clothing! Miniskirts, sequined T-shirts, tight pants, dizzyingly plunging necklines. They're in teetering heels, of course, and when they walk it seems like they're going to fall over at any moment. Looking at them, you could write an anti-style guide.

At the table next to us is a group of boisterous fifty-some-things. The waiter tells us they're celebrating because one of them is getting divorced. What an idea, to come here as a pub-lic demonstration that divorce is no big deal and you're feeling freer and happier than ever! I'd like to know the real story.

We were going to order gin and tonics, but the waiter told us there's only one brand of gin, so Genoveva orders a bottle of Moët & Chandon to avoid any surprises.

Suddenly the lights go out and the show begins. The MC is horrible—old, really dodgy. The first number takes place in a school. It seems humorous. Genoveva hisses to me that one of the guys is the one I'm going to meet later, but she doesn't know which one. I examine them all; they seem pretty normal. By the end they're all naked, with only a tiny pair of briefs covering their genitals. They look ridiculous, but they have nice bodies. It would be pretty much perfect if they were wearing hoods too—their smiles seem kind of pathetic. I can't see them all that well, but they're just a bunch of hicks. When they're done, the audience applauds wildly and the divorcing ladies shriek at the top of their lungs.

In the second number, that guy Iván comes out playing a sort of comical Zorro. If this whole show ends up being humorous and tongue-in-cheek, we're in trouble. I'm rarely amused by that sort of thing—comedy films, jokes, any of it. Genoveva's really excited, like a mom whose kids are performing in the school play. She laughs, cheers, finds Iván just hilarious.

"Isn't he a hunk?" she asks. "Did you see the way he moves? He's fantastic!"

"Fantastic, absolutely," I reply, and take a sip so she won't notice what I really think.

Is he a hunk? Well, he's a hunk of *something.* He's fit and muscular, but his hair is cut so short and he opens his eyes so wide that he seems retarded. You could also take him for a crazy person. Even naked, you can tell from a mile off that he's from the wrong side of the tracks. I don't know what Genoveva sees in him. She says he's funny. If the other guy, the literature teacher, is as funny as he is, the evening will be ending soon.

There are breaks between each number to encourage the audience to drink more, and the numbers are all fairly similar, so the show starts to drag. The only entertaining aspect is that the spectators are getting more and more riled up, and at the end of some performances the dancers come down off the stage and circulate among the tables. The women shriek, cat-call, reach out their hands to touch them. It all reminds me more of a schoolyard than of a real striptease.

Only at the end, almost the end, does something interesting happen. The MC, the horrible, dodgy, paunchy old man, sud-denly comes out to perform. When I saw him getting ready, I feared the worst—the ultimate caricature, a parody to top everything that preceded it. But no, I'm amazed to see him move with a provocative and sensual grace. Not like the oth-ers—he moves like he means it, as if that striptease were his life's work. His stocky body exhibits the ravages of age and hard living, but I can't take my eyes off him. He disgusts me and, at the same time, pulls me in. His dance is the only erotic thing I've seen today.

When he finishes, the harpies who spent the whole show howling, only shutting up once he started dancing, burst into enthusiastic applause. All right, not bad, but is it worth endur-ing the whole tedious show just for those last few minutes of reality? I doubt anyone who's seen it once would go back to see it again.

As the audience starts filing out, Genoveva orders another bottle of champagne and four glasses. "They'll be here soon," she says.

The light in the room is flat and harsh, unpleasant. Maybe to highlight the arrogant beauty of our companions.

"All right," I respond, on the verge of grumpy.

* * *

"You were awesome, boys, both of you! The shows in Las Vegas don't have anything on this one. I loved it! So, Iván, are you going to introduce your friend?"

He's gorgeous today—it must be the adrenaline of the per-formance. He's got a riffraff vibe that I love. It's too bad he showered—he must be even hunkier when he's flushed and sweaty from exertion. It doesn't matter, though. I'll make him sweat later. Jesus Christ, what's wrong with me? Genoveva, control yourself!

"This is Javier."

"And this is my friend Irene. She really liked your dancing too."

"So you liked it, ladies. It's a sweet show, huh?"

Shit, they've ordered Moët! Awesome! There's class and some good dough at this table. I already knew this Genoveva bird made the grade. There's enough for everybody here. And the other one? She's not bad, though she's dressed like my grandma and has a little smile on her face that could mean anything. I'm sure the teacher will like her, since she looks like a little girl who's being raised by nuns . . . though the bastard still hasn't opened his mouth. If he screws up this plan, he's going to hear about it, or my name's not Iván.

"We loved it, right, Irene?"

"It was very good."

"It was amazing."

Jesus, she's so bland! And I'm so nervous! These things revitalize me, remind me of when I was young and we girls used to go out as a group and they'd introduce you to new boys. But she's so dry! There she is with that grim little smile she always puts on when we're with other people. And she didn't even go that far during the show—it was like she was at a funeral, motionless as a statue! And me laughing the whole time! Iván's friend is handsome—he looks like an old-school college type, very polite. To be honest, he's nothing like Iván. I wonder why they're friends and how this guy ended up here. If Irene snubs him, I'm never going out with her again! I don't have the patience for spoiled little girls who think they deserve it all. Has she ever thanked me for all the arrangements I've made? Not once. Naturally, she's on this planet for other people to serve her and make her happy. But if she ruins the evening this time, there won't be another one.

"Have you thought about where you'd like to eat, Iván?"

"Why don't you decide? We're flexible."

I hope she takes us to one of those posh places they must go to—though really there's no way she will, on the off chance her snooty friends spot them with losers like us. And teacher is just sitting there, mute as a mummy. I could kill him! Of course, Genoveva's friend doesn't seem to be all that into it either, though she is giving him sidelong glances with a greedy look on her face. Maybe that's what chicks like about him, that he sits there the whole time keeping quiet and pretending to be interesting.

"I know a brasserie that would be perfect. Do you know what a brasserie is?"

"Yeah, it's where they brass you off."

"Oh, Iván, you're too funny! You crack me up!"

It's obvious that if the two of us don't get it on . . .

* * *

All right, we're in the home stretch. We're in the hotel room and she's right there. She needs to tell me what she wants from me, at least give me a hint—but no, she's inscrutable, impenetrable. She isn't acting at all like a little dove. She brought me here without the slightest show of embarrassment or shame. She made all the arrangements at the hotel reception desk with the utmost confidence. She's no dove, but I have no idea what kind of bird she is. Her friend Genoveva is easy to classify—she reminds me of some of the mothers of the students at my school. She's older, probably about fifty-five. She speaks with that affected casual tone of the well-to-do. She's tiresome, shallow. She couldn't wait to take off with Iván even though that meant leaving me alone with this girl. This girl. There's nothing extraordinary about her, but she's not anodyne. Her eyes transmit an inner strength. She hasn't said a word all night. She doesn't smile. Anyone would say she's doing this out of obligation, though that's a ludicrous idea. She must be sad about something—but that's not my problem. My only problem right now is figuring out what she wants me to do.

"Get undressed, please," I tell him.

I can see he's started getting nervous. They all react the same way, feeling awkward until they're sure of what I want from them. In other respects, though, this one seems different: he's not dressed like a lowlife, he's reserved, he doesn't say much and says it quietly, he takes off his clothes slowly and neatly. The others always toss them brusquely to the floor as if they were pissed off. It pisses them off to have to strip naked with you sitting there, not moving, just watching them.

And then he's naked. He's lanky, not at all ugly. He's got a normal body—he hasn't gotten all buff at the gym. Not much hair. A large penis, but it's not erect.

"Now what?" he asks.

"Now nothing."

"All right. I'll stay just like this."

Fine, I'll stay right here—though I would like to know what the nub of this all is, how this sexual conduct is described in the user's manuals. Static voyeurism? Staring at a naked guy. Maybe it should make me uncomfortable, but I just feel ridiculous.

"Aren't you going to get undressed?" I ask.

She opens her eyes wide. How dare I speak to the goddess?

"No."

"Why not?"

"Because I don't feel like it."

What does this guy think? That we're pals, that we're spending some time together as friends? It's not too late to kick him out.

"This all seems really weird to me."

Nobody's told me to keep quiet, and I'm feeling muti-nous—I'm not a doll in a store window.

"That's not your concern."

"Depends how you look at it. We're about the same age. We're in the same room, but I'm naked and you're dressed. I'd like to know why."

"Because I'm paying you and I'm the one who decides what happens next."

Because she's paying me, of course. The two of us are here, ludicrously motionless, because she's paying me. Her dressed, and me buck naked. It was a mistake to come here, an absurd mistake, and I should have known it. They pay me to waggle my ass in a crappy show. They pay me to fuck. And I do it—I do all of it and then charge afterward—but no snooty little girl is going to have me at her service just to humiliate me.

"I'm sorry, but I think it was a mistake to come here, a sim-ple misunderstanding. I'm going to get dressed and go. Don't worry about the money—consider my time a gift."

"Didn't they tell you what you'd be doing?"

"It doesn't matter, seriously. It's not worth talking about it any further. It's been a pleasure. If you tell me how much din-ner cost, I'll pay my part and then we'll be square."

"We're already square. Dinner was my treat."

"Well, thank you very much. Good night."

He got dressed and left. He shook my hand goodbye! Who is this guy? What was it about the situation that he couldn't bear? Maybe he doesn't do this professionally? Maybe it was his first time? But he's a stripper at the club! He was probably expecting me to succumb to his charms once I saw him: "Oh, baby! I want you so badly! Take me, please!" Idiot! A total waste of time.

\* \* \*

"So it didn't go well. So what? Come on, man, you're a fucking stud! The grand dame just called me—they want to go out with us again. Both of them! It hasn't even been a week, and I can tell you these arrangements don't tend to go for a second round. Irene's the one who's requested a replay—it's not that Genoveva's wild about me. These broads who've got their lives all sorted out don't get hung up on some lowlife— or anybody, for that matter! They're living it up, and relation- ships would just create complications! These birds don't feel trapped or lonely—they do their own thing. I don't know if Genoveva has any grandchildren, and I'm not about to ask; I don't want to get her all upset over the age thing. But I've been doing this a while, so I've met a few ladies who show you pho- tos of their grandkids after you screw. Holy hell! And they're so goddamn satisfied. That's because you don't count—you exist for as long as the two of you spend in the sack, and that's it. They're free as a bird, man—they don't give a rip about any- thing. Money gives you freedom—you can just buy it off the shelf, man. 'Give me ten pounds of freedom,' and they fucking giftwrap it for you."

He gives me a look that says, "That's not my thing." The hell with the teacher! He's such a pain in the ass, goddamn weird. Just when you think you've got the hang of him, he comes out with something totally unexpected. There's no get- ting anywhere with him. It's like he still doesn't get that these are the things you do for money so you can have your nice apartment and all the rest. I'd like to know what happened the other day with Irene. Sure, the chick seems kind of prissy, but if it's true what he says, the only problem was his own hang- ups. "I can't take getting undressed and having her just sitting there, fully clothed, looking at me like a zoo animal. She just wants to humiliate whatever guy is there in front of her, and I have my dignity." When he said that about his dignity, I got pretty pissed. Does he think he's the only one with dignity, and I don't have any? I've got it just like everybody else, damn it. But if you're a guy trying to make ends meet, you have to just close your eyes and put up with a lot. Plus, we're just talking about getting undressed here—being in your birthday suit. He's got to stop being so squeamish, because life's a bitch. I've had to do a lot of things I really didn't want to: having some awful, raunchy chick slap me on the ass, rimming a couple of nasty fifty-somethings. But that's the business. Every job has its downsides—or does he imagine it's a fucking joy to wake up every day at six in the morning, get on the subway, change lines twice, and clock in at the factory at eight so you can spend the whole day locked up in there like a goddamn prisoner? Come on, man! And then live in a goddamn hovel on four euros a day. If you think about all that, it puts dignity in perspective pretty quickly. Plus, the teacher should already know that chicks are filthy and impulsive, even poor ones. Why does he think I won't commit to anybody? And then on top of it, he doesn't even charge the broad. The guy's a real piece of work, seriously.

"Look, Iván, I don't want you to be mad, but I don't think I'm going to go this time."

"Listen, Javier, we've been lucky so far and you've been able to pick and choose: a private party here, a couple of tourists there . . . but we're heading into winter now, so there's not so much tourism, not so many parties. If you start with this bullshit, you're going to end up dead-ass broke and not even be able to make your rent. And then what will you do, turn back? Is that what you want?"

"No, of course not."

"Well then, man, be responsible and come with me."

I burst into laughter. His solemn invocation of responsibility seemed hilarious coming from him and applied to such circumstances. The sound of my own laughter made me realize I was making a mountain out of a tiny molehill. Iván was right. I pondered: it wasn't that I was especially protective of my dignity. Maybe I'd just been annoyed by that cold, contemptuous woman. My reaction was unsettlingly like that of the typical macho Spanish male. And of course—and it was here that Iván's reasoning was most persuasive—I was going to have to pay my rent, eat, buy books, get dressed, pay for those lines of coke I was snorting more and more often, and which gave me the strength to keep going.

"Let's make a deal. I'll go to the next appointment, and you promise to finish reading *Crime and Punishment*."

"Shit, teach, you're a real brain-teaser! But OK, it's a deal. I'll finish that punishment business, though you're more than enough punishment for me. What do I need fucking Raskolnikov for when you're around?"

Who knows what the hell goes through this dude's head. Definitely not me. Here he is voluntarily changing his mind. Maybe he set this up just to get that chick all hot to trot. Everybody knows chicks are all about having a good time, and when you mess with them they come slinking back with their tail between their legs, begging for more. Is the teacher that devious? Maybe so.

* * *

The room isn't the same one we were in the other day—we aren't even in the same hotel. I had a lot to drink at dinner. I'd glance over at her from time to time, briefly, against my will. She always looked the same: serene, mostly quiet, barely smiling. Iván and her friend were taking care of the carousing: jokes, laughter, toasts . . . I tried not to reveal my curiosity.

Now I'm here with her, animated by booze and coke, firmly

resolved to do what I have to do without making a big deal about it. She's wearing a black pantsuit, a scarf knotted at her neck. She's elegant—a bourgeois sort of elegance, unimaginative. What is it that's brought her to this room? Why is she doing this? I remove my pants. I shrug off my sweater. I stand there. I look at her.

"I'll just do the usual, ma'am?"

"Yes," she says tersely.

Either she found my irony too on the nose or she has no sense of humor.

I casually finish getting undressed, making no effort to be sexy. She watches me, expressionless. Good poker face. I ask, "Do you want me to sit down, or should I stay standing?"

"Sit in that chair. Pull it in front of me. Not there, farther back."

"Great, I'm a little tired."

"Spread your legs, please."

Here he is, sitting naked in front of me. I wonder how I can have become suddenly so uninhibited, how I'm able to play this game so calmly, so coolly. With the other men I found it more difficult, but not with this one. I am aware of his shame, his nervousness, his discomfort, and that reaffirms me.

It's strange—I've spent the whole week thinking about this man. I had the feeling he was a fantasy, an unreal being, as if my memory of him had been a sort of hallucination. But no, he's just as I found him the first time: slender, not very muscular, with a boyish quality. He doesn't at all seem like the kind of guy you rent by the hour, paired up with that bum Genoveva's so crazy about. His reaction the other day was odd: in high dudgeon like your classic Spanish gentleman. He left without taking my money, indignant and dignified. He doesn't fit into any of the categories of men I expected to encounter in this underworld. I always imagined immigrants with hardened faces, marginal people who spend their earnings on drugs, hustlers who've learned to live off of women because they don't want to work. What box can I put him in? At first I was angry about his reaction the other day, but afterward I felt curious enough to ask Genoveva to set up another date. And here he is again, naked in front of me. I thought he wouldn't come, but here he is.

Today he's changed his strategy. He's ready to fulfill his obligations without a murmur, but his attitude is the same: defiant, irritated, rebellious, as if he were demanding an explanation for why I'd hired him. He can't possibly behave like this with all the women who request his services. So what's going on? Is he angry with me? Is there something about me that drives him crazy? Regardless, I've made him get undressed and sit just the way I want him. He's got to understand that I'm the one in control here.

"You're not going to ask me to get undressed too this time?"

I'd sworn to myself that if she said anything to me, I'd respond with vague statements or giggles. But I'm an idiot, and as soon as she opened her mouth, that was that. I was even grateful she'd spoken!

"I didn't ask you to get undressed."

"You certainly insinuated it."

"You want to know the truth?"

"All right."

"It seems ridiculous to be naked in front of a woman who's fully clothed."

"And if I were naked too, it would seem less ridiculous?"

"Look, seriously, this whole thing is absurd: me sitting here, whether naked or dressed, and you there looking at me. It's not just absurd, actually. It's crap. So don't ask me anything or make me talk. When you get bored, I'll get dressed, you pay me, and I'll leave."

I'm sitting on the bed, and I stand up. I start getting

undressed. I didn't think I was capable of such a thing, and I don't know why I'm doing it, but I am. I'm calm; I feel relaxed. I don't pay attention to him while taking off my clothes, but when I'm done I see he's watching me, disconcerted. He's not smiling—he's still got that expression of an angry, self-righteous little boy. Now naked, I sit back down. He closes his legs. I let him do what he wants.

"Better?" I say.

"Yes."

This chick's making me nervous. She really has gone off the rails now. What does she want from me?

"Why do you do this, Javier?"

"What do you think?"

"For the money?"

"Of course I do it for the money!"

"You don't seem like the kind of guy who does this sort of thing because he's broke and doesn't have another option."

"Well, I am. People who have money are always surprised to find that other people don't have it."

"And do you enjoy it?"

"No, no way, not at all. I hate it. I'm a literature teacher, you know? That's my real profession. But I got laid off from the convent school where I was working, and this allows me to make enough to live on until I find another job doing what I'm supposed to be doing."

The chick starts laughing. It's the first time I've seen her laugh or smile. I'm an even-keeled sort of guy, but right now I'd like to slap her. What's so funny, that they fired me?

"All the guys who do this say they've got intellectual jobs or really important jobs."

"I don't care. I am a teacher, and that was a really rude thing to say."

It's amusing that he's so ill-tempered. I get up and go to the minibar. It does take an effort to walk around naked in front of him, but I don't care too much as long as I'm in control of the situation. I pick up two glasses and pour a small bottle of sparkling wine, splitting it evenly.

"If we have a drink, maybe we'll stop arguing."

"Listen, Irene, I don't want to give you the impression I argue all the time. I imagine you've hired me to have a nice time, but to be honest, you don't make it easy for me."

"Drink."

I obey my customer and drink. I guess things are finally going to go back to normal: we'll have a drink, look at each other, kiss . . . I'm getting an erection, and I don't know whether to cover it up or just let everything flow, maybe it will all go as it should. But she's still imperturbable and silent, so I ask, "What about you? What do you do?"

"Me? I've been idling away for a while now. I don't feel like working."

"Are you going through a rough patch?"

"I don't feel like talking about myself either."

"Of course."

"Don't ask your customers personal questions. Isn't that right?"

"Who cares! We don't know each other, and we're not going to. We can talk and it won't matter a bit."

"You're right about that. I am going through a rough patch. I'm seeing a psychiatrist."

"Oh, wow!" Jesus, and now what do I say to her? "We all go through bad spells."

"Let's drop it. It's better if we don't talk."

"You're right."

I interpret her "better if we don't talk" as a signal, so I stand up and walk toward her. My intentions are obvious, but she doesn't move, doesn't bat an eye. I'm an inch from her and she still hasn't reacted at all. I notice how beautiful she is: intense red lips, shiny hair. She's got fantastic tits. I put my hand on her shoulder. I bend down to kiss her on the mouth.

"Please don't touch me. You can get dressed and leave now."

"Have I done something to upset you?"

"No. My head hurts. Thanks for coming."

His face has tensed in an expression that looks almost like pain. It seems like he really wanted me, but maybe he's such a professional that he's able to fake it perfectly. He gets dressed hastily, his back to me. He waves at me and turns to go. I call out to him:

"Javier, I didn't pay you!"

"Give the money to Genoveva when you see her. She'll pass it on to Iván. We always do it that way."

He's said that last bit with contempt, as if emphasizing that I'm just another customer. What a peculiar man.

Back at home, alone, my head is spinning with thoughts I should control, discard. In all the time that's passed since David and I split up—or, rather, since he left me—I haven't resolved a single problem that's come up in this new life. My work is hanging by a thread, with me unable to make any decisions. I go to the psychiatrist, but I never tell him anything important or follow his advice. He tells me over and over that I need to set up a daily routine. He harangues me about how I need to analyze my past so I can understand what happened. He thinks I'm an idiot. I don't need to analyze anything—I'm quite clear on what happened. I married a man who was interested in me only for the money, social position, and professional advancement I could offer. He didn't love me. He probably wasn't even attracted to me. When things started to go south, the man left. Full stop. It's easy to understand what happened. What I'm finding more complicated is figuring out why I want to see this guy again. Is he handsome? I don't know. I suppose that after the ones Genoveva's been introducing me too, he seems, quite simply, civilized. He belongs to an unfamiliar tribe. I'm sure we've never frequented the same places, even though we've been living in the same city for years.

That guy. Javier. I don't think he's lying. When he told me he was a teacher who'd lost his job, he was telling the truth. He's well spoken, cultured; it's obvious he's educated. I shouldn't be, but I'm curious. The next time we meet I'll try to get him to tell me a little about his life. Maybe if I know more about him, he'll stop haunting my mind like a ghost. Getting to know him better will confirm that he's like all the other men. Because he's doubtless no different. He relied on clichés: "People with money think," "I'm doing this because I have to." Clichés. If he were as pure as he pretends to be, he wouldn't dance at a strip club or sleep with women for money, and he definitely wouldn't be friends with a guy like Iván. A man like any other. The first thing he did when we were both naked was try to touch me. I shuddered. If he'd pushed it, I might even have called reception for help. But now I want to see him. I'm going to call.

"Genoveva? It's Irene. I just wanted to know if we're going out with those guys this week."

"Oh, no, sweetie! I can't this week. I'm going to a wedding in Marbella. My niece, my brother's daughter, is getting married. It's going to be such a drag! I've got to start thinking about my dress, my shoes . . . and the trip there! And since I have friends in Marbella, I'll be staying a few days longer, of course. If you want, I can give you Iván's number, and he can put you in touch with Javier and the two of you can go out."

"No, not the two of us alone, no. We'll go out next week."

"Irene, if I ask you something about that guy, will you get mad?"

"Almost certainly. Best not to ask."

* * *

How about that. Turns out he's taken a shine to the girl. Why else would he ask if Genoveva's called to set up another night out? And when I told him no, he got all pissy.

"Listen, Javier. You like Irene, right? I'm sure that whole business with having you stand there naked and not move is over now. I bet she's wild in the sack. That's awesome. What's not so awesome is the other stuff. If a chick comes to me and tells me to strip and that's it, I'll tell her to go to hell. Maybe once she'll get a pass, but twice . . . If she wants to look at statues, she can go to a museum. A screw is a screw, and a man is a man, and you can't screw around with men. Her making you stand there in the buff, as if she had nothing to do with it—it's like she's telling you, 'You ain't worth shit, man. I'd rather do it with a vibrator than sleep with you.'"

"Let's just drop it, Iván."

"All right, kid, it's none of my business, huh? I was just saying it in a general way, professionally speaking. But if you don't want to talk about it, we'll drop it."

And now what the hell's wrong with him? Maybe he thinks it isn't nice to discuss screwing your customers. I'm not the kind of guy who's always talking about what I do or don't do with women, but I don't hold back if there's something weird going on, and this Irene business is really weird. If I end up making out with a chick who's been acting like a goddamn holy virgin, that's unusual, right? It bears mentioning. But if he doesn't want to talk, I'll keep my mouth shut.

"Just drop it, Iván."

"It's dropped, man. Don't get mad—your blood pressure's going to go through the roof."

As far as I'm concerned, though, I can't stand this fucking Irene chick. And not because of what she does or doesn't want to do in the sack—I don't give a damn about that. What pisses me off is it seems like she looks down on everybody. She's stuck up, silent, with that good-girl vibe but always looking at you like you're a piece of shit and she's got to endure the smell. I've never put up with that crap from a chick—much less from a dude, of course. And I've been with chicks who had money coming out their ears, but as soon as they started acting superior, I was out of there. Because in bed, man . . . I'm the one in charge there, and they can ask for weird shit or make me suck whatever they want me to suck, but there's no way I'm letting them look at me like I'm a loser. No chick is going to reach for the sanitizer after touching me. I may not be educated, I may have to hustle for a living, but I'm nobody's inferior! No way! Plus, if a chick's paying to sleep with you, she's got to have something wrong with her, right? With guys it's different—the more they sleep around, the better. But women? Not having a dick available must be really sad. In Genoveva's case, it's kind of to be expected. She's getting up there, she's divorced, and she likes sex. What choice does she have? Hire a male escort— that's it. But she doesn't act like a goddamn princess! In fact, she's well aware her body is past its prime, and she doesn't just pay you, she thanks you for fooling around with her. She's grateful, goddammit, and horny. Now that's satisfying work. But if you get some snooty-ass prude, just take a pass, man— that's what I'd do. But I have no intention of telling the teacher any of this. Anyway, it works out better for me if things stay the way they are. The four of us go out as a group, I earn some money, and we're all good.

* * *

She's a strange woman. I like her eyes—they're strange too, cold, intense. I don't know what they're expressing. Something potent and unidentifiable, maybe despair. At first

I wasn't that into her, but I've gradually started finding her more and more beautiful, elegant, special. When she got undressed, I didn't want to stare at her too much. Given the situation, I have to be careful. I don't want her to get scared or think I'm some kind of insensitive brute. She must have a completely distorted concept of me. She didn't believe I was a teacher. It makes sense—I don't blame her. If I could, I'd explain my circumstances in more detail, but for the moment it doesn't seem possible to share such confidences. The only thing we have in common is a hotel room, and we each have a role to play with the other. I play mine without conviction, and I could swear it seems like she's not all that committed to hers either. My previous experiences sleeping with women for money have been very different: the Russian and Scandinavian tourists sometimes speak to me in incomprehensible tongues while we fuck. I barely remember any of them. But Irene is too similar to the kind of women I've always been with. It makes me a little uncomfortable, even though it's with her that I've been the most natural. I wish she'd give me some sort of clue as to her personality. But no, she watches me with her frigid eyes, and when I speak, her replies are vaguely mocking. I really should just never see her again—one less complication in my life, which is already far too complicated. But I want to meet up with her again. I want to know. Who is she, really? Why does she want to look at naked men? Why did she get undressed with me? And above all, what's behind that tragic air of hers?

I'm a dumbass who's getting lost in his fantasies. I'm transporting my fictions into the real world—which is what you'd expect from a man for whom books have been his succor and his guide. Absurd clichés: the enigmatic woman who conceals secrets and life experience, tumultuous passions. The lady with the dog, the vampiress who bears life's stamp. Cheap symbolism. Irene is a rich girl from the upper crust—that's how she was presented to me. All you have to do is take a look at her companion: Genoveva, the prototypical wealthy woman, the grandest of grandes dames. The only things she worries about have to do with her personal care: fashion, hairdressers, spa treatments. I assume she also cares about her stock portfolio. Irene is probably exactly the same way. Although . . . what if I'm letting myself get taken in by stereotypes? Maybe she reads Schopenhauer, recites Rilke at her mirror, and thrills to the music of Gustav Mahler when she comes home at night. If I'm inferring that Irene is just a rich girl because of her association with Genoveva, then by that same logic I'm a hustler like Iván. And I am, of course I am, I'm an escort and prostitute, but with less property than Iván, the hustler king. That's my hope: that Irene may be well heeled, but not as much as Genoveva. I think that tragic quality of hers frees her from that. Rich women can be pathetic, but never tragic.

Where does that pained grimace on her face come from? Can divorce really mark a person so deeply? It all depends on who it is that's having the experience, rather than on the experience itself. She must be a sensitive woman despite her sour humor, her frostiness. I have no idea what the hell she's like—she's got this inscrutable quality to her. I'd like to know her story and—no point in denying it—I'd like to fuck her, overcome her resistance, scale the wall, reach the treasure chamber. Other people would probably say I'm driven by the same desire that drives any man: to seize what is forbidden, prove that no woman can resist me, invade sanctuaries, triumph. But that's not true, I don't think that's true.

\* \* \*

The wedding was really nice. The bride was stunning, in a cream-colored, strapless Cavalli gown, just perfect. I didn't have a bad time. Even so, I'm less and less inclined to attend these kinds of events. Once you reach a certain age, you don't get excited about things unless they're real firecrackers. And then there's the whole business of being with your family, which never changes. I don't get it. Other people in the world change, right?—but your family never does: they say the same old things, tell the same old stories . . . You know it all by heart: children, grandchildren . . . Only the ailments vary: slipped disc, high cholesterol . . . a real drag. When I'm at one of those family gatherings, I feel like I've aged ten years. I leave the event and *bam!*, the decade falls away. Luckily, I met up with a couple of friends at the wedding, and the partying and the gin and tonics helped me hold out till the end. Otherwise I would have ended up going back home in a massive funk. I don't see my family much, but they make me incredibly claustrophobic. It always feels like I'm in a cheesy illustrated story like the ones we used to read when we were little: the father duck, the mother duck, and all the little ducklings trailing behind. All so predictable, so normal, so atrociously commonplace! And then you remember the awful things they've done to you!—my sister-in-law always spreading dirt about me, my brother trying to pull a fast one with the inheritance after my parents' death . . . I don't hold a grudge, but once you go through certain experiences, you realize who you're dealing with. And the worst part is that the exact same things happen to poor people. Puri, who was my assistant for so many years, was always telling me about her life. Well, turns out her family problems were very similar to mine: her sister-in-law was badmouthing her, her sister was angry about the distribution of the inheritance their mother left them when she died . . . On a different scale, but exactly the same crap. So this family stuff doesn't just suck—it's also incredibly mundane.

I've experienced it before: coming back from a family event, I want a man! I guess I get the urge to act naughty to make it clear I'm not like everyone else: no kids or grandkids or sad weddings full of flower girls with beige ribbons in their curls. Oh, please, no, those things are out of another era! My family hasn't figured out we've entered a new age, one with Internet and women's liberation. I'm a person who lives in the moment, more modern, more open. And as soon as I got back from Marbella, I called Iván so the two of us could go out— but on our own. I've had enough of double dates.

I had a great time. I'm crazy about this guy. The first thing he asked wasn't how the wedding was but what kind of car the newlyweds drove off in. Well, at least he's original. We met up at my house, and we spent the whole afternoon in bed, non-stop. I love sex with him! He's self-assured, commanding, imposing. You feel like you're in the hands of a real man. He doesn't display any pleasure himself, but it's almost better that way—it's like screwing a machine that'll never wear out. He restored the years of youth I'd lost at the damn wedding. Later, we got to talking. He told me his friend the teacher wanted another group outing, and I told him Irene did too.

"Seems like those two are getting along," I remarked.

"Like a house on fire. Let's hope that friend of yours moves past just wanting to see guys naked."

"God, I don't know what to tell you! She's so weird!"

"So's he—the teacher's a weird dude! But he's a good guy."

"Can you imagine if they fell in love? That would be so funny!"

"I don't see what's funny about it. Hey, your friend's not a ball-breaker, is she?"

"A ball-breaker? What do you mean?"

"One of those women who like causing destruction, seeing men suffer."

Because if she is, I'll smack her. I know all about those broads: neurotic, high-maintenance, demanding . . . They like playing with guys, reeling them in and then once they're hooked . . . never seen 'em before. I don't like that chick—she gives me the creeps. Seems spoiled to me. Javier's a little clue-less, totally oblivious—he can't fathom that there are people out there with bad intentions. He goes around with his heart on his sleeve—he's a fucking chump. If this chick messes with him, I'll make her pay. She'd better not try it.

"Irene, a femme fatale? Honey, I don't know. She doesn't give me that impression, but who knows. She never says what she's thinking or feeling."

\* \* \*

I'm nervous, and angry about being nervous. It's not stress—it's expectations. I don't know why it throws me off so much to be alone with this guy. There aren't going to be any surprises: he'll do whatever I say. Maybe I'm unsure what I want to have happen. The other day I got undressed in front of him without even thinking. I've got to be careful, take things slow. I don't have a lot of experience with men. I never dated boys when I was young. I'd see my girlfriends, listen to them talk about their relationships. It didn't seem appealing. They lost their personalities, turned into other people, foolish girls with no will of their own. I just couldn't imagine myself acting like such an idiot: rolling my eyes heavenward, writing my crush's name on all my notebooks, crying whenever we argued. I had Papá—we spent the weekends together, went to the club, idled our Sundays away in each other's company. It was all sim-ple and peaceful, no problems or surprises. And my obligation, my sacred obligation, was to be with him. Papá had devoted his life to taking care of me. He never remarried, didn't go out with women. I was always by his side. He took up all the empty space in my heart. I didn't need anything else.

I met David at the club. He was friends with one of Papá's friends. My first boyfriend, and my last. Our relationship progressed as if the stages had been planned out in advance.

He was the one who fell in love, and I let him love me a little more every day. Papá would have rather I found a wealthy man, one who had his own company, but he was always very pragmatic, and he quickly realized he could hire David at the factory and secure his future. He sat me down and persuaded me it would be to everybody's benefit if David and I got married. My friends were already married. Though he was a modern man and believed women should make a living, he also thought marriage offered additional protection. He wanted to continue to protect me even after his death. Poor Papá—if he could see the way things turned out: our factory hanging by a thread, David sprinting out the back door as everything was crumbling around our ears, and with another woman. A disaster—total collapse.

Papá was never wrong, but he was wrong when he advised me to get married. The two of us were good on our own. If I'd remained single, maybe I would have put more effort into our business. If I hadn't gotten married, I wouldn't have had to suffer through having my husband leave me. If my marriage hadn't fallen apart, I wouldn't be where I am now, paying guys to undress in front of me. Papá was wrong, and I was an idiot who didn't feel secure in my own desires. That's the truth of it.

There's only an hour till Genoveva comes to pick me up. I'm not nervous anymore. It's been good to think about the past. Memories keep you from deceiving yourself, they put everything back in its place. You're humming along in your mind, you get distracted, and gradually you veer off the road. But suddenly you remember and reality comes rushing back—a firm jerk on the wheel puts the car back on the highway. My expectations are gone. I'm not going to meet up with an attractive young man I'm excited about. I'm going to pay to be with a naked man.

Today Javier's had a bit of a haircut, just a trim. He's wearing a navy-blue sweater that looks brand new. I'd swear he's gotten dressed up for the occasion. My memory of his facial features had gotten blurry. I confirm now that he's pretty good-looking, maybe even handsome. He doesn't take his eyes off me, a conspiratorial smile on his face. I don't smile back. I don't talk to him either, addressing Iván instead, though I'm repulsed by his cocky hood-rat look, so coarse and vulgar.

"Do you like the place I chose for dinner, sweethearts? It's really hot right now, but it's nice and cheap. That way you won't spend a lot and we can go have some more fun afterward. You can't say I don't look out for your finances."

"Don't call me 'sweetheart,'" I tell him.

He can call Genoveva whatever he wants, if she lets him, but not me. There's a moment of intense quiet. I don't regret saying it. All of us need to return to our proper places. Iván glares at me, but he doesn't stop smiling.

"I didn't mean anything bad by it. That's the way I am—I use pet names with cool people, just for a laugh. But if you don't like it, no problem. I'll just call you by your name. Or 'ma'am'—I can call you 'ma'am' if you prefer."

Sensing the threat of a serious clash looming, Genoveva starts chattering away. She babbles about nothing, laughing wildly for no reason. I'm in a foul mood, wanting nothing more than to get up and leave. What am I doing here? Why the hell is this lowlife calling me "sweetheart" while the other one's looking at me like we've known each other all our lives?

We order dinner: appetizers and pasta—it's an Italian restaurant. The red wine starts flowing. Javier doesn't say a word and has stopped gazing at me so insistently. He's probably noticed I want to get out of here, and he must be feeling exactly the same way. Genoveva and Iván talk on and on, meaningless chitchat. To think I'm paying to put up with all this! Forget it! This is the last time I'm playing this game. This kind of entertainment isn't for me. It was fine for a while, but I'm through.

Time passes slowly—it feels like this godawful dinner will

never end. My mood isn't improving. The swell of deep rage that flooded me has left aftereffects that I can't shake. As soon as we finish dessert, I get up and announce that I have to leave. Genoveva's so invigorated and happy, she doesn't even blink. Iván looks at me sardonically.

"Are you feeling all right?"

"Just a little tired."

"Of course," he says, and his mocking smile turns to a sneer.

Javier practically leaps to his feet, determinedly leaving the table. "I'll go with you," he says.

We exit the restaurant and start walking. He doesn't ask anything, doesn't speak, for which I'm infinitely grateful. I gradually relax; my bad mood dissipates. I stop thinking of Javier as an escort. He's a man walking beside me, and the sensation is a pleasant one. I'm struck by an unexpected thought: I may never have walked with a man before. David and I never took walks. We would go to the club, the office, friends' houses . . . always by car. We'd host dinner parties . . . No, I'm sure we never walked together. We didn't dance either; he didn't like dancing. Strange things to realize at this point.

"I'm going to take a taxi," I tell Javier. "I'm sorry, but I don't feel like doing anything tonight. I'll pay you just the same—I don't want you to waste your night because of me."

He stops and turns toward me, a look of frustration on his face.

"I wish you'd stop saying that."

"What?"

"You keep talking about paying me. I'm not a hooker you pick up on a street corner. I'm a normal person."

A normal person! So stupid—I can't believe I said that. I'm embarrassed, painfully so. But how can I explain it to her? What should I explain? I charge money, but I'm not a prostitute. She didn't find me on a street corner, but she made contact through a friend who does these sorts of things. I'm not what I seem, but I am. Yet there must be some way to make her understand, because she's probably going through the same thing: she doesn't visit brothels, but she's paying to be with a man. She's not a slut, but she gets turned on looking at naked men, probably because she doesn't dare go any further than that.

"I didn't mean to offend you."

"Look, Irene, why don't we go and get a drink somewhere and talk for a while?"

"On one condition: you let me pay for tonight. Otherwise I won't go."

"All right."

An ambiguous condition: I don't know if she's insisting on paying because she doesn't want to put my finances in jeopardy or because she's afraid of losing control of the situation. It doesn't matter.

"Do you know of a place around here where we can talk?"

He wants to talk so he can tell me about himself and rationalize his lifestyle to me. Fine, let him talk, let him say what he wants to say—sure, he's a respectable teacher and he doesn't enjoy this work he's doing. The more excuses he makes, the more ridiculous he'll seem. Maybe that way I'll be able to get him out of my head when I'm not with him.

We go to a bar he's suggested. It's packed. We sit at a table where we can talk. We order two gin and tonics.

He goes first:

"Do you want to tell me what you do for a living?"

"No problem. I run the factory I inherited from my father. And you're a teacher."

"They let me go—I told you that part already."

"Why are you friends with Iván?"

"We met when we were kids. I didn't see him after that, and later we met again through various circumstances. He's helped me out a lot. You don't like him, do you?"

"He's a little annoying."

"He can be, yeah, but underneath that hyped-up exterior, he's a pretty cool guy. His life hasn't been easy. His mother's in the psych ward at a prison. His father left them and then died of an overdose. He had a rough childhood."

"How awful!"

"He did what he had to do to get by."

The tone of her "How awful!" was distinctly sarcastic. Where does this chick get off? Does she think everybody inherits factories? Doesn't she know terrible things happen in life, that some people are really fucked up? Does she think I'm making things up for her entertainment, to disguise the fact that I'm a depraved prostitute, a randy satyr? Why doesn't she like Iván—is he too rough for her delicate skin? I'd like to smack her! Damn right she's going to pay for the whole night, down to the last penny!

"Are your parents still alive?"

"You'll probably think it's funny, but they died in a car accident when I was young."

"Why would I think that's funny?"

"You think everything I say is a lie, a tall tale. You don't believe I have a normal life, or that Iván's hasn't been normal. Who do you think you are? Tell me."

"Nobody. I don't think I'm anybody anymore."

"Well, I don't believe you're an innocent girl too shy to sleep with a man either."

I've overstepped, but I just can't take it anymore. Everything's ambiguous and weird, and talking is pointless. She's lowered her eyes and is staring at her lap. She's probably counting to ten before telling me to go to hell.

"I've changed my mind. I don't want to go home anymore. Let's go to a hotel."

I want to see him naked now. I want to watch him strip in front of me.

"All right. Your money, your call."

What should I brace for? Is she going to pounce on me like a wildcat to show me what she can do in bed? Really, I'm the one who should go home right now—but I'm curious, so I decide to wait a little longer. I'll go to the hotel, and then, whatever happens, I won't see this woman again. She's nuts, she's dangerous, she doesn't act like a normal person.

We reprise our little hotel routine: she gets a room while I wait off to one side. We go upstairs. When she closes the door, I mechanically start undressing. I don't look at her for a good long while, and when I finally do, I see she's undressing too. She gives me time to observe her small body, slim but not angular, white but not milky, as sculpted and perfect as a marble statue. I take a chair and sit down, the same distance away as on our last encounter. I cross my legs to cover my genitals; seeing her has turned me on. She sits on the bed across from me. We look at each other, not speaking, but it's so awkward that it's impossible for me to keep quiet.

"What now?" I ask.

"We can talk."

"We talked earlier, and the conversation didn't go that well."

"Not anymore."

"Not anymore. Are you sure?"

The way she said "not anymore" was sensual, almost affectionate. Her voice has dissolved in her mouth. I feel the level of desire rising in the room like a dense fog. I get up and walk toward her. I touch her shoulder, touch her breast. I bend down to kiss her. I kiss her. She has fire on her lips, blazing flames. Passionately, she kisses me back. Her breathing is smothered with desire, panting. I gently take her by the arms and tug on her to lay her back on the bed, but she suddenly lets go of me.

"I can't, I'm sorry."

I take her arms again, smile, say quietly, "Come on, baby. It's OK."

She blanches as if she's been stung by a scorpion. She pulls away with startling abruptness.

"I'm not your baby!"

I try to get the seduction back on track, stroking her face with the back of my hands. She scrambles away from me, and I stay still, holding my dick and feeling like an asshole.

"I'm sorry, I'm not mentally prepared for this today. Please go."

Angry, I quickly put my clothes on. Stay cool, though, you knew it—you knew something like this might happen, so don't say anything. Nothing and then goodbye.

"Goodbye, Irene."

"I'll call you another day."

"Don't call—I won't answer."

"Maybe next time I'll be ready."

"Tell Genoveva—she'll find someone else for you. I'm sure she won't have much trouble."

The carpeted hallway generates a sensation of freedom in me that swells when I reach the street outside. I am free.

I'm not far enough along in my prostitution career to be able to handle these situations gracefully. If I'd met that nut-case later on, maybe I would have been less flustered, but not today. I feel humiliated, anxious. Nobody has ever treated me like that before. And yet . . . what did I expect—a housewife who would whisper sweet nothings to me? Iván wouldn't have allowed all of this to happen. If only I could go out tomorrow and find a teaching position! I walk to my apartment. I'm tired, sleepy. I hope I fall asleep as soon as I go to bed—I won't fight it.

\* \* \*

Baby—how dare he call me baby? Who the hell does this guy suppose he is? I think back carefully to see whether I did anything that could have inspired him to call me "baby," but I can't identify anything. Everything was quite clear on my end: I told him I was going to pay for the whole night, and I made no promises. Even more concerning, though, is my reaction there at the end: Why did I say I'd call him? What was I thinking, implying that next time I'd sleep with him? I even apologized! Since when do you apologize to someone who works for you? I've never apologized to the workers at the factory! I must be going crazy.

The day after the disastrous encounter with Javier, I went back to my psychiatrist, whom I hadn't been seeing the last few months. I told him I was in a bad place, having trouble sleeping again after a period of improvement. Of course, I didn't say a word about my run-in with the teacher, or renting male companions, or my private life.

The poor psychiatrist is used to my silence at this point. He looks at me in frustration, as if to say, "If you aren't going to talk about the main issue, why the hell do you bother coming here?" Obviously he doesn't say that out loud, however much he thinks it, since I pay an astronomical amount for our sessions. To be fair, I should note that he tries his best to get me to open up; since he's been unsuccessful, he merely gives me general advice. That day, after the misunderstanding with Javier, he made a basic and nonspecific suggestion:

"Don't punish yourself all the time, Irene. Allow yourself a bit of happiness—allow yourself that."

The problem with recommendations made blindly like that is that a person takes them and applies them according to her own reality, just like newspaper horoscopes.

In any event, I've decided that, as part of allowing myself a bit of happiness, I'm going to call Javier. I'll call him because I feel like seeing him again, and when I see him I'll probably be happy, despite his gaffe. Maybe the psychiatrist's one-size-fits-all suggestion isn't so far off after all.

\* \* \*

She called me directly for the first time, without Genoveva as a go-between. I told her no, I don't want to set up a date with her. That kind of relationship hurts people in the end. Just because someone's paying you doesn't mean you can simply expose yourself to whatever squalls and storms they unleash on you. I'm have feelings. I'm not made of stone. I said it politely but firmly: "I'm sorry, but no. Maybe another time." My curiosity about her is gradually dissipating. The woman is profoundly disturbed for reasons I do not understand. That's enough for me—I have no wish to find out more.

I talked to Iván without telling him about Irene's exaggerated reaction. I asked him if he had any work for me.

"Actually, I do!" he said. "There's this foreign lady who wants to go out to dinner and a hotel on Friday. Unfortunately, I have a previous commitment. I hadn't mentioned it to you in case you wouldn't be interested."

"Is there a reason I wouldn't be interested?"

"The broad's getting up there in years."

"How old?"

"Her seventies are in the rearview mirror, but she pays well. I'd planned to tell her we should meet another day, but if you go, that would be even better."

"No problem."

"Really?"

"Really."

She turned out to be a charming Frenchwoman who spoke Spanish pretty well. She was impeccably arrayed: elegant and sophisticated, still attractive. And she was poised and cheerful. I liked her, and she liked me. We laughed a lot at dinner, and were passionate in bed. I gave her pleasure. It was all very simple and natural; I didn't feel spurned as a monster. She thanked me for the evening before she left. She gave me two tender kisses on my cheeks. She told me she'd always remember me.

Then it was time for her to pay me. I found it jarring to take the money right from her hand; I'd never done it that way before. She kindly asked me to count the bills to make sure she hadn't made a mistake, which of course I refused to do.

After that night, I felt better, even more reconciled to my job as an escort. Not all women despise the men they buy, I decided.

\* \* \*

Mariano has worked out all of the choreography himself. And the man's got a lot of skin in the game: in addition to the club décor, he bought our new outfits, which cost a shit-ton of money. He's paying us for the rehearsals because they last so long, and he's also doing advertising to make sure people find out we're changing up the show.

Personally, I'd rather dress as Zorro than as a Roman gladiator; Zorro had that heroic thing going on. But I don't really care, since by the end, when we're all in the buff, we're dressed the same: like men, in all their glory. Javier's happy as a clam. I'm happy he's been put in the same dance number as me, just the two of us. He's thrilled, not so much because he's been promoted from a dancer in a group number to one of the stars, but because he gets to ditch the schoolboy uniform, which has always bugged him. His new outfit makes him feel more important. Though to be honest, given how skinny he is and with those huge clodhoppers of his, he looks more like a Roman soldier from a Holy Week procession in some tiny-ass village. But whatever, we're all stuck with the looks God gave us.

The number is fine, maybe a little complicated. We two

gladiators come out and fight for a while. I've got a sword, and he has a spear. The complicated bit is when we have to remove each other's clothes with the tips of our weapons. It's a real nightmare, because if you don't get the exact spot with the automatic zipper, the clothes don't come off. Ultimately I win, pushing the teacher to the ground and placing my sword against his throat like I'm going to polish him off. But suddenly Mariano appears, dressed as an emperor, and gives a thumbs-up, the signal that he's sparing Javier's life. To celebrate, everybody gets buck naked. I think this show's going to be a raging success. We've certainly rehearsed enough.

It's opening night, and Irene and Genoveva are coming to see us. Apparently, I'm not supposed to tell the teacher because it's a surprise. Genoveva told me things have been weird between him and Irene for a few days now. She calls him to go out, and he tells her to fuck off. I'd like to know what the hell happened. And Javier's got some balls on him not to have mentioned it. It's the least he could do! I'll confront him about it, see if he snaps out of it. If the problem's that the chick wants to make love, it's no skin off his back to tell me. If it's something dodgier than that—I don't know what—maybe he could use some advice. But no, the guy's not opening his trap. Well, fine, things'll get messy for him tonight when we go out to eat and whatever happens after that. I haven't said boo to him. I'm playing dumb. If he's not telling, there's no reason for me to know. I imagine the scene: "We wanted to surprise you on opening night for the new show." I don't think he'd get pissed off in front of them—he's too polite. He'll just endure it, weather the storm, and maybe that way I'll find out what the hell is going on. It's easy here to go from being the one calling the shots to being the low man on the totem pole—it's a rough business.

The new show was a hit! It just ended, and people were whooping and clapping like crazy. The teacher and I were really tight, sparring like ferocious beasts. I'd say we got the most applause of anybody in the club. We didn't make a single mistake—it came off without a hitch. The other acts were great too. After all, we're fucking professionals. Mariano looked happy, so happy that he told us afterward, "Nicely done, boys, you killed it," and when he calls us "boys," that means he's as happy as a goddamn piranha in a river full of vacationers. He passed out hundred-euro notes to us as a tip. "Go have a drink to my health." Absolutely—I want his health to last a hundred years, one for every euro! Actually, it's a shame about the date with Genoveva, because there might be some hot babe in the audience, and since I'm on my motorcycle, I'm sure I wouldn't have had any trouble hooking up. But no worries, there'll be other opportunities, and with that gladiator costume highlighting my package and leaving my pecs bare, I'm going bag more chicks than George Clooney. I think I'm going to buy a new car—it's time.

But now comes the hard part: I've got to tell uptight teacher-man that we've got a date with the girls. Well, screw him—everything he's got in life is because of me. If I hadn't lent him a hand, he'd still be there in his lame apartment, depressed and unemployed, living with that harpy Sandra and taking out the trash every night.

"Javier, man, I didn't have time to tell you earlier what with all the rehearsals and being so nervous about the opening, but I had to set up a date with Genoveva and that other chick tonight. I didn't have a choice, man. They insisted, really drove me nuts. They found out we were premiering the new show, and now they're waiting for us out at one of the tables."

Shit, what a look! I don't know if I'd dare go up on stage to fight with him after a glare like that. The dude's spear doesn't have a real point, but he might impale me with it anyway. But the worst thing is he just says, "You should have told me." That's it. That's the teacher's damn problem—he's one of a

kind. If he were like everybody else, he would have gotten
pissed off and yelled at me. And then you give it right back to
him, yelling too, so you end up even. But no, the guy just looks
at you like he wants to kill you, leaves you feeling like shit and
not knowing what to say or do.

"So you're not going to leave me high and dry, then?"

"No, if you set it up, I'll go with you."

"Hey, man, it seems like I missed something. What's going
on with you and that chick? You used to like her! Did something happen? Things get weird?"

"Drop it, Iván."

"I'll drop it, but if we're friends, it doesn't really make sense
for you not to tell me things—especially if those things are happening with chicks we've been going out with together the
whole time."

"I said drop it, Iván. I'll go with you and that's that. That's
what you want, right?"

"OK, OK, man. Forget I said anything."

The hell with the teacher and his shitty temper, goddammit!
Better just leave things alone—it's not worth getting pissed off.

Anyway, I thought my bosom buddy might blow me off, but
no, it was OK. He didn't scowl when we went over to their
table. I imagine it was also because Irene wasn't dressed like
she usually was, like a secretary on her day off. No, she'd done
herself up all super sexy in a lowcut black minidress and black
fishnet stockings, wearing black eyeliner and red lipstick. I'd
never noticed she was so hot before. I was almost sorry I
hadn't told the teacher I'd take care of both of them.

We went out to eat. The teacher was good, as usual: courteous, gallant . . . not exactly a bundle of laughs, pretty serious,
but no bad vibes. And the two women, especially Genoveva,
going on and on about the performance: you were great, what
an original number, those Roman costumes, blah blah blah.

We had a hearty dinner, but we only had a few drinks in

case something sparked later. As we left the restaurant, where we'd all go our separate ways, I thought: now's when the teacher says goodbye and leaves the three of us to figure something out on our own. But no, not at all: I went off with Geno, and Javier stayed chatting with the chick on the sidewalk like it was no big deal.

I'm not nosy. I don't generally give a crap what happens to other people, and I don't even look at those gossip magazines that are always shrieking about who's getting married or divorced. What do I care? I actually find those people who want to know everything and go around butting into other people's business really embarrassing. But this is different— I'm dying to know what's going on with Irene and Javier, what's going on right this moment. I asked Genoveva, and she said Irene hadn't let anything slip either. Something really big has happened, is happening, or is about to happen—though it could also be rich kids' bullshit.

\* \* \*

"Shall we go to a hotel?" Irene asks.

"No, Irene, not this time. We're practically old friends at this point, so why don't you come back to my place for a drink? If you don't want that, we can just go our separate ways right now."

"Do you not like hotels?"

"There are lots of things I don't like, hotels among them. Are you coming?"

"All right, but let's make one thing really clear: I'm still paying, even if we're at your house."

"No problem. You want to pay, and I want to charge. Works out perfectly."

We hail a taxi. She's not nervous, and neither am I. She's really dressed up today—she's wearing makeup and a sexy dress. Why? Ever since Iván told me about this surprise encounter, I've been determined to do things the way I want. First, in my own home. I'm tired of going up to a room that this girl's rented for the sole purpose of watching me take off my underwear. I can take them off here, just like I do every night before bed. I'm done with these tired routines. Beforehand, I'll offer her a drink, and while I'm pouring it she can check out the bookcases in the living room, which are full of books. She'll also see that my apartment is clean and tidy. Maybe that'll show her I'm not a slum kid, a cheap whore.

Just as I imagined it, the first thing that catches her eye when she walks in is my books. She goes over and examines them a good long while. I leave her there and head to the kitchen to make our drinks. I realize that I'm tired. My arms hurt. We've had a number of days of intense exercise getting the gladiator number down pat. I go back to the living room holding a glass in each hand and—oh, delight!—she is still absorbed in looking at the books, the only difference being that she is now naked. Her black dress and her underwear are lying on the sofa. I don't say anything. I put the drinks on the table and start to remove my clothes. I lean against the wall, watching her. It's strange to watch her slowly move, distant from me, to watch her pick up a book, page through it, and then put it back, and at the same to be able to see her straight back, her firm butt, the soft curves of her hips. Finally she turns around.

"You really like reading."

"Don't you?"

"I haven't read many books in my life. I always had my work at the company. I figured I could read when I was old."

"Irene," I tell her. "I'm going to come over to you. I can't stand this anymore. If you don't want that, please just get dressed and go."

"I don't want to leave."

He does what he's said he's going to do: he comes toward me. He presses his body against mine, and I feel his penis against my belly. He kisses my lips. He kisses my entire body, kneeling before me. Then he pulls me to the sofa. I start to desire him, as if something were gnawing at my insides. It's an overwhelming sensation, one that makes me tremble, makes me dizzy, frightens me, staggers me. I no longer see the room, reality, my own identity. I don't know who I am or who he is. I don't care. And then heat, a heat that uncoils the entrails. There is no longer him or me—we are one, and on fire. I return to the protection of the maternal cloister, where nothing exists yet.

"Irene," I murmur in her ear.

She doesn't answer, doesn't breathe. I look at her.

When I penetrate her, she emits a sigh, a growl, a yelp. I don't know what kind of sound it is—it's something animal and yet also spiritual, almost mystical. We are lying on the sofa, one on top of the other, spent. Her eyes are closed; she's congested, still panting a little. Looking at her, I am amazed. What life experiences has this woman had? Am I the first man she's been with? Is this the best sex she's had? I tenderly kiss her hair. I am moved—she's like a little girl who's fallen asleep. She doesn't move at all; she's still deep within herself, in her atmosphere, swaying in the air or floating in the sea.

Our position is unnatural, and when I sit up a little, we both roll off the sofa onto the rug. I start laughing. I want to laugh: I'm euphoric, full of life, contented to my core, drugged by her sensations and mine. She opens her eyes, as if she'd suddenly awakened, as if she were returning from far away.

"Are you OK?" I ask.

"Yes."

But it's not true—I'm not OK. I would have liked to stay up in the clouds a little longer, not coming back down to earth, not existing. I'd never experienced such agonizing sensations in my life. For the first time in my conscious existence, I was able to escape myself, escape the past and the future. Now I just feel cold. I don't know what time it is. I have to leave.

"That was wild, huh?" Javier says.

And I don't know how to respond. I am once more in my own skin, once more myself though not entirely. I've got to finish pulling myself back together, take the reins again, regain control.

"Yeah, it was fantastic. And you didn't call me baby, which is a plus."

A chilling response. Strange sense of humor. She dresses quickly. She looks for her purse, places the money on the table. She asks me where the bathroom is.

While she's out of the room, I try to get a handle on her reaction. She's ashamed, overwhelmed by having allowed herself to be taken beyond her limits. She's a businesswoman, an executive, a frigid woman who wanted to see men naked only to demonstrate her power, her control. This behavior after such mind-blowing sex doesn't surprise me. It certainly doesn't offend me. She uses her phone to call a taxi. She shakes my hand goodbye. I'm still naked. I start laughing again. She smiles faintly.

"We'll see each other again soon, I hope," I say, and grab one of her hands.

"Genoveva will call you."

Genoveva! What does Genoveva have to do with this? Whatever—she has the right to keep the fiction going a while longer. But if everything that happened tonight was real—and it was—she'll be back soon. And that'll make me happy because now I definitely want to see her again, and screw again like we did today.

* * *

I went straight to the factory this morning, though I'm not really sure why. All I do when I go there is listen to complaints and get bad news. If it weren't for Papá, for Papá's memory, I'd have sold the place already. But today when I woke up I felt energized, wanting to do something, to act. Maybe so I could stop thinking about what happened last night. As soon as I opened my eyes, yesterday's sensations came flooding back. I started feeling prickling in my ovaries, chills all over my body, weakness in my legs. I'd never experienced something so intense, so brutal. I'm all mixed up. I'm forty years old. How have I lived this long? I'm a forty-year-old woman who's basically just lost her virginity. It would be funny if it weren't so pathetic. Luckily, I lost it with a prostitute. It could be a lot worse: with an old friend I hadn't seen in years, with a divorced man I'd been set up with in the hope I'd rebuild my love life, the way Genoveva had planned. No, at least I took care of it myself—I paid for what I wanted, didn't let myself get carried away by a supposed love story. Still, I'm surprised. I hadn't realized that desire could be so intense and the fulfilling of it so animal.

Still in bed, having only recently returned to consciousness from sleep, I focus on all the pinpricks of pleasure that my body is magically keeping alive. I haven't tried to shake them off. Quite the opposite: I've let myself float away on them. Maybe in sexual terms I've been cold my whole life. But it's clear I'm not frigid. I used to think about the issue a lot, though it didn't really bother me. I had everything that people considered the keys to happiness: money, a husband, an important job, social prestige . . . and yet now I find that I lacked that element that anyone can enjoy: pleasure.

Impulsively, I picked up the telephone on my night table to call Javier. Thankfully, I've still got half a wit about me, and I aborted the operation. I can't allow myself even the slightest bit of fantasy. Javier is an escort—I mustn't forget that. He charges for his sexual services. What for me was a profound encounter is a humdrum routine for him. Every night he goes to bed with different women he doesn't even know. I can't think of him the way I would a normal man. He isn't one.

One thing is more important to me than anything else in the world: maintaining control over myself. I'm on my own. Papá doesn't live with me anymore. Beneath my feet yawns the void. One misstep on this slender tightrope, and I'll fall and fall, never hitting anything solid. Just falling.

I'm not going to call Javier for now. The sensations he awoke in me and that persist in my body are mine alone now. I think I can live off of them a while longer, summon them rather than chasing them away, keep them under my control.

\* \* \*

When I woke up this morning, I almost called her. It would have been the usual thing to do after last night's torrid sex. Couples generally talk about these subjects with a certain intimacy, celebrating having squeezed every drop of pleasure out of a moment of life together. But I immediately discard the idea. She may have given herself to me utterly, but she'd swiftly pulled herself back together. I still remember her stony satisfaction that I hadn't called her "baby," and her goodbye: "Genoveva will call you." Just because we had a great time in the sack doesn't mean any social barriers have tumbled down: she's still a lady, and I'm still a whore. That's what's at the core of her reaction, even apart from whatever shame she feels at having let herself get carried away. Then I realized I couldn't call her anyway: I don't have her number. I'll ask Iván to get it, and then I'll call her. That way I can hopefully avoid having that woman act as the intermediary between us again. I think it would be better if she and Iván didn't take care of setting things up for us anymore, though maybe I'm wrong.

Iván calls to invite me out for a beer. I figure he wants to gossip, and sure enough, we've hardly sat down when he asks how things went with Irene yesterday. I'm tired of playing cat and mouse with him on the subject, so I tell him it was awesome and that I need her phone number so I can call her. He looks startled. He doesn't have her number; he'll ask Genoveva. Then he pauses.

"But you're not getting hung up on her, are you?"

"No, man, no way!"

"Good."

That's good, man, because if you swear undying love to the first chick you screw a couple of times, you're in trouble—you're going to fuck it all up. I think at a fundamental level the teacher still hasn't realized how this movie plays out. Being an escort allows you to have a different kind of life from your average working stiff. If you surveyed all the guys who dance at the club, how many of them are going to turn out to have a girlfriend or a steady chick? Not one, man—the club isn't an office or a bank branch. And we're not like everybody else. You can't live like other people if you spend your weekends shaking your naked ass in a club. He saw that firsthand with that goddamn pain in the ass Sandra, who put him out on the street quick as a flash. When you do this for a living, you can't have a partner—it causes too many problems. That goes double if, besides being a stripper, you're also an escort and screw other chicks during the week. But that's the good part, right?—not being tied down like a goddamn schmoe every day with the missus, the mother-in-law, the kids, the dog. We're free—we can do whatever the hell we feel like, take care of ourselves and not have to worry about anybody else. But if the teacher doesn't get that and just wants to go back to having what he had when he was with Sandra, we're in trouble.

Iván forgot to ask Genoveva for Irene's number. I had to remind him the next day. He didn't call me with the number until eight at night. I was at home, reading. I sensed a hint of insolence in his voice—it's clear he doesn't want me to have direct access to the girl. Maybe it's just his fear that I'll get "hung up" on somebody, or maybe he likes to be in control of things.

At last I could call her. She answered immediately. "It's Javier." A moment of silence, and then a cool "Oh, hi, how are you?"

"Did you know I was going to call?"

"I figured you would. Genoveva asked me permission to give you my number."

"And you gave it to her."

"Evidently."

"Did you want me to call?"

"Listen, Javier, I can't really talk right now. I'm very busy."

"Sorry, I didn't know you were still working."

This was a mistake. A bad move. If I want to see her, I'm going to have to change strategies fast.

"Work comes first, dear."

"Absolutely. That's why I thought maybe we could get together tonight or tomorrow."

"Do you need money?"

"Yes."

"I can't tonight. Tomorrow . . . let me think . . . I'll check my schedule. I'll give you a call."

Perfect. As long as I don't give up my official role as an escort, she's OK with it.

The phone rang at ten in the morning. Her schedule! Such a conventional fib.

"Let's meet at nine tonight at Saisons, a French restaurant. If you don't mind, we can go back to your place afterward. Hotels are a nuisance, and I have to stay in them so much for work that I've come to loathe them."

Sick of hotels! The packed schedule, the work trips . . . The truth is she wants to see me as soon as possible, right? I've been thinking about that amazing sex constantly. I'm sure she'll be counting the hours till tonight. She might be a strange woman, even a little unstable, but crazy or not, sex like we had the other day isn't so easy to find. Neither of us is a kid at this point—we both realize there's a special chemistry between us.

Her schedule—such a childish pretext! She shows up for our date dressed to the nines—she's gotten dolled up to see me. She's classy, that's for sure, with a delicate silk scarf around her neck and tiny gleaming earrings. She didn't choose the restaurant at random either: widely spaced tables, white tablecloths, candles . . . I've never been in a place like this.

"It's a very intimate space," I comment.

Unwilling to admit she's put a lot of thought into choosing it, she says curtly, "Maybe—I don't know. I just heard the food is good. Plus, they don't know me here, which is a plus."

"Of course," I say. "You don't want anybody to see you with me."

"Nobody knows what you do, but next time you should wear something a little more formal, if you don't mind."

"A suit jacket? I don't have one."

"Well, buy one. It's more appropriate than a T-shirt and sweater."

The point of her rude remarks is to put me in my place and keep me there. I could get offended, but the upshot of what she's saying suggests that we're going to see each other again and she doesn't want us to stand out—she wants us to seem like a real couple.

We place our order, and she has them bring a bottle of wine. It's spectacular, the best I've ever had: smooth and flavorful. My first impulse is to toast, but I refrain, fearing it'll turn out she doesn't toast with peons—or worse.

We begin to eat. We don't have anything to talk about. She avoids looking at my face. I try not to take my eyes off her even for a second. She's a hard nut to crack! Maybe we should have started off in bed.

By the time our entrees arrive, we've almost finished the

bottle of wine. I'm in high spirits, but I still don't know what to say. Impassively cutting her steak, she suddenly goes and asks:

"Tell me about when you were a teacher."

Maximum confusion on my part.

"So you believe I'm a teacher now?"

"You do have a lot of books."

"What do you want to know?"

"I don't know, what your students were like, what happened in your classes . . . "

"I taught at a Catholic girls' school, but I wasn't a full-time teacher; I taught supplementary classes. Some of the parents wanted their daughters to get exposure to good books so they could talk about literature and be more cultured. The school was full of wealthy young women—daddy's girls."

"I'm a daddy's girl too."

I start laughing and give her a sympathetic look.

"Then you know what I'm talking about."

"No, my father didn't care whether I could talk about books. He just wanted me to finish my economics degree so I could run the family business one day."

"The girls in my classes didn't care about literature at first either, but that changed when they really learned how to read it. I guided their reading at first, and eventually they realized that novels and poetry were talking about life, love, human relationships, things that they were experiencing. I showed them that even though the stories were fiction, they were simply depicting reality."

"It sounds like fun."

"We had a good time—but things changed, and after a while it didn't seem to matter whether they were cultured or not. The important thing was to study so you could get a top-tier job."

"And then they let you go."

"Yes."

"Would you recommend a book for me to read?"

I can't believe what I'm hearing. Practically euphoric, I say, "Of course!" I keep talking, my tone utterly transformed, expansive and animated:

"Do you know I lent Iván a book? *Crime and Punishment.* And he started reading it! Though I'm not sure he actually made it to the end. I'm afraid Dostoyevsky didn't do it for him."

She's laughing, she's laughing! What is this—a metamorphosis, merely a truce? She has a pretty laugh, with her straight, white teeth and her eyes narrowing mischievously. She's so beautiful when she laughs—why doesn't she ever do it?

"You're really beautiful when you laugh."

It's as if I've splashed her with ice-cold water. Her face darkens. I've got to be careful—it's not enough to avoid calling her "baby." The slightest suggestion of intimacy is going to put her on guard, drive her away.

As we leave the restaurant, I ask her gravely, "Shall we go to my place?"

She nods. A taxi takes us to the door. We're silent the whole way there. I'd love to kiss her, to hold her hand. I'm feeling aroused, my body is exuding desire, but I don't dare even brush up against her.

When we arrive, a neighbor has left the elevator door open somewhere above us, so we have to climb the stairs. I'm walking in front, and she's trailing a good bit behind me. I'm afraid to look back at her in case I discover she's disappeared. We're panting a little as we reach the sixth floor. I insert the key in the lock and pause. I glance at her conspiratorially and smile, but she looks away. As soon as we enter the apartment, she springs at me like a mugger. She's thirsty, starving, out of her mind. She yanks at my clothing, pushes me against the wall. I'm caught off guard by her aggressiveness. I try to calm her a little, whisper in her ear, caress her. No dice—feverishly, she starts undressing, throwing her clothes to the floor.

"Get undressed!" she commands me.

"Should we go to the bedroom?" I suggest quietly.

I think I see her shake her head in the dim light of the entryway. I take her in my arms and lift her a little, and we bump against the wall. Forcefully, I penetrate her. I come quickly. She moans gently, as if she were injured.

All at once, the situation feels awkward: the clothing scattered across the floor, the darkness . . . It's cold. Irene tries to go to the bathroom, but she doesn't know where the light switches are. "Turn on the light," she says in a tense voice.

I go into the living room and pour myself a finger of whiskey while I wait. I see her glide toward the entryway like a shadow. I look to see what she's doing. She's gathering up her clothing, her shoes, her purse. She starts to get dressed.

"You're leaving already?"

"It's late."

"It's not that late. Have a drink, and I'll look for a book for you to read. Remember? You asked me for one."

"All right," she says, almost reluctantly.

"Pour yourself a drink. I'll be right back."

I go to the bedroom and pull the bedspread off the bed. I drape it over my shoulders. I don't have a robe. She's surprised to see me wrapped up that way, like a victim after an earthquake. I go over to the bookcases, pull out *La Celestina* from the rows of books, and sit down on the sofa.

"Most of my students never understood this book."

"Why not?"

"They were young—they'd never experienced passion, and sexual passion is at the heart of the book. Listen."

I read the first encounter between Calisto and Melibea aloud. They meet by chance, and Calisto is enthralled by her beauty. He immediately attempts to seduce her, but she rebuffs him with all the phrases you'd expect from a decent woman. But a moment later, without prior warning, she eggs him on explicitly: "You will have much more if you persevere."

"It's odd, right? She says what she's supposed to say, but she doesn't want to risk losing him. It's a direct, forceful seduction technique that leaves no room for ambiguity or misunderstanding."

She's listening with great attention, hanging on my words. I keep talking about *La Celestina*, even recall things I used to tell my students: the lovers' great passion, similar to romantic love but always limited to sex. Suddenly, she shivers. She's half dressed.

"Are you cold?"

"A little."

"Come here." I open the cocoon of the bedspread, revealing a space next to my naked body.

She hesitates, uncertain, but finally comes over to the sofa.

"Take off your shirt," I say quietly.

She hesitates again, but she takes it off. I put my arm around her, covering her. We sit without moving. She's holding her head uncomfortably upright to avoid resting it on my chest. Feeling her there, naked, warm, soft, I want her again. This time with tenderness, emotion. We make love slowly, deliberately, deeply. She is lost in pleasure, moving in slow motion with her eyes closed, her body as sinuous and sensual as a cat's. We last a long time. I hear her dark, muffled orgasm. She collapses in my arms. I go next, trembling violently. We lie there, still and quiet. An ambulance siren filters in through the window, moving off into the distance.

A light punch in the stomach awakens me. She is getting up and hit me without meaning to.

"We fell asleep. It's five in the morning. I'm going to go."

"Stay. We can get in bed, and I'll wake you up at eight."

She is hastily dressing. "No, I have to be at work really early tomorrow."

She comes back from the bathroom with her hair combed and her face washed. She picks up her purse and retrieves her wallet.

"Do I owe you the same as usual? We've been together longer this time."

I leap to my feet, filled with a surge of indignation.

"It's a set price. It doesn't matter how many times we fuck."

I hope my harsh tone and ugly language will make her react somehow, argue, demand an explanation, even an apology. But no, she just shrugs her shoulders. She leaves the money on the table, puts on her coat, and leaves.

"Goodbye," she says before closing the door.

I don't respond.

Now alone, once more I sense my intuition warning me that I mustn't see this woman again. Not ever.

\* \* \*

I have no need for magical or romantic explanations. It's actually quite logical that it's taken me so long to discover sex. I've spent my life so focused on my work that I didn't have time to think about anything else. That might seem strange in a married woman, but that's how it was. I was wrapped up in my work, and my husband was busy mooching off of me, so who had the space to think about sex? Routine sex just for the sake of it: him with me and me with him. I never missed it. My life was full already: the factory, Papá . . . Things are harder now—I've started seeking out pleasure, even though I'd do just fine without it. Ultimately, it's a destabilizing element, provoking thoughts I'd like to banish from my mind. I'm going to the psychiatrist more often. He's a nitwit. Yesterday I mustered some nerve and said to him, "I've just discovered sex." After all those sessions of my sitting in silence, he should have changed up his reaction a little, but he went back to his old standard: "Tell me about your marriage."

"What do you want me to tell you? That's in the past."

"And our project here is to analyze the past."

"There's nothing to analyze. I got married because my father thought it was best for me and I didn't want to disappoint him."

"Your father was an enormous influence on your life."

Of course he was, dummy—he took care of me and loved me more than anyone else. I owe him everything I have.

"He was a great man."

"Have you ever found any flaws in him?"

"My father is dead. I don't think about him looking to find flaws."

If he thinks he's going to dazzle me with the four basic concepts from a psychology manual, he's in for a surprise: Electra complex, omnipresent father . . . I know about all that already, and it doesn't apply to me. Why do psychiatrists put so much emphasis on the past? My head's never worked that way. At the factory I had to prioritize the present to make sure some possibility of the future still existed. Thinking may be important, but acting is even more vital. That's the sign of the times we live in. If we spent our lives analyzing what we'd done previously, the world would come to a standstill. It's crucial to develop new ideas quickly and execute them fearlessly. That's how Papá did things. But I don't have his fortitude. If he saw me right now, he'd be ashamed of me. And with good reason. Here's the big director of his big factory with no idea what the hell she's doing. Look at her, observe her new habits: she goes to the psychiatrist, and she likes fucking. My lamentable situation does have one redeeming aspect: I'm paying for sex. I'm not going out with some moron I met on the Internet, I'm not seeking consolation in an artificial romance, I'm not willing to put up with the first asshole who comes along and offers me tenderness and companionship. No, I pay to fuck, and I find that comforting. The only problem is I like fucking Javier so much. I'll get over it. And as for the psychiatrist, it's ridiculous, I know, but it gives me a certain confidence to go to his office, even if I don't say anything.

Yesterday I went out to eat with Genoveva. She rattled on about her usual topics: beauty, fashion, well-being. Afterward, when they brought the coffee, I asked, "Genoveva, do you get the feeling you've missed out on anything in life?"

"Oh, honey, good Lord, where did that come from? I'd have to think about it."

"Think about it."

She performs a caricature of deep thought, resting her chin on her hand and narrowing her eyes, and eventually I can tell from her expression that she actually does start thinking.

"I don't know, so many things! If I'd been born later, I could have been a fashion designer and led a more interesting life. I'd have gone on business trips, met famous people . . . But back in my day women didn't have a choice. All we had was the sacraments: baptism, confirmation, communion, and marriage."

"But living the life you've led, do you think you've lacked anything?"

"Sure, lots of things. For example, I'd have liked to have had a husband who wasn't such a pain in the ass. Most importantly, I'd have loved to have a love story like the ones you see in the movies, where a man really fell head over heels for me."

"What kind of man?"

"A millionaire. A powerful man who, being totally smitten, would take me sailing around the Greek isles. A wild, sensitive millionaire who'd sweep me away to the Paris Opera one night. What do I know! But to be honest, it doesn't bother me

298 · ALICIA GIMÉNEZ-BARTLETT

too much that I never got to live out those dreams, especially at this point in my life. I'm a realist, and I've lived what I've lived. I'm not complaining. If I want anything extra, I just pay for it. As you know quite well!"

She winks at me and starts laughing. Genoveva and her Hollywood dreams! Compared with my own aspirations—to screw more often and better—hers seem like foolish whimsies. And they are.

\* \* \*

I call her at lunchtime. She doesn't sound at all excited to hear my voice. Concerned she might think I want to suggest another date so I can get more money out of her, I quickly ask, "Did you finish reading the book?"

Silence. Then she replies: "Yes."

"What did you think?"

"I don't agree with what you said."

"Why not?"

"Let's talk later—I'm at work right now."

"Do you want to get coffee this afternoon?"

An extended silence. I brace for one of her rude comebacks. Finally, it comes:

"Coffee? I thought you weren't going to waste your time."

"Just because I do what I do for a living, that doesn't mean I spend all my time in bed with women. I get coffee with friends, go to the movies . . . have a private life."

"And what does your private life have to do with me?"

"Just a coffee—a coffee and a chat about books. If you're interested, great. If not, no problem."

"All right."

I give her the name and address of a bar downtown, and we set a time. She's the most unpleasant person I've ever met. Incredibly hostile.

At the bar, I'm feeling nervous as I wait. What's going on with me—do I like this woman? I like her, yet I'm also aware she can be as deadly as poison. I imagine she's got her reasons for acting the way she does, but I have no idea what they are. Does she like me—does she really like me? What I like about her is the way she seems so normal. She looks like a normal girl I could have met at any point in my previous life. I also like the way she has sex with me: her complete dedication, the strength that thrums through her body combined with her vulnerability. It's as if she's trying not to feel what she feels and at the same time is letting go, almost ready to die. None of the other women I've slept with have reacted this way, not ever. The hard part is that when the party's over, she turns as prickly as a sea urchin. If I could at least learn a little bit more about her, if she just relaxed for once . . . I'm such an idiot. What would I do if she did relax—ask her to be my girlfriend, my best friend, my wife? I don't seem to realize what I am: an escort. I haven't managed to process that my new job comes with a new identity. I keep feeling like I'm subbing in for another person, and that sooner or later everything will go back to normal. But I shouldn't fool myself: the more time I spend in this role, the less likely it is I'll find a direct, obstacle-free path back to a normal life.

Through the bar window, I see her arrive. She comes in and walks straight toward me. Not even the hint of a smile. She says hello, sits down. She eyes me with an inquisitive look on her face. I can read her thoughts: "Now what? You called me here for this? Don't you see we have nothing to talk about?" To fend off her silent reproach, I launch into a ridiculous speech about why I've chosen this place: the selection of beers and the solemn, ritualistic way they're poured. She listens, wearing a pointed expression of endless patience. The waiter arrives and we order two beers, selected from among the many types I've rattled off like a parrot in a cage.

This woman makes me so nervous, I'm acting like a total jackass. I pull myself back together, try to be energetic and forceful. I called her because I want to know more about her, right? I spit it out:

"I want to know you better."

She takes a long pull from her glass. A smile! Hallelujah? No, it's a hard, mocking, cynical smile.

"I thought we were here to talk about *La Celestina*."

She's right, I'm a moron—I'd forgotten.

"That's true. You said you didn't agree with my interpretation, and I'd like to know why."

"You explain everything in terms of passion: you see desire and sex as the key theme. But I think there's something far more important: social differences. The two lovers are from the upper class. The others are commoners: the old procuress, the servants . . . they're just after money and that's it."

"But they know passion too."

"As a weapon they can wield against the powerful."

Where the hell is this coming from? Who is this woman, a slaveholding business owner? Is she implying I'm just a libidinous servant? But she's given me ammunition for an attack. I'm sick of being beaten up on, so I use it:

"Well, Celestina herself nostalgically recalls the time when she used to enjoy sex. Not to mention the servants, who screw like bunnies."

"Exactly, and they never dress sex up as love."

"Irene, do you realize what great chemistry we have in bed?"

I've caught her off guard. She blushes. She clenches her jaw and looks at me furiously, her eyes narrowed to slits.

"That's not in the book."

"No," I answer, and hold her angry gaze.

She reaches into her purse and looks for the check to pay it. I cut her off: "It's my treat."

"Great. Oh! and if you don't mind, the next book you rec-ommend, try to have it be about politics or war or religion. I'm not interested in ones about sex and love."

"I'll keep that in mind. You're leaving already?"

"I have a meeting."

"When will we see each other again?"

"Genoveva will set it up."

I start laughing.

"Of course, we've got to include Genoveva!"

She ignores me and leaves, muttering a goodbye. In this moment, I hate her like I've never hated anybody in my life, and I barely know her.

\* \* \*

He's still going out with that chick. I know because Geno figured it out, not because the chick's told her anything. But Genoveva's a smart cookie, so something's up. I don't care, obviously. I'm not his father or his brother, much less his pimp. If he wants to set things up on his own, I'm not going to demand a cut. I'm just pissed he hasn't said anything. Why is he hiding it—is he afraid of me? I'm a straight shooter, damn it, and it makes me crazy when people do things behind my back. If the teacher's earning some scratch off of her, that's great—he can just tell me. But if he's being all mysterious because he's hung up on her and is afraid to admit it, then he's screwed—he's going to get gored like a bull runner at the fes-tival of San Fermín.

But I have no idea what's going on now. Yesterday Genoveva called me to arrange for the four of us to go out again. What's up with that? If those two are screwing on their own, why do we have to all go out as a gang? Maybe Genoveva's wrong. What the hell do I know. I'll just keep doing my thing.

Dinner at an Argentine place. Awesome plan. I polished off a massive steak with mushrooms and roasted potatoes on the side. I was so hungry after the show that I didn't pay attention to anything else: I just tucked right into the cow. Then, over dessert, I start to notice a couple of things. There was a good vibe going, with teasing double entendres about tenderloins. Genoveva loves that crap—despite her age, sometimes she seems like a little kid.

As I ate my chocolate mousse, I started really pricking up my antennae: the teacher was gazing moonily at the chick—so was she, though not as much. Little glances, little smiles . . . it's clear they've got something going on besides our double dates, but I have no idea what. One possibility is that this dumbass has gotten himself hung up on that ditz, but maybe he's actually a goddamn genius and he's screwing her to finagle a car out of her or something. I really wouldn't advise that, though; big gifts can end up really tying you down afterward. If you accept a car from a chick, you're basically at her beck and call. That's the worst, a total bummer—the chick gets all bossy and demanding, and you just have to sit there and take all her crap. It's a goddamn nightmare, not worth getting involved.

After that last supper at the Argentine restaurant, I called Javier so we could get a kebab and a beer at the Arab place. And I asked him. Hell, there's nothing wrong with asking!

"Hey, teach, what's up with you and that chick?"

He starts laughing, but he's faking it—I know him well.

"You're still harping on that, Iván? You're a broken record, man!"

"Shit, though, you'd have to be blind not to see it! Makes no difference to me—I'm just asking to make sure you don't get in too deep, buddy."

"No worries, man. I've got it all under control."

I wish what I just told Iván were true, but it's not. I'm not in control of anything, and I don't even know it is what I'm sup-

posed to control. I'm liking Irene more and more. She's a hurri-
cane in bed, but it's not just that. Right when you least expect it,
she transforms into one of those first loves from your youth: inex-
pert, frightened, tender, a little girl you're holding hands with.
And then her other face suddenly appears: aggressive, distant,
sour as a lemon, tormented. That torment doesn't dissipate until
she places the money on the table to pay me. Still, lately she's
agreed to go out with me a few times just to have coffee and talk.

"Do the two of you meet up to have sex every day?"

"No, Iván, Jesus. We meet up every once in a while, and not
always to have sex. Sometimes we just talk."

"Talk about what?"

"Books, movies . . . The other day we went to see a movie.
Then we got a drink and talked about it for a while."

"When you do those things, does she pay you?"

"No."

"And when you sleep together?"

"Yes, she does then."

"That's weird."

"Well, it's like if you had a friend you . . . "

"Yeah, a friend you occasionally sleep with for money. Sure,
I get it."

I don't get it at all. It's a goddamn mess. Today we go out
and take in some culture for free, and tomorrow we knock
boots for cash? How does that work? Really, though, good for
the teacher. He's got some massive balls on him. He sleeps with
her before she pays him, and then the guy goes and tops it all
off with a bunch of books. And she loves it: cock and brain for
one low price. The combo would never have occurred to me!
Maybe I should be offering these two-for-one deals. Not with
books, obviously, but tell the girls I'll change the oil in their car
for the same price as a lay. Get a load of the teacher! The guy's
amazing! A goddamn genius!

* * *

"We've got to sell the company, Irene. We don't have a choice. If we wait another month, it'll lose all its value. The crisis is global, and it's lasting longer than we expected. It's time."

"Let me think about it."

"There's nothing to think about. We're totally bankrupt."

"I said I'll think about it! I'll call you when I've made a decision."

So long to everything. I have nothing left of my father. I have nothing left of my life. I have nothing left of me. Selling is easy for this guy, but for me . . . I want to curl up and hide somewhere where I won't feel anything, where I can wait quietly for the very end.

I've agreed to go out and have coffee with Javier a few times. At first we acted strictly on that plan, but not the last few times. When it comes time to say goodbye, something prevents us from separating, and we end up going back to his place. I'm starting to think I'm sick—just the way he smells makes me want to jump on top of him. I'd never thought anything like this was possible. It's not normal. I can still feel the sensations of sex with him for hours afterward. I wake up in the middle of the night, wild with desire. It's not normal. It scares me—maybe I'm developing a pathological obsession. It's as if I no longer belonged entirely to myself. For the first time in my life, I sense a danger that Papá wouldn't be able to protect me from. Javier is unquestionably that danger. He knocks me off guard, derails me, makes me dependent. He's destroyed my willpower. And he's a prostitute too, a guy who charges money to sleep with women. Some days, I can't believe this is happening to me. How far I've fallen.

I decided to tell the psychiatrist about some of my fears. I thought I wouldn't be able to be honest with him, but then I figured I was paying for his discreet listening skills.

"I've met a man, and I'm obsessed with having sex with him."

He asked me about the man. I told him he's polite, cultured, good-looking, pleasant. He started laughing.

"I don't see the problem."

The problem is the obsession, you damn idiot. The problem is I feel trapped in a spiderweb. The problem is my hunk is a hooker. I wasn't able to tell him that part—the words refused to come out.

"Maybe you've been too sheltered, Irene. Often, without our realizing it, our refuges become prisons, and the people who protect us become our jailers."

He's not just an idiot—he's an asshole too. He's referring to Papá and me. Anything I tell him, he connects it back to Papá and me. As if relationships didn't contain nuances, special circumstances, infinite variations. No, we always end up right back in the psychoanalysis manual. He has no idea how perfect my father was. He doesn't realize the complications and pain my father saved me from. And as far as my current situation, if I told him what Javier does for a living, he'd understand I actually do have a problem, and one that's not easily solvable. But why tell the truth? The man's an idiot and an asshole.

He ends the day's session by placing a decorative cherry atop his psychiatric cake.

"Look, Irene, you'd be surprised if you knew how many wealthy women with quiet lives discover sex and love late—or never discover them at all. You're lucky. Enjoy it. Don't put up barriers—let yourself go. Don't be afraid. Just stay calm."

I'm just another wealthy woman—that's how he sees me. A woman who's led a conventional life with her husband, playing tennis, drinking tea with her friends, buying a million Christmas presents. But none of that is true: I grew up without a mother, worked like a dog at the company, endured a husband who married me purely out of his own self-interest, suffered a humiliating divorce, stopped seeing my friends, and go out with male prostitutes for sex. I'm on my own. If you call that a placid, bourgeois life, then yes, I guess I'm just another wealthy woman.

When I left his office, I'd already made a decision. So long to the idiot asshole. No more therapy—shame about the money wasted. I'm going to use only one bit of his advice: enjoy it. I swear up and down I'm going to try. For starters, I'll agree to put the company up for sale. I can't fight it anymore. I have and will continue to have money to spare. The hell with everything! This wealthy woman's going to wage her own little revolution.

\* \* \*

Nothing is written—everything develops little by little, and we can give it whatever shape we choose. I've never believed in destiny, but I vaguely remember my mother telling me, "Everything's going to be OK." Then I never saw her again because she died in that ridiculous accident. But I'm still alive. Everything's going to be OK. I'm not depressed like I was when I lost my job, like I was when Sandra left me, kicked me out. I've fought tooth and nail. I'm a stripper and a prostitute, but the only thing that should count is that I'm still myself, regardless of what I do for a living. Plus there's Irene. We see each other almost every day now. We make love, but we also talk about a million things. She remains an enigma, never tells me anything about her life, but I can tell she's moving closer to me; she's more open, more real. She's starting to smile, and the other day she almost laughed out loud. Her face is beautiful when it lights up, when it loses its tragic aura. I like her more and more all the time. She's brave, mysterious, elegant. I get goosebumps seeing how she gives herself to me when we have sex, like a virgin bride, like a wild woman I've found on a desert island. Afterward, she pulls herself back together, turns cynical and aloof again. But that mask, too, will fall one day, a defense she'll no longer need when she's with me. Everything's going to be OK.

There are some things I'm having a hard time accepting: her money when she insists on paying me, the company of women that Iván keeps finding for me. Irene asks me about that sometimes, seemingly casual—"Have you seen anyone else today?"—or tinged with sarcasm—"How's business?" I'm sure pretty soon she's going to ask me to see her exclusively. And when she does, will I agree to it? Because if I see only her, my income will depend on her. Maybe she'll offer me a set amount per week, per month. If I go along with that, our relationship will be forever tainted: the lady and her rent boy. Just thinking about it turns my stomach, but I'm trapped in a labyrinth that has no way out, at least for the moment— nobody can predict what might happen in the future. Today I have to move cautiously: no scaring her, no losing ground on the progress we've made, no driving her away with some clumsy gesture. Everything's going to be OK.

The phone rings. It's her. She wants me to go out to dinner at her club, with her friends. I'm so surprised, I don't know what to say. Is it a test? Does appearing with me in polite society mean we're moving up another rung on the treacherous ladder of our relationship?

"What should I say if they ask what I do for a living?"

"Tell them the truth."

"That I go out with you for money?"

"Is that the truth?"

"Yes, but no."

"What do you mean?"

"Well . . . "

She understands exactly what I mean; she's just trying to get me to talk. I'd like to know what it is she wants to hear.

"Don't worry about it—it doesn't matter. Just tell them

you're a teacher. That's true too—or is that another yes but no?"

"Actually, that's a yes but no too."

"It's pretty ambiguous, what we've got going on here."

"Yes but yes."

I hear her laugh on the other end of the line, and it is a beautiful, clear, happy laugh. We agree to meet at eight that same night. She doesn't tell me to dress appropriately.

\* \* \*

Shit, man, I can't believe what I'm seeing! Well, I'm not actually *seeing* it, but the teacher told me about it. Irene invited him to dinner at her private club with her fancy friends. A real sniffy place where you can play a ton of sports—it's even got an indoor pool—and they also hold galas, banquets, cocktail parties . . . real blackout ragers. He got all dressed up for the occasion. It's like *Pretty Woman*, but the other way around: the rich woman marries the poor prostidude. But maybe there's something fishy going on here! When Javier started telling me about it, everything sounded great: how everybody was looking at him with curiosity, her all affectionate and putting her hand intimately on his knee . . . It was pretty intense for him, of course, because apparently the rich folks kept staring at him, smiling as if to say, "Get a load of Irene—she finally hit the jackpot." And she goes and snuggles with him in front of everybody and asks whether he enjoyed the food. The teacher says she's never that attentive when they're alone because she's shy—but I think she was putting on a show for her audience so they'd all believe the teacher was her new fella. If I were him, I'd have been really pissed, but he's patient and never thinks ill of anybody. He must be thinking something, though, otherwise why the hell is he telling me all this? He usually never tells me anything.

Just in case, since I don't want anyone talking smack about my friend, I called Genoveva to go out for a beer and just came right out and asked her:

"Hey, Geno, did you know Irene invited Javier to her club?"

"It's the first I've heard of it."

"Well she did, and apparently she turned all lovey-dovey for the occasion, even though she never acts like that in private."

"Wow, everybody at the club must have practically died of shock. The curiosity must be driving them crazy. I'm surprised nobody's called me to find out more. Irene's cut off contact with all our friends, so you can imagine what the place must have been like after that performance. Do you know how she introduced him—as a friend, boyfriend . . . ?"

"No idea, babe, no idea. And to be honest, I don't really give a crap what they think. What I want to know is what your friend is up to with Javier. It seems like things have gone a little beyond the usual arrangement. She can go out with him, fine, but why introduce him to her friends and start making out with him in front of everybody, when she doesn't usually do that?"

"What do you care?"

"I care. Javier's a good guy, a really good guy, and he doesn't have as much life experience as me."

Shit, what the hell is up with her? Glaring at me like she wants to leave—really? Doesn't she get that that's what this meeting is about, that we're here about my friend?

"Whereas you're more of a dick, huh, Iván?"

"It isn't a matter of who's more of a dick or more of an asshole—that's no contest. I'm worried my friend is getting hung up on Irene, and it seems like she's toying with him: today I love you, tomorrow I won't. Today I'll show you off to people like a monkey in the zoo, and tomorrow I won't even say hello."

I don't think goddamn Genoveva's even listening. She pouts and looks at me and wriggles her foot toward my crotch under the table. I could punch her, I really could! She doesn't have a clue, goddammit, doesn't give a shit about anything but fucking.

"And aren't you a little hung up on me, darling?"

"You know me, Genoveva. The only thing hung up around here are those hams dangling from the ceiling. Plus, I'm in a hurry here. I'm trying to ask you if you have any idea what Irene's plans are, if she's said anything about the teacher."

She's not happy about being given the brush-off like that, but screw her—she was getting on my nerves. She offers up a vicious smile.

"So you're Javier's protector now?"

"Something like that. I was the one who got him involved in stripping and all this stuff."

"And you feel responsible."

"Well, yeah."

"Very considerate of you. Look, if you're in a hurry today, we're both wasting our time. I don't have the faintest idea what Irene is thinking or planning. She's locked as tight as a fire-proof safe, and she never talks about personal stuff. You can believe that or not—I don't care."

"But female friends always tell each other things."

"Sorry to disappoint you, but Irene isn't a close friend of mine. Our relationship is more one of convenience."

"What's that supposed to mean?"

"We keep each other company, go out together if we need to. But we don't share confidences. We do our own thing. And if you don't have any other questions, we should wrap this up: you're in a hurry, and I've got an appointment at the spa."

That's women for you—doing their own thing, just like she says. They don't give a crap about friendship or what happens to other people. All they care about is their figure and their pocketbook. They disgust me. But she's out of luck today—she wanted sex and didn't get it. Maybe she'll figure out she's not going to manipulate me the way that shrew manipulates the teacher.

\* \* \*

Inviting me to her club, with her friends—there are a lot of connotations. If she's trying to demonstrate that her relationship with me is more than just sex for pay, then the invitation is important. But maybe she just wants to show me off as a trophy, as proof she's remade herself after her divorce. I'm never quite sure how things stand with her, and I don't know which of the two possibilities is true.

After the dinner, when the two of us were alone again, her actions clearly indicated that the situation hadn't changed a bit: she's the boss and I'm her playmate. Serious face, chilly demeanor, and an obsession with immediately paying me for my services. There's no doubt what kind of connection we've got. She didn't want to make love that night, and when I asked her, "Do you think your friends liked me?" she grudgingly replied, "I'd rather just watch the game. Let's not talk about it." Brutal—having her put me in my place like that really hurt. Sometimes it's hard not to be cruel in return. It's a shame, because during dinner, when she was being so nice to me, I felt really good. I'd never seen her play at being a woman in love, a girl who's full of dreams. Funnily enough, she was great at it. Maybe she's not as cold as she seems. She's been married—maybe she's felt affection before, even love. I'm convinced her ambivalence toward me comes from the walls she's erected inside herself. Who knows! If she gets over her psychological issues and I'm there . . . maybe it could work.

I made the mistake of telling Iván about the dinner. I should have foreseen his reaction. Iván hates women, and Irene's no exception. He got really pissed off: "Shit, man, can't you see she's messing with you?" He gave me the same advice as always: "Tell her to go to hell. She may be a good customer, but it's not like you don't have others. If what you want is a stable gig, I'll find one for you, honestly. Ditch that chick soon as possible or she's going to ruin your life."

But it's impossible to listen to someone with whom you've got nothing in common.

\* \* \*

I loved it. It was so much fun seeing the dumbfounded look on everybody's faces. You don't have to be a superspy to realize that one of my friends at the club has found out we've started drawing up the paperwork to sell the company. And if one of them finds out, they all do. So A+ for me! After months and months without hearing from me, the first thing they learn is I'm getting rid of the company. "Poor thing!" they must be thinking gleefully, "she just couldn't hack it." The hell with them! I'm putting the company out of its misery! I'll be rolling in money, and no more manager hounding me like Jiminy Cricket. I know my father would be upset about this decision, but I don't care. This is no time for sentimentality.

The whole while I've been seeing the psychiatrist, he's kept insinuating that my father has been harmful to me. His words are still ringing in my ears: "Love is sometimes abuse," "Affection can be a need to control," "Protection becomes a prison" . . . I'd love to call him up and tell him, "I sold the company my father founded, Doctor, the one I fought for my whole life. You see, I wasn't his little doll after all—he didn't leave me so appallingly traumatized that I can't make my own decisions. I know what I want, and I act on it." Of course I won't call. It's better to just forget about morons as soon as possible.

Taking Javier to the club was a master stroke. The rumors

had probably started already, the comments, the phone calls: "I heard Irene's selling the factory." And with the hive all abuzz, *boom!*, my e-mail to the whole group: "Anyone up for dinner at the club?" Their first thought must have been that I wanted to tell them about the sale, but then I go and show up with a guy. Amazing! I disappear, and when I reappear I do it with a high school teacher by my side. Not a lawyer, an economist, a banker, an executive, a tycoon. Nobody from our tribe, no. A literature teacher! Lanky, but good-looking. Well mannered and friendly. With bookish glasses. I loved seeing the look of surprise on their faces! But watching them try to hide it was even better. If only I'd been able to overcome my own prejudices and invite Iván instead of Javier. That would have been the ultimate victory. But it's easy to gaze lovingly at Javier—I could almost say I enjoyed it. I can't imagine pulling it off with that trained monkey he calls his friend. And I have to say Javier was perfect: reserved, aware of his role, without trying to hog the spotlight, seemingly unfazed by my affectionate attitude . . . like a professional actor. Maybe he's acquired some theatrical abilities from spending so much time up on stage. And I didn't feel weird acting like we were a couple. In a way, we are. But afterward . . . what came afterward was all too predictable. When you play a role well, you can end up believing it. That's what happened to Javier: he was clingy, demanding affection, as if he wanted to our playacting to continue in private. And that's not an option. I shut him down quite sternly—and paid him, obviously. I paid him as usual, every last cent.

Not even twenty-four hours later, I get a call from Genoveva.

"Geno! How are you? What are you up to?"

My effusive tone sounded fake. Hers was dry, sharp.

"Listen, Irene, is it true you took Javier to the club and introduced him to the group?"

"I see the gossip network is still up and running. Who told you that?"

"It doesn't matter."

"Your information is correct. So what?"

"I'll remind you that I'm involved in all this too, sweetie, and the group knows we go out for drinks together. It's one thing for people to know I'm a free spirit who's up for anything, and another thing to give them details about my affairs."

"Your name never came up, and I introduced Javier as a friend."

"The person who called me said he was your boyfriend."

"And did this person call just to tell you that?"

"Of course not. He wanted to know more about your relationship: whether you live together, where you'd met—to gossip, basically."

"And what did you say?"

"Nothing, I ended the conversation."

"So what's the problem?"

"Please be careful, Irene. You can't play around with this stuff."

You can't play around with this stuff, you spoiled child, because going out with male escorts, depending on how you shade the nuances, can meet with open disapproval. Let's hope my ex doesn't end up getting wind of this and cutting off my alimony because of this ninny. Anything's possible. I've always been big on discretion. I do what I want and people know it, but I don't flaunt it or shamelessly violate norms. We're part of a society, and if this girl wants to destroy everything she's got left—the factory and her social standing—she should go for it, but I'm not going with her. I'm doing great the way I am.

"Listen, Irene, can I ask you something? You aren't falling in love with that guy, are you?"

"No, I don't think so."

"Remember he's a lowlife. If you give him an opening, he'll try to bleed you dry, take all your money. He could be dangerous. You have to keep your distance from that kind of guy—you never know how they're going to react. They're not like us, Irene. They're trash."

"I hear you. Stop worrying, Genoveva."

I love that too. The daddy's girl has surpassed the experienced woman. The great Genoveva, paralyzed with fear! I can't help it—I love it.

\* \* \*

The phone wakes me up. It's seven in the morning. I fumble to answer and try to understand all the information that comes flooding over me, information that isn't part of my daily life and eludes easy identification. Little by little, I manage to organize what I'm hearing. They're calling from the prison psych hospital. Iván's mother just died. They've informed him, but he gave them my number and hung up. He wants nothing to do with it. I understand the words but not the situation, so I don't know what to say. Was Iván drunk? What does "wants nothing to do with it" mean? I ask for some time.

"I'll be there in a couple of hours."

Shower and coffee. Clean shirt and jeans. I still have no idea what to do. I sit down to smoke a cigarette, and eventually a light bulb goes off. I've got it. I call Iván. He doesn't answer. Once, twice . . . I leave a message, my voice serious: "Iván, are you home? Please pick up." I hang up, and a few seconds later, he calls back.

"Listen, man, I'm not up for any bullshit. You go see what the hell's going on."

"Iván, please don't hang up. Hang on, we have to talk. Don't leave the house—I'm coming to see you."

I'm not sure he's going to answer the door, but he does. It's eight o'clock, and he reeks of alcohol. He's in pajamas. He's out of his mind, furious. I try to speak, but he doesn't let me.

"Look, Javier, I know the score here, and I have no intention of showing up. They're the ones who had her locked up. It's their problem if she kicked the bucket, not mine."

"Calm down, Iván. You don't know what they want from you. They're just letting you know your mother died. You have to go. I'll go with you if you want."

"Bullshit! I know what they want! They want me to go and pay for the funeral and cry. And I'm not up for that shit. I didn't give a fuck about my mother when she was alive, and I'm all out of fucks now that she's dead. I'm not going to go there and squeeze out some tears and say, 'Poor thing, she was so alone, what a terrible life she had!' We're all responsible for our own fate, and she's responsible for hers."

"You're not being reasonable, Iván. I'll tell you what: why don't you get dressed and we'll go to the hospital, show up, do what has to be done, and come home again? No problem. It won't take long, you'll see."

"Look, teach, I know I always rope you into my funeral shit when I'm the one who should be dealing with it. But you know me—I'm no use with that stuff. You go on your own and pay for the funeral, which is what those bastards are after. Don't worry about the money—I'll take care of it. Then you just split. You don't have to stay and wait for the goddamn priest to give a eulogy. We're friends, right? So let's make a deal: I'll help you out with your life, and you help me out with my deaths. You're coming out ahead on this one, since I don't have anyone left alive."

This preposterous perspective on things makes me laugh. I walk over to him, grab his arm, and propel him toward the bedroom. "Come on, man, don't be a dumbass. Take a shower and get dressed. I'll make you some strong coffee. The sooner we get moving, the sooner we'll be back."

He pushes my hand away so forcefully that it actually hurts. "Leave me alone! I said I'm not going! If you want to go, great. If you don't want to, don't, but I'm staying right here. You do what you want."

I'm taken aback by his crazed eyes, his aggressive tone. I look down. Nod. "All right, I'll go. I'll come by this evening."

When I'm at the door, he calls to me. "Javier!"

Slowly, I turn and face him.

"Buy her some flowers, OK? The price doesn't matter. Whatever you choose will be good. And have them cremate her—no cemeteries or crosses."

I hail a taxi and get out at the address they gave me over the phone. I don't want to look at the place for long: it's gray, ugly, impersonal, depressing. A woman meets me.

"You're not her son."

"No, I'm a friend. Iván's in bed."

"He's not coming?"

"I don't think he can—he's got a high fever."

"Right."

The monosyllable contains the full truth of the situation: the son doesn't want to come. From that moment on, her tone is more direct, less restrained. The dead woman has nothing to do with either her or me, so we can carry out the protocols without the need for emotional palliatives.

"She was found dead this morning. She had gone to the bathroom and collapsed there. It was probably a heart attack. Do you want them to perform an autopsy?"

"No."

"Burial or cremation?"

"Cremation."

"Will you be attending the funeral service?"

"There's a funeral service?"

"The priest says a few words and commends the soul to God."

"No, I won't be attending."

"What about the ashes?"

"You can dispose of them."

"All right. Do you want to see her?"

I'm caught off guard, and for some reason I answer in the affirmative—maybe out of curiosity, maybe a faint twinge of pity.

The two of us walk down the endless corridors together until we reach a small room. Wood-paneled walls and some benches arranged like pews. In the middle there's a sort of tiny altar, in front of which is a coffin. The hospital's funeral parlor. The coffin is a simple one, and the upper part is made of glass so you can see the dead woman's body. I go up to it. I recognize the woman who ate with us on Christmas. The skin of her face is pale blue, and her features seem sharper. Her nose is a knife that could cut through something. They haven't put any makeup on the corpse, just brushed her hair back. She's wearing a white tunic. She's like a dead bird: small, fragile, a shadow of what she was. I feel an immense sadness, not for her but for me. "I'll end up the same way," I think. Not in a prison psych ward, but in some home for elderly people who are indigent and lack social security, like me.

The woman is waiting for me outside.

"When the family doesn't have means or doesn't want to cover the expenses . . . "

I don't let her finish. "Her son will pay for everything through me. Can you add some flowers?"

"Of course, no problem."

We go to a tiny office and she gives me the account information so I can make a bank transfer. She keeps a photocopy of my ID. She calls the bank to confirm that there are funds in my account. We shake hands. Thank you. Goodbye. She doesn't say she's sorry for my loss because there's no need.

I go to a bus stop and take the first one that comes by. I

don't know where it's headed, but I want to get as far away from there as I can. I get off after ten minutes. I find a bar and order a beer. I'm terrified—I don't want to die like Iván's mother. Starting tomorrow I'll do whatever I can to find a real job. I can't keep going like this. My hand that's holding the glass is shaking, but I quickly tamp down my hysteria. "I'm still young," I think, growing calmer. I'm positive I'm going to find a decent job, take back up the normal habits of a normal man. The ghosts that just visited me have made me long for something I've never wanted before: to die in bed, surrounded by my children, my grandchildren, a professional mourner hired for the occasion. I want to stop being a social pariah. I want to possess a man's dignity again. And I will.

Perhaps inspired by the solemn ceremony, I decided I should do things right: I'd wait until evening and go to Iván's house to tell him that everything had been taken care of and his mother was resting in peace. So instead of throwing dirt on what had happened and forgetting about it, I showed up at precisely eight o'clock, ready to carry out my obligation.

When Iván opened the door, he was naked. His expression went blank, as if he'd never seen me before in his life. He left the door open and muttered "Come in" as he headed back to his room. I stood there alone, uncertain what to do. I called out to him, so he could hear me, "If you're resting, I'll come back tomorrow. See you!"

I heard him shout. "Hang on! I'm with a hooker. I'll be right there."

My heart clenched up. I realized what a mistake I'd made in coming.

"No worries, I'll come back!"

I was almost to the door when he reappeared.

"What the hell are you doing, man? Where are you going? You can't even wait five minutes? We're finished. I'll pay her, and we're all set."

I stared out the living room window, which didn't have a view. A short while later, the two of them emerged. She was young, Caribbean-looking, coarse and exuberant. He was still naked.

"Come on, girl, get a move on. It's late, and my friend's waiting!" he said.

"Will you call me again?"

"Call you? I'd rather get an impromptu blowjob on a street corner somewhere!"

"So you're going to be nasty, huh? Well, let's hope that street corner is well lit, or they might not be able to find your dick."

I watched in a panic as Iván raised his hand to strike her. I leaped forward and grabbed his arm in the air. "That's enough. Come on, let her go."

The woman spat on the floor and left. I was still gripping my friend's arm. He looked at my face and, with a tense smile, said very softly, "You can let go, buddy, the assault's over."

"I should come back tomorrow."

"No way, man! Let's have a drink and you tell me how the old lady's bonfire went. Want some whiskey?"

"I'll take a beer."

He disappeared into the kitchen. My heart was hammering, my chest squeezed by an enormous pressure. I tried unsuccessfully to calm down. He came back with the drinks.

"First of all, man, tell me how you paid them at the prison."

"With a bank transfer."

"Well, give me your damn account number and I'll make the deposit now."

"There's no rush."

"No way, I'll do it online right now."

I got out the receipts and documents and handed them over. He sat down at the computer and tapped away at the keyboard for a while.

"All right, we're square now. What the hell is this paper?"

"A copy of the death certificate."

He tore it in half without even looking at it and threw it on the floor. He sat down on the sofa, still naked.

"All right, now tell me."

"Why don't you get dressed, Iván?"

"Making you uncomfortable? It's not like you're queer!"

"It's awkward talking to you like this. We're civilized people, right?"

"Hell, man, we're totally freaking civilized! All right, there you go. Better?"

He'd placed a cushion over his crotch. Hostility was emanating not just from his eyes but from every pore of his skin, from those white teeth bared by his ferocious smile. Immediately, my only desire was to get the hell out of there, but I stifled the urge and asked, "What is it you want to know?"

"I don't know, man. Were they rude to you? Did they badmouth me for not going myself?"

"No, not at all. Everything was very orderly, very professional. I signed a few documents on your behalf. They told me she'd had a heart attack during the night while going to the bathroom. They found her on the floor, already dead. They asked me if I wanted them to perform an autopsy, and I said no; I'm not sure if that was right."

"Great, man, that's great. Why slice up dead people? Better to just leave them alone. By the way, did you see her?"

"Your mother?" I paused a moment. I looked down, lowered my voice. "Yeah, I saw her."

"And?"

"Nothing, really—she was there. It was a very nice funeral parlor."

"What about her body—how was it?"

The fury and sarcasm were gone from his voice. He was looking at me with wide eyes, immensely anxious.

"Well . . . you know what I thought, Iván? I thought she

looked like a little bird that had fallen from a tree: small, parched, with dull, colorless feathers. It made me sad."

His face twisted in a strange grimace, completely distorted. He was unrecognizable. He let out a pained wail, got up, and went to his room. I heard his desolate sobbing, the sound of him pounding his fists on the mattress, or maybe the pillow. I got out of there as fast as I could. I know I should have stayed to try to comfort him, but how do you remove that kind of pain from a man's head? And what did it have to do with me? What do I have to do with a man who tries to hit women?

Things happen to me, it seems, without my being able to avoid them or have any influence on them. When I got home, my nerves were shot—I was tired, disgusted. Surprisingly, I fell asleep almost immediately.

* * *

It's strange—I feel free as a bird, and at the same time it's as if I'm no longer part of the world around me. The company was so important to me! It was the center of my life for a long time, and now it's nothing, just smoke. I don't feel any regret or guilt about selling it. Business is business—everything else is outmoded romanticism. Nobody gives their soul to their work anymore. To be successful and ride out this crisis would have taken all of my time and energy. Exhausting! I don't want to struggle anymore.

I should be happy: I'm free for the first time in my life. I don't have any ties or obligations; nobody depends on me, and I don't depend on anybody. I feel like running out into the street and shouting it to the world. Stopping people on street corners and telling them I can do whatever I like, rubbing their noses in it. Shaking them to make sure they understand. It's frustrating to know that nobody cares what happens to me. It makes no difference to them whether I'm free or a slave, and that makes me angry. A contradiction.

A while back I would have gone to the psychiatrist and told him I live in that contradiction: I'm free, and being free pisses me off. No doubt he would have given me some kind of relaxation pill. Not today—today I know how to relax on my own, the natural way. I'll call Javier and hire him for tonight—assuming he's free, of course. Maybe I should make some sort of arrangement with him, free him of other commitments and have him work for me exclusively. He might not accept; sleeping with other women may earn him not just money but pleasure. Does he feel the same pleasure with others that he does with me? He's not faking it with me, I know that. He convulses, moans, collapses afterward. I never saw my husband experience that kind of pleasure. If he gives the same performance with the other women he sees, he's a real pro.

"Javier?"

"Irene, what a surprise!"

"Are you free tonight?"

"Of course!"

"Shall I come over around ten?"

"Come earlier if you like!"

"No, I have to work."

"All right, perfect. I'll make us some dinner."

He'll prepare a dinner with the whole pseudoromantic she-bang. He's done it before: candles on the table, mood music . . . It all seems quite tacky in his rattrap's tiny living room.

When he opened the door, I leaped at him. I yanked on his clothing and started to remove it. He was laughing, but I wasn't. I wanted to fuck like never before. It was a hunger, a thirst. I'm an orangutan in heat, an animal. We roll around on the floor. I don't want words or kisses or caresses or foreplay. I want to fuck. And we fuck. I get on top of him. I open my legs, close my legs, plunge down on his cock. We come almost instantly, both of us at the same time. Panting, sighs. When we've calmed down again, he looks into my eyes and starts giving me little kisses all over: my eyelids, my cheeks, my forehead. He moves to my neck and gives me chills. I pull away, trying to elude his mouth. He laughs hard and crushes me in an enormous hug, folding himself around me.

"You're wonderful," he says.

I try to stand up, untie his knot. He stops me.

"I won't let you go," he murmurs.

He's acting the part of the playful boyfriend, and it makes me uncomfortable. I don't know if the terrible anger I was feeling when I came here is gone yet. I get to my feet and pick up the clothing scattered around us.

"Can I take a shower?"

"Of course. While you shower, I'll make dinner. A perfect arrangement."

He's euphoric. I'm embarrassed about my recent effusion. I go into the bathroom. I can hear him humming in the kitchen. Yes, he's euphoric. I poke through the things he has on a glass shelf: shaving cream, electric shaver, a huge bottle of cologne, some ibuprofen . . . Not much. I'd assumed a man who dances naked in a show would use fancy skin products, perfumes, massage oils. But no.

I shower. My muscles gradually loosen under the hot water. I dry myself off with a towel that's hanging on a hook. All the cells in my body are mine again and under control. As I'm rubbing myself with the towel, I remember that it's used and feel squeamish. It's silly, and I know it: you have sex with a man but are disgusted by his used towel. Of course, with Javier there's sex but no intimacy. With David there was intimacy, but no pleasure. You can't have it all at the same time. It doesn't matter—we can take turns. Suddenly I realize my rage at my contradictions has evaporated. The natural method has been more effective than a psychiatrist's pills.

I go out into Javier's living room. It's so austere, so tiny, so full of books. In one corner he's set the table for dinner. Just as I feared, he's lit a candle.

"Dinner's ready," he says, poking his head out of the kitchen.

Salad and pasta. He must have had it all prepared in advance, because he got it ready really quickly. A bottle of white wine in a bag to keep it at the perfect temperature. I've seen this set piece in plenty of those American movies they show on TV. They're for young people. Boy, girl, lit candle, wine. Something unexpected always ends up happening. It can be good or bad—doesn't matter. It just has to surprise the viewer. And the outcome is always a foregone conclusion: they fall in love. I've never seen a movie where the girl pays the boy for sex.

"Do you like the spaghetti?"

"It's great."

"I didn't make the sauce. I bought it this afternoon in an Italian import shop."

She's gorgeous like that, fresh out of the shower. The makeup she was wearing is gone. I like her better without it. Her features have also softened. When she got here she had sharp lines around her mouth, stress lines. She must be more relaxed after our intense hello. And now here we are, having dinner like any other couple.

"I'm really happy you came, Irene."

"Thanks," I respond, not knowing what else to say. I hope this doesn't turn into an attempt at romance.

"I actually needed this visit. I had a rough day yesterday. Iván's mother died—she was in a prison psych hospital. He asked me to take care of everything because he didn't feel capable of dealing with it. It was really depressing."

"Why did you have to do it?"

"Iván's relationship with his mother was pretty unique. Dysfunctional family, love/hate relationships . . . Things were complicated."

"Your friend isn't a child anymore. He's had time to work through his traumas."

"Easier said than done."

"You're very supportive."

"Are you not?"

"To be supportive, you have to be either really happy or a really good person. Otherwise it's better if you don't get involved."

"Which quality are you lacking?"

"Both. I'm not good or happy."

If I don't shut this conversation down, he's going to start asking personal questions that I don't want to answer.

"Is there any dessert, or am I being punished?"

He rushes off to the kitchen and brings out a tub of ice cream. As he serves it, I have time to observe him at leisure. His hair is gleaming in the lamplight. He's handsome today. We eat in silence. Suddenly he looks at me, very serious.

"Yesterday I saw Iván's mother in her casket. I started thinking I'd end up the same way: abandoned, alone in a corner, without anybody who cared whether I was dead or alive."

"That's a horrible thing to say."

It's like being stabbed with a knife. It catches me off guard, and my voice almost cracks. He notices. He gets up and comes over to me. He takes my hand, and we go over to the sofa and sit there, our arms around each other, in silence. After a while, I start feeling sleepy and let myself drift off.

I awake with a start in the middle of the night. There's no light in the living room. I've fallen asleep on the sofa, and Javier is lying on the rug. Nervous, I get up and try to step over him without waking him. I go to the window to peer at my watch in the light from the streetlamps.

"It's four o'clock," I hear him say from the floor.

"I'm sorry, I didn't mean to wake you, but I have to go."

"Why? Go ahead and sleep here. If you want, I can give you my bed and I'll sleep on the sofa."

"I have to go."

When he sees me move to take out my wallet to pay him, he jumps to his feet.

"Not today, please."

There's such authority in his voice, such desperation, such violence too, that I decide to obey and put the money away, even though I know I'm making a mistake I'll come to regret.

"Do you want me to call you a taxi?"

"I'll call one down on the street."

"Whatever you prefer."

He moves toward me, evidently to give me a kiss. I back away, trying not to seem like I'm rejecting him. I raise my hand to wave goodbye. I smile.

"I'll call you. Thanks for dinner."

It doesn't really matter whether he kisses me in and of itself. But right then I couldn't have borne even the slightest bit of intimacy. I went down the stairs and called a taxi from the sidewalk. When I got home, I found it lonely and silent, as always.

* * *

I should have given the teacher some kind of gift. He deserves it after that bullshit with my mom. Maybe I could give him one of my good contacts, the ones I keep for myself. Puri, for example, who's a gold mine. The problem is, since we've been screwing around for almost three years, she might say she doesn't want to switch. Though most likely it'd be the teacher who'd say no. He just wants to see tourists, do parties with large groups of women, and go around with that pain in the ass Irene. If I propose a divorced hairdresser, he'll tell me he's not interested. Doesn't matter if I insist she's the owner of a fancy salon and has a shit-ton of money and buckets of style—he'll

say no. He doesn't give a damn about style. Just look at Irene—
always so buttoned up, in flats and secretary blouses. Now that
he's earning a decent living, he could go out and buy a nice
shirt or some Armani jeans. But no, he still goes around in his
department store duds. Thankfully I made him pick up some
black pants and a white shirt for parties, or the bastard would
show up in a tracksuit.

No, I'm going to forget about hooking him up with Puri. I
should just go to a bookstore and buy a gift certificate. Then
he can go and choose the books he wants. He might be excited
about that, and I really want him to be happy. I want him to
know I'm super grateful to him for dealing with that crap with
my mother. I just didn't have the stomach for it, no matter how
the hospital people acted. Going there, enduring their platitudes, all of them lies, and then putting up with that rude
director looking at me as if to say, "You never came to see her,
you asshole." No way. And I didn't want to see her dead. I
guess that crap about how "A mother is a mother" has some
truth to it. Though mine was a sorry excuse for a mother.
Maybe she did used to love me and would gaze at me proudly,
saying, "Look at this squirt—he's my own son." But just a
while isn't long enough. I remember one day when one of the
priests, back when priests still got on my nerves, goes and says,
"You must always be grateful to your mother for bringing you
into the world. You owe her your existence. Her and God." I
thought: So mothers are like cats, right? They take care of you
for a while, and then they just leave you to your own devices,
and that's apparently something to be grateful for. And let's not
even talk about God, always watching you in case you misbehave. You can all fuck off!

Back then when my grandma used to take me to see the
priests so they could counsel me, I'd really kick up some major
hissy fits. I was always pissed off inside, and eventually I'd lose
it. I was like those guys in the movies who've experienced some-

thing really brutal and they're eaten up inside until they finally manage to get their revenge and are able to rest. But I didn't have anyone to get revenge on. My parents? They were just a couple of losers, total trash. So I spent my life angry, and that anger came back to bite me in the ass. Things got worse and worse. Until one day I saw it all clearly and said to myself, "You've got to chill, man. The way you're going, it's just a matter of time before you crash and burn." I started making my own way, leaving the past behind and taking care of myself. It's true I'm still a bit of a hard-ass because of that time in my youth. I don't like people's bullshit, though instead of going for the jugular when somebody pulls some nasty trick, I turn on anyone who puts up with it. I can't stand it when people just sit there and take somebody's shit and don't say anything! It pisses me off!

I didn't bother with any of the advice I got from my grandma, the priests, or anybody else. "You have to behave." Screw that! "You have to go to school and study hard." Up yours! "You have to get a decent job." Buzz off! "You have to choose a good girl and start a family." Get stuffed! I gave all that a hard pass, but I worked things out on my own, took care of myself. And here I am! Nobody can say anything now: I've got a cool apartment, a computer, a car, designer clothing, enough money to pay for my lifestyle . . . and all the chicks I want, whether they're paying or I am.

The bookstore gift certificate idea is the best option—I'm sure he'll like it. The teacher really loves reading. He picks up his book, hunkers down somewhere where there's not too much going on, and forgets the world. The rest of us can get stuffed. He's lucky. I may spend hours on Twitter, Facebook, and all that crap, but it's not the same, damn it. He gains culture with those books, while I just interact with a bunch of dipshits and assholes I actually can't stand. But reading bores me. I couldn't keep it up with that Raskolnikov pain in the ass. If the policeman doesn't stop coming after him and hassling him,

I say he should get pissed off and beat the crap out of him, or maybe even bump him off, shit, put an end to the whole business. But no, Raskolnikov just broods and doesn't do anything. It's goddamn boring, man—I can't help it.

The teacher's lucky despite everything he's gone through lately. For example, it's a goddamn lucky break his parents kicked the bucket in a car wreck when they were young. And that's not me being delusional. This way he can remember them as being great parents and make up whatever story he wants: they bought him toys, tucked him in, kissed him goodnight . . . That's the way it works: you might not buy into your own lies at first, but after a while you get sucked in and end up believing they're the God's honest truth.

I'd have done anything never to have met the folks I scored in the parent lottery. At least my asshole father kicked it early on, but my mother . . . I've lived my whole life knowing she was out there, a fucking mess, out on the street with nobody giving a shit about her. Not to mention the last few years. The last few years I've had her camped out in a corner of my head, constantly busting my chops: "I'm in a crackbrain warehouse at a prison." Shit, man, what more can you ask for? She hit absolute rock bottom, down in the goddamn basement. And me there, gritting my teeth knowing she was still alive. I fucked up, really. I should have just gone ahead one day and shot her in the face. But I held back, even invited her to my house on Christmas. The hell with it! That's why I say the teacher's had it easier—and he likes to read too.

\* \* \*

It's a pretty confusing situation—ambiguous at the very least. I really wanted to call her to set up a date, but in theory she's the one who should be requesting my professional services. But the other night she didn't pay me, and we had a wonderful dinner.

She was relaxed, cheerful . . . you might even say she seemed loving. Though she did end up deciding to go home in the middle of the night. But apart from that, our relationship took a big step forward. Toward what, though? I'm not sure. Irene's unfriendly, contemptuous, contradictory, with one of the strangest personalities I've ever encountered. Trying to understand her has become a sort of challenge for me, but it's a nearly impossible task because she never tells me anything. How can I even guess what she's thinking or feeling if she refuses to talk about herself? And I'm not supposed to ask her questions. I'm convinced any curiosity on my part might scare her off. She's like one of those thoroughbred mares, high-strung and wary; you can't make any sudden moves around her. But I'm certain she's got a tender core, a treasure that can't find its way out.

In the end, I called her.

"I can't today. I have to work. Maybe tomorrow."

"But tomorrow's Friday and I'm performing at the club. I have to be there early."

"We can see each other after your performance."

"I'd thought maybe we could do daytime activities."

"Daytime activities?" She laughs, and I still like the way it sounds.

"You know, take a walk, get coffee."

Her silence stretches out for a moment, but she accepts my proposition and we agree to meet at a café. Apparently, her work can wait.

She looks carefully made up, very elegant. One day I'd like to see her dressed in jeans and a simple T-shirt, like me. We kiss each other on the cheek, almost timidly. She sits down and remains quiet. Those moments when nobody's talking don't make her uncomfortable, but they do me. We order coffee.

"You thought 'daytime activities' was funny."

"Yes." She smiles vaguely.

"I didn't know quite how to say it. The thing is, I like it

when we get together and do things that people normally do. Do you know what I mean?"

"Yes, take a walk or get coffee."

"It's more than that. What I'm trying to say here is I like being with you, Irene, night or day."

I expect her to react badly or change the subject without responding, but she looks down and says, "I like it too."

It's a pretty vague statement, but it's heartening enough to encourage me to continue:

"I can't stand being an escort. I just can't get used to it. Everything feels cheap and sordid. Maybe I'm just a dinosaur, but I miss other kinds of relationships: being in a couple, the intimacy that develops between two people, the sharing of lives, mutual support . . . Do you know what I mean?"

"Yes."

"Do you ever miss those things?"

"No. I'm good the way I am."

"You're stronger than I am."

"I don't know."

"You know something? I've started looking for a job again, and not just as a teacher. I think I could do well working in a bookstore, as a librarian's assistant . . . I don't know, I've been sending out my CV. It's hard, but it's not impossible. I stopped trying a while back, but now I have new incentives; I feel more motivated."

"Are you tired of us?"

"Us?"

"Your customers."

She knows how to get to you—she throws that dart at just the right moment and with perfect aim. But I'm not going to lash out. Maybe I've been too pushy, tried to go too fast. That's enough for today.

"What do you think we should do, Irene? Take a walk?"

"I'd like to go to your house."

I smile and nod. She smiles too. I keep going.

"On one condition."

"I can guess what it is. But if I don't pay you, what are you going to live on?"

"I have other income. You're the only one I don't want to charge."

Surreptitiously, I watch her face settle into a stubborn micro-pout. If she asked me why, I'd seize on it as an invitation to express greater commitment, take a giant step forward. But she doesn't ask. She stands up and searches for her sunglasses in her purse.

\* \* \*

The closing scene with the factory manager at the notary's office was quite unpleasant. We'd already talked many times, gone over the numbers, signed a million documents. So why does he have to go and kick up a stink in front of the notary and the buyer?

"I'd like to speak to you in private for a moment," he tells me.

We go out into the hallway. He looks at me intently.

"Irene, are you positive you want to sell?"

"Where is this coming from? You know I do."

"I'm obligated to tell you how bad things are, and I did that—but there's still a chance, with a little effort on your part . . .

"Let's go back in, please."

"Irene, it's your father's company. This work has meant everything to you, and when we leave here it will disappear from your life forever."

"You know what I think? My father's company has been responsible for every bad thing that's happened to me since the day I was born. Let's go back in, please."

Given the look on his face, I might as well have plunged a

dagger into his heart. Very melodramatic. He wants to make it very clear that he tried to change my mind. He wants to point out my mistakes, my lack of courage to keep running the company, my inability to fight.

As we left the building, he suggested we get lunch together. I took great pleasure in blowing him off. It's over.

I considered calling Javier. A surprise. An impromptu meal as a "daytime activity." Was it enough? For once I didn't care. I needed company.

"I can't today, Irene. Iván and I are performing at noon."

"Noon?"

"A cosmetics corporation is having its annual convention. Since almost all of the executives are women, they decided on a striptease as the final event. It pays really well. I can't leave Iván in the lurch."

"It's OK. Another time."

"Tomorrow, if you want."

"I can't tomorrow. I'll call you."

I met up with Genoveva instead. I didn't feel like eating alone today. We drank champagne and toasted the sale of the company. When we were done, I was pretty tipsy, and I was tempted to call Javier again. But he wasn't available, of course—he was stripping naked and acting like an idiot in front of a bunch of shrieking girls. Actually, I didn't want to have sex with him either. The only thing I wanted was for him to silently stroke my back the way he does sometimes. In those moments, my mind goes blank and I rest, finally free of thoughts.

* * *

We've seen each other with increasing frequency over the past few days. Sometimes she pays me and sometimes she doesn't. It's good to have her pay every once in a while—I need to cover the expenses of daily life. My job search hasn't led to anything—and it's not going to. Who needs a college graduate during a recession? I could try getting a job in a factory or warehouse. But do I really see myself unloading boxes from a truck eight hours a day? No. I don't see myself doing anything eight hours a day. I need time to read, to think. My grandmother supported me while I was a student, and after that Sandra did some too. I'm not used to working full-time. I'm not brave, not a fighter. Being an escort has allowed me to have free time, to maintain the lifestyle I've always had. The world's a complicated place—more so all the time. You can't have everything, though sometimes I'm convinced that with a bit of luck I could have a lot more.

Irene called one morning and we arranged to meet up for dinner. We went to a Japanese restaurant and then to my apartment. We had another glorious round of sex, intense and wild. Afterward, almost without thinking, I asked if she wanted to spend the night. She never does, but that day she said yes. I was astounded. A giant step forward.

I lend her a nightshirt that's so huge on her it makes both of us laugh. She lies down beside me. I turn out the light. I don't even touch her—I'm scared of her. I'm always afraid she's going to take off running. After a while, I hear her steady breathing. She's asleep. I'm filled with a sense of well-being I haven't felt for a long time. I'm sleeping next to somebody again. A woman. Hardly any light is coming in through the window, and I can't make her out in the dark, but I hear her, calm, peaceful. I feel like sobbing with emotion. I've been so alone the past few months, but today I have a priceless treasure: the gentle, almost childlike breathing of a companion slumbering beside me.

The next day I open my eyes and she's gone. Nothing's wrong: she awoke early and left for work, trying not to disturb me. I smell the pillow, which is infused with her scent. I toss and turn in the bed, stretch my limbs . . . I feel good. Suddenly

I'm filled with doubt about a potentially meaningful detail. I look on the nightstand. I go out to the living room and search everywhere. No, she hasn't left me any money. Good! She must have debated what to do and made this decision—she's not the kind of woman who acts without considering things carefully.

I hum as I make breakfast and eat it in the kitchen, filled with calm and a growing sense that my life is falling into place. Who knows! Maybe a parenthesis is closing and from here on out everything can go back to the way it was, or even better. All at once, without logical cause, I am gripped by unease: what if all those tender moments from last night were a way of saying goodbye? It's not impossible—after all, I barely know this woman. Foolishly, I pick up the phone and call her. She doesn't answer. I leave a message: "I'm not calling for any particular reason—I just wanted to hear your voice. I'll call you later."

I shower. I go out. I buy a newspaper and sit down to read it in a bar with a good cup of coffee. The absurd anxieties I was feeling just a moment ago evaporate. Even so, when the phone rings and I see that it's her, I swell with joy.

"Sorry. I didn't call because I was in a meeting. Will I see you later?"

Impulsively, I say yes, then immediately realize I can't. I've got a rehearsal at the club, and it's going to last longer than usual because we're changing a few things in our number. We agree to meet the next day, though there's some disappointment in her voice.

Incredibly, she's smiling when she appears, and, also incredibly, I greet her with a hug without worrying that she'll reject me. We're at a high-end Italian place she picked. We study the menu, but then both of us look up at the same time. Neither of us looks away. I'd swear she seems more frank, more direct, almost conspiratorial. Maybe I'm about to discover the real woman who's hiding behind the mask I've seen so far. It's a critical moment. I don't think I'm wrong about her: she's got a "tender treasure at her core" that sooner or later—or right now, maybe—will blossom.

We have a quiet dinner. I tell her about the changes we've made to the performance: the spear is too long, and Iván's gotten a little scratched up . . . Silly details that I relate in a comical tone. I watch her laugh. The woman who never even used to smile is finally laughing. Suddenly she says:

"Maybe there's a way we can fix your job problem."

My heart pounds, and I wonder if she's about to say the words I want to hear. She's a little nervous, and she doesn't meet my eyes as she speaks.

"I know you're not planning to give up performing at the club, but maybe you could stop going out with other women. I don't know how much money you earn that way or how much you need for your living expenses, but we could come up with an estimate and . . . um, I could pay you a sort of salary. You'd be free of those obligations and be available to me at all times. Within limits, of course."

A bucket of cold water? I'm not sure. At any rate, now's my chance, now or never. After all, she's the one who broached the subject.

"Irene, I've been thinking about this issue for a long time, though I'd never have dared bring it up. You own a company, right?"

"Yes."

"Well, maybe it would be possible for . . . for you to find me a job there. I don't know how to do much, but just a part-time job in the office would be enough. You know I've been looking for a while, but there's nothing out there. If we follow your suggestion and pay me to . . . to go out with you, I'll have to keep being what I am now. Plus, our relationship will never be able to evolve naturally. I don't want to be your escort—yours or anybody else's. It's humiliating; I'll never get used to it. If I worked for your company and things went well, I could even stop dancing at the club eventually. You and I could live a normal life like normal people. There's something between us, Irene. I don't know what it is exactly or where it's going, but it won't be anything at all if we don't give it at least a chance."

I've spoken with restrained vehemence and complete honesty. Her expression hasn't changed, which isn't surprising. I've made an unexpected counterproposal, and she needs to think. Indeed, a moment later she says:

"I'll think about it."

"All right. Let's drop the subject for today, if you don't mind. Shall we go back to my place?"

We go back to my place and make love. I don't want to keep overanalyzing her behavior and getting myself worked up, so I focus on my own pleasure. I have a good time. The idea of finding a solution for my life relaxes me rather than sending me into a tizzy.

At one in the morning, Irene says she's leaving.

"You're not going to spend the night?"

"I have an important meeting first thing in the morning," she says. "At the company," she adds.

Her scent floats in the air for a good while after she leaves, and I fall asleep.

* * *

I get home at one thirty. I take a shower and put on my pajamas. Instead of going to bed, I sit down on the sofa in the living room. I turn off the overhead light and leave on just a small lamp that glows only dimly. Semi-darkness, good. There's a fifth of whiskey nearby. I don't feel like going to fetch a glass, so I drink straight from the bottle. I start laughing. It's really incredible—it must be fate, or karma, or my guardian angel, always steering me down the same paths. The guy doesn't want a salary for his exclusive services; no, what he wants is to work for me in a respectable job. He wants to work at my company, the one I just sold. It's a perfect setup for him. That way our relationship can evolve, an evolution not even Darwin himself could have conceived of. I'll attempt to imagine it: he'd start out as a hotel porter and end up running the place. That's how it always goes in old Hollywood movies. Old Hollywood movies also feature fortune-hunters pursuing the dull, ugly rich girl. Excellent. So I find him a part-time position that won't wear him out, and he starts rising through the ranks of the organization chart. In the meantime, our relationship also develops toward its apex, and I keep giving him a boost up until he eventually triumphs. Once he's reached the very top, we get married. Then my guy will have two coveted roles: manager and husband of the owner. It's a great plan for him—and not just for him. Do I get any benefit from this arrangement? But of course! For starters, not only do I get to assuage the social sting of having been left by one husband, I also snag myself another one, brand-new and in mint condition. And as for the company, what more could we ask for? We gain an amazing literature scholar, such an invaluable skillset for financial dealings. And on top of that, he's an unemployed teacher, striptease dancer, and professional prostitute. He really checks all the boxes! It's a shame I sold the business. With a new employee like that, we might have been able to get things afloat again.

I stand up and go to look for my wedding photos. I considered throwing them away when David left me, but instead I buried them in a drawer. Here they are, and here I am in a white raw silk dress and a tulle veil secured with a wreath of flowers. I have no idea who tricked me into wearing such a traditional look. If my mother had been alive, she wouldn't have let me dress like that. I'm sure she was more modern—or maybe not. How would I know? I never met her. Here's Papá, dapper and proud, of course: he was marrying off his only daughter and gaining a splendid asset for the company in the figure of the young lawyer who would work for him from then on. The company. You really screwed me with the company, Papá. A perfect prison for me. An apparently surefire husband-snaring trap. And here's David, all serious in his morning coat. He'd probably written it in his agenda: "Wedding at noon." All these marvelous images could soon reappear for an encore. With new characters, of course. Papá wouldn't be in the photos because he's dead. David's with a woman who's not me. The groom would be Javier. How would we dress for the nuptials? He'd be in that gladiator outfit he dances in at the club, and I should match: maybe a vampire-red dress with a thigh-revealing side slit and my foot sheathed in a silver stiletto heel. Spectacular! The best man and maid of honor would be Iván and Genoveva. Even more spectacular!

I take a big swig and then pour two drops of whiskey onto the photo. One on my father's image. The other on David. I want them to drink a toast with me to my new marriage, which will never take place.

Everything could have been different this time—in fact, it was starting out that way. I never asked Javier questions. I didn't want to know anything else. We were fine the way we were: casual conversation and sex. Every once in a while, sleeping contentedly beside each other after screwing. I'm grateful to him for opening the doors of sexual pleasure to me. And I can't complain about the rest: he's been polite, kind, caring, and fun. But I wanted more—exclusive access to him at an agreed-on price that worked for both of us. A civilized arrangement, and I could start living. With the company sold and money in the bank . . . free for the first time! But it was an unforgivable misstep. In wanting to have him all to myself, I gave him an opening to want it all: a steady job, an evolving relationship, and a normal life.

Maybe I should have told him, "The company's no longer part of the package," but I kept that information to myself, and that's how it's going to stay. It's such a crock! There are only a few women whose value comes from themselves alone; the rest of us are always part of a package.

Tomorrow I'll call the psychiatrist and tell him to go to hell. Oh, I did that already? Doesn't matter—I'll tell him again. I'll say, "You were right. I've been living in a cage made of fatherly love and money, but I'm not going to escape it by taking pills and trying to make do. I'll get out my own way. Dumbass!"

It'll be fun, it'll be great. I'll call him tomorrow.

I'm sleepy, but I won't go to the bedroom. No, I'll stay right here, spend the whole night on the sofa. I don't want more order in my life. For me, order has been chaos.

\* \* \*

I figured I'd put my foot in it for real. She didn't call me for two weeks, and when I called her, she always told me she was busy: a series of problems at the company that required her attention. Until yesterday. Yesterday she called me, sounding upbeat: things at work have finally cleared up and she can go back to normal. I'd been almost positive my proposal had set back our relationship to the very beginning. All gone, bye-bye. I told Iván I'd asked for a job at her company, and his reaction didn't cheer me up.

"You're nuts, man. You really thought you could look to these broads for professional advancement? Just thinking about you working at her company must have freaked her out. And then you go and suggest the two of you should be a couple! I bet my balls once she was alone in her house, she pissed herself laughing at you. You really don't get it, teacher. These chicks think we're a couple of losers, the bottom of the barrel, pure cannon fodder. What's that country where everything's organized around social classes and the ones on the bottom can't even be touched? China or India, I think—I don't remember. Well, it's basically like that here too. Don't tell me you believed that crap about how in a democracy everyone's equal and all that jazz."

I couldn't reply that I'm not him, that my relationship with Irene isn't just sex. I made an attempt:

"Look, Iván, I'm not saying Irene's in love with me, but I think I mean something to her—she treats me differently."

"Oh, yeah, I'm sure she pines for you every night. Probably kisses your photo. So she proposed you fuck her exclusively— that doesn't mean anything. These chicks get selfish—all of them do. They don't like to share. They want a cock of their own. But to go from there to giving you a job and getting serious with you . . . Get it out of your head, man. Get it out or this chick is really going to screw you up. And my advice is to tell her you won't go exclusive, no way. You be the boss. I warned you right from the start, if you stay with just one chick, you're screwed."

Iván's changed since his mother died. He's more aggressive, more insulting toward women; he snaps at me a lot and is always in a bad mood. He must feel guilty he didn't go see her, or angry he never got revenge on her. Who knows! In any event, though, Irene's call dissipated all my doubts. We agreed to meet that night.

She's radiant in a low-cut blue dress. She's acting completely normal, as if we saw each other just yesterday. She smiles, makes small talk—she looks so happy that I wonder whether she's about to tell me she's got a job for me. It's not like I'm asking for anything excessive or immoral. I'm not trying to take advantage of the situation. I like her, she likes me— why not give it a shot? If I worked for her company, I'd make sure to do a good job. I'd never look for extra privileges or special treatment. And I'm not hoping to get ahead or earn a ton of money, just a fair salary that's enough to live on, pay the rent, buy books . . . I've never been an ambitious man, and I don't understand people who are. My little apartment is enough for me; a bit of free time, and I'm all set—guaranteed happiness. I'd give up my job at the club—I've had enough—and my nights out with women, which I find more and more unbearable. I don't regret what I've done: the situation was out of my hands and I didn't have another option. But I have to escape the fringes of society at some point. I don't want to end up like Iván, like his mother. As far as my relationship with Irene . . . we'll see. For the moment, we have our own places. We'll evolve or we'll remain stalled, but at least we'll have things clear, and maybe, just maybe, something lasting will come of it. Stable relationships aren't based just on violent passions or romantic love. After being together according to other rules, it's still possible we might get to know each other well, maybe even love each other. It wouldn't be hard if she were always the way she is today: beautiful and happy. Today she's looking at me in a special way; it takes my breath away. I want her. I'd like to get up from the table and drag her home with me. The sex today is going to be explosive.

And it was: explosive and all-encompassing, hungry and passionate. Afterward we had coffee in the kitchen, an intimate little ceremony. With my cup steaming in my hand, I asked her:

"Have you had time to think about a job for me?"

"Of course! I've given the relevant instructions to have them look for something for you."

"Look, Irene, I don't want you to think . . . "

"No need to explain. It's all very clear. I thought to celebrate I could invite you all to dinner at my house. It would be the usual foursome: you, me, Genoveva, and Iván."

I've never been to her house. She hasn't said what it is exactly we'll be celebrating. Maybe she's referring to the changes that will be taking place in her life and mine going forward. That must be it. I've never heard her sound so professional either: "I've given the relevant instructions." She must be a very different woman in her work environment. I have no idea—come to think of it, I just know her in bed and across a restaurant table . . .

She insisted on paying me tonight. That's OK—I'll let her be the one to set the pace for the changes in our situation.

\* \* \*

It was awesome, just awesome. Really amazing. I was surprised she invited us to her house—that doesn't usually happen—but there we were at the indicated time for dinner. The house was freaking huge. The living room's as big as a nightclub. Armchairs everywhere and a sofa as long as a train. And paintings, and antique and modern furniture all mixed together. All of them good quality, top-of-the-line stuff—I don't know much about that, but I know a little. A low dresser or whatever you call them—when I opened it I was blown away: bottles and bottles of whiskey and gin, a million different kinds, and other liquors too, who knows what all of them were. I'd never been in a rich person's house, as a guest like that, I mean. I'd seen plenty of nice houses when we performed at parties, but never one like this. Hell, at first it pissed me off! If we'd known these broads were such high rollers, the teacher and I would have charged them more. Of course, rich people are known for haggling, being stingy—after all, they got rich some way. And the situation itself pissed me off too: why the hell does this chick get to live like a queen while the rest of us are scraping by as best we can? It's massively unfair. I know there have always been rich people and losers, and that's not going to change, but when you see it up close and in person like that, it really cheeses you off. At least she was treating us like VIPs: "What would you like to drink?" "Please have a seat." All very sophisticated and polite. Even the ice they put in the glasses looked different from the kind you take out of the freezer at home. It made a fantastic noise when it hit the bottom of the glass: *clink, clink* . . . It sounded posh, as good as the honey-colored whiskey trickling down afterward.

The four of us sat down and started making small talk as usual. Just to be a pain in the ass, I said I didn't feel like whiskey, wanted a beer instead. I didn't want them to think I'm a bum who was seizing an opportunity—I can have whiskey whenever I want. The lady of the house went off to get one, and when she came back with the bottle and a chilled glass, Genoveva asked her if the maid had the day off. Irene probably got her out of the way so she wouldn't see us.

Every once in a while I'd look over at the teacher and signal to him with my eyes to check out the luxury around us, but he didn't notice. He was in a daze, sitting with his knees together like the old people in the waiting room at the public hospital. He looked as crumpled as a recently discarded cigarette butt. Not me—I was cool as a cucumber, drinking my beer like I was at the corner bar. I don't crumple in front of anybody.

We stayed there chatting idly until it was time to eat and Irene said we should move into the dining room. Shit, it was like being in a goddamn movie! The dining room featured a sideboard loaded with canapés on trays covered with white cloths. You just had to remove the cloths and chow down. The maid had probably left everything all ready so Irene didn't have to do anything. It was an awesome dinner, the kind you don't see every day. There were even goose barnacles, which I'd never tried before because they kind of gross me out. I didn't try them that night either. I just can't bring myself to gulp down some animal where you can't identify its head and feet. But there were some other shellfish I did eat. Genoveva was babbling on the way she does: "God, this dinner is just orgasmic!" I used to find her funny, but she's starting to get on my nerves. I'd like to punch her. Or kill her, even. But I just chilled, got up to fill my plate when it was empty and laughed and watched the teacher, who was less nervous now—he looked goddamn delighted with life, toasting with his glass and gazing at Irene as if we were celebrating a goddamn marriage and she was the bride.

Irene was starting to fall apart. She hit the wine hard and then moved on to the Moët. The maid had left a huge bucket full of ice and bottles of alcohol so we wouldn't have to go to the kitchen to get them, in case we were completely pooped. We made full use of it. And Irene was holding her own, though she remained as buttoned up and occasionally rude as ever. The chick bugs the hell out of me. You never know if she's screwing with you or doesn't mean anything by it. My money's on the first option. "What a lovely shirt, Iván!" she says suddenly. "Is it a name brand?" I longed to shoot back, "Shove it up your ass, sweetheart," but I kept quiet because she's a customer and the teacher is my friend. Come to think of it, how is it he's hung up on a hussy like her? Cold, always looking down on you, nasty, a total weirdo . . . Aren't there any other chicks out there?

She can't stand me, so I wonder why the hell she invited me to dinner. I guess she likes screwing with people.

Anyway, when we were many bottles in, the lady of the house goes and says she's got a surprise for us. She takes out a bunch of cocaine wraps.

"Get out of here! What did you do to come up that kind of supply?" I said.

"You think I'm just a dumb girl, don't you, Iván?"

"I didn't say that. You said that."

"We're talking about thinking, not saying."

Iván's a real champ, just a gem. Aggressive, boorish, lazy, macho, imbecilic. Pure trash. The king of the lowlifes, number one. An anthropological treasure.

"I always say what I think!"

It's a good thing I wasn't carrying a gun or I'd have plugged her right there. Seeing that the situation's getting ugly, the teacher makes a couple of silly comments to calm things down. We all laugh. Even Genoveva laughs. The poor woman's so wasted, she seems like she might pass out at any moment.

We do a few lines, some high-quality stuff. We chill out a little. We talk about the usual bullshit, nothing special. Then Irene gets up and puts on some music. She starts dancing sexily around the dining room. What the hell is she doing? Today's full of surprises. The coke has put her in a good mood, brought out her hidden side. Genoveva starts dancing too. Between how hammered she is and how she's getting up there in years, she's about as graceful as a breakdancing bear. The teacher, who's a goddamn prince for life, keeps sitting there, very upright and faintly fake-smiling. I join the party and start horsing around, though I have no idea what this is all about. What comes next? Has she gotten two rooms ready, or are we having an orgy today? Just to test things out, I grab one of Genoveva's tits; she shrieks playfully, picks up a piece of bread from the table, and throws it at my head. When it seems like things are finally getting going, Irene breaks in and asks, "Does anyone want a gin and tonic?" The teacher says he does, and goddamn Irene leaves us all taken aback because she goes and says, "Well, let's go to a bar. It's really hot in here." Javier's thrilled—what a relief, right, teach? You didn't really see what was going on. So we gather up our things and the wraps we haven't snorted yet, and head out into the street.

Almost immediately, Irene, who's high as a kite, spots a bus approaching a stop and takes off running. "Follow me!" she shouts. We get on the goddamn bus without tickets, of course, through the back door. The driver doesn't say boo, and the few people on the bus at that time of night eye us listlessly. We're

not the least bit funny: four jackasses, obviously stoned, looking to make a scene. I'm getting fed up with that bullshit—I've
never liked calling a lot of attention to myself. And I don't like
having a hot chick leading the group. But all right, I'm down
for whatever. Plus Irene's got the blow in her purse, and a line
here or there will keep me going. Javier's chipper but surprised. He laughs at all of his girl's antics—he's probably never
seen her so happy.

Downtown, we go to a cocktail bar. Four gin and tonics and
laughter and "the night is young" bullshit, and Genoveva saying it reminds her of her youth. The hell with her youth—there
were probably dinosaurs roaming the earth back then! We
take turns going to the bathroom for a supplementary line of
coke. We're totally buzzed, smashed. I'm so high, I'm not even
pissed anymore.

All of a sudden the chick, our activity director for the night,
tells us to knock back our drinks and come outside with her
because she needs some air. That's no surprise—I've never
seen her drink so much, let alone put anything up her nose. We
go out and head down the street, the four of us looking like
freaking zombies. We walk through some plaza, no idea—the
one with the huge fountain in the middle of it.

"Anyone feel like a dip? It's hot—I'm really hot."

No sooner said than done. The girl goes and starts getting
naked right there. And I do mean naked: she takes off her bra
and panties and stands there in her birthday suit.
Unbelievable—what the hell is up with her? I never would
have expected that. Shit, people are always surprising you. She
looks at us, wobbling, with the same superior air as always.

"What are you waiting for? Come on, guys, strip down and
get in!"

I immediately go after her and take it all off. I'm not about
to be intimidated, especially not in front of this goddamn
annoying chick. And it's fun. Shirt, pants, boxers, and splash!

Shit, it's cold! I look out and there are Genoveva and Javier, fully clothed. The teacher is smiling strangely. Genoveva looks really pissed. She goes up to her friend and starts saying, "Irene, please, please."

Lots of pleasepleases but she didn't say anything else, though it was clear she was asking Irene to drop the cavewoman routine and wrap things up. But Irene had no intention of it— there she was, splashing the water with her feet like a kid at the beach. And I was having a great time! It had turned out to be an awesome party. I looked at the teacher again, and the bastard wasn't moving a muscle—he had on a poker face, though it was a little glum too. I guess he was taking it hard seeing his little angel going wild and making a buck-naked spectacle of herself. I warned him to watch out, but he just refused to see it.

While this is going on, a taxi comes by. Genoveva doesn't hesitate.

"Well, kids, it's been great. I'm taking off."

And she ups and leaves. All right, I think, but I'll call you tomorrow because we haven't settled the bill yet, unless the invitation from the bathing beauty here also includes our fees for the night.

The teacher gets nervous when he sees a car and launches another set of pleasepleases at the mermaid.

"Irene, please."

Looking to ease the tension, just fooling around, I shout, "It's the cops!"

The car kept going, but Irene was already out of the water, howling with laughter. Still dripping, she put on her shoes, tucked her clothing under her arm, picked up her purse, and started running, cracking up and without a stitch. The teacher called out and went after her, but I jumped out of the fountain and grabbed him by the arm.

"Where the hell are you going?"

"She's naked, Iván."

"Let her go, damn it. She'll go into some doorway and get dressed. Then she'll catch a taxi and go home. She's got money—there's nothing to worry about. The party's over."

I started getting dressed, and he just stood there like a twit, his face gloomy.

"Come on, teach, let's go. Feel like having one last beer? Come sleep at my place tonight."

"No thanks. I'm going home."

He started walking like he was coming back from a goddamn funeral, poking along all hangdog and dragging his feet.

"Who's going to pay us for tonight?" I call after him.

"I don't know, Iván, I don't know."

Like I say, worse than a funeral director. Oh, love! A little white dove, huh? You're screwed, dude. But that's life—as a man who spends all his time reading should know. Though I'm no dummy, and I get the impression that people who read all the time end up losing sight of things. Maybe books don't paint life prettier than it is, but they do make it seem more important. And there's no such thing as important shit in the lives of everyday people. Nothing is important, nothing. Well, except for earning money—so tomorrow I'm going to call Javier to see when these broads intend on paying us.

* * *

I was pretty upset after the party the other night. Irene's behavior didn't exactly seem like that of a woman who was laying the groundwork for a new life. If her plan is to give me a job and start a future with me, why did her fun have such a desperate edge to it? It's clear she's not in the mental place I'd expected. Indeed, her mind never is where I expect it to be. Taking a glass-half-full view of things, I can decide that the other night was a sort of farewell to the seedy world we've been circulating in. Saying goodbye to our prostituted relationship with a drugs-and-alcohol–fueled bender. Or maybe I'm being foolish, trying to change facts through sheer will. Iván tends toward this latter option, but he doesn't realize what's happening between the two of us. Irene needs me more than I need her, and I'll be by her side when any obstacles come up in life, which they inevitably will. She's insecure, fragile, neurotic. It may seem like her life's been easy, but it hasn't. She's endured a lonely childhood, a broken marriage, a demanding job. She's been surrounded by frivolous, superficial people with enormous wealth but very little to offer her. With me her life would be different: I'll make sure everything around her is simpler, more authentic, more harmonious. We'll read books and discuss them afterward. We'll go out for pizza on Saturday nights, like other couples do. I don't want to make plans on where we'll end up living because that would be premature, but the ideal, I think, would be to get a new house. A house that's new for both of us, not as fancy as hers but less spartan than mine. Starting over. I'm laid back and rarely get angry, and the person I'm with tends to appreciate that quality. Working and living with your partner. It's quite simple and can go really smoothly.

I call her on the phone. I have a rehearsal tonight and won't be able to meet up. I pay close attention to her tone of voice, which sounds normal.

"How are you doing, Irene?"

"Good. I've got a bit of a hangover."

"Last night was pretty over the top, huh?"

"Over the top? I don't know, it was fun."

"How should I interpret what happened?"

"What do you mean?"

"I was surprised you organized a party like that. Not that there's anything wrong with painting the town red, but it seemed like we were taking a step backward. Going out with Iván and Genoveva again, causing a scene in the middle of the street . . . I don't know, it had felt like we were starting a calmer phase, just the two of us.

"It's not that big a deal—there was no real reason. I just felt like it."

What did this guy think? The bastard! Calling me to demand explanations for my behavior! He's a lot dumber than I thought. Next he's going to ask about the job I'm supposed to find for him. It's all so tacky!

"Yeah, but I want to make sure you're OK, that everything's on track."

"I don't see why anything has to change, Javier."

"Can we see each other tomorrow?"

"I've got a lot of work at the factory tomorrow. Let's do the day after."

"Just the two of us, OK?"

"Great. Now I've got to go—somebody's calling on the land line."

Everything's still the same. Everything's still the same? Maybe if my situation were different it would be time to break up with Irene. Too much uncertainty. But my only hope for the future depends on her.

\* \* \*

"Yes, Iván, yes. I've got your money for the other night. Irene transferred it to my bank account—it was her treat. It's the least she could do after the way she acted."

"She was off her gourd."

"It was just awful, and I told her so, believe me. I'd already warned her on a couple of occasions, just as a good friend, but she went way too far that night. I'm a respectable woman, and I've got a reputation to uphold. Plus I depend on my ex-husband's alimony. I can't mess around with stuff and nonsense. And I really don't see the fun in it, honestly:

getting high, sure, but what's so great about swimming naked in a fountain?"

"It wasn't that bad!"

"Maybe not for you, Iván, and I hope you won't be upset by what I'm about to say. You two were in your own world, doing your own thing, and what you do in that context isn't so important. For a man, it could even be a notch in your belt, something to tell your friends about afterward. But things don't work that way for women. You understand where I'm coming from, right, Iván?"

"Yeah, of course."

You think I won't understand, you damn hussy? I hear what you're saying: we're trash, so if we want to get buck naked outside a cathedral in the middle of the day, it's no big deal. At most, a police officer comes along and runs us off like the dogs we are. But not you ladies—you're the goddamn cherry on the sundae, always perched at the tippy-top. I'd love it if your reputations were actually affected by going out with riffraff and getting hammered. No, man, I understand you just goddamn fine. The only one who doesn't get it is the teacher. But me? I've understood this crap since birth. I was weaned on it. First I learned I'm a piece of shit, then that everybody else was better than me. Finally I got sick of it and started doing whatever the hell I felt like, no matter what. But that doesn't mean I can change reality. Reality is crystal clear: you're a couple of rich-ass women, and we're goddamn losers. That's the way it's been since the dawn of time. And what can I do about it, grab a shotgun and start shooting? Who would I shoot at, you? You're just a dumbass—I feel sorry for you. But a guy can't get cocky the way teach has. Get laid a few times, charge your fee, and fuck right off! But this business of going out and getting drinks and hooking up . . . no goddamn way! The ladies can go play at the lady daycare and leave us the hell alone.

"I was really clear with her. I'm done. I can't risk going out with her and having her make a spectacle of herself when I least expect it."

"Is she really that out of control?"

"She's getting worse and worse. She was already odd, very much a daddy's girl and in her own world. But now she's had all these problems—her father dies, her husband leaves her, and her company falls apart and she has to sell the business . . . She hasn't gotten over any of that, and she's going a little crazy."

"She sold the company?"

"Just a little while back, and from what I hear she got a good price for it. I don't think she'll ever lack for money, but of course her work was her life, and now she doesn't have anything to do. I told her to see a psychiatrist and she did start going, but . . . "

"I'm sorry, Genoveva, I've got to run. Want to get together one day, just the two of us?"

"I don't know, Iván, I don't think so. I've got a bad taste in my mouth. Let's give it some time, all right? Maybe fate will bring us together. I'll wire you the money really soon."

"Bye, Geno."

Goodbye. Fate's crystal clear: I'm never going near her again. Even though she's a cool broad, unlike her crazy-ass friend. So she sold the company—that's news to me! And the bitch is still telling the teacher she's going to hire him to read books to her employees or whatever. What is she after, what does she want—to totally fuck him up? How am I going to tell Javier? Regardless, it's got to be soon so he can finally rip the wool from over his eyes and stop living in a fantasy world.

I told him to meet me in a bar before the rehearsal. That way, however hard he took the news, he couldn't get too upset because he had to work afterward. I didn't know how to go about broaching the subject. I'm paralyzed. The broad is super sketchy—dangerous even. A person can go through a rough patch and fuck things up. I've been in a pretty bad way myself since my mother kicked it. But deliberately screwing with someone, deceiving them . . . and with Javier being such a good guy on top of it. The chick deserves to die—or worse.

I just give it to him with both barrels as soon as we sit down.

"Your friend Irene sold her company, Javier. Did you know that? Did you know?"

"That's not possible."

"All right, it's not possible, but she sold it. Genoveva told me."

"You must have misunderstood."

"You're the one who doesn't understand, teach. This chick is lying to you out of pure spite, I'm telling you."

"It's not possible."

"Fine! Why don't you call her up on the goddamn phone and ask her if she sold the goddamn company?"

"We've got dinner plans."

"That's the perfect opportunity."

I hope my numbnuts friend figures out that if you want to live off of women, you have to be the one to set the rules.

\* \* \*

So it's true. She's right here in front of me and she just confirmed it: she's sold her company. And now what do I ask? What do I tell her? She looks at me calmly, as if nothing had happened, or as if whatever had happened were no big deal.

"So I can't work for you now."

"Not at the company. But you can do other things—you can give me literature classes or anything else you come up with. Any ideas?"

"It's not funny, Irene."

"There are some things you've proven you do very well."

"I don't want to be your hired whore! I thought you understood. I asked you for a job so I could leave that life behind."

"But what's the difference? You can leave the club, stop seeing other women, and just go out with me. I give you a salary, and we're set. We both win."

"That doesn't lead anywhere. That kind of relationship is rotten, dead, and it wouldn't last. You'd never treat me like an equal, and I wouldn't feel good about it. I want a normal life, Irene, a real bond between us."

"I'm offering you an exclusive bond with rules that are easy for both of us to satisfy."

Men are just unbelievable. I'd been so removed from them thanks to Papá and my fake marriage that I never realized it before. But yes, they're unbelievable. This guy, whom I met while he was stripping in a club, whom I've been paying for his sexual services for months, is demanding I solve his economic problems in a way he finds morally and socially acceptable. He's reproaching me for having sold the company my father founded and I helped build! He's blaming me for not asking his permission to sell the business, not giving him the chance to lead a respectable life! He's right, I should have preserved a failing business structure just to be able to hire him on as a janitor. It's so over the top that it's actually getting interesting.

"You're refusing to understand my perspective, Irene. I think it's best if we stop seeing each other."

"I do understand, Javier. You don't like being a prostitute or a kept man. Fine, let me try to find you something with someone I know. I've got a lot of contacts in the business world—that's an option we haven't explored yet."

"If you cared, you'd have explored it already on your own."

I've got to stay firm. In fact, this is my chance to get out, since this ship isn't headed for any port. I know it—I'm almost positive. But any ship is better than the raft I've been clinging to, totally adrift.

"I've been really busy with the damn company. Do you realize what selling a company involves? And I'm not just talking
about in economic or legal terms. Have you stopped to think
about the emotional cost of all this for me? That factory has
been my life's work; it was my whole world. I understand
you're worried about your future, but I have problems too."

"I'm sorry, Irene, you're right."

She's right and I'm an idiot, but it still seems to me that no
matter how many problems she has, the platform she's building her life on is level and unobstructed, while I'm stuck at the
bottom of a pit.

The rest of dinner flows through calmer channels. We both
try to move past the conflict and avoid setting off the argument
again. When we leave the restaurant, we head to my house. We
screw passionately, as usual. We clasp each other as if it's the
last time we'll have sex. It's almost as if we've overcome all the
difficulties between us. Sex always offers the appearance of
normality, of true closeness. Even when I sleep with a tourist,
there's a moment of mutual appreciation, of total peace.

Before leaving, Irene pays me. I look at her with infinite
weariness. I don't have the energy to fight her on it again, to
explain what I've already said a million times before. She
smiles at me.

"Everything's going to work out, Javier. Give me a little
time. I'll see if anyone I know has a job for you, if that's what
you want."

*If that's what you want.* She still thinks this is some whim of
mine, one option among the thousands available to me. She
just doesn't get it. She has no idea what it means to a man to
have the woman he's with pay him for sex. Still, maybe this
time she'll look for a job for me. She's realized I'm ready to
bolt, and she doesn't want to lose me. I'm sure of that. And
maybe it'll be better not to work directly for her company anyway. I'll feel freer, under less pressure. Afterward, once things

are in place, I can make sure she changes, discovers what a real, sober relationship means. Neither of us has any reason to be bitter. Whatever the circumstances, we've found each other. The two of us may have been abandoned by fate, but we have the power to change that. And I know how—Irene just has to go along with it, to trust me.

The next day Iván called. I almost didn't pick up, but it would have been pointless.

"Well, teach, what did the bird say?"

"Don't call her the bird, please."

"Fine. What did she say? Is it true she sold the company?"

"Yeah, it's true."

"What about that job she was planning to give you?"

"Look, Irene's had a lot of difficulties lately. The company was really important to her. Being forced to sell it because of the crisis has been a terrible blow. She wasn't in a place where she could think about my needs."

"Shit, man, you're tripping! She could have told you she'd sold it, right? Why did we have to find out about it from Genoveva by pure chance?"

"OK, she didn't tell me, but we've cleared things up. She's going to ask her contacts to see if anyone's got a job for me."

"Well, that's just perfect!"

What's wrong with the teacher—is he a moron, or a sucker for punishment? He may be hung up on this chick, but he's got to realize she's just screwing with him. No, she's not just screwing with him—she's going after him, she's trying to destroy him, she wants to make him pay for all the shit her husband pulled, or all the men she's ever met in her fucking life. It's so obvious to me. And what for does Javier want a job anyway? He's already got one! Is dancing at the club really so awful? Is it that much of a drag to sleep with chicks and have them give you money? If you ask me, all chicks should have to pay for sex! So what does my buddy think of me, then? I can imagine:

I'm a total shitbag, without even the smallest shred of dignity. But what's the difference between stripping and working in an office? There's only one: if you work in an office, you don't even make enough to eat—you're a fucking slave. And who likes being a slave and having rich guys cruise past you in their luxury cars while you're pedaling a goddamn bicycle? The teacher does, that's who! And nobody else.

"'Well, that's just perfect'? Is that meant to be sarcastic?"

"It's a reaction, dammit! All I'll say is this chick has got you by the balls, Javier. But if she wants to find you a job at some friend's company, that's great. That way at least you won't have all your eggs in one basket. Because if a chick's both your boss and your girlfriend, you might as well go jump in a river wearing a boulder as a necktie."

I start laughing. Iván is Iván, and he's never going to change. The only thing he'd have to do to be the perfect friend is realize I'm not like him.

\* \* \*

My relationship with Javier is like a sociological experiment. I don't really know what it is, but I like it—it makes me feel good. When I get up in the morning, I've got some motivation to face the day, something to think about that's not just totally overwhelming or depressing. I never imagined it would be so exciting to delve deep into human relationships. I guess you can only enjoy them if you're convinced nobody can hurt you. And I'm convinced of that. I'm immune to the pain others can inflict. My transformation has been swift, almost startling. I've gone through the stages set out in psychology books for abandoned women: numbness, sorrow, anguish, shame, rage, anxiety about the future . . . But I've experienced them all out of order, sometimes all at the same time. Now I find myself in excess, in anarchy. I'm happy this way. I no longer want to build anything nor am I obligated to preserve anything: The factory's gone. Everything that tied me down and held me back is gone. I'm free.

Meeting Javier has turned out to be providential. I've really enjoyed sex with him, and I've come to understand a lot of things. Like, for example, that love doesn't exist. Once upon a time I felt cheated because I'd never experienced or inspired love, but I can relax now. Couples are just seeking a balance between what each partner has and lacks, that's all. And I'm no exception. David was seeking professional success in being with me. Javier is satisfied with much less. I even feel a little bad for the guy! For my part, I was gaining status by marrying David, and bolstering the company. There was a balance between what the two of us wanted and had to offer. But Javier . . . He wants to put his dream of happiness—so modest and humdrum—in my hands: we'll live happily together, go out for dinner with friends on Saturdays, go to the movies, do our grocery shopping once a week. A wonderful plan, but far too late for me. For him, it's a way of getting away from stripping and being an escort, which he finds deeply humiliating. I wonder why. If he were a woman I'd understand, but a man? Just look at Iván. He knows a thing or two about life, and he understands the price of freedom. He's as free as I'd have liked to have been.

Well, there's nothing tying me down anymore. Not even friendship—my friends were the first people to drop me after my husband left me. I don't have children. I never wanted them—that was the only element of Papá's plans that I opposed. He wanted an heir for the factory, to leave a legacy. But he wasn't pushy about it; we never talked about intimate matters. An heir for the factory! Poor Papá! I feel a little bad about that too. Poor men, really! Always doing what's expected of them. David craved social success, Papá had taken on the tasks of building a successful company and raising me, and Javier needs to have a respectable job. Poor men, stripped of free will, naked! Always pursuing achievements the world has created for them.

I'm over forty, and only two things have mattered to me in life: the company and my father. The company was swept away on the winds of this damn crisis. As for Papá, ever since that numbskull psychiatrist suggested that his affection for me was a type of aggression, I don't dare think about him. Despite everything, I'm very happy. When anything bothers me, I just do a line of coke. I don't depend on anybody else. Everything is under my control. I have power.

I call Genoveva to ask for Iván's number, and then I call him. He's dumbstruck when I identify myself. It's the first time we've spoken on the phone. I remember his naked body in the fountain clearly: slim, muscular, energetic.

"Are you aware Genoveva doesn't want the four of us to go out together anymore?" I ask.

"Yeah. She's afraid we'll ruin her reputation. But it's no big deal. We had a great time the other night."

"Javier didn't come into the fountain."

"That's the way he is. You know that I better than I do."

"No, not better than you. I'm calling to suggest that the three of us go out. If Genoveva wants to stay out of it, that's fine, but that's no reason to ruin everybody else's fun."

He's silent a while, long enough that I think the call's been dropped. But no, at last I hear his swaggering voice:

"Wouldn't it better for you and Javier to go out by yourselves? I don't want to feel like the odd man out."

"No way, a night out is a night out."

"You're right about that."

Shit, man, I never expected this! I wonder what this chick's after. Is she looking to sucker-punch the teacher again? I'm sure she is, but I have no intention of being played for a fool. I say I'll have to ask him. I accept my own invitation with pleasure, but I want her to know I'll be charging. Javier can do whatever the hell he wants, but I'm not interested in that bullshit. Just in case it's not clear, I say, "The usual fee, right?"

"The usual."

Good for Iván. No trembling in his voice. The usual fee. All clear and concrete. Much better.

* * *

Dammit! What kind of bullshit is this? Why am I the one getting nervous? They can just screw off—that crap's not for me. I do my own thing. The teacher didn't say anything when I told him the chick had called me to arrange for the three of us go out. I guess she'd called him too—hope so. I don't want to get dragged into the middle of something without realizing it. If this girl's counting on me to participate in some plan of hers, like making Javier jealous or some other bullshit, she can forget it. My friendship with Javier comes first.

Trying to be slick, I asked him, "Hey, teach, you know the three of us are going out tonight, right?"

"Yeah, I know."

"What's up with that?"

"Genoveva doesn't want to come."

"Right, but are you and Irene fighting?"

"No."

"Are you sure I won't be in the way?"

"Yes."

Well, there you have it: yes and no! And if you don't know what those words mean, do a fucking Google search. Christ, couldn't the dude elaborate a little? But no, he doesn't feel like it.

Anyway, that night the chick invites us to a French restaurant. Lots of lit candles and wine tasting, but at the end of it all, I'm still hungry. It doesn't matter—I'm just curious to see what will come out of our three-person night out.

The chick was normal, the usual, wearing that mask of hers where you can never tell what's going through her head. We were talking all sophisticated, about food, booze, how white wine is good going down but can really fuck you up . . . It was pretty boring, but I was tense thinking that at any moment they were going to start arguing right in front of me. I was ready, my speech all written out in my head: "Look, guys, if you two are having problems or are just itching for a fight in general, go ahead and kill each other for all I care, but please wait till I'm not around. I get faint at the sight of blood." It was pretty good, I thought, not too pushy but putting them in their place. But it turned out it wasn't necessary—we spent the whole night talking about white wine, red wine, and whatever the hell else.

When we were done, the chick paid the bill, and before anybody could ask what we were doing next, she suggested we go do some lines back at her house. Javier got all sullen and said reluctantly, "But no fountains." She looked at him the same way she'd looked at the waiter all through dinner, like she didn't give a crap what he said or did.

I remembered the house really well, though it didn't seem as beautiful the second time around. It looked super generic, like they'd just shoved in the furniture they needed and nothing was really theirs. For one, it didn't have framed photos all over the place the way fancy houses generally do. I'd have loved to get a look at that husband, or her family—anything that might give me some clues as to what the chick had been like before she turned into the cold fish she was today.

She put on music and poured some whiskey. She pulled coke out of a drawer, and we did a bunch of it. Who was she buying such good stuff from, and for how much? I didn't intend to ask her, in case she took it wrong.

Things started perking up a bit. We were laughing and making fun of Genoveva: "I'm not getting in that fountain—I can't swim" and "Just call me Saint Genoveva" and "I'm living off my ex's alimony; he's supporting me even though he's a fag . . . " We all got in on it, trying to one-up each other with our crudeness and cruelty. Laughing and doing bumps of coke. Finally, Irene, sitting next to Javier on the sofa, took off one of her shoes and started sticking her big toe in his ear. It was time for me to beat it, so I stood up and said, "Guys, it's been a blast, but I'm going to take off. I've got to be up early tomorrow."

Then the chick goes, "No, you can both leave now. The night ends here. I'll deposit your money tomorrow." Some balls.

The sentence hit us like a bucket of cold water and an electric current. I stood there in shock, not saying anything, waiting for what was coming, but the teacher got to his feet with great dignity, a fury on his face I'd never seen before, and headed for the door.

"I'm the one who's taking off. Good night."

I raced after him, but he spun around angrily and said, "I'm leaving on my own, Iván."

I still went after him, even started down the stairs to catch him, but he was really booking it and there was no way to nab him. Plus, I'd left my backpack in the living room, with everything in it: ID, cash, car keys . . . I turned around and went back into the living room. She hadn't moved from where she was—she even still had her leg stretched out from when she'd been provoking Javier by touching his ear. She was smirking. I felt like smacking the shit out of her. No, what I really wanted was to drag her off the sofa, push her to her knees, and start whaling on her with a baseball bat till her head lolled to one side like a dead chicken's. It wasn't just a thought that flitted through my mind—I really wanted to do it, right there and then. So much so, it actually scared me and I cranked my powerful imagination into gear like I always do when I'm in a blind rage. I picture a waterfall and get under it. The ice-cold water runs down my body. I raise my wrists together above my head, and the chill starts to seep into my veins. Calm down, calm down. I take a deep breath. I'm calmer now. I think, "This isn't your battle, Iván."

"Look, Irene, what's your deal with Javier?"

"What's Javier's deal with me? Have you asked him?"

"No, and I don't want to overstep here, but it seemed like you were trying to get under his skin tonight. You flirt with him and then tell him to get lost, just like that, out of the blue and in front of me."

"Want another drink?"

We had more drinks. I kept objecting to the way she'd treated the teacher, the way she was screwing with his head and playing him for a fool . . . until she gets real serious and says, "You think Javier's crazy about me? Well, he's not, make no mistake. Javier's just like everybody else—he wants something. He wants me to give him a job that makes him feel like a normal, respectable man. He wants my money, but without having to take it from me directly. He wants me to be his good and virtuous girlfriend, like the one he had before he met me. Can you believe it? The poor guy's totally lost the plot. So don't come to me with all this crap about how he loves me and I'm making him suffer by toying with his emotions—it's just a cliché."

Shit, man, that's rough. She's saying all the same things I do. But she's trying to tell *me* this stuff? Me? Me, who takes off running whenever I hear the word *love*.

"Did you tell him all this, straight up like that?"

"No, why should I? He concocts his fantasies and I let him. He wouldn't listen if I were frank with him anyway."

"Damn!" I said, not knowing what to say. Not like I had the chance anyway, because then the chick grabs my arm and pulls me down on the sofa and kisses me and we start getting it on. It was really hot! The chick's totally wild, a firecracker in the sack. I got totally into it. A primo lay, no games. I start to understand why the teacher's hung up on her. I never just let go during sex—I always stay a little detached—but this time I did, and when we were through I couldn't even remember my own name. Then, all cool, the chick says, "You'd better go now, Iván. I'll pay an additional fee for the sex."

"Let's keep this between us, OK, Irene?"

"You can count on my discretion."

What a sentence, right out a movie! She smiles at me, I smile at her, and I leave.

I start the car. A wave of fatigue sweeps over my body. I could fall asleep right there. I bet I won't remember a thing when I wake up. Did I have sex with Irene? How did that happen? Fatal attraction? Anyway, I don't feel bad about it. The teacher was asking for it. Why the hell is he letting this chick make a hash of his life?

\* \* \*

I'm home alone, very laid back. It's a rainy Tuesday. I don't have any performances, rehearsals, or dates. I'm reading a book on personality disorders, really interesting. Everything I'm learning about in its pages seems applicable to Irene. She's not in her right mind, definitely not. What happened yesterday is a clear example. At first she acts with what we might call "good intention." Feeling relaxed, she cooks up plans, calls me on the phone, wants us to have a good time. But afterward some emotion intrudes in her mind, and she tries to hurt me. I don't think it's anything premeditated; it's just a reaction to the contradictory impulses roiling inside her.

Yesterday I didn't have the patience and left in a huff. I should have endured her needling and confronted her with her own behavior, but it's hard being treated with such disrespect. She threw us out like dogs, Iván and me. "I've had it," a voice inside me said. I was ready to break off our relationship right there. But this morning when I woke up, I felt at peace again.

Now our relationship is in my hands. If I don't do anything, she won't call me and that'll be the end of it. If I go back to her, everything will continue as it has been. I should think about it carefully before making a decision. Going back to the way things have been seems pointless, absurd, a continual source of stress and servitude. I should make things change, find a solution. I discard the idea of having a long, deep conversation with her—it wouldn't do any good. The key is to try to help her without her realizing it, gradually unblocking her emotions, subtly guiding her toward positive, luminous thoughts. To be patient, really patient. Never to think that she's trying to wound me on purpose. Indeed, to be positive that her lashing out is, at a fundamental level, a cry for help.

I could help her. I'd offer her a simple, quiet life, sharing good and bad alike. With me she'd emerge from her swamp of unhappiness, forget the past, start over again.

Thinking about all this, I doze off. A ringing sound wakes me up, and the book falls from my hands. It's her on the phone.

"What are you up to, Javier?"

"I'm reading."

"You left in a hurry last night."

"That was what you wanted, wasn't it?"

"I started feeling really tired all of a sudden—I needed to sleep."

"Do you always boot your guests out like that? Of course, the two of us were just a couple of employees. I guess that's the real issue."

Why am I saying this to her? Didn't I decide I needed to be patient? Didn't I intend to withstand her attacks, redirect her moods toward tranquil prairies and flowering fields? Is that the option I've chosen: continuing on with the affair?

"Don't take it so personally. I was curt, but you reacted really badly. In any event, I'm not calling about that. I just wanted to tell you that one of my contacts has offered me a job interview for you."

"What?"

"It's a job as a document retention specialist at a company. You know, organizing and storing: files, e-mails, contracts . . . Do you think you could do that?"

"Well, yes, of course, if they tell me what they're looking for . . . "

I'm shocked—happy. Before I can ask more, she says, "I don't have any information about schedule or terms. Not a thing. And of course the job isn't guaranteed. Do you have something to write with? I'll give you the name of the company and the address."

After this bombshell, I feel drained. I sit down to think. Fortunately, I've made the right decision: to stick it out. I've got to be patient, tolerant, understanding with other people. I need to analyze everything dispassionately, be adaptable: one idea opens a path among all the others—you can change reality. My life will change, and Irene's too.

That afternoon, Iván shows up at my house unannounced. He's come to tell me he's lined up a great gig for us the next day. An all-women's corporate conference. It's a lingerie firm where all the employees are women, and since the numbers this year have been really good, they're being rewarded with a dinner followed by a party. That's where we come in.

"They want the gladiator number, of course. It's going to be in a hotel ballroom. And you know how much they're paying us? Four hundred each, man! Not a bad haul for a little partying, huh? We have to cut in the guy who gave me the contact for fifty apiece—he's good with a hundred."

"And afterward?"

"Nothing, man, nice to have met you and ciao. At most get a drink with them just for PR purposes, but after that we collect our money and vamoose: best of luck and keep selling bras by the bushel."

"I don't know."

"You don't know, teach? What don't you know?"

"All those women out for a good time . . . they're going to be a real pain, try to feel us up, act all innocent."

"So what? You've been doing this a while now—you know how to put them off gracefully."

"I really don't feel like it."

"Stop screwing around, Javier, this is work, not a wedding invitation. Are you going to say no to three hundred fifty smackers because you don't feel like it? You think you're the king of mambo or something? Plus, if you don't come, you'll screw it up for me too. Who am I going to find for tomorrow if you don't agree?"

"Don't get upset."

"What do you mean, don't get upset? This is how I make a living, man, so tell me: are you in or are you out?"

"Well, that's just it, Iván, maybe soon I won't be in at all."

"Feel like telling me what you're babbling about?"

"Irene got me a job interview with a friend of hers who owns a company."

"Aha! And what sort of job is it, if I may ask?"

"Recordkeeping—organizing, digitizing, and storing all the papers."

"And do you have the job already?"

"For now I have to do an interview, but it's very possible they'll give it to me. Irene recommended me."

"Right."

The hell with her recommendation! The chick doesn't even tell him she sold her popsicle stand and now she's finding a job for him. In the meantime, she goes and sleeps with me. I don't get it, man, not a goddamn thing. If I were in the teacher's shoes, I wouldn't be able to sleep at night.

"You hadn't told me any of this."

"I just found out. It was a surprise to me too."

"Well, it's a drag you're going to dump all this."

"If you're my friend, you should be happy for me. I always intended to leave, Iván, from the very beginning. I can't get used to it—it's not for me. Every time I strip naked in the club, it's traumatic, every damn time. Not to mention everything else! It's humiliating to sleep with women for money. Understand? It's humiliating—it's tearing me up."

Listening, Iván has grown somber. He seems not angry but incredibly sad. My words have wounded him, it's clear. We're back to the same old thing. I'm telling him, "You don't give a crap about anything, but I'm better than you." I hasten to speak again:

"Anyway, count me in for the gig tomorrow. It may be the last one, but I'll be there."

"All right, thanks a lot. I hope you won't leave us in the lurch at the club. I was the one who brought you in, and I don't want any problems with the owner."

"Don't worry, I'll give plenty of notice. I'll do things right."

He says good night in a very quiet voice and leaves without adding anything else.

\* \* \*

I passed out last night. I guess the combination of coke and booze knocked me out. This morning I woke up with dark circles under my eyes—it looked like I had holes in my face. One of these days my assistant is going to find me lying on the floor without a pulse. The thought doesn't frighten me much. A doctor will come, maybe the police, or a magistrate. People will think I committed suicide: "Things started going wrong for the poor woman all at once. Her company failed, her husband left her . . . and most likely she hadn't gotten over her father's death either. Her mother died when she was a little girl . . . Lives like that always come to a bad end." That sort of nonsense, and probably more besides. Those kinds of comments are annoying, but since I'll be dead if anyone makes them, it won't matter.

Javier calls. He wants to see me and get some advice before the job interview. Standard sorts of things: what to wear, how to act . . . Poor guy! He's like a monkey that never learned to swing from branch to branch, but is eager to learn how the other monkeys travel through the trees so he can be just like them. He wants to be just another monkey.

I meet up with him and give him a couple of pointers on how to do a job interview, nothing he couldn't read in the Sunday supplement. He thinks they're marvelous anyway. Then, since he's not one for artifice, he asks if his potential employer is really a good friend of mine and if I've recommended him enthusiastically. I say yes to both questions. With the pragmatics out of the way, he assures me that if he gets this job, everything is going to change. His life will turn around, and, strangely enough, apparently so will mine. We'll enter a higher plane of tranquillity and normality. He speaks in a soothing, paternalistic tone. It's clear he sees my life as a disaster from which he intends to rescue me. Men have come into this world to rescue women, to implant a bit of rationality in our poor weak heads, which are so full of romantic garbage. My situation must seem particularly complicated—it's no mean feat to rescue me from myself—but he's put all his hope in the transformation that will take place. Luckily, he doesn't mention those aspects of my personality that will need to be eliminated. I'm grateful for that small courtesy. Even so, I picture the general setup he's proposing. We live together. He gets home from work and sprawls out on the sofa in my living room. He tells me all about his exciting work day organizing invoices and memos. We eat the dinner my assistant's prepared and go to bed because we have to be up early the next day. Maybe we'll watch a TV program? Read for a while? It sounds like a great new life.

What fun! After gray years of integrity and submissiveness, I've finally taken a few steps over to the dark side. And when I hire a male prostitute, an honest-to-God prostitute, he wants to rescue me and deliver me right back to the straight and narrow. Praise the Lord! I'm headed for paradise, whether I like it or not.

* * *

I was pretty anxious—I thought in the end he wasn't going to show, leaving me up shit creek without a paddle. But no, the teach is the teach, and there he was, like he'd been nailed in place, right where we'd arranged to meet. He was carrying a little briefcase that held his gladiator costume. He hadn't failed me. The face he had on was something else—as grave as a corpse.

I had him meet me a little early so I could do a little psychological prep on him, just in case he still wanted to bolt. I wasn't planning to say anything against the girl or the job she'd found for him. I've warned him a million times already—that's plenty. I'm not his fucking mother.

We had a couple of beers at a bar and took turns going to the bathroom to do a line. The mood improved a little, and the teacher's face got more and more relaxed. Good thing, too, because performing with that look on wasn't an option. The subject of his new job didn't come up until I asked him about it directly:

"Hey, teach, if they give you that paper-pushing job, how much will you make?"

"I haven't asked yet."

"Oh!" I said, and I said it in a way where you could tell I thought it was dumb not to have asked. The dude's getting ready to leave the club and the nights out, and he doesn't even know whether he'll make enough to keep living like this. The pompous ass. Right now, between one thing and another, he's making some good scratch every month, and I don't know shit about it but I'm pretty sure shuffling papers doesn't pay much. Just a normal salary, that's it. Of course, evil-minded guy that I am, maybe if he lives with Irene and she pays all the bills, he's got enough already. After all, that's what they did when he was with Sandra—she was the one supporting the two of them.

"If I were you, I wouldn't leave the club job until I had the other one lined up for sure."

"Of course."

He says "of course" so I'll shut up, but he's not really listening. The guy's asking for trouble! If he leaves the club and doesn't end up getting the job and the chick dumps him, he'll be totally screwed. I won't be able to do anything for him anymore, since I don't know any other way to make a living. Smart people have no goddamn clue how things work! I feel bad for him—he's a good guy.

When it's time, we head to the luxury hotel and I ask at reception for the chick who's going to be meeting us. After a while, a posh-seeming chick with her lips pumped full of silicone appears. She scans us up and down to assess what's on offer and gets this look on her face that suggests we're less impressive than she was expecting. I start feeling miffed. The chick, whose name is Mila, is painted up like a goddamn door and has bleached blond hair. The first thing she says, no hello or anything, is:

"What about your costumes?"

"We've got them here."

"I thought you'd be wearing them already."

"This isn't Carnival, you know—we dress like normal people out on the street."

"Well, I don't know where you're going to change."

"Isn't there some kind of little room near the ballroom? You could have thought about this!"

"No, look, I didn't think you'd need a dressing room like a couple of Hollywood stars!"

I could have smacked her right then. I move toward her, not knowing what I'm going to do, but the teacher grabs my arm and asks, "Is there a bathroom nearby?"

"Yeah, there's that."

She accompanies us down the hallway. We're off to a bad start, and it bugs me, because of course it's today, when the teacher didn't want to come in the first place, that we end up with a bitch. When we're alone in the damn bathroom, I start flipping out.

"Goddammit, teach, let's get out of here if you want to! This chick gets on my damn nerves! I'd like to punch her!"

"Calm down, Iván, chill. No violence. We'll do our performance, have a drink with the girls at the end, and leave. No drama—total zen. It's not worth making a scene. There will be a lot of girls in the room, and not all of them are going to be like that."

I'm going to miss the teacher. If he leaves this job, I'll remember him fondly. He always says what needs to be said. He calms me down. I listen to him.

We get in our gladiator outfits and head into the ballroom, which is labeled with a golden plaque: "Hermitage." As soon as we set foot inside, the chicks—there are a ton of them—start squealing like pigs. They're all sitting at a long table and have finished dinner. There are glasses everywhere and empty bottles of sparkling wine. They're probably tipsy already. The waiters swoop around and eye us mockingly. They whisper to one another. I'm pissed they're having a laugh at our expense.

We huddle in a corner. An older woman comes over to us,

all gussied up and dressed in black—she must be the real boss, because the bitch moves aside.

"Good evening, how are you? Welcome, I'm thrilled you're here. I hope you give the girls a good time. They'll serve you a drink later."

After her spiel, she sits back down and leaves us with the bitch, who's still looking at us like we're pure shit.

"Do you need anything for your performance?"

"Yeah, somewhere to plug in the music, and have them turn off all the lights except the ones in this corner."

"OK, I'll let them know."

"Oh, and get rid of the waiters!"

"That won't be possible. The waiters have to keep serving."

"No way. While we're performing, nobody moves but us."

"Listen, honey, who do you think you are, going around giving orders like that?"

"Look, darling, either you do as I say or we're out of here, and you can just go visit the chimp exhibit at the zoo if you want to see some balls."

The chick flushes as red as a goddamn tomato. It looks like she's going to explode or come after me, but she holds back. What else can she do at this point, with the girls and her boss waiting for the show to start? She doesn't say anything and leaves. She speaks to the head waiter, and they all exit the room. The lights go out. I put on the music at top volume, and the girls look over at us. The teacher's really tense, I can tell, but I pretend not to notice. The last thing I need right now is to have to worry about him.

We start the Roman number, which we know by heart at this point. We fight, our movements rehearsed down to the millimeter. We remove our clothes up top, down below, all over. It's going well, the room in silence. Once we're in our briefs, we dance around a good long while, and nobody moves

a muscle. We're going to have to strip naked. I look at the
teacher.

"Are we doing it, Javier?"

"We're doing it."

We're doing it, Iván, we're doing it, but I swear it's the last
time. I swear I can't take it anymore. I can't take any more misery and humiliation. It's the last time.

Ta-da! Final chord, full nudity. The girls applaud—in the
end they always applaud—solemnly, like they're at a concert
with violins and bow-tied musicians. It's freaking them out to
see a guy buck naked in front of everybody like that.

We strut our stuff a little, showing it all off, and that's when
the fun begins: shrieks, wolf howls, shouts of "Studs!," clapping, pounding on the table, a chair crashing to the floor . . .
Like it's no big thing, we just pull our briefs back on and
saunter over to the table. They calm down. We go around the
table, talking to each girl: "Hi, having a good time?" and that
kind of bullshit. There's always a class clown making lewd comments: "Come here, hot stuff, I'm going to rock your world!"
Standard crap, but things don't get out of hand because their
boss is right there.

Then people start gathering into little knots. The waiters
reappear. We have a drink. They put on background music.
We've stopped being the main event. The teacher goes for his
Roman cape and puts it on. I don't—let them look as much as
they want, they must be starving. I've left a little stack of business cards for the club by the door in case we get customers.
I'd be surprised, though—they're all factory girls, total losers.
The youngest waiter tells me, "I'll switch jobs with you." "You
wish!" I reply so he'll keep his distance. I glance at my watch.
We've been there more than two hours. We've fulfilled our
contract. I go straight to the bitch with the sausage lips and tell
her we're leaving, we want our money. She lets me off the hook
and hands me an envelope; my contact and I agreed they'd pay

us in cash. I say, "No. Bring it to us in the bathroom. I want to count it, and I don't want to do it here in front of everybody."

But she's no longer worried we're going to leave her hanging, so she says, "Listen, sweetie, no more demands from you. Here's the money we agreed on. If you want, you can count it right here, and if not, you figure it out. I'm not going to carry it to you on a platter."

Fuming, I go ahead and count it. In front of her, in front of everybody, everybody but the teacher, who, delicate as ever, has disappeared. When I finish counting, I say, "For a little bit more, the two of us can get it on too."

She shakes her head in disbelief, smears on a superior little smile, and says something in English like "cash" or "trash" that I don't understand.

When I go into the bathroom, Javier's practically dressed already.

"Hey, smarty-pants, this chick said something to me like 'prash' or 'trash' . . . That's English, right?"

"'Trash' means garbage."

"Well, that's sweet, huh? You want me to go back there and give her a pounding? Huh?"

"The only thing I want is for us to get out of here, the sooner the better."

"Fine, it wouldn't be worth my time anyway. Want to get a beer, or are you going straight home?"

"Let's get a beer. I need to decompress."

We go to a hip bar nearby. It's hopping. The teacher seems sad and kind of grumpy. I prod him to find out what the hell is going on.

"Are you feeling sick or something?"

"That was awful."

"Shit, man, it wasn't as bad as all that! The girls were nice. The only negative was that goddamn bitch who had it in for us. She probably hasn't had a good lay in years."

"I'm sick of all this, Iván, seriously. You saved my life by giving me the chance to earn an income, but I'm at a point where I'm realizing that this isn't for me. I can't take it anymore."

"That's because you take it too seriously—if you were a little more laid back . . . "

"But I'm not, and it's too late to change personalities. You get it, right? Tell me you get it."

"Of course I get it, man! But you can't always choose what you want in life. Maybe you say, 'Look, I've always done whatever the hell I wanted.' But then you think about it some more, and it's not true. Can you choose your father and mother? No, right? So you're screwed right from the beginning. If I'd been able to choose, there's no way mine would have been the way they were. For starters, they would have been loaded, and then all the rest of it. So screw freedom—we're all just getting by however we can, and that's that."

The teacher looks at me as if he finds what I'm saying quite bizarre. Then he starts laughing. Who the hell knows what's so damn funny! He says, "You're the best, Iván!"

Well all right, yeah, I am. No idea why he's laughing, but at least he's laughing, damn it!

"What's so funny?"

"It's just . . . the things you say have been written down for ages and . . . the thing is, the people who wrote them took a long time to come up with them."

"Well, shit, that's because they were dumbasses. Give me an example."

"Well, Freud, for one."

"Well, that Freud dude must have been a damn moron, because that business about being stuck with your parents is pretty obvious. Those intellectual types are lame, man. Like fucking Raskolnikov: just because he kills a disgusting old lady who totally deserved it, he spends a thousand pages being gnawed at by his conscience."

The teacher laughed like a little kid, so I kept spewing bull-shit a while because I like seeing him happy, which he never is. Then we split the money from that bitch who'd made me want to kill her and went home to sleep.

\* \* \*

It's an office building with a façade of steel and glass. I look for the company's name on some metal plaques in the lobby. Seventh floor. Once I'm in the elevator, I have a hard time getting it to work. I stare helplessly at the buttons for the floors. A guard yells from behind a counter, "Pull on the security lever!" I take a minute to figure it out, but I finally get it. I go up alone, fortunately. I'm wearing khaki pants, a white shirt, and a warm jacket. I guess I'm dressed all right, though I don't imagine it matters much, since a records retention specialist isn't a public-facing job.

There's a girl at the reception desk. I tell her my name and that I have an appointment for a job interview. She starts hunting around in the computer. Then she smiles. "Mr. Guzmán will see you personally."

That must mean that with the other applicants, if there are any, Mr. Guzmán doesn't see them personally. Good for Irene. Everything's off to a good start.

The receptionist accompanies me down the hall. To one side are cubicles with smoked glass walls that don't go up to the ceiling. I hear the clatter of typing, a phone conversation . . . These are the offices where the employees work. We go into a little room with some rows of seats. They each have a little platform where you can put your papers. I remember having sat in something similar back when I was in high school.

The girl hands me a stack of papers. "You'll need to fill out these questionnaires. When you finish, press this button. Can I offer you anything to drink—water, coffee . . . ?"

"No, thank you. I'm good."

She leaves me alone, and I start examining the papers. It's a large stack. The first ones are pretty standard: name, birthday, address . . . Then there are questions about my professional life: education, experience . . . Then they move on to my personal life: spouse, children, hobbies . . . The third one gets a little more complicated: they ask if I belong to an athletic club or NGO, if I have a pet, if I'm a member of the Civil Defense or a city volunteer. I don't really understand how any of these things help indicate whether a candidate is ideal for the job. But the worst is yet to come. The final section of the questionnaires is totally crazy. There are a ton of ridiculous questions you have to answer at length. For example: "Which is more valuable, a snail or a rock? Explain." "Where do you prefer to swim, in a river or in the ocean? Explain." I work my way down the list, uncertain whether my responses are the right ones. Iván's right— you're never able to choose. If I could, I'd take off and leave this stupid questionnaire unfinished. But I stay.

By the time I check my watch, I've been answering that nonsense for more than an hour and a half. Maybe how long you take filling it out counts too. Bad if you're really slow, too much hesitation when answering. Or the opposite—if you're really fast, you demonstrate you're not a careful thinker. My head hurts, and I'm anxious. I press the button and, endless minutes later, another girl appears. She introduces herself as Mr. Guzmán's secretary. She asks me to come with her and leaves me in another small room with armchairs and magazines. I have to wait there till the boss can see me. She offers me something to drink again, and this time I ask for coffee, which she brings immediately.

Mr. Guzmán is about the same age as me and looks like a numbskull. He's wearing a silky, light-gray suit with no tie and has three or four days of stubble. Suddenly I get the feeling I've seen him at the club, watching the show from the front

tables. He flashes a quick, professional smile. I calm down—
it's extremely unlikely that this man has been to the club, just
me being neurotic. What would a handsome modern guy, an
executive and boss, say if he knew the applicant sitting before
him is a stripper at a club and sleeps with strange women for
money? I try to banish that question from my head.

The interview begins. Guzmán comments on a number of
my answers from the questionnaire. He asks several questions
about my experience as a literature teacher. He's not as dumb
as he seems, and we hit it off. He explains in detail what the job
entails and asks why I want it. I tell him I've been unemployed
for several months and, though I'm not in dire economic straits,
I'm looking to go back to work. I stress how important work is
to me, tell him I need to be part of the social fabric. I insist that
changing professions and no longer being a teacher might even
be good for me. It'll open new possibilities, do away with the
dull routines that developed during my pedagogical period. He
nods, as if my presentation had convinced him. He tells me
what I'd earn, which isn't much but isn't too bad either.

It's been half an hour, and we're done. He stands up energetically, and I follow suit. He shakes my hand, a firm squeeze,
firmer than when I arrived.

"Now we'll be taking a look at your application as a com-
mittee. We'll let you know in a few days."

He hasn't mentioned Irene. I want to make sure he knows
who I am, so I tell him she says hello.

"Yes, Irene, of course, a great businesswoman. Such a
shame she had to sell her company."

"Times are hard," I say stupidly.

"They're terrible!" he says, and moves off.

I'm back in the hands of the secretary, who escorts me to
the reception desk.

When I step outside, pleasant sunlight warms my face. I feel
like sitting on the terrace of a bar and having a beer. I walk

until I'm a good distance away and choose a place at random. It's quiet. The beer is good. I think back on the interview and decide that not only did it not go badly, but in fact it went quite well. As for the job, I could do it with my eyes closed, and I think I'd even grow to enjoy it. I feel contented; in the end, things will fall back into place, and this strange period of my life will be just that: a strange period. I call Irene.

"Hi! I finished the interview not long ago."

"How was it?"

"Honestly, I'm pretty happy. It went really well. Your friend and I hit it off."

"He's a very nice man."

"What do you say we have dinner together and I'll tell you all about it?"

"Oh, no, I can't! Today I'm very busy all day! I'll call you tomorrow or the day after and we can have dinner then."

I hang up, surprised and a little annoyed. Very busy? Why does she have so much going on when she isn't working at the company anymore? She must mean she has to go to the hair salon or the gym, but she could postpone those things and meet up with me to talk about the interview for a little while. Doesn't she realize how important this is for me? Well, it's not worth getting angry about it—she'll respond in her own time.

I'm still eager to talk about what happened, so I call Iván, who's my only friend at this point. He immediately agrees to have lunch. We meet at a German restaurant near his place.

"What kinds of things were on the questionnaire?"

"At first, the usual: education, experience, age . . . Then they started asking these bullshit questions."

"Like what?"

"Oh, I don't know. Like, for example, which is more valuable, a rock or a snail?"

"You're shitting me!"

"I'm totally not."

"What did you say?"

"I said a snail is worth more because it's a living creature."

"Shit, I wouldn't have known what to answer!"

"It seemed like that was the way to go, show you're a person with humanity."

"Well, I don't know what to tell you—maybe they'll think you're a total moron. What if the rock's a diamond? Don't tell me that if you had to choose between a diamond and a snail, you'd go with the goddamn snail, no matter how alive it is."

"Man, if you look at it like that . . . But in these kinds of interviews they want you to say what's politically correct. Companies these days are all ecological and into social justice."

"You're kidding! Seems to me companies are just looking to make a killing and the hell with the rest of it."

"Well, sure, but you can't say that."

"I guess. I'm sure if I did one of those interviews, the cops would be waiting to scoop me up and dump me in jail when I came out."

I laugh hard, laugh for real. Iván's a phenomenon. I'm going to miss him when we're not working together anymore. It's the only good thing I'm going to miss. I toss him a compliment:

"No way, you'd could do any job better than anybody if you put your mind to it. You've got higher than average intelligence."

"Damn, teach, nobody's ever told me anything like that before! What are you after—trying to get me to pay for your meal?"

He's blushing and proud. Poor Iván! I guess people really haven't said many nice things about him in his life. I'll try to keep seeing him from time to time, find a moment for him.

"And how much are you going to be making, Javier, did they tell you?"

"Enough."

"Oh, well, that's great!"

If he doesn't want to tell me, it's because he's not going to be earning shit. I hope he's done his calculations carefully. The teacher's lifestyle probably costs more than some paltry little salary, so the girl might have to cover the rest. If I were him, I'd keep working at the club a while to see how things went. But if I tell him that, he'll tell me to fuck off, so I'd better just keep my trap shut and we'll see.

"A toast, Iván?"

"Absolutely!"

We toast, raising the German restaurant's steins. They're old and very colorful. They look pretty clinking together in the air. The custom of toasting is also lovely.

The telephone startles me awake. It's eleven o'clock. I didn't hear my alarm, which must have gone off at ten. On Mondays I'm always really tired after the weekend at the club, and yesterday I was particularly tired, who knows why.

"Hi, it's Irene. Don't you recognize my voice?"

"Sorry, I'm still in bed, a little groggy."

"I'm sorry. Maybe it's not a big deal, but I wanted to tell you right away. A little while ago I called my friend to ask him about your job interview, and he told me you made a great impression."

"Really?"

"Yes, really. I don't know how much that matters—you'll have to wait till the company makes its final decision—but I thought you'd like to know you were a hit in the interview."

"That's wonderful!"

"Would you like to get together to celebrate?"

"Of course!"

"Shall we go out to eat somewhere?"

"Come by my place. I'll make something nice and buy a bottle of sparkling wine."

"I'll be there around two."

She's coming to eat here. A celebration. It can't rain all the time—occasionally the sun finally comes out. The sun shines for everybody, and for me too. If I let myself get carried away with what I'm feeling, I'd leap up and pump my fist in the air. Everything's going to be OK. Fate doesn't always move in a straight line; instead, it meanders, does somersaults, retreats into its shell like a snail. But in the end it unexpectedly starts moving forward again.

I take a long shower. I get dressed. I go out and get a cup of coffee with a couple of little sponge cakes. I go shopping at a high-end supermarket with a nice deli. I take my time selecting smoked salmon, Jabugo ham, Gorgonzola cheese, cherry tomatoes, a bottle of champagne, and French cookies. A gourmand's grocery haul.

Back home, I make the bed, sweep the living room, clean the bathroom . . . and then make the salad. I make sure the kitchen is tidy. If I had to leave this apartment, I'd miss it. I've grown quite fond of it. It's best not to get ahead of myself, though. One step at a time. I've held out so long, it would be stupid to grow impatient now.

Irene arrives right on time. She looks beautiful. Have I really never noticed how gorgeous this woman is? She's wearing a dress with little flowers on it and a white collar that gives her a childlike air. I open the door, and she hurls herself into my arms. I'm not dreaming—she's hugging me tight. She's maybe happier than I've ever seen her. The situation seems so new that it makes me feel a little shy, as if I'd just met her.

She moves around the living room, smiles, looks at the table I've prepared. She seems to approve. She comes over to me and kisses me on the mouth. We tangle in a long, deep kiss that ends in panting and sexual hunger. I pull away from her a little and look into her eyes: "Before or after we eat?"

"Before and after."

I laugh and take her in my arms, carry her to the bedroom. It feels as if the sour air that was smothering our relationship has suddenly dissipated. I inhale the new breeze.

We intertwine on the bed—intensity, pleasure, happy ending. The strange, brusque, elusive, difficult, cynical, sad woman has disappeared. Maybe, I like to think, she's seen a future with me and it doesn't seem so bad.

We eat, talk, drink. I long to discuss the changes that will take place in our lives if they give me the job, but I'm still afraid when I'm with her, afraid of her panther swipe that can so easily destroy you. There will be time to make plans.

When we finish eating, we're tipsy, indolent. We go back to bed and make love again. Afterward we fall asleep. When I wake up, it's dark out. I get up and make some tea. As I'm drinking it in the living room, she appears, still naked.

"I want to talk to you," she says, and I feel all the alarms in my brain going off at once.

"Go on, I'm listening."

"I feel like you're never going to be my escort again."

"I'm happy you said that, because it's true. That's over—I'm not going to be anybody's escort anymore."

"I'll never pay you again."

"Never."

"I've never told you this, but you've helped me discover an aspect of sex I never experienced before."

I'm so moved, I'm unable to answer. I place my hand on her cheek, caress it.

"But there's something I want to ask from you, Javier, something specific."

She's silent, looks at me steadily. She's serious now. Finally she says, loud and clear, "I want to have a threesome with you and Iván."

I'm flabbergasted. I giggle foolishly. She continues, her tone unchanged. "I've always had that fantasy: what would it be like with two men at the same time? Just once would be enough. If I feel uncomfortable or overwhelmed by the situation, I'll put up my hand and we'll stop."

It's going to take me a minute to figure out how to react, what I should say in response. I'm so startled, I can't get my thoughts in order. Take it easy, I've got to tread cautiously; now that everything's all set up, it would be a disaster to make it fall apart. Let's see. At its core, her request indicates trust and complicity. It's a way of bidding farewell to the past. The dark period is being left behind, but before the light begins, I have to make an offering: a threesome. The threesome is a goodbye, a fireworks display. The future will begin very soon. The evolution of my relationship with Irene has been hard, slow, painful, but it's reached its culmination.

Seeing that I'm not answering immediately, she says, "You won't be jealous, right?"

I tell her no, we'll have the threesome, and in fact I'll suggest it to Iván myself.

* * *

And this—how am I supposed to take this? At first I'm totally freaked out thinking she's told him about our wild sex. But no, as the teacher explains the situation, it's clear he knows nothing about it. Whew!

So this threesome business is for real? I don't get it.

"Things are going to change between us. It seems like the job is going to come through, so . . . we'll have a different kind of relationship."

"Are you going to live together?"

"That might happen in the next phase. First, a change of social and professional contacts. After that we can change our habits."

"And between phases, a nice ménage à trois."

"That's not funny."

"Don't be mad, teach! It's just that this all seems really weird."

"It's her way of saying goodbye to the world of male escorts."

"A fling."

"A fling too. An endpoint."

"You're going to be her boyfriend now."

"I don't know what I'm going to be: her partner, her boyfriend, her significant other . . . the label doesn't matter."

"But she won't be paying you."

"No."

"What about me? Will she pay me when we do the three-some?"

"If she doesn't, I will."

"That's not funny either. Look, I'm willing to do whatever favor you need, but not for Irene. I hope that doesn't piss you off."

"I'll tell her to pay you. There won't be a problem."

Shit, I just don't get it! Fine, the chick wants a wild night, but why do I have to be the third party? They should pick somebody else! The bitch is just looking to drive a wedge between Javier and me. First she sleeps with me, and now this. And it's brutal, a real shitstorm. If I get really turned on, that's a problem because he's there. But it's worse if I don't. To be honest, I'd rather take a pass on the whole business, but now that things are in motion, I'll do what I can, pocket the cash, and jet. I don't give a crap what happens afterward—those two can figure their weird shit out. The only thing that's a bummer is when the next stage begins and they go off and live together, I won't see the teacher as often. We won't work together any-more, and we definitely won't go out as a threesome. I can't hang out with this chick—I might end up losing my temper and smacking the crap out of her. That's life, man: fucking weird.

* * *

I'm having them meet me at my house. Better here than at Javier's apartment. I'm nervous. It's my first time being with two men. I don't care who they are. I should have arranged to have this experience with strangers, but I don't think I could do it. I know my limits. Even with these two, whom I've slept with already, it's going to be tough. I'll drink liquor and do some lines before they come. I have to act totally normal, in control: my money, my commands. Two men at my service. It's going to be hard. The mind, already formed, keeps functioning, telling you what your identity is. Today I want to erase myself, not be me or another person—not be anybody, as if I'd never existed.

The doorbell rings right on time. I've gotten myself dolled up: dress, makeup, perfume. When they come in, they look at me, kiss my cheeks in greeting. Maybe I'm too stoned. Maybe I calculated wrong when I was trying to figure out the right quantities to put me in the mood. Maybe I got ahead of myself and it would have been better to do the coke with them, as a team, all together.

Today's arrangement didn't include dinner, so I've just prepared some snacks. Javier looks awful: upset, agitated, pale. He's going to have a terrible time. I should send him away and just be with Iván. Iván's a bastard without scruples, morals, or fear. He knows his life is shit, but he doesn't aspire to anything better. If I'd hooked up with him instead of Javier, we wouldn't have made it two weeks. He doesn't have the patience it takes to deal with me. Javier does—he wants a better life, so he's prostrated himself, agreed to anything I wanted. He's a sheep.

We spend a while drinking and chatting idly. I quickly start feeling drunk. Inevitably, Iván's the one who initiates the action. He looks at Javier, and Javier looks at me. Iván gets up from his chair and takes off his shirt; his torso is as slim as in a crucifixion icon. Then his pants, his underwear. He's naked. Javier and I look at him, but he goes straight for his target: he pulls me to my feet, removes my sweater, unfastens my bra, sucks hard on each of my nipples, making me shiver. He pulls down my panties and starts tonguing my genitals. I feel my legs wobbling. Suddenly Iván kicks Javier.

"Wake up, man!" he mutters.

Javier gets undressed and comes over to me. He grabs my shoulders from behind with both hands. I feel his hot mouth along my neck, while the other man is still between my thighs. I fall, literally fall on the sofa, my legs weak. I hear them whispering. One of them grabs my arms, the other my feet, and they carry me to the bedroom. They lay me down on the bed. I let them. I have no will of my own. Then the assault begins. Mouths suck me. The tip of a penis trails up and down my spine. They penetrate me. They thrust in and out, they lick me. I don't know what part of my body is boiling; I feel something like a river of hot lava flowing from between my legs. I can't stop, I don't want to stop. I forget who I am. I'm facing a powerful monster, a monster with a thousand limbs. It's impossible to fight it.

I've come so many times, I end up as limp as a wet rag, unable to move. I don't hear anything, don't open my eyes. I remain curled up in a fetal position. I think I fall asleep, but I'm not sure. I hear them murmuring, very far away.

I'm thirsty, really thirsty, and I wake up searching for water in the darkness. I think I'm alone, but I'm not. The light in the hall comes on, and I see Javier go out, naked. He comes back with a glass of water. He helps me sit up; I drink.

"Are you OK?" he asks.

"Yes, I'm fine."

"Iván left."

Unfortunately, he stayed. What I need is to be alone in my house, resting, reliving the experience I've just had.

"Wouldn't it be better for you to come back tomorrow, Javier?"

"It's very late. Can't I stay and sleep with you?"

"I'm worn out."

"I thought we could wear you out a little more."

He comes nearer, starts caressing me between my legs, kisses me. He's like a dog: he needs to mark his territory, eliminate the traces left by the previous dog, reclaim his property. I cover myself up with the sheet.

"No, please."

"Sweetheart . . . "

"Leave me alone, Javier, I'm begging you."

"All right, don't worry. I'll just take up a corner of the bed; you won't even know I'm here."

"I'm asking you to leave me alone, to go home. I'll call you."

"But Irene, if we're going to start a new life, why do you care if I sleep here? I won't bother you, and in the morning when you wake up, I'll be here."

I got up, went to the living room, and opened the box where I keep a duplicate set of house keys. I grabbed them and stuck them in the pocket of his jeans, which were lying on the floor. I looked up to find he'd followed me and was watching me in disbelief.

"See? You have the keys to my house now. Happy? You can come over tomorrow and have breakfast—you can even take out yesterday's trash. Do you feel more fulfilled now that you've started your new life? Now please leave."

"I don't understand your attitude, Irene. We talked about this."

I see her in the half-light, naked. Her hair is tousled, the makeup around her eyes smeared. I see the expression on her face, and it's rage that she seems to feel, overpowering, unbridled rage.

"We talked about what, Javier?" she yells. "It's no use talking to you. You don't understand, you don't listen, you just stick with the bullshit in your head. You don't care about other people—you set up a parallel reality and live there, happy as a clam. You don't even see yourself! That's how you're able to be so ridiculous."

"Where is this coming from, Irene? Is something bothering you, something I've said or done . . . ?"

"You, you bother me! Always making plans for new lives, always trying to redeem me like a missionary! Don't you remember who you are, what you do for a living, how we met, what we just did with your buddy?"

I honestly didn't know how to process what I was hearing. I decided the most important thing was to remain calm. Irene was angry. After our three-way, the intense pleasure, she was now feeling guilt, shame, all the sensations she thought she'd left behind.

"You know what I think, Irene? I think we should have some tea and calm down a little. And maybe it's better if I don't sleep here tonight. I'll go home."

I expect her to unleash more abuse, but she doesn't. She opens the wardrobe and puts on a robe. She goes to the kitchen, and I follow. I see her put water on to boil and prepare the teapot. Great, the storm is over, the clouds are clearing. I go to get dressed—having her see me naked will only make things more complicated. When I return, she's sitting there at the kitchen table. Wrapped in her robe, with her hair tousled and a steaming mug in her hands, she looks like a housewife who's recently gotten out of bed. I smile at her. I stand in front of her, where my tea is waiting for me.

"Feeling better?" I venture to ask.

She doesn't respond. She looks at me, expressionless, but she seems to have exorcised all her demons, to be at peace.

"Look, Irene, I think these kinds of sexual experiences are always a bit traumatizing. It's left a sour taste in my mouth too. In the heat of sexual passion everything's fine, but afterward . . . "

She interrupts me with a chuckle. I don't know what to make of it. She keeps wordlessly drinking her tea. Her expression has gone blank again. I feel a vague twinge of fear. I finish my tea in a hasty gulp. I get up and give her a kiss on the forehead. As I head for the door, I say, "I'll call you tomorrow. If you want to see me before that, call me any time."

Before I cross the threshold, I hear her voice: "Javier!" I turn around and see her enigmatic smile.

"They didn't choose you for the job."

I have a hard time understanding what her words mean, but it finally clicks.

"How long have you known?" I ask.

"Don't you want to know why they didn't choose you?"

"Go ahead, tell me."

"My friend called—you didn't have the right profile, which is a nice way of saying you didn't measure up. I asked why not, and he answered, very contrite, 'What's the firm going to do with a high school teacher, Irene?'"

"How long have you known?"

"Since yesterday. I didn't want to ruin our fun."

Now what I see on her face is a smile of simple mockery, pure spite. I snatch up the sugar bowl from the table. It's metallic and solid, weighs a lot. I go up to her and hit her on the temple with the dense, heavy object. Sugar flies everywhere. She doesn't cry out, doesn't try to defend herself. Her face crumples and her body slides off the chair onto the floor. I crouch down and keep hitting her in the same place, harder and harder, with increasing intensity. I'm not nervous or upset. I'm calm. I hear her skull crunching, her temple is swollen, blood is trickling from her ear, her eyes are rolled back. The smell of blood makes me stop. I start shaking uncontrollably from head to foot, especially my hands.

Standing up, I suddenly feel unable to move. Just like in nightmares, I'm nailed to the floor and my legs refuse to obey me. I take a number of deep breaths, shake my head, and start running.

\* \* \*

Holy hell, where am I, who am I, and all that jazz. I look at my cell phone, which is charging on the nightstand. 5 A.M. 5 A.M. and the teacher is calling. It hasn't even been two hours since I went to bed, three hours since I left him—what the hell does Javier want? I decline the call, but then the doorbell starts ringing and the telephone again too. I go to the intercom.

"Please open up, it's Javier!"

"Shit, man, it's 5 A.M., I'm zonked. I'll call you tomorrow."

"Please open the door!"

The tone of his request worries me. I open the door, and he gallops in like a runaway horse. I'm alarmed—I've never seen the teacher so nervous, so out of sorts. He's as white as a goddamn wall and panting like a tired dog. I could tell things were fucked up, so I started up my good-dad act and invited him inside.

"Oh my god, oh my god!"

"All right, man, calm down. Come in and have a seat. Do you want a drink?"

But he was in no mood for calming down; his hands were shaking.

"I killed her!" he blurts out.

"What the hell do you mean?"

He dropped onto the sofa like a bale of hay and covered his face with his hands. He sobbed like a child, but he didn't answer me, the bastard. I started to get pretty anxious too, so

I said to myself, "Calm down, Iván." I thought about the icy-cold waterfall tumbling onto my wrists. What does "I killed her" mean? Knowing the teacher, it could be anything. For example, maybe the chick said something rude, he roughed her up a little, and that seems to him like the ultimate aggression. He feels like he's practically left her half dead, but she's maybe just a bit bruised.

"How did you kill her, Javier? Tell me what happened."

"With a heavy metal thing—I hit her on the head over and over again. Blood was running out of her ear."

"Holy shit!"

Holy fucking shit! The dude really offed her! If what he's saying is true, he offed her, damn it. The quiet ones are like that—when their rage finally spills out, they turn into real monsters.

"Where did it happen, at her house?"

"In her kitchen."

"And you left her there? You shut the apartment door and left her there?"

He weeps and keeps weeping, without answering, but it seems like he's nodding. Jesus H. Christ! Suddenly I realize I'm in my pajamas, the ones with Donald Duck on them. It feels inappropriate. I go to my room to change and think about what the hell to do.

When I return, the teacher hasn't moved. He's still saying, "Oh my god, oh my god" and making a sound like a wounded animal.

"You don't have the key to her house, do you, Javier?"

He reaches into his pants pocket and pulls out some keys. Lucky thing, too!

"She gave me these keys before . . . She told me I . . . "

"Stop thinking about what she told you. You need to drink some coffee and smoke a joint—you're useless like this. Come on, hurry up! And stop fucking crying!"

"Are you going to call the police?"

"Are you nuts, man?"

I quickly make two cups of coffee, asking him if he ran into anyone, if anybody saw him. He says no.

We headed to the chick's house. I parked a few streets over and we walked the rest of the way. Nobody was out at that time of night. We went up the stairs to the apartment. I was carrying rubber gloves in my pocket that I'd grabbed from my kitchen. I opened the apartment door. Total silence. The teacher went in ahead of me. And there she was, yeah, lying on the floor, her skin white or greenish . . . dead. The first dead body I'd ever seen, holy shit. She looked pretty rough, with dried blood gumming up her hair. A goddamn slaughter! The hell with the quiet, polite ones! The hell with bookworms!

I rummaged through the kitchen cabinets and found more rubber gloves under the sink. I handed a pair to Javier. In another, larger cabinet were the vacuum cleaner and the mop, along with a few bottles of bleach and rolls of paper towels.

"Now let's get to scrubbing, man! We don't have police records, and we need to keep it that way. I'll take care of the kitchen, and you get the living room. Everything we've touched, everything. And then bleach the hell out of the floor. And focus, man! Save the freak-out for later! By the way, you were wearing a condom tonight, right?"

"I flushed it down the toilet."

"Great, perfect, me too."

We started cleaning like a couple of deranged housemaids. The entire kitchen. The entire living room. I finished first, so I moved on to the bedroom. When I saw the bed, with its tangled sheets, the hairs on the back of my neck stood on end. The three of us had been having sex there just hours earlier, and now she was lying in the kitchen, stiff and cold. I went to look for a garbage bag and stuffed the sheets inside it; we were taking those with us.

Two hours later, we were done. They'd have to search hard to find any trace of us, and neither of us had a record. Clean as a whistle.

We tossed the keys down a sewer grate and went back to my place. I cut up the sheets and burned the pieces in the bathtub, one by one so we didn't smoke the place out. The rubber gloves too. Maybe we didn't need to take so many precautions, but it couldn't hurt—I've seen a lot of movies, and they can nab you over the tiniest thing.

The teacher did OK during our cleaning frenzy, but afterward he started to fall apart, muttering, "My god, my god, what have I done?" Before he took up crying again, I said to him, "Look, it's eight-thirty in the morning. Let's take the car and go get breakfast across town to clear the air a little."

Clearing the air wasn't my only goal—out in public, the teacher would have to pull himself together and stop bugging me with his whining.

We went to a bar near the wholesale food market where you can get a great meal. It was packed with office workers. The truth is, after all the work we'd put in on so little sleep, I was starving.

We sat down at a table in the middle of the bustling crowd. The teacher said, "Now they're going to find her."

"But it'll take a while. She said the maid was on vacation. Anyway, don't worry. Nobody's going to report her missing— she doesn't have any family. They're never going to connect her to us."

"What about Genoveva?"

"Genoveva? You think she's going to go to the police and tell them she suspects two prostitutes that she and Irene were screwing? No way, she'll keep as quiet as a fish."

"What about Irene's friend who gave me the job interview?"

"Shit, teach, that dude's never going to figure it out! He's not going to make a connection between the friend of a friend and a killer who snuffs her during a wild night of sex and alcohol. And we left the liquor bottles and coke there, so the police won't dig too deep. A girl without any family who's living that kind of lifestyle is basically asking for it, right? I don't think they'll worry about it too much."

We ordered two plates of fried eggs with potatoes and bacon. The yolks were runny and split open over the potatoes, and the bacon crunched in your mouth. And the beer—the beer was cold, powerful, went down cool and refreshing and warmed you up at the same time. What a breakfast, man. The best one I'd ever eaten! Then we got some nice strong coffee and two spectacular slices of Galician almond cake.

The teacher tucked into the food as eagerly as I did. He was hungry too, what the hell. He was looking better, so, while ordering another coffee, I thought it was time to ask him:

"What happened back there, Javier? What did she do to get under your skin like that?"

He hung his head. I thought he wasn't going to answer me, but eventually he looked at me sheepishly and said, real quiet, "She told me they hadn't picked me for the job, and then she laughed at me. Then I realized she'd been laughing at me the whole time, from the very beginning."

"Well, these things happen, man. Don't worry about it, don't think about it anymore."

That's all I said. There was no point in repeating what I'd told him a thousand times, because he knew it and I know it: rich people are from another planet, and any sucker who thinks otherwise is going to regret it.

"My god, Iván! What am I going to do with my life now? What am I going to do?"

That did piss me off, and I was tempted to tell him to go to hell. I looked him square in the eyes and said the only thing I could say:

"What are you going to do? You're going to hang in there, man, hang in there and keep going same as everybody else! What do you think the rest of us are doing?"

\* \* \*

Police blotter:

*Irene Sancho, a forty-two-year-old businesswoman, was found dead this morning in her home. Her assistant notified the police because she showed signs of having been brutally murdered.*

*Police sources speculate that the death may have occurred during the course of a night of sex, alcohol, and drugs, though they admit that they currently have no evidence or witnesses and cannot dismiss any line of inquiry.*

*Some neighbors have reported seeing individuals of North African descent walking through the neighborhood in recent weeks, but they are unable to provide any precise information.*

*Of course, the more time passes after a crime is committed, the harder it is to solve it. The woman had been dead for three days by the time she was found, so solving the case will be enormously difficult. The judge immediately issued a gag order.*

## About the Author

Alicia Giménez-Bartlett is one of Spain's most popular and beloved crime novelists. She was born in Almansa, Spain, in 1951, and has lived in Barcelona since 1975. In 1997, she was awarded the Femenino Lumen prize for the best female writer in Spain, and in 2015 she was awarded the prestigious Planeta Prize for her novel, *Naked Men*.